NOV 2007

MALICE

ROBERT K. TANENBAUM

MALICE

ATRIA BOOKS

New York   London   Toronto   Sydney

ATRIA BOOKS

A Division of Simon & Schuster, Inc.
1230 Avenue of the Americas
New York, NY 10020

Library of Congress Cataloging-in-Publication Data is available

ISBN-13: 978-0-7432-7119-6
ISBN-10:   0-7432-7119-X

First Atria Books hardcover edition August 2007

ATRIA BOOKS and colophon are trademarks of Simon & Schuster, Inc.

Manufactured in the United States of America

10 9 8 7 6 5 4 3 2 1

For information about special discounts for bulk purchases,
please contact Simon & Schuster Special Sales at 1-800-456-6798
or business@simonandschuster.com.

*To those most special, Patti, Rachael, Roger, and Billy;
and to my legendary mentors, Coach Paul Ryan, Coach Rene Herrerias,
District Attorney Frank S. Hogan, and Henry Robbins*

ACKNOWLEDGMENTS

Wendy Walker and Espey Jackson deserve special recognition for their invaluable assistance. The superior quality of the manuscript is directly attributable to their devoted and brilliant contributions.

Prologue

November 17, 1603
Westminster, England

"THOU ART A MONSTER!" THE PROSECUTOR ROARED OUT HIS accusation and pointed at the defendant as the judges and jurors in their satin doublets and embroidered waistcoats shifted uneasily in their seats. "Thou hast an English face but a Spanish heart!"

The defendant, Sir Walter Raleigh, remained calm despite the worst insult to someone who had spent much of his life fighting against Spain. But, forty-nine years old, his hair and the distinctive goatee shot through with gray, he now stood accused of treason.

"Let me answer for myself," Raleigh demanded.

"Thou shalt not," Prosecutor Sir Edward Coke thundered back.

Raleigh turned to the jury. "It concerneth my life," he pleaded, though he knew the men before him were not sympathetic to him personally or interested in a fair trial.

The hearing was a specialized sort of court procedure. In later years, it would be inaccurately referred to as a Star Chamber, a fifteenth- to seventeenth-century English court comprised of judges appointed by the Crown. The Star Chambers, so named because the courtrooms were decorated with stars, were notorious for being conducted in secrecy and were given to arbitrary procedures. They were a convenient way for the Crown, and its supporting nobles, to get rid of rivals and enemies both real and perceived.

What Raleigh faced was actually a "special commission of oyer and terminer." Similar to the Star Chambers, the commissions had been created for the sole purpose of trying people accused of treason. However, unlike a Star Chamber, juries sat on these commissions and weighed what evidence was presented to them. The trials were also supposed to be governed by the rules of law, and the proceedings were followed with great interest by the general public. However, the method and outcome were still heavily weighted in favor of the Crown's wishes.

The prosecutor, Sir Edward Coke, would someday be noted in legal circles as a man of substantial courage who in his waning years actually stood up to the Crown on behalf of English common law, which would become the basis of the American legal system. But at this time, he was not well liked by the general public because of his involvement two years earlier in convicting the popular Lord Essex of treason on orders of Queen Elizabeth. On the other hand, Raleigh was not universally liked by the common man either.

Soldier, ship's captain, adventurer, poet, and courtier, Raleigh was one of the most famous men of his time in both his own country and among England's enemies, especially Spain, whose treasure ships from the New World he'd plundered on behalf of his Queen and himself. He was also one of the wealthiest men in England.

With his taste for fine clothes and armed with charm and wit, he made a dashing knight in Elizabeth's court—with a reputation as a ladies' man—and occupied a special place in the heart of the Queen. Legend had it that he had once laid his cloak over a mud puddle so that Elizabeth would not have to dirty her royal feet. But it was his charms with the ladies that also got him in trouble with

Her Majesty when he married one of her maids of honor—the lovely, and much younger, Bess Throckmorton—without the Queen's permission. The Queen had him thrown into the Tower of London, but she eventually relented when she realized that the couple truly were in love.

Her Majesty's court was notorious for its intrigues and plots, with the various courtiers vying against one another for the position as her favorite. Lord Essex, Robert Devereux, a descendant of King Henry VIII, had been one of Raleigh's chief rivals.

Devereux was a hero to the masses for his military successes against the Spanish and also a favorite of the Queen. However, he saw himself as deserving of the throne and was accused—with reason—of conspiring against her with King James VI of Scotland.

Tried by Coke, Devereux was convicted and executed in February 1601. It was this execution that also would cast Raleigh in a bad light with the public. Although he had nothing to do with the trial, he held the title of Sheriff of London, which meant that he had the duty of presiding over the execution. The public saw this as a devious way to remove a rival, and he was reviled for it.

In 1603, Raleigh's fortunes took a definitive turn for the worse when the Queen died. Soon thereafter, none other than King James ascended to the throne. And not long after that Raleigh was himself arrested for treason—accused of plotting with his friend Lord Cobham and with Spain against James.

When the trial began that morning, Coke was faced with a dilemma; he had very little evidence, only an unsigned letter supposedly written by Cobham that accused Raleigh of being part of the conspiracy. On the other hand, the commissions of oyer and terminer were not known for their objectivity. The judges were selected from officers of the state—nobles and judges appointed by the King and his councillors, all with a stake in the survival of the current political structure, and therefore antagonistic toward anyone who might be a threat to the King or their positions.

There was no attempt at impartiality for Raleigh's trial. The commissioners, or judges, included Secretary of State Sir Robert Cecil, Sir William Waad, who was Raleigh's jailer, the Earls of Suffolk and Devonshire, Lord Wotton, Lord Henry Howard, and Sir John Stanhope, many of whom disliked Raleigh and had envied his status with Elizabeth, or held him partly responsible for Essex's death. They sat with the Chief Justice of the King's Bench, Sir John Popham, who hated Raleigh, as well as the Chief Justice of the Court of Common Pleas, Sir Edmund Anderson, and Justices Gawdy and Warburton.

The jury was handpicked in advance. Comprised of four knights, four esquires, and four gentlemen, this deck of King's men, too, was stacked against the accused. Yet, when offered the chance to challenge the seating of any juror, Raleigh shook his head. "I know none of them, but think them all honest and Christian men. I know my own innocency and therefore will challenge none."

Coke opened the trial by pointing to Raleigh and sneering, "I will prove you the notoriest traitor that ever came to the bar."

"Your words cannot condemn me," Raleigh responded easily. "My innocency is my defense. Prove one of these things wherewith you have charged me, and I will confess to the whole indictment, and that I am the horriblest traitor that ever lived, and worthy to be crucified with a thousand thousand torments."

"Nay, I will prove all," Coke promised, and introduced the unsigned statement of Cobham implicating him in treason.

When he got the chance, Raleigh pleaded to be allowed to answer the charges by calling the only witness against him, Cobham, to the stand. "My Lords, let my accuser come face-to-face and be deposed."

Raleigh knew that if he could get Cobham on the witness stand, he might have a fighting chance. While he was in the Tower of London, a letter wrapped around an apple was thrown through the window. It was signed by Cobham and recanted the earlier accusation. If Cobham testified to that in court, public opinion would surely swing in his favor, Raleigh thought.

However, Raleigh was not allowed to confront his accuser, or call any other witness who might have vouched for him. In fact, only one witness was called to the stand during the entire trial and that by the prosecution. His name was Dyer, and he claimed that he'd once visited a merchant's house in Portugal where he was asked by an unknown gentleman if King James had been crowned yet.

"And I answered, 'No, but I hoped he should be so shortly.' "

According to Dyer, the gentleman then said, "He shall never be crowned, for Raleigh and Cobham will cut his throat ere that day come."

Dyer's statement was hearsay; in fact, it was hearsay several times removed from the source, if there was one. And even if the "gentleman" existed and had made the statement, there was no evidence that the conspiracy existed anywhere but in the man's mind. But the testimony was allowed anyway.

Hour after hour passed in the courtroom, and it became increasingly apparent that Coke could not win the case with his evidence. So he resorted to name-calling and insults, which he repeated over and over again, as if repetition gave weight to his words. Raleigh, he said, was the "absolutest traitor that ever was" and "the notoriest traitor that ever came to the bar. Thyself art a spider of Hell."

But Raleigh remained cool. "You speak indiscreetly, barbarously, and uncivilly."

"I want words sufficient to express thy viperous treasons," Coke shouted.

"I think you want words indeed," Raleigh countered quietly, "for you have spoken one thing half a dozen times."

It was well into the night when the trial drew to a close with both men trying to get the last word in. Raleigh insisted that it was his right. "He which speaketh for his life must speak last."

When the judges agreed, having perhaps been shamed by Raleigh's spirited defense, Coke sat down and refused to give his closing argument. The judges finally prevailed upon him to finish, which he did by reading a third letter that he'd forced Cobham to sign, which rescinded the retraction letter sent via apple to Raleigh.

Finished, Coke sat down again, at which point Raleigh stood and with the flourish of the old courtier produced his own letter from Cobham. He prevailed upon Lord Cecil to read it:

" 'Seeing myself so near the end, for the dire charge of my own conscience, and freeing myself from your blood, which else will carry vengeance against me; I will protest upon my salvation I never practiced with Spain for your procurement; God so comfort me that this is my affliction, as you are a true subject for anything that I know. . . . God have mercy upon my soul, as I know no treason by you.' "

After the letter was read, Raleigh argued that the prosecution had not proved its case, despite the disadvantages he'd had defending himself.

"Consider my disability, and their ability; they prove nothing against me. Only they bring the accusation of my Lord Cobham, which he hath lamented and repented as heartily as if it had been for a horrible murder—for he knew that all this sorrow which should come to me is by his means. Presumption must proceed from precedent or subsequent facts."

Noting that without him his wife and son would be penniless, Raleigh asked the judges and jurors to put themselves in his shoes before convicting him based on the scant evidence presented by the prosecutor.

"If you would be contented on presumptions to deliver up to be slaughtered, to have your wives and children turned into the streets to beg their bread; if you would be contented to be so judged, judge so of me," Raleigh said, and sat down.

It was a valiant battle, but of little use. The trial had lasted for sixteen hours—from 8:00 a.m. to midnight—but it took the jury only fifteen minutes to reach a verdict of guilty. Lord Cecil then pronounced the sentence: death "in the full magnitude and horror" the law then required, which meant he was to be hanged, drawn, and quartered.

However, Raleigh's spirited defense had one unforeseen impact. Though his perceived role in the death of Lord Essex had made him an unpopular character among the general public, the obvious injustice of his trial and the noble manner in which he'd conducted himself now made him a national hero.

King James and his councillors recognized that executing him at this point might cause a general uprising worse than any treason Raleigh had been accused of. In fact, the King conceded that "by his wit, he turned the hatred of men into compassion for him." The king decided to grant Raleigh a stay of execution.

For the next thirteen years, Raleigh remained a prisoner in the Tower of London. He was legally dead but was able to write and even have his family around him. Then in 1617, in an effort to gain his freedom, he proposed a voyage to the New World to find gold. He promised he could do this without attacking the colonies or shipping of Spain, with whom the Catholic King James intended to remain at peace.

However, once in the New World, Raleigh's men attacked a Spanish community while he was laid up in bed. There were two major consequences for the action. One was that Raleigh's son was killed in the fight; the second was that Raleigh knew that his own life might be forfeited. But he sailed back to England and, as expected, was arrested.

King James received a letter from the king of Spain saying that Raleigh would not—if the occasion arose—be executed in Madrid. However, the letter added, should he be beheaded in England, it would "please his most Catholic Majesty."

As attorney general, Coke was asked to render an opinion on what could be done with Raleigh. It was a chance for revenge against the man who'd made a fool of him in the courtroom, and he took full advantage, noting that Raleigh was already "civilly dead," and therefore his execution had merely been postponed.

On October 28, 1618, Raleigh was taken from the Tower of London to Westminster Abbey, where after another quick show trial he was placed in the gatehouse to await his death. He spent most of his last night in the company of his beloved Bess and writing his final letters.

On the morning of his execution, Raleigh ate breakfast and smoked a little of the tobacco he'd made popular in England. He then dressed magnificently, the dashing courtier one last time as he was led from his cell.

The Old Palace Yard was packed with spectators, many of whom jeered as he climbed the scaffold. There he gave one last eloquent speech that ended, "So I take my leave of you all, making my peace with God." He then removed his cloak and doublet before asking the executioner to show him the ax. "This is sharp medicine," he said approvingly, "that will cure all my ills . . ."

With that, Raleigh refused the blindfold and laid his head on the block. Composing himself, he gave the signal that he was ready. The executioner, however, hesitated. Then Raleigh gave one final command. "Strike, man! Strike!"

The executioner followed his orders and Raleigh's head was shown to the crowd. They had fallen silent, but then one man spoke up.

"We have not such another head to be cut off."

1

BUTCH KARP WASN'T SURE WHAT IT WAS THAT WOKE HIM. He'd been dreaming of murdered schoolchildren and gun-toting terrorists. But it was something else that pulled him from sleep, something to do with unfinished business.

Disoriented, he lay quietly trying to remember where he was. It wasn't at home where he belonged—in bed with his wife in their Lower Manhattan loft. That's for damn sure, he thought, fighting off a small surge of apprehension.

As a prosecutor for the New York District Attorney's Office, and as *the* district attorney for the past couple of years, he had a reputation among friends and opponents for his ability to concentrate on "what really mattered" to the exclusion of all else. It made him a formidable adversary in the criminal courts where in a nearly thirty-year career he'd lost only one homicide trial. But for that loss, Karp tried successfully a who's who of major league evildoers: assassins, career criminals, contract killers, and your classic Gotham homicidal sociopaths. Now he called upon that famous focus to clear the cobwebs.

Breathing deep, he let the anxiety subside and thought, Okay, you're in Beth Israel hospital. You were shot. . . . What month is this? . . . Mid-October? Time they let me out of this place.

Karp looked around the room. Or at least tried. Except for a diffused glow from beneath the door, there was little illumination beyond the small green blips that stared out from the machines next to his bed like the eyes of lizards caught in a flashlight beam. All he could see were shadows within shadows, and there was nothing there to cause alarm or disturb his sleep.

Yet something wasn't right. He sniffed the air and would have sworn that the usual antiseptic bouquet of the hospital room now carried a faint earthy odor, like the windowless basement of his parents' home in Brooklyn when he was a boy. He held his breath to listen. But all he could hear was the death rattle of a fluorescent bulb in the hallway and the far-off voices of the late-night shift hovering around the nurse's station. He could make out a male voice engaged in banter with a bevy of female voices and supposed that the young police officer who'd been assigned guard duty outside his door was taking a break.

Flirting with the nurses, Karp thought. *Good for him. I don't see the point of wasting the night, sitting in a chair to protect me. Never wanted it, but that damn mother hen Clay Fulton . . .*

Detective Clay Fulton was the head of the DAO's criminal investigations unit, a squad of NYPD officers and detectives assigned to the DA's office to provide investigative and protective services. He and Karp had been friends for three decades, but the big detective—a former fullback for the Syracuse University football team—sometimes treated him more like a witless child than the top law enforcement official in Manhattan, or his boss.

Karp glanced at the digital clock on the nightstand across the room: 3:00 a.m. The witching hour . . . try to go back to sleep. He tired easily and had been sleeping a lot over the past couple of weeks since the shooting. I guess that stands to reason after being shot three times, he thought.

Karp's memory of the attack was a series of surreal vignettes— like watching one-act plays from just offstage. He remembered that he was leaving the Manhattan Criminal Courts Building at 100 Centre Street, which housed, along with the courtrooms, the Manhattan House of Detention for Men, affectionately referred to as the Tombs, and the Office of the New York District Attorney. He and his longtime colleague, Ray Guma, had just won a murder conviction against political power broker Emil Stavros, who'd murdered his wife a dozen years earlier and buried her in his backyard. As he walked down the steps of the entrance, he'd glanced with satisfaction at the inscription carved into the marble on the wall: "Why Should There Not Be a Patient Confidence in the Ultimate Justice of the People." Why not indeed, he'd thought.

When he looked up, he saw his wife, Marlene Ciampi, waving to him from across Centre. They were going to go out to celebrate the victory with an expensive Italian dinner—on Marlene's dime—at Il Mulino on West Third Street, not too far from the West Village. He remembered smiling and distinctly recalled the warmth that coursed through his body whenever he saw her petite but well-proportioned frame—at least when they weren't fighting like bantam roosters—even after nearly twenty-five years of marriage. He'd had no clue that danger was approaching, not until he saw Marlene's attention suddenly shift to some point farther up the street.

Karp thought that he would have developed a better sixth sense for impending peril. After all, he'd grown up across the East River in a fairly rough-and-tumble Brooklyn neighborhood, and then spent most of his career working at the DAO putting assorted murderers, rapists, sociopaths, thugs, and terrorists in prison. But it was Marlene, a former Catholic schoolgirl, who had discovered a latent talent for recognizing the pungent aroma of danger before anyone else caught a whiff.

Karp had followed Marlene's glance to a sedan with dark-tinted windows that was pulling away from the curb and rolling slowly toward him. He heard her shout something—a warning that he couldn't make out over the din of taxi horns and human voices—and then watched her dash into the street with a gun in her hand.

Drivers slammed on their brakes to avoid her and hit their horns. Marlene was pointing her gun at the sedan. He looked and saw that the window on the passenger side was down. But he never saw who shot him, just flashes from the gun.

The force of the bullets striking him in the chest, leg, and neck propelled him back across the sidewalk on which he'd landed with a bone-jarring thud, like the morning delivery of the Sunday *New York Times*. Pedestrians around him screamed and ran to get out of the way.

Then he was just lying there, looking up at the sky and remarking to himself how white the clouds looked against the blue background, while around him there were more shots and more screams. Marlene's face appeared above him. She was yelling something and crying. He wanted to tell her that it was all right: Don't cry. I love you. He tried to say the words but his mouth was full of warm liquid that he realized was his own blood.

Then something was pulling at him, lifting him from the sidewalk. He looked down and was surprised to see his body lying in a spreading pool of red as his wife and a man he didn't recognize pressed at his wounds. He noticed the sedan was partly up on the curb, stopped where it had run into Dirty Warren's newsstand.

Vaguely, he heard Marlene calling him back. *Butch! Butch Karp! Listen to me. You're not leaving me, Karp! Please don't leave me, baby.*

It was difficult to keep his eyes open. He was so tired; he just wanted to rest. His mind filled with a white light. So that part's true, he'd thought. I wonder what's next.

He felt at peace and was ready to go. But Marlene's pleas were irritating him when he just wanted to be left alone. Opening his eyes, he'd looked at her with annoyance. "What?" he complained. "Can't you see I'm sleeping?"

Somebody else was pressing on him, and it hurt. It was the man he hadn't recognized, who now looked at him and smiled. The stranger had a thick crew cut of pewter-gray hair that matched his eyes, which were kind and steady, as if nothing fazed him. Then Karp glanced down and saw the collar. A priest?

"I'm Jewish," Karp had croaked through the blood in his mouth, thinking the priest meant to administer last rites.

"That's okay, Mr. Karp," the priest answered. "I'm not trying to convert you. But do hang on, I believe you have some unfinished business here."

The next thing Karp was aware of was waking up at Beth Israel with Marlene's head on his chest and the voice of the priest in his head telling him that he had unfinished business. It ain't over till it's over, he'd thought, recalling one of the aphorisms of Yogi Berra, a New York Yankee and boyhood hero. He'd stroked the short, dark curls of Marlene's hair until she gradually woke up. First covering his face with kisses, she'd then run out of the room to announce his return to the world.

"What happened?" he'd asked after a half dozen doctors and nurses who'd flooded into the room to verify Marlene's happy prognosis had left again.

"Rachel Rachman shot you," she'd replied tersely.

Karp caught the hitch in her voice but was too stunned by the identity of his attacker to do much more than stare at his wife with his mouth hanging open. He could have understood if it had been some killer he'd put away in prison and was out on parole. Or maybe some terrorist belonging to a group whose plans he or his family had foiled. But Rachman? The same woman who'd once been Marlene's protégé when his wife was running the Sex Crimes Bureau for the DAO?

It didn't make sense. Sure, she'd been abrasive and aggressive and wasn't well liked in the office. But she'd also been a good prosecutor, tenacious in her pursuit of convictions for sex offenders. Unfortunately, at some point her dedication became an obsession and justice had flown the coop. He'd had to fire her and even tried to bring charges of malfeasance against her for lying and hiding evidence in her zeal to prosecute an innocent man.

Party politics had saved Rachman from an indictment. The state attorney general had declined to prosecute under smarmy political pressure after Karp had recused his office to avoid any appearance of a conflict of interest. But then she'd announced herself as a late entry into the race for the district attorney seat. She'd immediately tried to make up ground by running a vicious, mudslinging campaign. In particular, she'd repeatedly accused Karp of being soft on sex offenders, part of the old-boys network that supposedly cod-dled rapists and blamed the victims for the crimes.

One of her main political backers in her party had been none other than city power broker Emil Stavros. When Karp's office brought a murder indictment against him, she howled that the charges were trumped up and "dirty politics."

Still, he'd never figured her for a nutcase, much less an assassin.

"I think she heard about Emil's conviction and knew that she'd look like she'd supported a killer. I guess at that point the only way to win the election was by killing her opponent," Marlene said when he'd wondered aloud what caused Rachman to snap.

"What happened to her after she shot me?" he asked, then wished he hadn't when he saw the look on his wife's face. That was the first time he recalled the image of her running into the street with a gun in her hand.

"I killed her," Marlene confirmed, her eyes dropping. A tear rolled down her cheek and fell on the bed. He reached up and brushed away another. He knew the tears weren't for Rachman; they were for her own seeming inability to escape the cycle of vio-lence that had taken over her life. She'd been trying to put that be-hind her with varying degrees of success, but in general seemed more at peace than she had in years.

A burst of hushed laughter and giggles from the nurse's station brought Karp back to the present. Clay would cut this young bull's balls off if he pulled a surprise inspection and caught him away from his post, he thought.

Fulton's already overprotective nature had only been exacer-bated by the shooting. Hard to believe, but true, considering he'd already gone overboard following the murderous escape of the so-ciopath Andrew Kane from a police motorcade while being trans-ported to a psychiatric hospital in upstate New York. Even though he was blameless, the detective, who'd been shot during the es-cape, wore the guilt like a coat of lead on his broad shoulders.

The thought of Kane's escape brought back the images of the

children from Karp's dream. He could see the photograph from the crime scene of their bodies lying next to an overturned bus. He knew each of their faces from the school yearbook photographs kept in the evidence file back in his office. Smiling, happy children with freckles and ponytails who'd been butchered by terrorists as a diversion to ambush the police escort and free Kane.

Lying in the hospital bed, Karp felt anger rise in him like bile as he returned to the question that had haunted him for all the months since: Who else was responsible? Kane didn't do it on his own.

The last time Karp had seen him, Kane was diving into the turbulent waters where the Harlem and Hudson rivers meet—a place called Spuyten Duyvil, or the Devil's Whirlpool—to avoid recapture. He'd been followed into the depths by the half-mad vigilante David Grale. But neither man—nor their bodies—had been found despite an extensive search of the heavily wooded shores of the Hudson to the waters of the Atlantic Ocean. But that was not a big surprise, according to the NYPD harbor patrol team leader.

"We've pulled strong swimmers from those waters," the officer had told him before the shooting. "Some of them dead by the time we could get to them. It doesn't look bad on the surface, but the combination of all that water coming down the river and the pull of the ocean tides makes it damn nasty underneath. It's like jumping into a big washing machine; it's not easy to tell which way is up. These two you're looking for—both fully clothed and not exactly Olympic swimmers—they're dead. And with those tides, their bodies could be ten miles out to sea."

He knew they were dead, but the lack of closure troubled Karp. He'd made the mistake before of assuming that Kane was finished. He would have rested easier seeing his body.

On the other hand, Karp was torn in regard to his feelings toward Grale. He'd first met him several years earlier when Grale was a young Catholic layman working in a soup kitchen for the homeless. Actually, it was then that teenaged Lucy, Marlene and

Karp's daughter, who'd been working in the soup kitchen, had developed a schoolgirl crush on the handsome social worker. She'd even brought him home to meet her parents.

Grale had been intelligent, personable, and gentle. So it had come as a surprise to all of them that he turned out to be a killer who'd been hunting down men who preyed on the homeless. He believed that the men he hunted were literally possessed by demons and that God had appointed him to the task. But while there was little doubt that his victims were themselves murderers, there was no provision in the law that allowed for the summary execution of demons or unconvicted killers.

Grale had become a fugitive, wanted for murder. He'd fled underground, literally, living in the labyrinth of tunnels and sewers—some man-made, some natural—beneath Manhattan. There he'd become the spiritual and temporal leader of an entire population of societal refugees who lived beneath the streets and called themselves the Mole People, or sometimes "underworlders."

In the dark, Grale had devolved further into madness until he saw himself and his followers as the vanguard for God in an upcoming apocalyptic battle against the gathering forces of evil. In his worldview, Manhattan was at the epicenter of Armageddon, and events such as the September 11, 2001, terrorist attack was proof to him that the final war had already begun.

"The demon's face that was seen, and even photographed, in the smoke rising from the World Trade Center was not an accident, or trick of lighting, or the caprice of the wind," Grale had once told him. "It was a warning."

Karp knew that Grale was dangerous, a killer and therefore subject to prosecution under state law in the County of New York. But time and again, this madman, this cold-blooded killer had shown up to rescue some member of the Karp-Ciampi clan, and in fact, thousands of people owed him their lives for his actions against terrorists intent on attacking Gotham.

Grale's alleged death had brought a mixture of relief and sadness. Karp was no longer going to be faced with the prospect of prosecuting him for murder. But part of the unfinished business alluded to by the priest was the desire to simply thank him for the lives he had saved.

As if he'd summoned a ghost, Karp was startled by a sound that emanated from the darkest corner of his room. It sounded like a man trying to suppress a cough. "Who's there?" he demanded.

A tall, thin shadow removed itself from the dark and moved toward him. "Please, not too loud, Mr. Karp," the shadow said.

"David Grale," Karp replied as a pale, hooded face appeared in the minimal light. "We thought you were dead."

"Yes," Grale whispered. "But I can assure you that the rumors of my demise were once again greatly exaggerated . . . though, perhaps, that is no great comfort to you."

As usual when it came to David Grale, Karp found himself in a conundrum. He didn't know whether to shout for the police officer or listen to what his visitor had to say. He decided to wait.

Grale seemed to sense both the debate and its outcome. He smiled, an act that showed his once perfect smile was now marred by gaps. "Thank you," he said. "I'll take your silence as meaning you won't turn me in. I have what I think is an important warning."

Whatever he was going to say next was interrupted by more deep, wet-sounding coughs that Grale tried to cover behind the sleeve of the monk's robe he wore. Karp recalled that the last time they'd talked, Grale had been racked by a similar bout, and he'd seen him wipe blood away from his mouth.

"Maybe you should get that cough checked out," Karp suggested.

Grale's haggard face softened for a moment. "Oh, this . . . just a summer cold." He laughed lightly. "But thank you for saying that—the elixir of human kindness is the best medicine. A few more years in the sewers and I'll be better than ever." He tried to laugh but was interrupted by another fit.

"Perhaps not," he added when the coughing subsided. "But never mind, I don't have much time before your guardian remembers what he's supposed to be doing. The truth is that I wanted to see you after I heard that you'd been shot and make sure you're okay. But I'm not exactly welcome around here, or anywhere, even during visiting hours. However, the more important reason for my visit is to warn you that there's a traitor in your midst. I don't know who yet, but it's someone close and they're working for someone or something with a lot of clout and no conscience."

"What makes you think there's a traitor?"

"Don't tell me that you haven't considered the possibility," Grale said. "But we can start with Kane's escape."

"We already know who betrayed us there," Karp said. "The FBI agent, Michael Grover."

"Yes, Grover was the guy on the inside. But who was he working with or for? He was obviously just an expendable pawn, otherwise Kane would not have been so cavalier about killing him."

"What makes you think Grover wasn't working for himself and just doing it for the money?" Karp asked. Even though he'd reached the same conclusions, he wanted to test the theory on Grale.

"This was bigger than one agent gone bad for cash," Grale replied. "Even Kane couldn't have pulled this off without a lot of help. I assume most of his assets had been frozen, so he probably didn't have the funds to pay for it. And even if he did, making arrangements with such disparate allies as Islamic terrorists and Grover was beyond the capability of someone sitting in a jail cell in the Tombs."

"Go on," Karp said.

"Whoever was helping him and the terrorists thought nothing of the consequences of murdering a half dozen schoolchildren, as well as nearly a dozen cops and federal agents, to do it. And it must have cost beaucoup dollars to finance and carry out Kane's plan to seize St. Patrick's Cathedral and hold the Pope hostage. You do realize the real purpose was to kill everyone, including the Pope, and create a terrorist public relations bonanza that would have made the attack on the World Trade Center look mild?"

"The thought's crossed my mind," Karp admitted. "But who? And to what end?"

"As for who, we don't know," Grale said. "The faces and names are unknown even to those of us who live in the shadows and make a living off of secrets. But whoever they are, they apparently can infiltrate federal law enforcement agencies and even the Office of the District Attorney of New York."

"No one in my office would reveal confidential information," Karp growled.

"Jesus might have said the same thing about his disciples," Grale replied, "until Judas took his thirty pieces of silver."

"Not my guys," Karp insisted.

Grale shrugged. "I'm here to warn you, not argue. But I can tell you that what I'm telling you is not just the opinion of your favorite mad monk, David Grale, but the collected wisdom of others who take an interest in your activities, as well as the safety of you and your family. But you're a grown man, what you do with the information is up to you."

"And this 'we' you mention," Karp said, "do 'we' have anything concrete to go on? This is all pretty conspiracy-theory stuff. Grassy knoll, two shooters, the CIA, and Castro."

"Yet, there are laws against conspiracy to commit murder, so sometimes conspiracies are real," Grale pointed out.

"Touché. Yeah, I know, 'You aren't paranoid if they really are after you,' " Karp replied.

Grale laughed. "Good to know . . . sometimes it seems that way. But back to your question about who might be responsible. We have one name linked to much of this—Jamys Kellagh . . . J-A-M-Y-S . . . K-E-double L-A-G-H. Ring a bell?"

Karp racked his brain for the name but drew a blank. "No, not that I can recall."

Grale nodded as if Karp had confirmed his suspicion. "We think that it's an alias for whoever pulled the strings on Kane. We also have allies in Brooklyn who believe that he was the liaison with the terrorists who helped Kane."

"So you think all this is being controlled by one person? This Jamys Kellagh?"

"No, no more than we believe that Kane was doing all of this on his own either."

Grale glanced over at the clock radio. "I haven't much time," he said, "but you'll recall that when Kane tried to flee upriver from the Columbia University boathouse, my people intercepted his band. We were able to capture two of them alive and take them back to our little underworld home where we . . . um, persuaded them to speak candidly about what they knew. One died before he said anything useful. But the other seemed to have been somewhat higher up in their food chain. He said that Kane was in contact with someone named Jamys Kellagh, who apparently was getting inside information from the authorities."

"Anything regarding his identity?" Karp asked.

"Nothing much," Grale said. "There is a photograph—perhaps someday you will see it. I'm told that it shows our friend, Kane, the Russian agent, Nadya Malovo, and this Jamys Kellagh. Apparently, it is not good quality, and its owners are trying to decide how best to use the information to derail Kellagh's plotting. His face is turned and it is difficult to identify him in the shadows, but he is wearing a short-sleeved shirt and a tattoo can be partly seen here. . . ." Grale touched the inside of his right bicep.

Karp contemplated the information. "Tell your source that the New York DAO would be happy to take the photograph and put it to good use."

"My 'source' is well aware of that," Grale said, "but is concerned with the security breach."

"Well, what happened to your prisoner, then?" Karp asked. "I'd like to talk to him."

Grale gave him an amused look. "I'm afraid he didn't survive our attempts to glean information from him. I can assure you, however, that he was an empty vessel before we dispatched him to the hell that awaits these demons."

Karp shuddered. *The bastard probably thought he'd already gone to hell before they killed him.* "What about Kane?" he asked. "You survived. Is he dead?"

A scowl creased Grale's face. He appeared to be weighing an old debate in his mind. At last he nodded. "Yes," he replied. "I believe that he is dead. We struggled beneath the water for what seemed like hours. He was fast and strong and knew what he was doing with a knife. He cut me here"—Grale touched his side—"but the wound was not fatal. However, I had the pleasure of feeling my knife go deep into his chest."

Grale paused to suppress a cough. "I would have liked to have questioned him about those whom he served. But the current swept him away, and I was desperate for air."

"Your people find his body?" Karp asked.

Grale shook his head. "We searched better than the cops. We also listened to word on the streets and in the dark places of our world. But there was nothing to suggest he lives. My mind tells me he is dead."

"What does your heart tell you?"

Grale grimaced. "It tells me not to stop looking for him until I have his skull in my hands."

Karp shuddered. A sociopath named Felix Tighe had once been about to rape and murder Karp's daughter, Lucy, until Grale showed up and put a stop to it. A few days later, the killer's rat-gnawed skull had shown up at the New York Medical Examiner's Office, where it was identified from dental work. Karp suddenly had a vision of Grale sitting on a throne surrounded by mounds of skulls like some Mongol king and flinched when Grale suddenly moved toward him.

Grale backed away with a look of sadness on his gaunt face. "I wouldn't hurt you, Mr. Karp," he said.

Karp relaxed, ashamed of his reaction. "I know that, David. I'm just a little jumpy. And it's Butch, okay?"

Grale smiled, moved again to the side of the bed, and reached above Karp's head to push the nurse's call button. A moment later, the buzzing of the fluorescent light in the hall stopped and the glow beneath the door disappeared. A red light appeared in the corner of the room indicating that the machines next to his bed were running on the backup power system.

"Good night, Mr. . . . Butch. I'll contact you again when we know more, though I may not have the pleasure of bringing it to you myself. Just be careful of who you trust."

Karp heard the door click open and remembered the thought in his dream about unfinished business. "Oh, by the way, David, I wanted to thank you for all you've done," he said. But silence was the only reply, and he didn't know if he'd been heard.

There was the sound of running feet and his door was flung open by the young police officer, who entered with his hand on the butt of his gun. The officer shined his flashlight directly in Karp's eyes and then around the room.

"Uh, sorry, Mr. Karp," he said. "I was, uh, down at the nurse's station making sure they were okay when your room buzzer went off and then the power went out."

"That's all right, Officer," Karp replied. "I must have hit the button by accident in my sleep, and these old hospitals are always dealing with little power outages. There's nothing to worry about."

The officer turned off his flashlight, wished him good night, and left the room. Alone in the dark again, Karp repeated himself. "Nothing to worry about at all."

2

"WHY DON'T I GO AND, YOU KNOW, SLIP INTO SOMETHING more comfortable," Ariadne Stupenagel purred, fending off the groping hands of her lover. "Now, now, no long faces . . . be a good Murry-wurry and fix us a couple of teeny-weeny martinis."

Gilbert Murrow pouted. It had been a long, frustrating day filling in for his boss at the District Attorney's Office, and he'd have just as soon forgotten the preliminaries with Ariadne and gone straight to the main event.

Then again—now that he had a moment to consider what she'd just said—it might be worth the wait. He never ceased to be amazed by her imaginative and ceaseless attempts to keep their sex lives ramped up. Which meant that he couldn't be sure if "something more comfortable" meant naughty silk undergarments from Victoria's Secret or something in leather and chains from the Kittens Toy Room catalog that she kept in her nightstand.

Besides, he thought, a martini might take the edge off the day and give me the courage necessary to keep up with Ariadne's more imaginative ideas.

"Make the drinks and meet me on the roof, sugar buns," she called over her shoulder. "I've been dreaming all day long about holding on to the railing and looking out at the lights of the city as you slip up from behind me and . . ." She purposely left the end of the sentence dangling, like Murrow's jaw, and disappeared into her bedroom.

With effort, Murrow willed his mouth shut and hurried to the "bar," which occupied most of the kitchen counter. He intended to make Vespers, the famous James Bond vodka martini from Ian Fleming's *Casino Royale*. "Three measures of Gordon's, one of vodka, half a measure of Kina Lillet," Murrow said in his best Bond, which wasn't very good. "Shake it very well until it's ice-cold, then add a large, thin slice of lemon peel. Got it?"

He'd just located the bottle of Kina Lillet when he caught sight of the *New York Guardian* newspaper lying off to the side. His attention was drawn to the top headline, Russians Implicated in St. Patrick's Crisis. Groaning, he read the first couple of paragraphs beneath Ariadne Stupenagel's byline.

A Russian agent allegedly working with the Islamic terrorists who took over St. Patrick's Cathedral and held the Pope hostage was captured by U.S. federal agents inside the cathedral last month at the conclusion of the hostage crisis, according to a well-placed source.

The public was originally led to believe that all the terrorists involved in the plot had been killed inside the cathedral, except for criminal mastermind Andrew Kane, who escaped only to drown in the Harlem River.

However, a separate government source close to the investigation, who asked to remain anonymous, confirmed that a "person of interest" had been taken into custody near the cathedral rectory.

Asked if the person of interest was one of the terrorists, the only response was "damn straight she was."

Russian government officials deny that any of their agents were in the cathedral when it was stormed by federal agents. And U.S. officials have declined to comment on the record. But the first source identified the "person of interest" as for-

mer Soviet KGB agent and current member of the Russian
secret police Nadya Malovo. . . .

Murrow rubbed his eyes, hoping that it might produce a miracle that would make the story disappear, but it was still there
when he looked again. He decided to add an extra jigger of vodka
to the shaker. His boss, Butch Karp, was sure to assume that he,
loyal and tight-lipped aide-de-camp Gilbert Murrow, was one of
the unnamed sources. Karp, who'd recently been released from
the hospital, was already too fond of accusing him of "sleeping
with the enemy," a journalist, and this was sure to add fuel to that
fire.

Karp had a love-hate relationship with Ariadne that went back
decades, before Murrow was even on the scene. Part of it was that
Karp considered most journalists in the same light as he did porn
stars and politicians; part of it was that Ariadne had been Marlene's
college roommate and there was the inevitable friction when a man
came between two female friends. Sometimes when Butch and
Ariadne squared off, it was all that Murrow—who at five foot eight
was four inches shorter than Stupenagel and nine inches shorter
than Karp—could do to step between them without being physically injured.

Karp had been surprised, and not thrilled, when Murrow and
Ariadne had become "an item." He'd warned Murrow that she was
a vamp—having allegedly bedded crown princes, athletes, and dictators (word had it that she'd broken Fidel's heart) to get her stories. But other than raising an eyebrow, he had not continued with
his dissection of her character when Murrow politely but firmly let
it be known that he did not appreciate any aspersions on his girlfriend's character.

In fact, Karp had even been willing to admit over the past couple of months that as journalists went, Ariadne was not the worst of
the lot. She did not burn her bridges for a scoop. And while she
could be a loud and abrasive advocate of the "people's right to

know," which did not always coincide with Karp's view of what they should know, she also knew when to keep a secret.

For the most part, Karp also seemed to believe Murrow when he said that he wasn't divulging any state secrets during pillow talk. *Name, rank, and serial number is all she gets out of me*, Murrow had promised.

I doubt that in a literal sense, but I'll take your word for it if it means not having to hear all the squishy details, Karp had replied, but with a smile.

The truth was that Murrow knew that she was working on another story about the attack, but he purposefully didn't ask what it was about. Nor did he know where she was getting her information. He didn't want to know. As a couple, they had an agreement: he wouldn't talk with her about anything confidential from the DAO, and she wouldn't stop asking him questions and promising exotic sexual favors if he answered them. So far he'd kept his side of the bargain. Then again, because she'd been generous with the favors on what she suspiciously referred to as her "investment plan," his resolve had never been really tested.

One of Ariadne's earlier stories about the St. Patrick's Cathedral attack indicated that the terrorists had helped Kane escape.

Sources say that the plan was for Kane to then assume the identity of a federal Homeland Security agent—including plastic surgery to aid his disguise—and breach the security surrounding the Pope's visit.

Having been deprived of his vast wealth by District Attorney Karp's motions to freeze his assets after being indicted, Kane attempted to ransom the Pope for one billion dollars, which he demanded from the Vatican Bank.

The Islamic terrorists at first demanded that Russia withdraw its troops from the Muslim-dominated state of Chechnya. However, they soon revealed that their real mission was to pull off an act of terrorism so shocking and heinous that it would rival the September 11, 2001, attack on the World Trade Center.

The cathedral was rigged with plastic explosives set to go off after Kane made his escape on the word of Palestinian terrorist Samira Azzam. The suicide mission would have been accomplished, except for the quick action of Marlene Ciampi, the district attorney's wife and a security expert. Along with other concerned citizens and federal agents, she prevented the murder of the Pope by Azzam and the demolition of the cathedral. All of the terrorists, including Azzam, were killed.

The rest of the media, of course, had had a field day with the events. But it was Stupenagel who'd broke the definitive story on what had occurred at St. Patrick's Cathedral, which had also been particularly critical of the Department of Homeland Security.

In the aftermath of the attack, there'd been a lot of finger-pointing at both the department and the FBI, each blaming the other for security lapses. However, Ariadne's story had revealed that it was the Homeland Security department that Kane had infiltrated. The breach not only had exposed the Pope and the hostages in St. Patrick's to a terrorism attack, but also had resulted in the earlier deaths of several federal agents trying to capture Kane in Aspen, Colorado.

According to a Department of Homeland Security press release issued in response, the agent whose identity Kane had assumed had come from another agency—the Bureau of Alcohol, Tobacco, Firearms and Explosives—and therefore wasn't personally known to Jon Ellis, the assistant director of special operations for the department. Ellis had been responsible for directing his agency's efforts to find Kane, as well as providing antiterrorism security for the Pope's visit, and he'd been taking the heat in the press for what had happened.

Public pressure mounted on the government after Ariadne's stories began to appear, and a U.S. senator from Montana, Tom Mc-Cullum, had been calling for a congressional hearing before the

Senate Intelligence Committee and threatening to subpoena "if necessary" the directors of Homeland Security, the FBI, the CIA, and others to testify. However, McCullum was in the minority party and so far his demands had been stymied by the majority party and the administration as "not in the best interest of national security."

Ariadne's last story had been published shortly before Karp was shot. After he recovered, Karp had not complained about the story. In fact, his off-the-record indication was that he was pleased that the information had come out.

Then Ariadne's second story was published when Karp was still in the hospital. In it, the complexity of Kane's plot was revealed. According to Ariadne's anonymous sources, Emil Stavros, a powerful banker and political kingmaker, was being blackmailed by Kane to wire the ransom money into offshore bank accounts. Kane had known of the murder of Stavros's wife and used it to force the man to cooperate or else spend the rest of his life in prison.

If that wasn't enough of a conspiracy, Ariadne had then linked Stavros to Rachel Rachman's campaign and implied that the assassination attempt on Karp had been motivated by revenge, not to secure the election for herself. The big question was—with Kane dead—who else would have had the motive and the juice to persuade Rachman to pull the trigger?

After Karp was shot, Murrow had gone into his office to secure whatever papers might have been left out and noted the school photos of the murdered children spread like a fan on the desk. Next to them was a yellow legal-sized notebook with a series of names and incidents with lines leading from one to the other. He'd studied the pad for a minute but concluded only that the names and lines were connected to the photographs.

Even in the hospital, Karp kept working the case. The day before he was released, he'd called and asked Murrow to quietly run the name Jamys Kellagh through the CCIC national crime computer. He'd had a few hits, including a Kansas City bank robber named James Kellough, who'd since had a sex change. However, none of the names matched the spelling, nor seemed to strike a chord with Karp, who was playing his cards close to the vest and didn't volunteer why he was interested in the name. But Murrow knew it had to do with the yellow legal pad and the murdered children.

While he had not criticized Ariadne's stories, Karp made it very clear to his inner circle that no one in the DAO was to comment to the press or provide information, even on background, regarding what they were referring to as the "The Kane Affair." He'd emphasized his point by giving Murrow the evil eye.

Recalling the glare, Murrow wondered if Karp would blame him for this latest story. He considered what it would take to keep Karp from ever seeing the new article in the *Guardian,* a weekly so-called alternative newspaper. But even if he could pull off that miracle, Murrow knew that the big dailies were sure to follow up on the story, and he'd be suspect again. In other words, he was doomed. There was bound to be a call from Karp in the morning.

Beyond his boss, Murrow had his own concerns about the stories. But it had less to do with incurring his boss's ire than being worried about Ariadne's safety. It was one thing to challenge the competence, and even integrity, of a U.S. law enforcement agency. But she was now intimating that a foreign government—the Russians no less—was involved.

He knew that his girlfriend had as much courage as any man. She'd written stories blasting dictators and mob bosses, corrupt politicians and dirty cops. She'd been shot at, beat up, and sued. She was no more apt to back off a hot story than Karp was likely to stop prosecuting criminals.

Murrow heaved a sigh. One of these days he was going to retire and write a series of books on the exploits of the Karp-Ciampi clan and their strange collection of friends, though no one would believe him and he'd probably have to publish their adventures as works of fiction.

In the meantime, the balancing act was wearing him out. Back at the DAO ranch, Harry "Hotspur" Kipman, the chief of the office appeals bureau and one of Karp's most trusted friends, was handling the business end of the office by overseeing the assignment of cases to the assistant district attorneys and running the weekly bureau chief meetings. But that left the actual running of the office—the telephone calls, the paperwork, the press conferences, and personnel matters—to Murrow.

By education and training, Murrow was also a prosecutor, but he had served as Karp's special assistant ever since Karp had been appointed to replace DA Jack Keegan, who'd left for a judge's seat on the federal bench nearly two years earlier. As the special assistant, Murrow's job had been to act as Karp's troubleshooter, keep an ear to the ground for what was going on in the office, and be the official keeper of Karp's time.

It hadn't left Murrow with much time to devote to the job he liked best, which was running Karp's reelection campaign. No swallow returning to Capistrano, no salmon swimming upriver had ever experienced a more instinctual homecoming than Murrow to the messy nest of politics. He so loved the battle that he'd even had to admit to himself that Rachman's death at Marlene's hands, and the opposition's failure to field a replacement candidate, had taken the fun out of election night.

In fact, that day he'd been feeling downright bluesy as he contemplated that the election was only a few weeks away and then they would all be back to the real business of the New York District Attorney's Office, which was prosecuting criminals.

Of course, they'd be doing that without the boss for a while. At least physically.

Karp had been ordered to stay away from the office by his physician, and he'd agreed in order for the doctor to let him out of the hospital. But he'd taken that to mean he wasn't supposed to physically go to the Criminal Courts Building.

Little by little, he'd been insinuating himself back into the running of the office. It began when he was still in the hospital and he'd call to discuss the bigger cases with Kipman or one of his other inner-circle bureau chiefs, like V. T. Newbury, the head of the bureau that investigated official corruption and malfeasance. Then he started hinting that he might "drop by" just in case some-one needed a little face time or even to quietly "catch up on some paperwork."

That afternoon, Murrow could have sworn that he saw Karp standing across Centre Street. The man had been wearing a broad-brimmed hat that he'd pulled down to cover most of his face, so it was hard to say for sure, but he had the same build, and when he moved, it was with a limp.

Murrow learned that his Karp sighting was the real McCoy a couple of hours later when he got a call from a terse Marlene Ciampi. "Gilbert, this is Marlene," she said, unnecessarily giving her name, as he would have recognized her voice, and been very afraid, in any dark alley. "I'm sitting here with my husband, Butch. Now, Gilbert, I'm going to ask you a question, and I expect you to answer me honestly."

Gilbert swallowed hard. He didn't need her to say "or else" to understand that this was an "or else" situation. The boss's wife had a temper straight from her ancestral home of Sicily and he wanted no part of it. "Yes, Marlene," he answered meekly.

"Gilbert, did you see my husband today?"

Hoping to be saved by a technicality, he answered, "I'm not sure."

There was a very pregnant pause. Then Marlene hissed. "Gilbert, are you toying with me?"

That's all it took. He cracked like a bad egg. "I think I may have seen him. . . . I was across the street, but it looked like him."

"Way to go down with the ship!" Gilbert heard Karp shout in the background.

"Tell him I couldn't commit perjury," Gilbert pleaded.

"No, Gilbert dear, you did the right thing . . . the smart thing," Marlene purred. "Now, if you'll excuse me, I have to cut a liar's tongue out of his mouth."

Gilbert had hung up the telephone feeling like a twelve-year-old kid who'd just ratted out his best friend to avoid getting grounded. And he should know, he'd been that kind of a kid.

❖ ❖ ❖

It was for his own good, he told himself as he carved a curl of lemon peel into a martini glass. There was nothing I could do. She knew. No sense both of us paying the price.

Still queasy at the thought of his close call with Marlene's temper, Murrow jumped at the sound of Ariadne's voice from the bedroom. "I hope the only reason you're so quiet out there is because you're stretching before the big game."

He paused to consider the merit of her suggestion. Not only was she taller, she outweighed him by fifteen pounds and, except for plenty of soft padding in the right places, was more muscular. Sometimes it paid to be limber when she was in one of her "moods."

"I'm shaking, not stirring, baby cakes," he yelled back. He cut the second lemon peel and plopped it into the other glass.

Murrow left the drinks on the counter and walked over to Ariadne's sound system—a Bose that could peel the paint off the walls when she was having a heavy-metal moment—and inserted a CD of Sinatra's greatest hits.

"These little town blues/are melting away/I'll make a brand-new start of it/in old New York . . ." Murrow sang along with Ol' Blue Eyes as he picked up the drinks.

A lot of people gave him and Ariadne one look and started to giggle. He figured other men were wondering what the voluptuous sex goddess saw in the pear-shaped little man in the wire-rimmed glasses whose taste in fashion embraced bow ties, vests, and tweed coats with a pocket watch.

To be honest, he'd wondered the same thing. But he gradually came to accept that for some unfathomable reason, she actually thought he was sexy, as well as smart. The fact was, however, that for all their physical differences, they had a lot in common.

For one thing, they loved the same music. Their friends might have been surprised if they'd seen them dressed in tight leather pants, leather vests, and dog collars at CBGB's, the seedy but trendy nightclub on the Bowery, attending a reunion concert of the Ramones. But they enjoyed a wide variety of music, including Sinatra and the rest of the Rat Pack, as well as big-band swing.

They were both also fascinated with American history. Anyone who ever listened to the way they talked to each other in some set-tings might have thought that the only book they had in common was the *Kama Sutra*. But the truth was that most of their evenings together were spent quietly lying in bed, reading aloud from some historical narrative like Ron Chernow's biography of Alexander Hamilton.

Who would have ever imagined that Ariadne could be turned on by a dramatic rendition of the Federalist Papers, he thought. Speaking of getting turned on . . .

"You coming?" he called back to the bedroom. "I think the Via-gra is starting to wear off!"

"You won't need any Viagra when you see what I bought at VS today," she yelled back.

Murrow smiled and grabbed the martinis before heading out onto the rooftop garden area that was the chief benefit of the loft apartment on Fifty-fifth Street between Second and Third av-enues. Ariadne didn't own the place—she couldn't have afforded it—it was on loan from one of her former lovers, a writer who'd "sold out" to author best-selling motivational books.

At first, Murrow wasn't thrilled about staying in the apartment of a former lover. But she'd convinced him that there was something particularly virile about having his way with her in the home—nay, on the very bed—of his rival, so he'd gotten over it.

Outside it was a lovely fall evening, and the air still carried a hint of summer. The roof had a nice clear view of the top half of the Chrysler Building and Midtown city lights, and was high enough not to be terribly disturbed by honking taxis and the smell of garbage. He placed the drinks on the ledge and reached up to ad-just his glasses.

Good thing, too, because at that moment, the garrote that dropped over his head would have quickly accomplished its task. As it was, his hand was caught between the nylon cord and his neck.

Back in the apartment, Ariadne paused her primping to listen. She thought she heard a glass breaking, but there was no sound other than Sinatra and the far-off noises of the city. Gilbert could be a little clumsy; she just hoped he hadn't dropped one of the martini glasses given to her years before by an enraptured British Member of Parliament when she was on assignment in London.

"I want to be a part of it/New York, New York," she sang as she brushed out her hair.

There was no one more surprised than she at her attraction to Gilbert Murrow. Karp's estimate of the number of notches on her bedpost was not totally inaccurate. She'd screwed some of the world's wealthiest, most powerful, and even best-looking men for the sake of a story, but she'd given them all up for a nearsighted intellectual who barely reached her chin.

However, she could not have cared less what people thought of her falling for Gilbert. He had a brilliant mind, was well read, and wasn't so in love with his own voice that he couldn't pause long enough to listen to her. And not just listen politely the way some men did when all they really wanted was to get laid. All of this made Murrow more desirable than any athlete with six-pack abs and buns of steel.

Along with the lovable personality traits, Gilbert had a few surprises of his own. For one thing, he was the most attentive and unselfish lover she'd ever known, and with the stamina to keep up with her own healthy libido. He claimed it was from all his years of abstinence. And he was delightfully funny for someone who came off even to his friends as such a straight arrow. He'd also discovered a latent calling for clandestine activities, whether it was assisting her with a story—as long as it didn't involve the DAO—or suggesting having sex in public places where they stood a decent chance of getting caught.

It was almost too good to last, and she worried what was next. Lately, she'd caught him looking at her as if weighing whether to say something, and she felt sure that a couple of times he was about to "pop the question." The idea had filled her with both dread—she'd avoided matrimony like she avoided stepping in the result of someone failing to curb his dog—and, surprisingly, excitement. She'd even tried out the name-change thing. Mrs. Gilbert

Murrow didn't work, but Ariadne Stupenagel-Murrow had a sort of magnificently multisyllabic cadence to it.

Ariadne knew that Gilbert was worried about her safety because of the stories. He pointed out a story in the *Times* that noted that journalism was one of the most dangerous jobs in the world.

"Yes, but not so much here in the United States," she assured him. "Don't worry, honey bunny, killing reporters only brings more reporters and most bad guys know that." She knew that only went so far, and he didn't buy it at all.

The truth was, she didn't know the identities of the men giving her the information for her latest series. One she figured was a fed, maybe FBI, maybe Homeland Security. Someone who didn't like what was going on in the aftermath of the St. Patrick's hostage situation.

The other source spoke with what sounded like a Russian accent. She pressed to meet with him, but he'd refused.

Okay, enough business for one day, she told herself. One last look in the mirror and she pronounced herself fit for duty.

Out on the rooftop, the assassin struggled to finish off the little man, who was putting up a surprisingly spirited battle—stomping on his feet, and fighting against the garrote like a marlin on the hook.

The job had been more difficult than anticipated from the beginning. The woman was supposed to have been alone and her murder staged to look like another Manhattan break-in where the tenant walked in on a burglar and was killed. He'd also intended on raping her for good measure. He supposed some of his colleagues in the assassination business would think that was unprofessional, but he was a man who liked a little fun with his job, and thought it worked well with the break-in scenario.

The assassin had reached the rooftop by first breaking into an apartment on a lower floor and accessing the fire escape. When the boyfriend arrived at the apartment, he'd cursed but hadn't panicked. If necessary, he'd shoot them both, though he hoped to catch them one at a time so that he could use his favorite weapon, the garrote. It was so much more personal.

The killer was a big man, six foot two and 250 pounds of muscle, but he was having a devil of a time trying to choke the life out of the little shit. Blood was flowing from a cut on his target's hand, and it made the rope slippery. He felt his grip giving way as they crashed into a trellis covered with the vines of a climbing rose. The thorns bit into his back as his arm muscles complained about the unexpected workout.

Maybe I'll just drop him over the edge, he thought. He forced the thrashing man over to the retaining wall. But just when he thought he could force him over, the punk-ass boyfriend put his feet on the ledge and shoved back.

"Oof," the assassin grunted as his intended victim landed on his stomach, but the effort seemed to have taken quite a bit out of his opponent as well. Furious, he rolled over on top of the man, and then knelt on his back to get more leverage as he pulled the garrote tight. "Come on, guy, let's just finish this," he pleaded, winded from the effort.

"Hey, asshole!"

The killer heard the voice behind him and reacted instantly by shoving his victim forward and standing. Without hesitating, he whirled with a back kick that should have caught the woman in the head. But she wasn't standing where she'd been when she spoke, and he struck nothing but air.

Then there was a moment when time stood still and he found himself facing a beautiful Amazon in a push-up bra, crotchless panties, garters, and nylons. But he also noted that the look on her face wasn't one of fear, as he would have expected; it was pure, unadulterated rage.

Only then did he see the baseball bat—the wooden Louisville Slugger. A baseball fan, he recognized Joe DiMaggio's signature on the barrel right before it caught him in the mouth, driving his front teeth down his throat, smashing his nose into a pulp, and propelling him backward toward the ledge.

Dazed, he was, however, not finished. He reached for the pistol in his waistband. But as well trained and fast as he was, he was no match for the angry woman.

"Nobody . . ." the big blonde snarled. The bat whistled down and caught him on the wrist, crushing the bone. The gun flew out of his hand.

"Fucks . . ." A backhand blow with the bat caught him on the elbow of his other arm, making it impossible to lift that hand to ward off the next blow, which caught him in the rib cage.

"With my . . ." The last blow caught him in the side of the head and sent him over the wall and into space.

"Boyfriend," Ariadne concluded as she looked over the edge at the body lying on the sidewalk five stories below. A woman who had been walking her poodle past the building started screaming and frantically yanked on the leash as her dog tried to inspect the pool of blood spreading from the corpse.

Ariadne turned and ran back to Murrow, who was staggering to his feet as he pulled the garrote off his neck and threw it to the ground. He pulled a handkerchief out of his pocket and wrapped it around his injured hand. Then, with her arm around his shoulders, they walked over to the wall and looked down.

A crowd had gathered around the body and several people were looking up and pointing at the faces of the man and woman on the rooftop of the building above them. Several were on their cell phones, apparently summoning the sirens that could be heard in the distance.

Murrow pulled back from the edge and looked at Ariadne. "Wow, that's some outfit," he croaked with admiration. "But the cops will be here in a few minutes. You might want to cover up."

"You think?" Ariadne asked as she went inside, picked up the telephone, and dialed 911, turning back to face him.

"Well," Murrow gulped, "only as long as you promise to wear it again sometime."

As Murrow and Ariadne pulled back from the parapet, a man who'd been sitting in the back of a stretch limousine down the block and on the other side of the street reached forward and knocked on the partition. "Let's go," he said when the driver lowered the glass.

"Yes, sir, Mr. Kellagh," the driver replied.

As the car pulled away from the curb and rolled past the crowd around the body, Kellagh shook his head and muttered, *"Myr shegin dy ve, bee eh."*

3

SURROUNDED BY DARKNESS, IT TOOK A MOMENT FOR LUCY Karp to realize that she was in the trunk of a car. Unable to see, she paid closer attention to her other senses—heard the whine of the wheels on the road, and smelled the old rubber of the spare tire and the fumes of a leaky exhaust.

Hope I don't die from carbon monoxide poisoning, she thought, then realized that she was not thinking in English. Euskara? Why am I thinking in the Basque language?

That she understood what she was thinking came as no surprise. She was a hyper-polyglot, a term used by linguists for someone capable of speaking six or more languages fluently. In Lucy's case, she was a hyper-polyglot times ten, having learned nearly sixty unique languages in her twenty-one years, plus a number of variations. In fact, her "gift" qualified her more as a language savant; unlike someone who studied and practiced languages to become fluent, she could pick them up simply by listening to others speak, sometimes in an afternoon.

But why Euskara? Maybe I got hit on the head?

Lucy didn't dwell on her mind's choice of language for long. She had a more serious predicament and needed to think clearly, but her heart was pounding like a drum. Taking a cleansing breath as she'd been taught by John Jojola, a Pueblo Indian police officer from Taos who had become something of a spiritual advisor to Lucy and her mother, she calmed herself and concentrated on noting details that she hoped might somehow help her situation. She could tell it was a big car from the size of the trunk and the heavy, solid ride. American-made . . . probably a Cadillac or Lincoln.

Lucy couldn't recall how she got in the trunk. In fact, there seemed to be several lapses in her short-term memory. She knew that she was living in New Mexico with her boyfriend, Ned Blanchet, after returning from Manhattan, where they'd helped foil a plot to kill the Pope.

No, wait, my dad got shot, she thought. Then Ned went back to Taos because the ranch needed him. . . . And he's probably grown a little tired of "vacations" with the Karps. . . . But I stayed until Dad was going to be okay, then I went back to New Mexico.

After that, her mind was drawing a blank. She wondered how long she'd been in the trunk. Hours, anyway.

The road apparently had a lot of curves, judging from the way she was jostled back and forth. And the sound of the tires was a monotonous whine broken only by the occasional growl of a car passing in the other direction. It all added up to the conclusion that she was being transported along a rural two-lane highway in the mountains of New Mexico.

Suddenly, the monotony of the road noise was broken by a thunderous rumbling, as if the car were passing through a storm. She was trying to identify the sound when a whistle shrieked, making her jump and bump her head on the trunk lid. A train. We're driving next to a train.

Soon thereafter the car slowed and turned left onto a gravel road, judging by the crunching sound beneath the tires. They didn't go far, however, before stopping, apparently to allow the train to pass. She could hear it thundering just in front of the car.

Remember all of this, she told herself in Euskara, it will be important later.

The train passed and the car moved forward again on the gravel road, but again, only for a few more feet before it stopped. Someone got out of the car and she could hear voices. Then someone got back in, a gate creaked open, and the car drove forward again.

After what she assumed to be a mile or so—given the time and her approximation of speed—the car swerved to the right and continued on for another mile or so. When it stopped, all four doors opened and she heard footsteps approaching the rear of the car.

Need to escape, she thought. Get to a telephone and tell the cops to drive several hours along a two-lane rural highway that at some point runs parallel to a train track. Then turn on the gravel road . . .

Lucy stopped, overcome by the realization that it was all useless. What she'd just described could have been anywhere, a thousand country highways, a million gravel roads. And her captors weren't about to just let her go.

She could hear men outside laughing and talking; their speech was slurred, as if they'd been drinking. Suddenly, the trunk opened, revealing that it was not nighttime as she had supposed. Instead, an intense afternoon sun blinded her, making it difficult to see the faces of the two men who leaned over and reached for her. Her eyes struggled to adjust, but everything seemed too bright, out of focus, and surreal. I must have a concussion, she thought.

All she knew for sure was that her tormentors were bald, which was odd, as they were obviously young. There's a reason, she thought, but it wouldn't quite come to her. The only other details that stood out were their cruel, smirking eyes and the smell of alcohol on their breath.

Lucy lashed out at the taller of the two men as he pulled her from the trunk, scratching at his face and kicking. Her knee caught him in the groin, and he fell to the ground, which made his comrades laugh and jeer. When he got up, his eyes were red with rage, and he began striking her in the face with his fist. The odd thing was that Lucy knew she was being hit but didn't feel any pain.

The tall man dragged her to the driver's-side door and shoved her down on the seat behind the steering wheel, to which her bound hands were lashed. She glanced at the steering column and noted the Cadillac symbol. Small consolation for being right, she thought.

Looking out of the side window, she saw that her abductors were standing in a line with their backs to her. They seemed to be posing; one was raising a beer and shouted something. Oh my God, they're taking pictures, like this is some sort of show!

The pounding of her heart sounded as loud as a drum. She peered between two of the men and saw the photographer standing on the little hill. *"Pikutara joan,"* she cursed the men. It meant "Go to hell," but they only laughed.

When they finished, the tall one she kicked in the balls walked back and leaned in the window past her and turned the keys in the ignition. The car roared to life. As he started to withdraw, he turned his face to her and tried to kiss her. But she spit on him and struck him with her forehead; her fingers wrapped around the chain that dangled from his neck and yanked hard enough to break it.

The man swore and grabbed her around her throat with his left hand while he punched with his right. He struck her again, and the fight left Lucy, who slumped in her seat, resigned to her fate. The man called her a name and reached back in and put the car's transmission into Drive.

The car crept forward but didn't have far to go. Immediately in front, the earth opened up into a six-foot-deep pit that had apparently been dug in the rust-red soil by the earthmover that sat belching black smoke off to one side. The car pitched forward and then rolled down a steep dirt ramp to the bottom, where it splashed through a shallow puddle of water before crashing into the far wall and coming to rest.

When it hit the wall, Lucy was propelled forward, striking her head on the steering wheel. Dazed, she tried to grasp what was happening. Then she realized she was in a car-sized grave; even the dirt walls around her wept groundwater as if in sympathy for her plight. Above her, the earthmover roared and a few moments later dropped the first massive shovelful of dirt and gravel on the car. She screamed in terror while the men on the edge of the pit looked down and laughed.

Lucy must have blacked out then because the next thing she knew, the pit and car were filled so that only her hands, shoulders, and head were above the gravel, dirt, and sand. The weight against her chest made it difficult to breathe. She opened her hand, the one that had torn the chain from the tall man's chest, and saw that along with the chain, she was holding a medallion made of three interlocking triangles. She turned her head to look up at the men taunting her from the edge of the pit.

"*Sasikumea*," she shouted, but the Basque word for bastard only provoked more hoots of derision.

She locked her eyes on the tall one to get his attention, then looked back at her hand. He stopped laughing when he saw the medallion; his hand went to his neck and he blanched, his face contorted by rage. He turned toward the earthmover as if to get it to stop, but then another scooperful of gravel crashed down through the broken windshield and flooded the interior of the car.

Entombed, Lucy tried to scream but her efforts were muffled, choked by the earth that clogged her throat, nostrils, and ears. Soon her body began to spasm from lack of air. My baby, she thought, my poor baby!

As she died, she could hear Jojola singing in Tiwa, the native language of the Pueblo Indians. "*May the gods bless me, help me, and give me power and understanding*," he chanted as the drum kept time with the thumping of her heart.

The singing stopped and Jojola's voice commanded, "Lucy! Lucy Karp! Listen to me. It's John Jojola. It is time to come back from the spirit world." Then he was shaking her roughly and patting her face. But she was dead and couldn't open her eyes.

"Inhale, Lucy, breathe deep and return," the voice of John Jojola continued. She smelled the fragrant sweetness of burning sage and took a deep breath despite the fear that she would inhale the rocks that filled her mouth. But when she did, the only thing that flooded her lungs was fresh air with a hint of sage.

Lucy felt Jojola's strong hands on her shoulders and wondered how he could have found his way into the car in time to save her. She forced her eyes open and discovered that she was not buried inside a car at all. In fact, she sat next to Jojola on a cliff of a mesa high above the New Mexican desert, wrapped in a Navajo blanket. It was daylight, but not the burning sun of a summer afternoon, just the setting sun of a chilly evening in late October.

The beauty of her surroundings slowly shooed away the horror of the burial. Nearby, Taos Mountain reached into the sky, its deep green, pine-clad slopes splotched with canary yellow and burnt-orange stands of aspen. The sky to the west was painted gold and purple, with the colors growing stronger as the sun slipped peacefully toward the horizon.

A strong hand gently turned her face from the sunset, and she found herself looking at the lined, bronze face of John Jojola. His dark brown eyes peered deep into her own, as if he were reading the fine print of a newspaper ad.

Jojola took her hand and placed something into it. "Sand," he said, "to bring you back to the reality of this earth." He then turned over her other hand and poured water onto it. "Wash with the waters from our sacred lake and be reborn."

Lucy felt the sand trickle through her fingers, aware of each grain. She splashed the water on her face and felt refreshed. "Where . . . where have I been?" she asked.

"Your body was here all along," Jojola replied as he picked up a piece of smoldering sage and waved it around Lucy, chanting something under his breath. "But your spirit has been far away."

The sage, she knew, was for cleansing. Then she remembered that the bitter, metallic flavor in her mouth was the aftertaste of peyote, a powerful hallucinogen found in the fruit of a cactus that grew in Mexico. It all came back to her—the dreams and going to the mesa with Jojola on a spirit quest.

Lucy had known that Jojola was a practicing member of the Native American Church, which had been organized by American Indian tribes so that the U.S. government could not stop them from taking peyote as part of their religious rights. He'd explained that peyote had been used by Indians of Mexico, where the plant grew, for thousands of years. Only in the past hundred years or so had American Indians used it as a path to the spirit world.

As such, peyote was considered sacred—not a toy for Anglo hippies who wanted to see a kaleidoscope of colors and go "on a trip." When Lucy broached the subject of using it herself, Jojola had at first rejected the request.

"Why do you want it?" he demanded.

Lucy replied that she wasn't some college kid looking for a high. "I'm searching for answers," she told him. She'd been having dreams in which she was suffocating and dreams in which she was burning, dreams filled with smoke and three triangular-shaped mountains. The dreams had filled her with fear and a sense that she couldn't trust anybody outside of her family and small circle of friends. But the worst dream of all—one she'd had with increasing frequency—was the one with Ned lying on the ground and a man pointing a rifle at him as his finger pulled back on the trigger.

"I think the answers might be important," she'd added.

Jojola hadn't replied right away. He knew that Lucy was different from most people and in tune with the spirit world. A few of the Taos Pueblo people had labeled her a *bruja,* a witch, and wanted her banned from the pueblo because she'd learned their secret language as if by magic. But most in the tribe who knew her as he did argued that her heart was pure, as were her intentions. And so an unspoken understanding was reached that no one would teach her the language, but if she learned it simply by listening, then the spirits must have wanted it to be so.

More than a year had passed since they'd met and Jojola found himself cast into the role of spiritual advisor to Lucy and her mother, Marlene. While it seemed an accidental meeting, he was sure it was not; the spirits had wanted it to happen and so it had. But even if he was willing to teach them his understanding of spirituality, the secret traditions of his people he would not reveal. His tribe was one of the few in the United States living on their ancestral lands instead of having been moved to a reservation. As such, they'd been able to keep most of their customs and language intact, in part because they did not allow outsiders to usurp them.

However, he reasoned, peyote was not a Taos custom; not everyone in his tribe or the other tribes belonged to the Native

American Church. He himself had come to it only out of desperation.

After two tours in Vietnam, Jojola had returned in 1969 to the Taos Pueblo only to discover that he had not entirely found his way home from the war. He became an alcoholic and deadbeat, especially after his wife, herself an alcoholic, left him with a young son to raise. Only his love for his son had saved him from drinking himself to death. But he couldn't overcome his addiction to alcohol by himself. Then one of the tribe's elders, who was a member of the Native American Church, suggested that he might ask the spirits to help by participating in a peyote ceremony.

Jojola was willing to try anything and begged the elder to set it up for him. But the elder said that his was a special case, and he would have to travel to Mexico and find the ancient roots of the peyote cult.

So he had gone with a letter from the elder introducing him to the Huichol people, the original practitioners of the peyote ceremony. He was in luck: they were preparing to go on their annual trek to find peyote, which they called *hikuri,* and invited him along.

Led by a *mara'akame,* or shaman, Jojola had to first pass through the rite of confession and purification. For each offense that he confessed, the *mara'akame* made a knot in a string. Some of the knots represented the guilt he felt over killing other men, even if it had been in combat, but mostly the knots represented mistakes he'd made as a husband, a father, and as a member of his tribe. Either way, his string was particularly long by Huichol standards, and filled with knots.

At the end of the ceremony, the shaman burned the string. When he woke the next morning, Jojola felt as if a weight had been lifted, but the shaman told him that his journey was not over.

In fact, it had only just begun. He traveled with the tribe to the sacred mountains of Wirikuta, where they prayed to the spirits and washed themselves in the waters of a holy stream. Only now, the shaman warned him, were they ready for the perilous crossing into the otherworld.

The tribe had then searched for *hikuri*. When they were through harvesting and ready to partake, Jojola was given twelve pieces of the mescal fruit that contained the peyote. It was considered a light dose for the more practiced Huichol, some of whom consumed as many as fifty pieces. But it was enough.

The journey began innocently enough with colorful lights and gentle hallucinations, as well as a general feeling of well-being. But that afternoon, the sky had grown dark, nearly as black as night, with frenetic blasts of lightning and thunder.

Coming out of the storm, he saw a dark warrior approaching from across the desert carrying a war club. The demon ran as fast as the wind, and Jojola could tell that it was coming to do battle and that if he failed, he would literally die on that mountainside.

Looking about for a weapon, Jojola saw the sharp-ended rib bone of a coyote and picked it up. Then the dark spirit was upon him. They struck each other with terrific blows, and then circled before striking again, before repeating their terrible dance.

Bloody and dazed, Jojola realized that the spirit was alcohol and it intended to devour him body and soul. Then it would take his son, and his people. Anger welled up inside of him and he raised the coyote rib, then plunged it into the demon with all of his might. The dark warrior collapsed to his knees but refused to die.

So with his remaining strength, Jojola lifted the demon and cast it down the mountainside, where it fell a thousand feet and struck with a sound like thunder rumbling through the ground. An avalanche of stone was dislodged and swept down, burying the demon.

Physically and emotionally drained, Jojola turned to see that the Huichol had gathered to witness the battle. Smiling, they came forward one at a time to embrace him. "You are free of the demon," the shaman, who approached last, said, "but only as long as you do not invite him back into your life. Return to the old ways. Reject him. Save yourself, your son, and your people."

Returning to the Taos Pueblo, Jojola was a changed man. He stayed away from bars and liquor stores in the city of Taos, and even shunned old friends who drank alcohol. Instead, he hunted

deer on the sacred Taos Mountain with a bow, swam in the holy
waters of Blue Lake, and communed with the spirits of the high
plains desert of New Mexico. He also taught his son the ways of his
people so that he would respect the culture and draw strength
from it. "We Pueblo Indians close our borders to outsiders every
winter and withdraw into our ancient adobe lodges so that we may
come together as a people and become stronger for being part of a
whole," he told the boy.

His tribe had rejoiced at his return to his place in the warrior
clan. When it had come time to name a new police chief, he had
been the only candidate they considered. Confident now in who he
was and with his past, he was a rare man who stood comfortably
and easily with one foot in the modern world—running a professional, modern police force—and the other foot in the ancient, returning every year to Mexico to join the Huichol in their trek to the
mountains of Wirikuta.

Jojola despised so-called Indian medicine men who sold peyote
and charged to perform the rites for Anglos who, dissatisfied with
their own culture, tried to become "white Indians." But he knew
Lucy was not trying to become something she was not, she was trying to understand who she was. When she talked about her
dreams, he saw the fear in her eyes and knew that the answers she
needed might be found in the otherworld.

So he'd led her to the desert butte where they now sat and up
the steep, narrow trail to the top. He'd often traveled there himself
because it was the home to eagles, who he considered to be messengers to the gods. There he'd heard her confession and tied
knots in a string, quietly amused at how few knots there were compared to his own first time. Then they'd burned the string.

When she was prepared, he gave Lucy six pieces of mescal. As
she sat looking at the cactus fruit, he told her to be careful not to
overanalyze the journey she was about to take. "There will be
things you don't understand or might misinterpret," he said. "We
believe that a powerful spirit resides in the peyote and that spirit
can be fickle. You may see visions that seem important, but aren't;
and often there will be experiences that don't seem like much, but

in the end are the most valuable to remember. Do you understand?"

Lucy nodded and began to place a piece of mescal in her mouth
when Jojola restrained her arm with his hand. "It is not too late to
turn back from the otherworld," he said. "People have lost their
minds to peyote or injured themselves. I will be here with you, but
I cannot protect you from everything in the spirit world."

The girl had held his eyes for a long minute, then patted his
hand. "I understand," she said, and placed the first button in her
mouth, making a face as the astringent chemicals hit her tongue.
An hour later, she became violently ill as her body tried futilely to
rid itself of the hallucinogenic poison. But it was already working
on her liver and coursing through her blood. And then she'd found
herself locked in the trunk of a car about to be murdered.

"What did you see?" Jojola asked gently. "I heard you scream and
you spoke in a language I did not recognize."

Lucy shuddered. "I saw my death," she said, and relayed what
she remembered though the details were already blurring in her
mind.

When she finished, Jojola was quiet for a long time. Death
dreams were not to be discounted. But he also knew that the visions could not always be taken literally. "Sometimes a vision of
death actually represents a new beginning, just as death is merely
the next step onward in our existence," he told her. "The spirit of
peyote is fond of symbolism."

Lucy was quiet. "Maybe," she said. "I hope so, but even if it was
literal, I still think it was important for some reason that I saw it
now." She looked out to where the sun was now a pastel memory
on the horizon and suddenly felt incredibly tired.

She yawned. "So what's next?"

Jojola smiled back. "Sleep."

As if he'd cast a spell, Lucy fell backward, but Jojola was ready
and caught her by the waist. He picked her up and carried her to a
bed he'd made of soft cedar clippings piled several inches thick.

She breathed deep the fragrant aroma of the cedar and began to drift off.

"Rest now, Lucy," Jojola said, covering her with a blanket. "You will dream because the spirit of peyote lingers in your blood. But I will be here."

Lying on her side with her eyelids growing heavier, Lucy watched him walk over to a ring of stones, where he lit a fire and sat down next to his hide-covered drum. Picking up a stick covered on one end with doeskin, he began to beat the drum softly to a rhythm that matched the beating of her heart. Then he began to sing in Tiwa. *"May the gods bless me, help me, and give me power and understanding."*

4

BUTCH KARP WINCED AS HE STEPPED UP ONTO THE CURB AT the corner of Grand and Mercer. The physical therapist at the hospital had suggested that he use a cane as he worked his wounded leg back into shape, but he was damned if he was going to hobble around Manhattan like an old man. Instead, he forced himself to walk without support, and as normally as possible, so that he wouldn't develop a limp.

He was making good progress, too, except for the occasional misstep that reminded him that a piece of metal had passed through his thigh at a tremendous rate of speed. It will take time, he reminded himself as he straightened and resumed his stroll down the sidewalk at what he considered a respectable clip for having been shot three times.

A second bullet had hit him in the chest, but he'd lucked out and the 9 mm bullet was deflected by a rib and so only nicked a lung before passing out of his back. It broke two ribs, and he might have bled to death if not for the quick reactions of his wife and a passing stranger. But once the bleeding was stopped, the danger had passed.

However, the third bullet was a killer. Almost . . . as in close only counts in horseshoes, dancing, and hand grenades. The bullet that hit him in the chest spun him so that the next bullet entered the back of his neck. It should have killed him—pierced his skull right where it met the brain stem and shut off the lights before he even hit the ground. But X-rays revealed that the bullet had miraculously stopped just short of doing any real damage.

No one—not the police investigators, not the emergency room surgeons who thought that they'd seen it all—could explain why the bullet stopped. At that range, a 9 mm could have passed through a two-by-four. In fact, several other rounds that missed him took out tennis-ball-sized chunks from the marble facade of the Criminal Courts Building.

"The bullet probably didn't get the right charge at the factory," Clay Fulton said, and shrugged. "Or maybe you tensed your muscles at the perfect moment . . . I heard there's guys in the circus who can do that."

"Bullshit!"

"Probably," the detective agreed, then gave him a meaningful look. "Or maybe it was a God thing. Maybe the Man upstairs wasn't ready to see your sorry ass."

"Maybe so," Karp replied with a smile.

That the bullet stopped short was the good news. The bad news was that it came to rest against the vertebrae and a major artery to his brain. Several surgeons had been consulted and he'd been offered two options.

Removing it was risky. The slightest slip of the scalpel or too much pressure on the bullet, and he could end up paralyzed or dead. Leaving it in was the other possibility; the hope would be that scar tissue would build up around the bullet and hold it in place. However, a blow to the back of his neck, an awkward fall, or even a sudden jerk of his head could shove the bullet against the artery and cause a stroke that could kill him.

After talking it over with Marlene, Karp had opted for the surgery. He just couldn't stand the thought of some evil piece of metal beneath his skin. Or the idea that some everyday event—even playing basketball with his two boys—could kill him. He would have to limit what he did, and that just wasn't in him.

Karp had gone into surgery wondering if he would wake up paralyzed, or wake up at all. He tried not to worry his kids or wife.
"This is nothing," he growled when their faces grew long and tears
welled in their eyes in the pre-op room. "See you in a few hours."
But when he was wheeled away to the operating room, he wished
he'd said something more memorable for his last words to his family. However, the surgery went well, and he'd come out of it knowing that his wife was holding his hand even before he opened his
eyes and saw the expectant, hopeful faces of their three children,
Lucy, Zak, and Giancarlo.

Not that someone had waved a magic wand and he was suddenly all better. During the first couple of weeks of recuperation,
it felt like someone was poking him in the neck with a red-hot
piece of iron. Now it didn't hurt as much, even when he felt for
the lump of the ugly purple scar just beneath the hairline. But at
times he wondered if he'd ever get strength back in his leg, or stop
feeling—especially late at night—the trajectory of bullets through
his body.

Still, he'd accepted that what he did now about his injuries was
up to him. He'd had plenty of experience with the process of rehabilitation, including when he was a highly recruited basketball
player at the University of California, Berkeley and a freak fall destroyed the ligaments in his knee. The injury ended his dreams of
a pro career, but it had taught him how to mentally, as well as
physically, recover from a devastating injury and move on with his
life.

Moving on was the toughest part. With his wife threatening to
finish the bullet's job if he got within shouting distance of the
Criminal Courts Building—ever since the little traitor Murrow
gave me up, he thought—he'd had to find other ways to occupy his
time and use up some of his prodigious energy.

After he was released from the hospital, the doctors had set him
up with a physical therapist who'd put him on a regime of light lifting to strengthen the injured muscles and frequent massages to
keep the scar tissue broken up, and encouraged him to "just get
out and walk." So he'd gotten in the habit of taking a long walk

every morning, often joined by Father Jim Sunderland, the Catholic priest who'd put pressure on his wounds as he lay bleeding on the sidewalk.

It was Sunderland's voice that had stuck in his head, reminding him that he had unfinished business. Then one day when he was still in the hospital, Sunderland had come by to see how he was doing. Karp had thought the name was familiar, but it took the sight of the priest's collar to put it together. Sunderland had angered his church and the U.S. government as a vocal antiwar activist during the Vietnam conflict; he'd also popped up in the civil rights movement, linking arms with the Reverend Martin Luther King Jr. in Mississippi to face the fire hoses, German shepherds, and the Ku Klux Klan. Time and again over the next forty years, if there was a war, he tried to stop it; if there was an injustice, he spoke out against it. His liberal ideology had often brought him into conflict with the conservative hierarchy of his church, as well as the Christian Right in general, and only his popularity with the masses kept him from formal censure. Most recently, he'd been organizing New York Catholics against the war in Iraq.

If they'd met in other circumstances, Karp might have dismissed him as a publicity seeker. Even now he didn't agree with all of the man's politics. But he found him to be sincere and committed in his beliefs. He respected that, and as a private individual, not the strident public activist, the priest was warm and caring, with a delightful and wicked sense of humor. He could also defend his positions on their legal and ethical—as opposed to emotional—merits as well as any law professor. In fact, to Karp's surprise, he had been a practicing attorney before "as Timothy Leary suggested to me in the sixties, I 'turned on, tuned in, and dropped out' of the rat race and became a Jesuit."

After Karp got out of the hospital, Sunderland had called to see if he wanted to go for a walk, and they'd spent several mornings wandering around Chinatown or Little Italy or Soho or the Village. Both men found in each other a worthy opponent and would become so wrapped up in their debates and conversations that they would walk for many blocks without paying attention to where they were going, until they looked up and had to figure out where they were.

As they strolled, they discussed a wide variety of topics, such as the death penalty. Sunderland, of course, opposed it on moral grounds. However, his opposition wasn't just a blanket "Thou shalt not kill," or even that state-sponsored executions were still cold-blooded murders that debased the society that perpetuated them. There was also no evidence, he argued, that the death penalty acted as a deterrent to other murderers.

By and large, Karp agreed that the death penalty was ineffective for those reasons, as well as costing the taxpayers "a bloody fortune" to prosecute and then defend on appeal. However, his opposition had a caveat. "There are times when the crime is so heinous, the perpetrator so depraved that society has the right to seek retribution by casting this evil from the circle of humanity," he argued.

"Oh really?" the priest said. " 'Many that live deserve death. And some die that deserve life. Can you give it to them? Then be not too eager to deal out death in the name of justice, fearing for your own safety. Even the wise cannot see all ends.' "

"Was that out of the Bible, I don't seem to remember the citation," Karp asked.

Sunderland laughed. "No, actually, I was quoting from *The Lord of the Rings*. But I think that even evil men may play out roles that neither they nor we can foresee may, without their choosing, work out for the good."

Over such discussions, the two had quickly become friends, and Karp looked forward to each encounter. That morning, Sunderland called and suggested that Karp join him and a small group of his friends—"all of us retired or semiretired with nothing better to do than discuss the great issues of the day; some might call them 'bitch sessions' "—for breakfast at a bustling little Tribeca café called Kitchenette.

"Even if the company is wretched, you'll love the peach and blueberry pancakes smothered in real maple syrup and washed down with Saxbys French Roast, which just so happens to be the finest coffee in the land," the priest added. "Or my current favorite, the 'Farmhouse' breakfast of eggs and bacon and the pièce de résistance, a huge, warm biscuit absolutely dripping with homemade strawberry butter. Anyway, we're commemorating an anniversary there this morning and you might find the conversation of interest."

"Really? And what anniversary is that?" Karp asked.

"Why, it's October 29, the black day in history when Sir Walter Raleigh was executed," Sunderland replied. "I'd have thought that a constitutional scholar such as yourself would be well aware of such an important date."

Karp chuckled. Every law student had the date drilled into his head at one time or another. The injustices of Raleigh's trial had been the fertile soil from which many of the U.S. Constitution's most important protections had sprung. "But of course," he replied. "It's just that the mention of the pancakes has driven all thought of history from my mind."

Throwing on a light jacket against the chill of the October air, he'd quickly left the loft and headed west on Grand Street past the Soho art galleries and, after the minor twinge at Mercer, continued to West Broadway where he turned left and headed south.

Although he'd never been to Kitchenette, Karp had heard of it as a locals' meeting place. Sunderland said that whenever the weather allowed, his friends liked to sit at the tables outside to discuss politics, the arts, "and pretty girls," while they ate what passed for down-home cooking in Manhattan. On less temperate days, the worthies crowded into the café to sit at tables crammed into the long, narrow corridor of the interior.

Even with the nip in the air, it was a beautiful fall day in New York City. The leaves had long since changed color and, except for a few stragglers, had fallen to the ground, but the skies were a bright blue and the air fresh with breezes blowing east from the nearby Hudson River. And really, the temperature was quite pleasant in the sun, which was what he spotted Sunderland enjoying as he approached the café.

After shaking Karp's hand, Sunderland led him over to a table where a group of older men were engaged in lively debate. Although Sunderland had not told him who they were meeting, Karp had figured that they would likely be an unusual group. He was not disappointed, identifying several of them as distinguished members of the legal profession.

The first face he recognized was that of a tall, lean, almost-to-the-point-of-gaunt man whose long silver hair was tied back in a ponytail like some aging hippy. He had looked quite a bit different the last time Karp had seen him, but there was no mistaking the deep-set probing eyes of Frank Plaut, a former federal judge with the Second Circuit Court of Appeals.

Karp was impressed. Plaut was considered one of the finest constitutional minds of his and many other generations. The New York DAO's appeals bureau chief—Harry "Hotspur" Kipman, a friend who Karp also regarded as one of the best legal scholars he'd ever met—worshipped the jurist. And Karp had argued several cases before him and learned, once or twice the hard way, to be on his toes when citing precedent or making an argument before Plaut.

By all accounts, Plaut had been destined for a seat on the U.S. Supreme Court. But for reasons known only to himself, he had one day stepped down from the bench and accepted a position teaching constitutional law at Columbia University. Now here he sat presiding over coffee and what appeared to be waffles at a Tribeca café.

Karp also recognized a second man as a former U.S. attorney for Manhattan, Dennis Hall. He was a conservatives' darling and a regular commentator on Fox, but he was not a poorly researched, mindless TV talking head. His arguments were always reasoned and based upon a strict interpretation of the Constitution.

Seated next to him was his legal opposite, Murray Epstein, a ferocious defense attorney who'd terrorized many an assistant district attorney of the New York DAO. The man could have made a living as a Shakespearean actor with his flair for language and dramatic gestures, but he was no empty suit. Epstein knew the law inside and out, and as a defender of the liberal camp of constitutional law, he'd argued, and won, his share of cases before the U.S. Supreme Court.

Some of Epstein's battles with Karp's mentor, the longtime New

York City DA Francis Garrahy, were the stuff of legend at the DAO. And he'd even put a much younger Butch Karp through his paces a time or two; in fact, he'd nearly won what had appeared to be a slam-dunk homicide case for the prosecution. Karp's bacon had been pulled from the fire only because Garrahy insisted on meticulous preparation and, conveniently, because the truth was on his side.

Karp didn't recognize the other men at the table. But if the company they kept hadn't already identified them as formidable thinkers, their conversation as Sunderland and Karp walked up certainly did.

"I still contend that the biggest impact of Raleigh's trial on U.S. constitutional law was the right to a fair and impartial hearing before a judge and a jury of one's peers," Hall argued.

"Humbug," Epstein replied. "The nut of this was the right to confront witnesses and present evidence."

"What good would it have done Raleigh to cross-examine Cobham and present his letter if the judges and juries were still predetermined to find him guilty?" a short man who looked somewhat like Albert Einstein asked.

"It was damned unfair," a heavyset man agreed. "Even Raleigh's judges and jurors recognized that—if somewhat too late. On his deathbed, Justice Gawdy said, 'The justice of England was never so depraved and injured as the condemnation of Sir Walter Raleigh.' And some members of the jury knelt before him and begged his forgiveness."

"I read that his widow kept his preserved head in a cupboard, which she would trot out to show visitors," said an effete-looking gentleman whose voice and mannerisms reminded Karp of Truman Capote. He obviously found the macabre more fascinating than the constitutional questions.

"Gentlemen, gentlemen, we digress from our topic," Plaut interrupted. "Today on the black anniversary, we were to stick to the impact of Raleigh's trial on the confrontation clause of the Sixth Amendment and how it applies, if at all, to the pretrial publicity surrounding the rape charges brought against members of the Duke University lacrosse team."

The admonition seemed to get the others' attention, but it was soon diverted again when a buxom fortysomething waitress with a lip ring arrived to take their order.

"Hey, babe," Epstein growled, wiggling his eyebrows, "if I told you that you have a beautiful body, would you hold it against me?" The others cackled at the old joke and sat expectantly awaiting her response.

Which was to roll her eyes and reply with a heavy Queens accent, "Not on your life, Murray. You'd probably have a heart attack and the cops would arrest me for moider."

"I'd sign a waiver for you, Marjorie," Epstein replied.

Marjorie the waitress was about to respond when she noted that the men had all stopped looking at her to watch a leggy model type in tight jeans walk past on the sidewalk to their appreciative wolf whistles.

"Hey, so what did I become, chopped liver?" Marjorie complained in mock seriousness. "I swear the minute I turn my back on youse guys, you're ogling some anorexic teenager with a bad dye job."

"Turn your back on us," the Albert Einstein look-alike replied, "and you can bet our eyes will be on you. That's one nice can you got there, sister."

"That's better," the waitress sniffed. "For a moment there, I thought you might all leave me for some floozy with a pair of plastic tits."

"As the old saying goes, 'Who cares if they're fake,' " Epstein said.

"That's an old saying? I think the copyright on it is a lot younger than any of you," she scoffed.

"Oh, so now you're a lawyer," Hall quipped.

"Well, I don't lie or cheat, so that rules out that career," Marjorie shot back. "Now, shall I call your wives and tell them to cut back on the vitamin E? Youse guys are getting a little too frisky, and you might fall and break a hip or something."

The men laughed and applauded the waitress's sauce and pleaded for mercy. That's when they noticed Karp and Sunderland standing to the side, enjoying the repartee, and waved them over.

"Ah, gentlemen, look what our good priest has brought us," Epstein said, clapping. "The district attorney of New York, Butch Karp. Have a seat, have a seat."

"So, Mr. District Attorney, did you overhear our topic of discussion on this auspicious occasion?" Hall asked.

"I did," Karp replied.

"Well, then, would you care to weigh in?" Epstein asked, shooting the others a sly glance.

The way the others suddenly grew rapt with attention gave Karp the impression that he was not so much being asked to weigh in as he was being weighed. Taking a seat, he joined the fray. "Well, prosecutors should do their talking in court. It's not advisable to engage in press conferences or encounter-type give-and-takes with the media. Just proceed in an orderly and fair fashion."

"Would you care to elucidate further on that position?" Hall asked, as if facing a witness on the stand.

The obvious challenge might have intimidated another man. But on the list of things Karp loved most in life were first his wife and kids, followed shortly thereafter by discussing the law. He shifted to address his opponent more directly and winced when the movement put a little too much pressure on the wounded muscle of his leg.

The others noticed the reaction and asked solicitously if he was all right. "We, of course, heard about the unfortunate incident," Plaut said.

"Hell of a way to try to win an election," faux Albert Einstein said. "And by the way, the name's Bill, Bill Florence. I used to be an editor on that fish-wrapper the *New York Post*."

"Guess she lost her head, and the name's Saul Silverstein, I was in ladies' apparel for a time," the heavyset man cracked.

The others groaned at the reference to the fact that by the time Marlene finished emptying her gun at her husband's assailant, there wasn't much left above her neck.

"Forgive my friends Mr. Florence and Mr. Silverstein for their tasteless senses of humor," Sunderland said, shooting the pair a dirty look. "They don't know any better. And by the way, my friend Mr. Silverstein is being unusually humble this morning. He wasn't just in 'ladies' apparel,' he practically invented women's slacks in the late forties."

"What? What?" Silverstein objected, as if Sunderland was reading something into his comment that he had not intended.

"My apologies, Mr. Karp, you'll find that the Sons of Liberty Breakfast Club and Girl-Watching Society is comprised of ancient cynics," Plaut noted. "The commentary can at times grow somewhat morbid or, as the good friar noted, a bit dark for some tastes."

Karp held up his hand and smiled. "No apologies necessary, gentlemen. No one understands more than those of us working at the DAO that if it wasn't for the ability to laugh at dark humor, we'd all go mad."

"The name's Geoffrey Gilbert," the effete-looking man said, laughing. "I'm an artist, which makes me 'the sensitive one.' But I'm quite sure that Mr. Karp understands satire, even if it's dark satire."

"Might I ask about the name of your group?" Karp ventured. "If my memory serves, the Sons of Liberty were a secret band of revolutionaries before and during the War of Independence."

"Very good, Mr. Karp," Sunderland said. "The name's a bit grand for the likes of us. But it does serve as a reminder as we have these little debates that we owe that right to other men who pledged their lives, their fortunes, and sacred honor to defend it."

"Hear, hear," Florence added. "The tree of liberty must be refreshed from time to time with the blood of patriots and tyrants; it is its natural manure."

"So spoke Thomas Jefferson," Sunderland pointed out. "But come, let's not be so dramatic with Butch, as he has asked me to call him, or he might not want to come out and play with us anymore."

Karp caught what seemed to be a meaningful glance between Florence and Sunderland.

"I was just staying with the revolutionary theme," Florence complained. "But fine, Butch, accept my apologies and do go on with your take on our question of the day."

Karp looked around at the faces of those who waited for him to speak. Their hair was gray, or they were bald, and the wrinkles aged their faces, but their eyes were bright with intelligence and so engaged in the debate that they seemed younger than their years in spirit. Not a fool among them, he thought.

"Well, the courts have held that part of the intent of the confrontation clause is that no citizen be deprived of his liberty interests without the right to hear the evidence against him, prepare his defense, confront any witnesses, and present witnesses and evidence of his own," Karp said. "So it's important that the DA proceed meticulously, cautiously, and prudently and avoid not only a rush to judgment but also the lamentable, egocentric, politically cool press conference that is unseemly and prejudicial to the accused."

"But how does that deprive the players of their liberty interest? They were all granted bail and free prior to trial," Hall noted.

"A liberty interest is not just whether a person has been deprived of his physical freedom," Karp replied. "The courts have also held that a Fourteenth Amendment liberty interest includes the right to pursue the career of one's choice. In this case, the young men in question were suspended from the university even though they had not been tried, much less found guilty, reminiscent of an act of academic McCarthyism that certainly could affect the pursuit of their chosen careers. Who is going to hire someone publicly branded a sex criminal? Even if later tried and acquitted, the stain will remain. They have been stigmatized by an avalanche of pretrial publicity. Prosecutors must be sensitive and professional to avoid that occurrence. It's why DAs should avoid press conferences and do their talking in court, not in front of the cameras."

"But the defense lawyers also made statements to the press that their clients' DNA did not match any samples taken from the alleged victim," Hall pointed out. "Wasn't this also trying the case in the court of public opinion?"

"Yes," Karp acknowledged. "But the defense attorneys made their statements only after the prosecutor went in front of the cameras to proclaim the players' guilt. Obviously, both sides are playing to the potential jury pool. But it seems to me that the prosecutor jumped to his conclusion despite the fact that this young woman showed up drunk at a party so that she could be paid to take her clothes off."

"So you're saying that strippers can be raped with impunity?" Florence asked.

"Of course not," Karp replied. "But look what came to light after the prosecutor made his comments to the press. It's not just the negative DNA tests either, or even that it took three days for her to come forward with these allegations—we can agree that victims of sexual assault may delay due to embarrassment or fear. But then her story kept changing. First she was raped by thirty men, then ten, then three. Then we learn that several years earlier, she accused three other men of raping her but nothing came of those allegations either. Also, there's the alleged timeline exonerating one of the accused. Perhaps all of this should have been ascertained and weighed before the lives of these young men were damaged without the benefit of a trial."

"But isn't the prosecutor supposed to take the side of the victim and be her advocate?" Gilbert asked.

Karp shook his head. "That's a common misconception created by television and by inept prosecutors. It is a defense attorney's duty to zealously protect the rights of the client and force the state to prove its case beyond a reasonable doubt before it can deprive that client of his liberty and sometimes even"—he looked at Sunderland and smiled—"his life. However, competent prosecutors engage in a two-step threshold analysis before charging anyone with a crime. First, you have to determine if the defendant is factually guilty. Once convinced that the defendant is a thousand percent factually guilty, you go to the next step, and that is: Is there legally admissible evidence to convict the defendant beyond a reasonable doubt? We may have factual guilt, but not have legally admissible evidence to convict. For example, we may have a defendant's statement that was taken in violation of a Fifth Amendment privilege, or we may have incriminating physical evidence, but there may be a Fourth Amendment infirmity that could prohibit admissibility. However, once there is factual guilt and legally admissible evidence, the prosecutor's duty is to go forward. He should be resolute and firm but compassionate and sensitive to the task at hand. It is a prosecutor's job to do this objectively, without taking sides."

"But in the Duke case how does the confrontation clause, which has to do with the right of a defendant to cross-examine witnesses during a trial, apply?" Plaut noted. "What does it matter if these statements are made to the press as long as the defendants' rights are protected at trial?"

"At trial, the defendants will have the opportunity to present evidence, confront witnesses against them, and have their fate determined by the rule of law as applied by an impartial judge and a jury of their peers," Karp said. "All those things that Raleigh was deprived of at his trial. But that due process fairness is compromised by prosecutors who engage in pretrial, win-the-hearts-and-minds of the jurors press conferences. The defense lawyers chimed in to proclaim their defendants' 'innocency,' as Raleigh did, but the damage to their reputations was done."

"I find this attitude surprising, and refreshing, coming from the district attorney of New York," Epstein said, grinning at Hall.

"Not really," Karp replied. "Mr. DA Francis Garrahy established the model here in Manhattan before I was born. He mentored us to understand that the unjustly accused must be exonerated, and that not to prepare thoroughly, and not to courageously and vigorously represent the people were the cardinal sins of prosecution."

When Karp finished there was a moment of silence. Then Plaut began to clap and was quickly joined by the others. With cries of "Hear, hear," they raised their glasses of orange juice and toasted his speech. Florence produced a flask of brandy and, after applying a generous dollop to his orange juice, passed it to the others, who spiked their drinks with an air of teenagers getting away with something.

The alcohol seemed to go straight to Karp's head and in the glowing effect he asked about the origins of the Sons of Liberty Breakfast Club. The answer was somewhat vague but essentially came down to their wives having grown tired of their postretirement hanging around the house and kicking them out. "We were driving them batty," Florence announced proudly.

However, there was a darker reason. "We were sitting right here when the bastards flew the planes into the World Trade Center," Gilbert said, pointing to the empty space four blocks to the south where the towers had once stood. "We thought that, perhaps, it was a good time to remember that during times of stress and fear, the protection of civil liberties is all that much more important."

"Well said," Karp responded. "To paraphrase Roosevelt, our greatest fear when it comes to liberty should be fear."

Most of the rest of the meeting was occupied by the arrival of breakfast and the group teasing the pretty girls who walked by. Full of pancakes and banter, Karp rose to leave and get the rest of his morning walk in.

"I think I speak for all of us, Mr. Karp, when I say that we enjoyed your company and your contribution to our little breakfast club," Plaut said. "Perhaps you'll join us again?"

"I'd be honored," Karp replied.

Florence passed a different silver flask to Karp, who unscrewed the top and sniffed. "Whiskey?" he asked, and then looked at his watch. "At nine a.m. on a weekday?"

"How do you think we lived this long?" Florence replied, and the others laughed.

Karp shook his head and raised the flask to his lips as the others shouted, "To Raleigh! This is sharp medicine that will cure all my ills."

"To sharp medicine!" the others shouted again.

As they watched Karp depart, Sunderland leaned toward Plaut. "Interesting fellow, wouldn't you say?

"Yes," the judge answered. "We've been following his career for quite some time." He turned to Sunderland. "Did you get the package off that our dear departed friend left in our care?"

The group fell silent and turned to the priest. "Yes. If you remember, that's why I was heading to see Mr. Karp on the day he was shot. But due to concerns over traitors and such, we agreed on this new route. It should have arrived already."

"Good, good," Epstein said. "That should get the wheels in motion."

"So now we just watch?" Gilbert asked.

"Yes, now we just watch," Plaut replied. "After all, that's what we've done for more than two hundred years."

Unaware that he was still the subject of discussion back at Kitchenette, Karp continued four blocks to Vesey Street and stood looking at the emptiness that had once been occupied by the World Trade Center. It wasn't just that the towers were missing, he thought, but it was as if their destruction had created a vacuum that pulled the eye to the hole in the ground and the mind to the numbing thought of what had happened.

Hard to believe that five years had passed. So much had changed. A war in Afghanistan. Followed by another in Iraq. All falling under the general rubric of the War on Terrorism. But were we winning these wars? Do we have the strength of character to win?

As many people had died that day as had been killed at Pearl Harbor sixty years earlier, launching the United States into a war that U.S. leaders had from the beginning said would end with one acceptable solution. Unconditional surrender. No negotiations. No allowing the enemy to keep the means to wage wars of aggression. It was surrender or die every last man, woman, and child if necessary. And they'd used atomic weapons to make the point.

What, Karp wondered, would U.S. leaders and, more important, a wavering public be willing to accept from al Qaeda, or an Islamic extremism in general that set as its goal a world caliphate? Unconditional surrender? The death of every Muslim, every man, woman, and child in those parts of the world that threatened the West?

And what would the United States and its allies be willing to accept in casualties to win? Not just in the lives of their young men and women, but in their way of life and their civil liberties. Tens of thousands of lives? A military government? A dictatorship that promised to keep them safe in exchange for their freedoms?

Watching the smiling, joking tourists standing in front of the observation area and snapping photographs as though they were at the Grand Canyon, Karp imagined the same scene at Fiftieth and Fifty-first streets, where there would have been a hole in the ground if Andrew Kane and the terrorists had succeeded in blowing up St. Patrick's Cathedral.

"BEHOLD THE DESTRUCTION OF THE TEMPLE . . . AS FORETOLD IN THE BIBLE!"

Karp whirled at the thundering of the voice behind him. A wild-eyed denizen of the streets stood there in a filthy yet colorful coat that appeared to have been sewn from the remains of many other articles of clothing. Beneath it, he could see a stained and faded T-shirt on which were stenciled the words Jerry Garcia Lives!

With his wild mane of wiry gray hair and a flowing salt-and-pepper beard, the man had always reminded Karp of some prophet newly arrived from the desert. "Well, Edward Treacher, imagine meeting you here," he said.

Treacher, a former philosophy professor of some note at New York University during the 1960s until a dose too many of LSD had addled his brain, was one of the regular street people who Karp often saw hanging around the Criminal Courts Building. He sometimes frightened the tourists with his vociferous biblical warnings, but he was harmless and from time to time, as one of Grale's Mole People, passed "street information" to Karp.

"Free country, the last time I looked, Mr. Karp," Treacher replied. "Though seemingly less free with each passing day, thanks in part to this." The old bum looked at the WTC site and then glanced around as if someone might hear.

"The government, of course, knew about the attack before it

happened," Treacher said under his breath, which smelled of cheap wine, marijuana, and poor dental hygiene.

Karp raised his eyebrows. Every New Yorker had, of course, heard the conspiracy theories that concluded that the U.S. government was in some way involved in the September 11, 2001, attack. The theories ranged from criticism that the intelligence community and the military should have known the attack was coming and that the 9/11 Commission was merely a cover-up for their incompetence, to allegations that rogue elements within the government either allowed the attacks to happen or executed them in order to pursue already determined foreign and domestic policies. One theory even had government agents planting bombs in the building to bring them down and then blame Osama bin Laden.

Although willing to concede the point of incompetence ascribed to an assortment of government intelligence agencies, Karp was one of those observers who was persuaded by evidence, not paranoia. "I didn't realize you were a conspiracy buff, Edward," he said.

"Believe what you will, Mr. Karp," Treacher replied. "But Satan prefers to corrupt from within before attacking from without."

Karp was about to reply, but Treacher had already spotted a likely gathering of tourists across the street and was hurrying toward them. "AND BEHOLD, A PALE HORSE. AND THE NAME OF HIM WHO SAT ON IT WAS DEATH . . ." he bellowed with his hand outstretched, hoping for a one- or two-dollar bribe that would send him away to the next unfortunate group.

Watching him go, Karp considered how the conspiracy theorists must be looking at Ariadne Stupenagel's stories about a possible connection between a Russian agent and the attack at St. Patrick's Cathedral. The Russian government's denials and the U.S. government's refusal to comment were sure to spark the conspiracy hotline.

Although officially, the police were treating the attack on Stupenagel and Murrow as a run-of-the-mill intruder assault, the reporter wasn't buying it. And for that matter, neither was Karp. She's onto something that's making someone nervous, he thought. He recalled a conversation before the attack that he'd had with his cousin Ivgeny Karchovski, a Brooklyn gangster with the Russian mob who was convinced that certain clandestine Russian and possibly U.S. interests were in collusion to, if not promote, then at least allow certain acts of terrorism to further their own goals under the guise of fighting the so-called War on Terrorism.

Karchovski's views had surprisingly meshed just a week earlier when Karp attended a meeting of the New York Bar Association to hear Senator Tom McCullum speak. The Montana senator was pushing for public support of his calls for a congressional hearing regarding the attack at St. Patrick's. However, the thrust of his talk that night had been to warn about government incursions into the private lives of citizens, using the fear of terrorism to thwart opposition.

"I understand that intelligence gathering in war is fundamental to winning that war," McCullum had said. "But I worry over the growing and seeming unilateral power under the Patriot Act of secret spy agencies and the placement of formerly independent departments under the single umbrella of the U.S. Department of Homeland Security. Where is the oversight when the administration cites 'national security' and keeps the other branches of government, as well as the public, in the dark? Who is watching the watchers? Who says that they are only inspecting the financial records of suspected terrorists? Who makes them follow due process before they subpoena the records of bookstores to find out what citizens are reading? And at what point will the government decide it would rather not have us read certain books?"

McCullum had urged those present "not to compound the tragedy of 9/11 with the loss of our fundamental liberties without a clear and present need to do so."

Not everything McCullum had said was popular with the association. At the cocktail party afterward, Karp had heard plenty of disparaging remarks about "bleeding-heart liberals who endanger us all."

To a degree, Karp agreed with the critics of those on the left who thought they could appease terrorists by talking to them. It reminded him of the pre–World War Two 1930s and Neville Chamberlain's attempts to appease Hitler. However, like McCullum, he was also concerned that the government seemed to use the specter of terrorism to justify tampering with civil liberties.

It was a difficult thought to deal with in front of the gaping hole across Vesey Street, and the sudden chiming of Beethoven's Ninth Symphony on his cell phone startled Karp. He pulled it from his pocket with a scowl. He hated the thing and only carried it to make Marlene happy. He looked at the number flashing on the panel but didn't recognize it or the area code: 208.

"Probably a wrong number," he muttered, but answered. "Hello?"

"Mr. Karp?" a male voice asked.

"Yeah, who wants to know?"

"Excuse the interruption, but your wife, Marlene, gave me your number."

"Who is this?"

"Mikey O'Toole. Fred's brother."

"Mikey O'Toole, what a pleasure!" Karp exclaimed. He and Fred O'Toole had been roommates at Berkeley, where they'd both attended on basketball scholarships. "This is an unexpected surprise, what's up?"

He heard O'Toole take a deep breath before answering. "Well, I'm in a little trouble out here in Idaho, and I was hoping I might ask you for a bit of advice."

Karp's stomach knotted up. Many years earlier, Mikey's brother had called with a similar request and that had ended badly. But there was a debt that remained, so he asked, "What can I do for you?"

5

WHEN LUCY AWOKE THE NEXT MORNING SHE THOUGHT FOR a moment that she'd slept her way into a Frederic Remington painting. A barrel-chested Indian stood quietly with his face pointed toward the rising sun and the gray-blue mist of the still slumbering west beyond him. A red Navajo blanket was draped around Jojola's heavily muscled shoulders, allowing his long, dark, gray-streaked hair to flutter in the morning breeze.

In the moments of sobriety when the peyote temporarily released its grip on her mind between hallucinations, she'd been sure that she was going to wake up with a hell of a hangover. But while her body felt drained, as if she'd run a great distance, her mind was crystal clear, sharp as a tack, a steel trap. All the clichés seem apropos, she thought.

However, her dreams had been troubled. She couldn't remember them all and something told her that those she couldn't were not important. The main one remained clear, a dream about crossing the desert by the light of a full moon with John Jojola as her guide. Only he was as he might have been four hundred years earlier, dressed in leggings beneath the traditional black skirt worn by Pueblo Indian men and carrying a bow and arrows. His face was painted dark on one side and light on the other, and he said little during the dream, leading mostly by pointing or going on ahead.

On the dream journey she'd come across St. Teresa, a fifteenth-century Spanish martyr who had been her sort of "invisible friend" since childhood, showing up in times of stress or danger with a warning or sometimes as a somewhat sarcastic witness. The saint had been standing behind a rock outcropping and might have gone unnoticed by Lucy if Jojola hadn't turned his head in that direction and stopped.

In the moonlight, the saint's face looked like porcelain, except there were tears running down her cheeks. Oddly, Lucy could see that there was a red feather in her dark hair.

Me aflijo para usted y su niño, the saint said in her native Spanish.

Why do you grieve for me and my child? Lucy asked. *I don't have a child.*

The saint reached for Lucy, but Jojola pulled her away. *We shouldn't linger with sad spirits, they want company and can sap your will to go on,* he said.

Later, as Lucy and Jojola were crossing a shallow oily stream, there was a disturbance in a pool and then an apparition rose slowly. It was Andrew Kane, though he was hardly recognizable; half of his face was eaten away, and seaweed was twined throughout what remained of his blond hair. A crab skittered out of his mouth and dropped back into the water. But she recognized his eyes—the cold, malice-filled blue eyes.

However, he spoke with the voice of a young boy that she recognized as Andy, one of the personalities of the schizophrenic Kane. Andy had briefly taken over from the murderous Andrew Kane during the St. Patrick's hostage crisis and revealed his alter ego's plans to Lucy that had eventually led to his downfall. *He will reveal himself when the assassin strikes,* Andy cried out. *He bears the mark that stands wherever you throw it.*

Shut up, you weakling! the sociopath Andrew Kane snarled as he took over from his weaker personality. Baring sharklike teeth, he took two steps toward Lucy but was brought up short as first one, then another of the arrows shot from Jojola's bow plunged into his chest. He clutched at their shafts and howled, then fell back into the roiling water and disappeared beneath the surface.

As frightening as that was, the next image was more disturbing. She and Jojola were approaching a path leading up a butte when their way was blocked by a swirling cloud of dark smoke. Flames could be seen inside the clouds and a menacing dark figure moved toward her. She wanted to turn around, but Jojola took her by the hand and led her into the cloud. *You cannot run from the dark warrior,* he said. *You must face him or he will defeat you in the waking world.*

Fear filled her as she felt a searing heat growing all around her. Then she lost contact with Jojola and fell to her hands and knees. Choking on the smoke, she was struggling to rise when a hand grabbed her arm and pulled her to her feet. Looking up, she saw that it was S. P. Jaxon, an FBI agent and friend of the family. She felt relieved as she'd known "Uncle Espey" many years as a colleague of her father.

Then she saw his eyes. They were angry and she believed that he was the dark warrior Jojola had warned her about. *The book, Lucy,* he demanded. *Where is the book?* His fingers dug into her arm like hot nails.

Lucy looked behind her and saw in the swirling black smoke an old book lying on a rock. There was a curious emblem in gold on the front, but as she reached for it, the book was consumed by flames while a terrified voice screamed in agony somewhere back in the smoke.

Lucy turned and ran past Jaxon, who reached out to stop her but missed. She stumbled blindly, falling again and banging her knee hard on a rock. Then two hands grabbed her shoulders from behind.

Don't hurt me, Espey! she cried out. *Please, don't hurt me!*

The hands turned her, but instead of Jaxon's eyes, she found herself looking into the calm brown eyes of Jojola. *It's okay, Lucy,* he said. *The danger has passed for now.*

Lucy looked around and realized that the smoke was gone, as was the unbearable heat. She was standing in the bright white light of a full moon that had risen above the New Mexican desert. A shadow passed across the moon. Looking up, she saw a snow-white owl drifting over her; its golden eyes met her own before it wheeled away.

"How do you feel?" In the clear dawn, Jojola's voice brought Lucy back to the present . . . the sober present. She looked at him again and saw that he was smiling at her, the morning sun defining the eagle's beak curve of his nose and casting shadows in the rugged contours of his face. She returned the smile and stood up to stretch, gritting her teeth at the sudden pain in her knee. Looking down, she saw that her pants were torn and the knee bloody from a fall.

But I was asleep, she thought. She looked around and her confusion grew. She didn't recognize the campsite. Yes, there was a bed of soft cedar boughs, but otherwise nothing was the same.

"Weren't we over there?" Lucy said, pointing to a butte in the distance.

"Very good," Jojola said. "It's important to remember landmarks when traveling on foot in the desert. To the untrained eye, the desert all looks the same, and distances can be tricky. Some things appear to be close and yet you can walk toward them all day and never reach your destination; others seem to be far away, but the next time you look up, they are right in front of you."

Lucy's jaw dropped. "But how? I don't remember you bringing me here last night. I must have really been tired. How'd you carry me so far?"

Jojola gave her an amused look. "An old Indian man carry a big strappin' white girl like you across the desert? No way. We walked here yesterday—actually, you slept all day and we walked all night. It's only about five miles, but you stopped a lot to talk to rocks and bushes and animals."

Lucy's brow knitted in disbelief. "We walked here? I mean, I dreamed we were walking in the moonlight, but it didn't seem real."

Jojola shrugged. "What is real? You were still under the influence of peyote, if that's what you mean. Lots of first-timers think that the journey is over after the first period of hallucinating. Occasionally, there are moments of sobriety, or in your case, you slept until I woke you to continue your journey. But sometimes it is so subtle when it decides to take hold again that you don't even know that you've stepped back into the otherworld. What do you remember from your dream that was more than a dream?"

Lucy recounted what she could remember. When she was finished, Jojola nodded. "Yes, there are good and bad spirits that take the form of people in the otherworld, just as there are good and bad spirits that inhabit human beings in this world, too. But that is the natural order of things—the balance of dark and light."

"Like the way you had your face painted," Lucy noted. "Black on one side, white on the other."

"I did not paint my face," Jojola responded. "However, under the influence of peyote you were able to perceive that within all men there is the potential for both good and evil."

Lucy nodded. They'd had the conversation before about the duality of the universe. Yin and yang. Right and wrong. Her father and Andrew Kane. One dependent on the other to provide context and meaning.

Tears came to Lucy's eyes as she recalled the angry look on Jaxon's face. "How will I ever face him without seeing that or hearing those screams when he reached for me?" she asked after describing the vision.

Jojola's face clouded for a moment. "I did not see what you saw," he said. "I heard you cry out." He was quiet for a moment, a frown on his face. "It is important to remember that some of what peyote chooses to show you can be taken literally, but more often it can't. Or, what seems to mean one thing in a vision quest may not mean that on this side of the otherworld. Even someone who seems to be doing evil may just be acting out a role that in the end accomplishes great good. And it can be unwise, even dangerous, to jump to conclusions."

"What about the owl?" Lucy said. "Aren't owls harbingers of death? Like the vision I had of being buried alive."

Jojola nodded. "Sometimes. But whose death is not always known, nor do they necessarily represent one's own doom. Remember, too, they also are the animal that can see in the dark, which means that they represent the ability to see what might not be revealed or clear to others. And if the owl is your totem, it has been since you were born, yet here you are more than twenty years later, a healthy, beautiful young woman."

"Yes, but the death of others has often been a major part of my life," Lucy pointed out. "Maybe I'm like the owl. Maybe I'm a harbinger of death." The lingering tears now fell from her eyes.

Jojola walked over and wrapped her in the Navajo blanket. "Lucy, listen to me," he said. "If you're going to mix your own spirituality with American Indian beliefs, then you should know that we believe that this life, and our deaths, are preordained. We are born into a life that has been laid out before us like the path leading up this butte, and we die when the path alters course and leads us into the next world."

"We're all just actors, right?" Lucy said. "The thought is not encouraging."

"Yes, Shakespeare knew that universal truth when he wrote it," Jojola said. "But that doesn't mean we just sit back and let fate come to us. A warrior goes out to meet his, or her, fate."

Lucy was quiet for a time, letting the sun warm the blanket around her shoulders and the light, cool breeze refresh her. "So am I done with the peyote?" she asked at last.

"I think for the most part, peyote is done with you," Jojola responded. "However, you may notice the presence of the spirit for several days in small ways. Sudden clarity of mind. A subtle difference in how you perceive colors or sounds. But we will hurry the process now by sweating it out of you."

Lucy clapped her hands. "You built a sweat lodge?" she cried happily.

Jojola pointed to a hunched-over piñon tree, the drooping branches of which formed a natural cave. He'd covered the branches with blankets and had a small fire going near the entrance. "It's a wickiup, more like my brothers to the north, the Utes, used instead of teepees or adobe buildings. I prefer the kivas of my people because they offer a place to sit while we sweat, but this will do."

Lucy understood. Kivas were pits dug into the earth, some of them quite large, and had been used for thousands of years. The Anasazi, a Navajo word meaning "the ancient ones," who had once lived in the American Southwest, had built kivas in their cliff dwellings before they'd abandoned their homes.

Anthropologists believed that the Anasazi were the ancestors of the Pueblo Indians of New Mexico, and Lucy figured that they must have shared a similar belief that kivas represented the hole from which they'd emerged to inhabit the earth in their creation mythology. The tribes clung tenaciously to that belief, which made them truly Native Americans, despite the efforts of scientists who contended that they were the descendants of people who had crossed into North America from Asia.

A few minutes later, Lucy and Jojola were sitting in the sweat lodge as he poured water on the rocks he'd been heating in the fire outside. There was an immediate rush of steam filling the lodge.

Lucy giggled at the thought that she was sitting naked next to a fifty-five-year-old man, a fact that would have thrown her conservative cowboy boyfriend, Ned, into a jealous pique, though he, too, adored Jojola. She'd felt a moment's embarrassment when she first stripped down outside the wickiup. But Jojola had kept his back turned until they were inside and then he busied himself with the preparations of bringing in superheated rocks from the fire and pouring water over them slowly. Soon, her body was drenched with sweat and she could almost feel the toxins from the peyote leaving through her pores.

"If you like, I can tell you a story about the owl," Jojola said. "It is from my cousins in the Zuni tribe. It is a sad story in the end. But it is also a love story and shows that the owl is a compassionate totem."

"Yes, I'd like to hear it," Lucy replied.

"Okay, then, once upon a time," Jojola said with a smile, "there was a young warrior whose beautiful and much-loved wife died. He was so devastated that he decided to follow her into the land of the dead and find a way to return her to the world of the living. The spirit of the young woman helped her husband by placing a red feather in her hair . . ."

Lucy's eyes flew open at the memory of St. Teresa with the feather in her hair. But Jojola continued with his story and in the comforting rumble of his voice, her eyes closed again.

"Spirits gradually grow invisible as they approach the land of the dead," Jojola continued. "So the feather was to help him keep track of her."

The spirit of the young woman and her faithful husband eventually came to a dark lake. She plunged in, but he could not follow. "As he sat in despair on the shore of the lake," Jojola said, "Owl Man saw how much he loved his wife and took pity on him. So Owl Man brought him to a cave in the mountains where his people lived and gave him a sleeping potion. 'When you awake, you will be with your wife. Take her back to your village, but do not touch her until you reach the village,' the Owl Man warned. As promised, when the young warrior woke up, his wife was there, waiting for him to guide her back to their village and the land of the living."

They almost made it, Jojola said, but as they drew close to the village, the warrior's wife grew tired and lay down. Soon she was fast asleep. As she rested, the warrior could not resist touching her. "Whereupon she woke, but instead of continuing on, she had to go back to the land of the dead, leaving her husband to grieve all the more."

"That's so sad," Lucy said. "If he'd just waited a little longer, they could have been together. What's it supposed to mean?"

Jojola shrugged his shoulders. "Different things to different people. Some might say it is a parable that love cannot exist without the physical side. Or maybe it is simply a reminder never to take those we love for granted because when they are gone, they are gone forever and no amount of wishing to touch them can bring them back."

Outside of the wickiup, an owl hooted. "See," Jojola said solemnly. "Your totem agrees with me."

6

BUTCH KARP STOPPED PACING LONG ENOUGH TO GLANCE OUT
of the big picture window of the loft at the apartment across
Crosby Street. A strikingly attractive dark-haired woman painted at
an easel, stopping every so often to look southwest as dusk settled
over Lower Manhattan. Dabbing at the canvas with her brush, she
tilted her head in an odd way that indicated that she saw better
from one eye than the other.

The painter, his wife, Marlene, finished a long stroke and then
turned in his direction. Seeing him, she smiled and gave a little
wave before returning to her project. He responded by raising his
hand, and with a sigh turned back to his own work, which was laid
out on the kitchen table across the room. He walked over and
picked up a yellow legal-sized notepad on which he'd written a series of names formed into columns.

Some of the names had been crossed out; others had lines connecting them to names in other columns; a few names were in multiple columns. He'd been trying to connect the dots and was
frustrated by the feeling that the forest was in front of him, but he
couldn't see it for the trees. What he could see were the faces of
the six children murdered during Andrew Kane's escape as they

had appeared in their school photographs. He'd arranged them on the table in two rows, like jurors in the jury box waiting for him to deliver his closing argument.

He wasn't sure why he'd asked Gilbert Murrow to bring the photographs from his office. If he did that with every murder victim he'd ever been connected to, he and Marlene would have had to add another room to the loft. Trying to explain it to her, he'd theorized that these victims were different because they'd been killed as a result of a decision for which he felt in some way responsible. It would have been different if their deaths had been committed within the jurisdiction of the New York DAO, and his office was simply pursuing murder charges. But these children had died because they'd been sacrificial pawns for Kane and security for the motorcade had been at least in part arranged through his office.

Maybe we should have fought harder to keep him at the Tombs and forced his psychiatrists to examine him there, Karp had said to Marlene, referring to the New York City jail.

But it was the FBI and U.S. Marshal's Office that had primary responsibility for transporting Kane, she pointed out. *And it was the FBI's guy, Michael Grover, who turned out to be a traitor. . . . You know, you're starting to sound like Clay Fulton, who was only riding shotgun because you asked him to and didn't even have his own guys. But I'm telling you, just like I told Clay, there was nothing that could have been done that would have made a difference. The judge was going to let them take Kane to his psychiatrists, and Kane had a guy on the inside who no one could have guessed at.*

I know you're right, Karp replied. *And it's not just the kids. They're the faces I can put on something deeper than an FBI agent who sold their lives for money. Grover already paid for his crime when Kane killed him. And Kane and the terrorists are all dead, too. But those photographs won't let me forget that Kane could not have pulled this off alone—not even with the help of Grover and his terrorist pals. Someone else, someone with a hell of a lot of pull and resources, did this and they're still out there.*

Are you talking about Grale's warning in the hospital? Marlene asked. *Look, I appreciate what he's done for this family, and for New York. But you do realize that he's at least half insane. He sees a conspiracy of evil behind every crime when sometimes it's just a bad guy doing a bad thing.*

Yeah, I know, Karp replied. *Still, I can't discount that most of his information has been right on the money; in fact, I've wondered how someone who spends his life underground fighting "demons" has such solid connections. I just hope that when we catch whoever it is pulling the strings in this puppet show, there'll be evidence that this conspiracy to commit murder was hatched in the County of New York so that I can have a shot at them in court.*

Aren't you taking this a little personally? Marlene cautioned.

Karp knew that her point was valid. His mentor, Francis Garrahy, had always warned about the pitfall of getting emotionally involved in cases, especially homicides.

Our job is a search for truth, not retribution, the old man would lecture. *We are not advocates for the victims. Our responsibility is to objectively weigh the evidence. Was the crime committed in our jurisdiction? Do we have legally admissible evidence that is likely to lead a jury to a verdict of guilty?*

Passion was okay, he'd say, if it was a passion for doing the job right. Emotion was human nature, and even a valuable asset in the theater of the courtroom during an opening statement or closing argument. *To care is human and juries like that. But not if it distracts from the central truth of the case.*

Garrahy's voice echoed down the long hall of time, and Karp knew that the old DA and Marlene were right, but still . . . *I'm just trying to connect the dots, Marlene,* he'd told her. *I know the answer is right in front of me, I just have to keep looking until I can see it.*

Marlene had stood on her tiptoes to kiss his cheek. *I know, babe,* she whispered. *You're still recuperating, and I was just trying to mother-hen you a little.*

❖   ❖   ❖

Alone in the loft, his wife across the street, painting, his twin boys at the movies, and Lucy in New Mexico, Karp glanced back at the legal pad. Each column of names had a heading. Under "Kane's Escape"—meaning those people who knew the route of the motorcade—the list started with himself, then Clay Fulton, V. T. Newbury, who had been investigating Kane's tentacles into the NYPD and the Catholic Archdiocese of New York, his appeals chief, Harry Kipman, who was also one of Karp's most trusted lieutenants, and Gilbert Murrow, who as Karp's aide had acted as the liaison between the feds and Fulton. After that, there were the possibilities outside his office: the traitor Michael Grover, followed by FBI agent S. P. Jaxon, who'd been Grover's boss, and a list of four names from the U.S. Justice Department to whom Jaxon and Grover reported. That was it.

Another column was headed "Archbishop Fey," a reference to the former archbishop of the New York archdiocese, Timothy Fey, who had looked the other way while his attorney, Kane, used the church to further his criminal empire. Fey had been awaiting the call to testify on a prison farm in California where he was living under a witness protection program alias. Yet, Kane had discovered Fey's whereabouts and sent an assassin, who strangled the old man in the barn.

Only a few people had known where Fey was incarcerated. That list included the same people from the DAO and most of the same federal names, except for Grover, who'd been killed after Kane's escape and had never been apprised of Fey's location. Unless Jaxon told him, Karp thought. Nah, there was no reason to tell him, and Espey knows how to keep a secret.

A third column was simply titled "Aspen." Acting on a tip, federal agents had surrounded the house of a Saudi Arabian prince in Aspen, Colorado, under the belief that Kane was hiding there, guarded by Islamic terrorists. However, it was a trap and an enormous bomb had exploded, leveling the mansion and killing the hostages, the terrorists, and a half dozen federal agents.

Again, those in the know were the inner circle from the DAO, as well as Jaxon and his superiors in the FBI and Justice Department.

New to the mix was Jon Ellis, the assistant director of special operations for the Department of Homeland Security, who'd stepped in
after Kane's escape.

Some of the names on the pad Karp had crossed off, especially
those who fell under only one heading, such as the prison farm administrator. He also would have crossed Ellis off, but he had not
and wasn't sure why.

Personally, Karp didn't like the man. He thought the agent acted
superior and condescending. Then there was the little matter after
Kane escaped yet again, this time from St. Patrick's Cathedral.
When Jaxon and Ellis, who had been outside directing the federal
response to the hostage crisis, learned that Kane was gone, leaving
the terrorists to blow the place up, Ellis had disappeared. He'd
later explained that he'd run to a different communications truck
to issue a BOLO, Be On the Lookout, to his agency for Agent Vic
Hodges, aka Kane, at the airports, train stations, and bus terminals.

Still, Karp had asked Newbury, who had connections at the State
Department and the Justice Department, to check Ellis out. The
report had come back spotless, if anyone in the intelligence world
could be considered clean. Ellis was a graduate of the U.S. Naval
Academy, from which he'd gone into the Navy's elite SEALs com-
mando force and served with distinction, earning a Silver Star and
Purple Heart. However, that was followed by a period of time for
which Newbury's sources could not account for Ellis.

*My guess is he went from military hero to spook—NSA or CIA,
maybe something even further off the map,* Newbury said. *My
sources indicated that Ellis was involved in some very nasty "wet
work" in trouble spots around the world that resulted in the early
demise of some noted terrorists. He reemerged after 9/11 in his current role with Homeland Security and, again according to my
source, has been effective at countering terrorist plans the likes of
which would terrify this country's citizens if they knew about them.*

You're convinced he's a good guy? Karp asked.

Newbury hesitated. *I've only met him a couple of times and I
also find him a hard guy to like,* he said. *Then again, he's in a business where maybe being likable is not an asset. I would say that his*

resumé suggests that he wouldn't be likely to consort with enemies of the United States. If anything, he's what you might call a "super patriot."

I don't know if I trust that sort either, Karp growled. *They all seem to know what's best for the rest of us, Constitution be damned.*

With his pen hovering above Ellis's name on the legal pad, Karp recalled the conversation with Newbury and wondered how his friend was doing. A longtime colleague, V.T. was obviously under a lot of strain after the unexpected death of his father from a heart attack two weeks earlier. Beneath his sometimes rigid blue-blooded exterior, Vinson Talcott Newbury was a gentle soul who'd loved his dad and grieved even as he went about his duties at the DAO. Karp had told him to take as much time as he needed; however, except for a day or two on either side of the funeral and memorial services, he'd preferred to work.

If anything, he's what you might call a "super patriot." Karp's pen moved to scratch out Ellis. The agent wasn't involved in the motorcade and wasn't privy to Fey's whereabouts. His explanation about running to a communication truck to issue a BOLO had checked out; a Homeland Security helicopter had been on the scene when Kane dove into the Harlem River and drowned. Karp lifted the pen and left his name on the list.

Glancing farther down the page, his eyes rested on one final name. Jamys Kellagh. Grale thought Kellagh was the man pulling Kane's strings. But extensive checks by Murrow and Newbury had not been able to turn up anyone with that name who could even remotely be tied to Kane or terrorists. He drew a circle around the name, but there was no sense drawing any lines connecting it to any other name or heading.

Frustrated, Karp rapped his knuckles on the legal pad. But at least he would have another four years in office to figure out who was responsible. Election night had come and gone, and he'd been elected district attorney in a landslide.

Of course, some of that had to do with the fact that he was un-opposed, an empty victory that had sent Gilbert Murrow into a strange melancholy. Even the attempt on his life, and subsequent death of an apparently prolific burglar with a long criminal jacket that included sexual assault, had not thrown Murrow in as much of a funk. When asked about it, he'd explained that it was because his magnificent plans for brilliant last-minute campaigning had be-come moot, the battle won without firing a shot. They'd watched the returns with a few close friends in the Karp-Ciampi loft, then everybody had gone home early.

Karp's concentration was interrupted when the lights went on in the apartment across the way. He'd leased the space and had it fin-ished for Marlene's art studio and given it to her as a present. She seemed to find real peace there, though he had yet to see one of her paintings.

Marlene walked back to the easel and picked up the paintbrush again. She looks . . . I don't know . . . content, he thought. It had certainly been a long road home. The funny tilt of her head was be-cause she'd lost an eye opening a letter bomb intended for him nearly twenty-five years earlier. The explosion that cost her her eye had also taken a finger, but most significantly it had been the begin-ning of her loss of faith in the justice system's ability to deal with vi-olent criminals. The ensuing years had seen her drawn into a world of violence as a sort of avenging angel for those unable to protect themselves, but also at odds with her Catholic upbringing in Queens and with her justice-by-the-book husband.

Watching her paint, he found it hard to believe that someone so beautiful and such a loving mother and wife was so capable of met-ing out deadly force. But during the past year, with the spiritual guidance of John Jojola, and her art, she at last seemed to be mak-ing peace with the past. She was still capable of swift violence, as she'd proved at St. Patrick's, but at least that had been in reaction to a situation she'd been thrust into and had saved many innocent lives. Not to mention the Pope, he thought.

Karp paced back into the living room, his hands behind his back, and then back to the kitchen sink to get a glass of water. Only there he was distracted again, this time by a blue note attached by a magnet to the refrigerator. It read: "Mikey O'Toole, Nov. 19."

Good, he thought, something to take my mind off Kane. He flashed back to the telephone call from Mikey. *Well, I'm in a little trouble out here in Idaho, and I was hoping I might ask you for a little bit of advice.*

Mikey's brother, Fred, had been one of Karp's best friends from his college days at Berkeley. They'd met shortly after they arrived on campus as highly recruited freshmen for the basketball team in the mid-1960s. In stature, they were bookends—both about six foot five and a rail-thin 190 pounds—and both loved basketball. But that's where the similarities ended.

Dark-haired and clean-cut, Karp had a round, Slavic face. His gray, gold-flecked eyes were somewhat slanted, as if one of his Jewish ancestors in Poland had been ravaged by an invading Mongol. On the other hand, O'Toole's ancestors were from Ireland and he had the wild mane of red hair, freckles, and sea-green eyes to prove it. A native of Mississippi, his southern drawl stood in sharp contrast to Karp's Brooklynese.

The difference continued beyond their looks and accents. Karp was a good student—thanks in part to his schoolteacher mother and his own drive to excel at everything he did, whether it was on the court or in the classroom. If something did not come naturally—a right-handed hook shot (he was a leftie) or calculus—then he worked at it until it did. He actually enjoyed practice and brought the same intensity level he did to games.

O'Toole, on the other hand, saved himself for game day. He had, perhaps, more natural ability than Karp, but he didn't work at it. He also was always on the verge of academic ineligibility, not because he wasn't intelligent, but because he placed a higher priority on chasing coeds and chugging beer. But during a game, O'Toole was a natural force, a dribbling, shooting, shot-blocking thunderstorm of a power forward.

Despite the differences in their personalities and personal habits, Karp and O'Toole had become fast friends, and then evolved into something more like brothers. Karp's college basketball career ended one day during a game when a tumble with another player resulted in a knee so badly damaged that the surgeon who opened him up said the joint "looked like a turkey leg after Thanksgiving." Nothing was still attached where it was supposed to be.

When he was laid up in the hospital, it was O'Toole who sat with him for hours to keep his spirits up. At one especially low point when Karp was lamenting that his basketball career was over, O'Toole grabbed him by the shoulders and shook him. "Hey pal, my basketball career was over the day you walked onto the campus," he said. "At some point we all have to hang up the Chuck Taylors and get on with our lives. It might be because of a lack of talent or maybe old-fashioned laziness, like me, or because of an injury like you . . . or maybe you just get too goddamned old, but it happens to every one of us. The only question is what are you going to do about it? The way I see it, you are meant for more important things than even the NBA, and basketball was just going to delay you from getting down to the real business of your life."

O'Toole had, of course, been right and with that Karp had turned his energies to getting through college and then law school. And O'Toole was the first to call and congratulate him after he passed the New York State bar exam and went to work for the DAO.

O'Toole had gone his own way. He graduated with a degree in physical education with the sole intent of coaching basketball at the college level. Over the years, he'd gradually worked his way from a small two-year community college program to an NCAA Division II team that he'd led to the National Invitational Tournament championship. That had landed him a job as the assistant coach of a Pac-10 Division I program. Then, when the head coach retired, O'Toole was the overwhelming choice to replace him.

In the basketball-crazy Pac-10, O'Toole's university had been a perennial basement dweller for at least ten years before he took over. In his first year as head coach, they'd played well enough to get an invitation to the NCAA's Big Dance. The next year, they got as far as the Sweet Sixteen.

Next year, the Final Four, and then who knows, he said when Karp called to congratulate him on getting as far as he had.

Life in general seemed to be going well for both friends. Karp was an up-and-comer in the District Attorney's Office and had met and married Marlene, with whom he'd had three children.

As for O'Toole, he'd fallen in love and married Jenny Dunlap, a pretty blond cheerleader at Berkeley. A bit on the wild side herself, Jenny had been a good match. They'd had no children of their own, but had pretty much raised Fred's kid brother, Mikey, eleven years younger, after the O'Tooles' parents were killed in an automobile accident during Fred's junior year.

If Fred O'Toole had one particular fault as a coach, it was that he spoke his mind and sometimes forgot who was listening. After another loss in the Sweet Sixteen, he'd complained in front of a sports reporter that it was hard to compete against some of the teams from back East because they were supported by mob money and that the NCAA, he believed, wasn't doing enough to counter it.

The story made for an instant scandal. But O'Toole had no proof. Stung and angry, the NCAA had called him on the carpet where he was "charged" with conduct detrimental to the college athletic community and especially that of the National Collegiate Athletic Association.

O'Toole's university had hired a lawyer familiar with the NCAA to represent him. The lawyer had assured him that if he kept his mouth shut at the hearing, except to apologize, the worst that would happen was he'd have to make the apology public and get suspended for a few games. But the NCAA wanted blood. O'Toole and his lawyer had sat in stunned silence when the hearing board handed down their punishment: Coach Fred O'Toole would be prohibited from coaching at the college level for seven years.

O'Toole wanted to fight it and demand a public hearing, or even take the NCAA to court. But the same lawyer had advised him to accept the punishment "for now."

"We'll let this die down," he said, his arm draped around O'Toole's shoulders. "Then when there's a few different faces on the board in a couple of years, we'll come back and convince them that the punishment was far too severe. But if we fight it now, the good ol' boys with the NCAA will make you pay. Those suckers can carry a grudge," the lawyer further opined, "and their word is law when it comes to college athletics. However, go along, don't say anything inflammatory to the press, and it will actually work in your favor. Those same boys will see that you can be a 'team player,' and they'll be more sympathetic after you've done a little penance."

Karp had only learned of his friend's treatment and the lawyer's recommendation to take his medicine after the fact. "You should have called me," he'd admonished O'Toole.

"I didn't want to bother you," O'Toole replied. "This other lawyer has spent his entire career handling cases with the NCAA and seemed to know what he was doing."

"But that's part of the problem," Karp had growled. "You were being advised by someone who has a stake in not upsetting the powers that be with the NCAA. He has to deal with them a lot, which means picking his battles carefully, hoping they throw him the occasional bone. He's not about to buck the system."

"What do you think I should do?" O'Toole had asked.

"You fight them," Karp replied. "There's no guarantee they're going to be any fairer in two years than they are now. From what you've told me, the NCAA board is the arresting cop, judge, jury, and executioner. They follow their own rules, no meaningful due process, no constitutional protection, which translates into precious little fairness."

O'Toole thanked him for the advice, but in the end he'd gone with the counsel of his attorney. The next time he and Karp talked, he tried to explain that if he stirred up a lot more press, it might be tough to find a job of any kind in coaching. He had the sound of a defeated man when he called a couple of weeks later to say that he'd accepted a position teaching physical education and coaching the boys' basketball team at a high school in Mississippi.

"It'll be fun," O'Toole said, trying to put on a brave face. "It will give me a chance to get back to teaching the basics."

Karp heard the lie in his friend's voice. Fred O'Toole was never going to be content to be a high school basketball coach. His dream was to coach a college team into the finals of the NCAA tournament and win it. Karp couldn't put his finger on it, but his friend's seeming acceptance of his punishment filled him with a sense of foreboding.

However, this was a time when they both had their families and careers to manage. Sometimes months went by between telephone calls and letters. Then it was mostly catching up through Christmas cards with an O'Toole form letter, and telephone calls to wish each other a happy birthday, which always ended with vows to not let so much time go by before they talked again.

O'Toole had waited three years before appealing his suspension to the NCAA. But it was rejected without even a hearing. Two more years passed. Another appeal was made and rejected. The good ol' boys really were carrying a grudge, so O'Toole thought.

Then came the Christmas when no card or letter arrived. Karp waited until early January and then called to see what was up.

"Jenny's dead," O'Toole said, his voice sounding hollow. "Ovarian cancer. They found it in October and she died the day before Christmas. Sorry . . . I just haven't had the heart to let everybody know." He'd then broken down and cried while Karp, two thousand miles away, could do nothing more than offer condolences.

The death of his wife left O'Toole alone except for his brother, Mikey. The two of them had come to visit the Karp-Ciampi clan in New York, where Butch got a chance to get to know the younger O'Toole. A polite, soft-spoken young man, Mikey had been a good student, "more like you than me in that regard," Fred had said, but instead of basketball, he'd been a college baseball player.

Mikey had no illusions about taking his game to the pros after graduation. Instead, he'd followed his brother's footsteps and became a coach, paying his dues at small schools until being offered the position of head coach at the University of Northwest Idaho in Sawtooth. It was a small Division II university, but had become a respected regional baseball school under Mikey O'Toole.

Meanwhile, Fred tried to make the best of coaching high school boys, as the NCAA had shown no sign of relenting. Seven years finally passed, but even with his suspension over, it was clear that Fred O'Toole's name was mud in college basketball circles.

The day before Christmas, on the fifteenth anniversary of his wife's death, Fred arrived back at the campus of the Pac-10 school he'd been forced to leave. He walked across campus to the gym and at center court blew his brains out with the gun he'd hidden in his waistband.

There'd been a sympathetic story about Fred O'Toole in *Sports Illustrated*, in which a bitter Mikey O'Toole was quoted as saying that his brother had been blackballed and treated as a pariah because he'd dared to question the NCAA about an allegation issue "everyone knows is true."

"The worst part is that there are rules and even laws being broken on college campuses every day that are far worse than anything my brother might have said," Mikey O'Toole went on. "But the NCAA will do anything to save itself from embarrassment or taking a good hard look at itself."

A spokesman for the NCAA had been quoted as saying the association felt for Mikey O'Toole, but also that he was wrong. "The NCAA had a duty to maintain the integrity of the system. Coach Fred O'Toole impugned that integrity and paid the price for it."

The last time Karp had seen Mikey was at his brother's funeral. Five years later, Karp was reflecting on a telephone call that, as Yogi Berra once quipped, was "like déjà vu all over again."

Mikey O'Toole told him that he'd been accused of recruiting violations and then suspended by the university pending a hearing before the American Collegiate Athletic Association, which governed the conference to which the University of Northwest Idaho belonged.

The ACAA hearing in Boise, Idaho, a short time later was "over before it began," O'Toole complained. He'd had an attorney with him—a friend from Sawtooth named Richie Meyers—but no opportunity to defend himself from the charges "or even a chance to have a public hearing at the university so that I could clear my name."

Instead, the hearing panel had immediately voted to suspend

him for ten years, after which the university had fired him. Meyers had since filed a civil lawsuit with the U.S. District Court in Boise, seeking reinstatement and damages. "But more important to me is the chance to prove I didn't do what they said I did," O'Toole told Karp. "If we don't win it, I'm ruined. No one will touch me. I'm damaged goods."

"Are you guilty?" Karp had asked.

"Hell no," O'Toole replied. "I'm being set up by a player I kicked off the squad for, among other things, raping a young woman. I think the ACAA's interest in going after me is in part because of my brother and also what I said at his funeral; they're a stepchild of the NCAA, abide by all of the association's rules and regulations, and they also get some of their funding from National Big Brother. There's also something funny about the university's attitude, too, that I can't quite figure out."

"So how can I help you?" Karp asked.

O'Toole cleared his throat, clearly nervous. "Well, to be honest, Richie and I were wondering if we could visit with you in New York," he said. "Richie's a good friend—he's been doing this on contingency to help me out. He's also a fine lawyer, but he's in private practice, which in Sawtooth mostly means divorce cases, DUIs, and property disputes. He'd be the first to tell you that he hasn't done a lot of litigation, and none at the federal court level. Meanwhile, as you can imagine, the ACAA has pulled out the big guns—some suit with a tough rep named Steve Zusskin—and the university has someone else as a co-counsel, too. Richie's game, but he's also feeling a bit in over his head. He knows you by reputation, and when he heard you were a friend of the family, he asked if maybe I could arrange it for him to run what we have past you."

Karp hesitated. He wanted to help, but didn't want to insert himself into a case where he really had no business. "Well, you know, most of what I've done is prosecute criminals," he pointed out. "I've done a little litigation, but there are more qualified civil attorneys."

O'Toole took the answer the wrong way. "Oh, you're right. Hey, you're busy. I'm sorry to have bothered you. It's just that my brother made me promise that if I ever got into trouble of any kind, and he wasn't around, I would go to you."

"Hey, that's not what I meant," Karp replied. "I'm glad you called, and flattered. I'd be happy to meet with you and your attorney and give you my two cents. Maybe we can go over a little courtroom strategy . . . that sort of thing."

"That's great!" The relief in Mikey O'Toole's voice was palpable. "We can fly out on the nineteenth if that's all right. And I promise we'll make it short and sweet; then we'll get out of your hair."

Karp laughed and said good-bye. But as he flipped his cell phone shut, he had a nagging feeling that there wasn't going to be anything short and sweet about his meeting with O'Toole.

7

"MY BUTT HURTS," LUCY KARP TOLD JOHN JOJOLA AS THEY walked past the front desk and into the saloon of the Sagebrush Inn on the south end of Taos. They'd just spent the day with her boyfriend, Ned Blanchet, rounding up cattle in the Sangre de Cristo Mountains in preparation for moving them to their winter range on the Taos ranch where Ned was the foreman.

Although she was getting to be a better rider—especially for a city slicker from Manhattan, she thought—she still wasn't used to a full day in the saddle. She was looking forward to a glass of merlot and a quick dinner with Jojola at the inn's great restaurant. Then it was shower, two aspirin, and off to bed to wait for Ned. Hey, that rhymes, she thought happily.

"You'd think with all that padding you wouldn't feel a thing," Jojola joked.

"Very funny, Jojola," she replied, sticking her tongue out. "And if I were you, I wouldn't be talking about 'extra padding'—I think you've been packing away the frijoles yourself."

Jojola laughed and patted his round belly. "Indians are smart like the animals," he said. "We put a little more on to stay warm in the winter."

Lucy was about to reply when she pulled up, sure that she must be hallucinating on residual peyote. At a glance, she'd thought the man sitting at a table in the cantina watching the door looked like S. P. Jaxon, the special-agent-in-charge of the FBI office in Manhattan. But then the hallucination stood and smiled at her and Jojola.

"Where in the heck have you two been?" Jaxon asked as he held out his hand. "We've been staking out the place all day waiting for you to show up. You know how much money you're costing the taxpayers?"

"You could have called the Taos Pueblo Police Department, but you feds probably don't bother to do any actual investigating," Jojola said, grinning as he pumped the agent's hand.

"Au contraire, my long-haired friend, we did inquire at the department as to your whereabouts," Jaxon replied. "The receptionist said you were out, but was a little tight-lipped as to where, and she didn't know, or wouldn't say, if you were with Lucy. No offense, but it's your partner there who I needed to talk to. So despite your snide comments about our abilities, we tracked down Ned Blanchet, who was still out riding the range like a good cowboy. I'm afraid we startled him some, swooping down in one of those black helicopters we're famous for. I was worried that he was going to put a hole in the fuselage with that thirty-caliber Winchester he carries before I could let him know we were friendly. He said you two were headed here. By the way, he said to say he was still going to drop by later, Lucy."

Lucy blushed. She was somewhat uneasy at Jaxon's sudden appearance following the peyote vision she'd had of him emerging from smoke and fire with an angry look in his eyes. Don't be silly, Lucy told herself. He's one of your dad's oldest friends. John said the visions couldn't always be taken literally.

Lucy had known Jaxon essentially since birth. He'd joined the New York District Attorney's Office a few years after her father and mother started working there and was still working there for the first few years after she was born. But "Uncle Espey" quit the DAO shortly afterward and entered the FBI Academy at Quantico. Her

dad said it was because there wasn't enough action putting criminals behind bars, "he wants to shoot some of them."

Except for the occasional visit over the years, Lucy hadn't seen
much of Jaxon, a tall man whose square-jawed face was neatly
framed on top by a gray crew cut. He'd recently returned to New
York City as the special-agent-in-charge and just in time to help
thwart an attempt by an Iraqi terrorist bent on exploding a "dirty"
atomic weapon beneath Times Square on New Year's Eve.

"You said 'we've' . . . as in 'we've been staking out,' " Lucy said,
hating what sounded to her like a suspicious tone in her voice.

Jaxon did not seem to catch it. "Huh? Oh, yes, that's Agent Octa-
viano Tavizon, formerly of the Albuquerque office," he said, pointing to the young Hispanic man in blue jeans and a denim shirt who
was watching them from the end of the bar.

Tavizon nodded but didn't smile or bother to come over and introduce himself. Instead, he turned his attention back to the big
mirror that ran the length of the bar so that he could monitor the
other patrons in the bar, the walls of which were decorated with
Navajo blankets, the namesakes of long-horned cattle, and various
examples of Western art, including several originals by the famous
Indian painter R. C. Gorman.

"He takes his job seriously," Jaxon noted, turning back to the
other two. "But I didn't travel all this way to introduce Lucy to
good-looking G-men. In fact, I suppose you're wondering what
brings me to Taos."

"I thought it was the silver-and-turquoise jewelry," Lucy teased a
little self-consciously, but determined to get past the strange feelings. "Or the green pork chile at Orlando's New Mexican Café? Or
perhaps you're in the market for a saucy little señorita?"

Jaxon laughed. "All except the last. My wife would kill me." He
hesitated, his face growing somber, then added, "And maybe one
or two other things. Would you mind if we went someplace
private . . . like your room?"

For an instant, Lucy saw again the man surrounded by the
smoke and flames and shuddered. "Of course," she said, then
added, "Can John come?"

Jaxon looked at Jojola and nodded. "That may be wise, in fact. But remember, this is top-secret stuff. I'd ask you not to talk about it even with your folks for now."

"I appreciate the vote of confidence," Jojola said. "But I don't need to—"

Lucy cut him off with a meaningful look. "I want you to. Please." She turned to the agent. "I trust you, Espey, but I've just been through hell back in New York, and I have a feeling that you didn't fly here in your black helicopter to give me an award from a grateful government. If you're here, there's trouble not far behind; you'll say what you need to say and then will leave to put out some other fire. I want someone here who I can trust to help stomp on whatever embers you leave smoldering."

Jaxon chuckled. "Fair enough." He gestured with his hand for them to lead out of the cantina.

Lucy looked back and noticed that Agent Tavizon was watching them leave in the mirror.

"Is Agent Tavizon a field agent or a bodyguard?" Lucy asked.

Jaxon gave her a sideways glance. "Your intuition is, as always, on the money," he said. "He's been assigned to watch my back. Good man for the job, too. He's a former U.S. Army Ranger with tours in Afghanistan, Iraq, and places that he won't tell even me about. My bosses have decided that it's not wise for me to travel alone. Plus, it lets me concentrate on what I need to without having to be concerned about security issues. There are a number of other agents stationed around the inn as well."

The trio left the back of the saloon and crossed the Spanish-style interior courtyard, heading for Lucy's room in an older—but more charming, she thought—part of the inn. The Sagebrush had been built in 1929 as a way station for travelers en route to Arizona and points west. It had also served as a magnet for artists and writers. The painter Georgia O'Keeffe had lived and worked there for a time, as had the novelist D. H. Lawrence, who began to write *Lady Chatterley's Lover* in one of the rooms.

The original building was now the cantina and lobby. The rooms were plastered with the ubiquitous adobe, featured ceiling beams of polished logs, and were furnished with heavy Spanish-style furniture covered in geometrical Southwest designs. The bathrooms were works of art with tiled floor and sinks, and many of the rooms boasted a small fireplace.

Another young agent was standing guard outside Lucy's room when they arrived. He nodded to Jaxon, opened the door, and then left without waiting for introductions or an explanation of how he got into her room.

In answer to Lucy's questioning look, Jaxon shrugged. "I'm truly sorry, but I took the liberty—in violation of your civil rights, I might add. I had to make sure that no one was listening in on any conversations taking place in your room."

Lucy thought of a few of the romantic nights she'd spent in the room with Ned and felt the blood rush to her face at the thought of someone listening to them. Call 1-800-RideEmCowboy, she thought.

"Boy, Espey, you're starting to scare me with all this spy-versus-spy stuff," she said. "I've had quite enough adventures for this lifetime. I'd just like to settle down with my cowboy and have lots of little cowboys and cowgirls—if he'll ever climb down from his dumb ol' horse long enough to ask me to marry him."

She's certainly changed, Jaxon thought. The girl he'd known for two decades had always been something of an ugly duckling—skinny and plain, with a beaklike, overly large nose. But during the past year of living in Taos, she'd filled out in the right places and was a tan, handsome, if not classically pretty, young woman. Even her nose seemed more suited to her face. Knowing her history, he thought it was a wonder that she was so well balanced. For some reason known only to God, she seemed to be a magnet for psychopaths like Felix Tighe and Andrew Kane. He had no doubt that settling down to life as a ranch hand's wife would suit her fine.

"I'm sorry, I don't mean to be so mysterious," Jaxon said. "The security is for me. Once I leave, so should the need for any concern for your well-being. I'm just hoping you can listen to something for me and, if you can, interpret it. You won't have to be involved beyond that."

"Yeah, right, not involved," Lucy replied sarcastically; then her brows knitted together. "Why do you need me to interpret something? You guys have linguistics experts at Quantico who are probably as qualified as I am."

"No one is as qualified as you are," Jaxon responded gallantly. He paused as if to think something over, then, apparently making up his mind, said, "Let me explain a little about what's going on."

Jaxon waited for Lucy to take a seat in one of the rustic aspenwood chairs that were standard for the room's decor. Jojola turned to the fireplace, which was Lucy's favorite feature of the room, and began to build a fire.

"Okay, let's have it," Lucy said.

"Well, first thing to get out of the way is that I'm no longer with the FBI," Jaxon replied. "In fact, officially, I'm not with the government at all anymore."

"Not 'officially'? So now you're a spook with somebody like the Department of Homeland Security?" Lucy asked, her voice harder than she intended.

She knew that her aversion to the department was unfair—that most people who worked for the department, which had been formed after the 2001 terrorist attack on the World Trade Center, had the country's best interests in mind. But there was something about the department's leadership that rubbed her the wrong way. They seemed almost cartoonish with their silly, different-colored "terror alerts" that had done little except raise fears only to call the all-clear with no explanations . . . sort of like the boy who cried wolf. But more than that, she disliked how they defended every gouge at civil liberties in the name of the War on Terrorism as if it weren't yet another step down the slippery slope. After all, it wasn't really spying on the American public as long as it was in everybody's best interest.

To her relief, Jaxon shook his head. "I'm not with the department either. Officially, my group doesn't exist and very few people know that we do. Even the director of the FBI knows only that I suddenly decided to take early retirement. Outwardly, my reason is that I'm blaming myself for Andrew Kane's escape and the massacre of those children and agents. But we've planted rumors that have more to do with me selling out for a very well-compensated position with a private security firm. The bureau isn't very happy with me because I hand-selected a half dozen of the best agents I knew and took them with me into 'private practice.' However, for your ears only, I remain a humble, underpaid public employee, as does my team."

Lucy frowned. It wasn't like Jaxon to make speeches, and this one didn't sound quite true . . . or maybe just not complete. "If you're still a fed, couldn't you use their resources?"

Jaxon shook his head. "As far as the bureau is concerned, I've gone over to the dark, well-paid side. We're mercenaries. They wouldn't touch us with a ten-foot stun gun. But that's intentional on our part."

"So I assume you're another government antiterrorism agency?" Jojola asked. "I thought the whole reason behind the Department of Homeland Security was to bring all agencies under one umbrella so that you guys would communicate and work together."

"It was, and still is," Jaxon said. "There are a lot of good people fighting a war that few members of the public know is happening, except as military actions in far-off countries and the occasional bombing in New York, Bali, Madrid, or London. But as for me and my people, we're not specifically antiterrorism but sort of trying to track organizations that might be using terrorism to further their own unrelated ends—like Andrew Kane demanding a billion-dollar ransom for the Pope while his terrorist pals planted bombs in the cathedral in the name of Allah. I can tell you that I was asked to take this assignment shortly after the debacle at St. Patrick's Cathedral, when it was clear that our agencies—including my own—had been infiltrated and compromised by traitors. I guess you could say we've been asked to watch the people who are supposed to be doing the watching."

Jaxon paused and shook his head sadly. "The truth is, maybe I should have retired after the St. Patrick's hostage crisis was over," he said. "A lot of it happened on my watch."

"That's nonsense, Espey," Lucy said. "Who could have guessed at Kane's intentions? So, then, who do you work for?"

"I can't say," Jaxon replied. "And if you ask elsewhere, the government will deny our agency exists."

Lucy whistled. "Like *Mission Impossible.*"

"Or when they sent us into Laos in sixty-nine," Jojola added softly. "We were to supply recon for marines, but the mission didn't officially exist. And if we were killed or caught, we would have simply disappeared in the eyes of our government."

"So who's behind this infiltrating and compromising?" Lucy asked.

"That's the million-dollar question, Lucy," Jaxon answered. "If we knew, we could cut the head off the serpent and the body would die. But we haven't been able to get anyone close enough yet to understand how they're organized or what their real aims are. Hell, we don't even know if they have a name they call themselves. They're not out there like al Qaeda or Hamas claiming responsibility for acts they did or even didn't do."

"If they're so secret, how do you know they exist?" Jojola asked.

"Good question," Jaxon answered. "I hope that my mission here tonight will help establish that. But up to this point, all we know is that there seems to be an organized group that is flying under the radar but manages to manipulate and use other people, even other organizations—including terrorists—to achieve its ends. One other thing we know is they are absolutely ruthless—so ruthless, if my guess is right, that they were willing to murder the Pope and a couple of thousand people as part of their plan."

"I thought Islamic terrorists and Kane were behind that—for their own ends," Lucy said.

"They were," Jaxon acknowledged. "But that doesn't mean that Kane and the terrorists weren't being assisted by someone else for purposes even they may not have realized."

"Do you have any suspects?" Jojola asked.

"Well, we have a name, Jamys Kellagh," Jaxon said. "Who he is, no one seems to know. However, we're told by informants that he seems to have been playing the middle man between Chechen extremists, Kane, and perhaps people in our own government, as well as the Russian government. But other than a name we have nothing—no photographs, no way of identifying him. We don't even know if Jamys Kellagh is a real name or an alias."

"So I assume all of this has something to do with what you want me to listen to," Lucy said.

Jaxon nodded. "Sorry to give you such a long story and provide so few answers. However, just a few days ago, we received a recording of a conversation purportedly between Jamys Kellagh and someone higher up in this organization. We're told it's important and may involve a plot in New York City."

Lucy sighed. "Of course. Why not? Just paint a target on Manhattan."

"I know how you feel," Jaxon said. "My kids are there now, too, living with their mother in Midtown. Unfortunately, as a symbol of the United States there aren't many better targets. But I have no idea what is being said in this message. That's why I've come to you."

Lucy looked up and had to blink away tears. She considered New Mexico her home now, but she'd grown up in Manhattan and that's where her family lived. She was tired of worrying about them. "So where's this message?"

Jaxon reached into his suit-coat pocket and pulled out a small device that Lucy recognized as an MP3 player. He reached into another pocket and pulled out a small plastic bag from which he removed a wafer-thin disc the size of a quarter and inserted it into the MP3. He handed the device, as well as a pair of earphones to Lucy, who put them in her ear and pressed the Play button.

Lucy heard two men talking in a foreign language with the apparent older man doing most of the talking. The message only lasted twenty seconds and ended with what sounded like, *"Myr shegin dy ve, bee eh."*

Lucy hit the Play button again, then a third time before placing it back on the table.

"So any ideas?" Jaxon asked.

Lucy pursed her lips. "It sounds Celtic . . . a very old archaic form if I'm right . . . but nothing I've heard before. That last bit, *'Myr shegin dy ve, bee eh,'* sounded like a sign-off . . . sort of like

'See you later, alligator,' though I suspect it's not quite so innocent."

Jaxon looked at her for a long moment, then nodded and picked up the MP3 player. "Well, thanks for trying. I thought I'd give it a shot."

"Hold on," Lucy said. "I said I didn't know the language. However, with a little help from someone I know, we might get a translation."

"Who is this person?" Jaxon asked.

"Just a guy I know in Manhattan," Lucy replied. "I wouldn't want to give up his name until I've spoken to him. But he's spent most of his life studying the Celts—their languages and history. An odd duck, but I'd consider him the foremost authority in the United States. I'll give him a call."

"You trust him?"

Lucy smiled and nodded. "This guy lives with his mind in the twelfth century. I won't tell him anything except that I need to see him about a translation. He'll be happy to help. Like all right-thinking men," she added with a wink, "he's madly in love with me."

Jaxon chuckled. "Certainly any man who never changed your diapers, which leaves me out." He was interrupted by a coded rapping on the door. "Come in," he said.

The door swung open and Agent Tavizon poked his head in. "Sir, the farmer we tracked down earlier is here asking to see the young lady."

"He's a cowboy," Lucy said. "Let him in."

Jaxon nodded and Tavizon stepped back. Ned Blanchet appeared in the doorway, scowling and looking like he was about to avenge the farmer remark with his fists.

"Anything wrong?" he asked, walking over to Lucy with an angry glance over his shoulder at Tavizon, who looked at him blankly, the way a shark looks at a fish when it's not particularly hungry.

"Not any more than usual," Lucy said, and gave him a hug and a kiss.

"Great." Blanchet scowled more. "Just what I wanted to hear."

Jaxon shook Blanchet's hand. He respected the young cowboy, who'd proved himself to be a man of action, certainly more than Agent Tavizon was giving him credit for.

"So, when do we leave to see my friend?" Lucy said. She was getting impatient to get rid of the G-men so she could devote her attention to Ned.

Jaxon looked at Ned. "Sorry, pardner," he said before turning to Lucy. "But I'm going to have to ask Lucy to go with us now."

8

GILGAMESH BARKED TWICE AT THE SOUND OF THE BUZZER announcing that visitors had arrived at the security door three floors below the Crosby Street loft. Karp scratched the dog behind the ears, got up from his easy chair to walk over to the apartment foyer, and pressed the intercom button.

"Hello?" he asked. The visitors were expected, as they'd called from LaGuardia Airport to say they were on their way, but at nearly midnight in Lower Manhattan, it paid to be safe.

"It's Mikey O'Toole and Richie Meyers. Have we come to the right place?" a voice replied from the speaker.

"You have, indeed," Karp said. He pressed the button to unlock the security gate and then opened the front door to wait for the elevator to arrive outside the loft.

When the elevator door slid open, two men began to step off with suitcases but stopped when they saw the enormous Presa Canario dog panting next to Karp, who noticed their expressions and chuckled. He thought of Gilgamesh as the family pet, but he sometimes forgot that many people took one look and immediately thought *Hound of the Baskervilles*, or maybe *Cujo*.

"*Trovisi giu,*" Karp told the dog, who wagged the nub of his tail at the visitors—he was a lover, not a fighter, unless commanded otherwise—and then trotted over to the easy chair where Marlene was reading a newspaper and slumped to his belly with a sigh.

"Holy cow!" the older and larger of the two men exclaimed. "We have bears smaller than that in Idaho. What was that you told him?"

Karp grinned mischievously. "These guys are not for dinner."

"Actually," Marlene said, rising from her chair with a smile, "that was poorly pronounced Italian for 'Lie down.' Otherwise, he would have said, 'Questi uomini non sono per il pranzo,' which doesn't mean anything to Gilgamesh. Unfortunately, my husband's fluency in Italian is about as well developed as his sense of humor."

The first man laughed and stepped forward, extending his hand. "Mr. Karp, it's been a long time." He was nearly as tall as Karp, and like his brother, Mikey O'Toole was a redhead with sea-green eyes and a constellation of freckles on his face.

"Too long, Mikey," Karp said, nodding and shaking his hand. "And I thought we agreed you'd call me Butch. That Mr. Karp business coming from someone I've known since he was nine years old makes me feel older than Methuselah. You remember my wife, Marlene Ciampi?"

"Yes, sir, Butch," Mikey O'Toole replied, turning to Marlene. "And of course, I never forget a pretty face."

"Ha! I see the apple fell from the same tree," Marlene said, laughing. "Your brother was a great bullshitter, too. And it's Marlene, before you 'ma'am' me again; then I'd have to hurt you."

"I meant every word," O'Toole said, then turned to the younger man, who stood behind him smiling at the repartee. "I'd like you to meet my attorney and, more important, my friend, Richie Meyers."

Shorter and muscularly compact, a former all-American collegiate wrestler and nationally rated chess master, Meyers appeared to be in his midthirties, although his short blond hair and tan face made him look younger. He shook their hands; then his eyes glanced to something behind Karp and Marlene. "And who are those two fine young gentlemen?" he asked.

Looking back, Karp saw the twins, Isaac and Giancarlo, peering from the hallway that led back to the bedrooms. "Gentlemen is a relative term when it comes to these two rascals, who by the way are supposed to be in bed and asleep," he growled. "But since they're here . . . Zak and Giancarlo, come on out and meet an old friend, Mikey O'Toole, and a new friend, Richie Meyers."

Pleased to be invited to join the party, the thirteen-year-olds emerged and shook hands, which gave the visitors a chance to appraise the boys. Born only minutes apart, they were alike and then again, not so much. They both had curly dark hair, like their mother—Giancarlo wore his somewhat longer, while Zak kept his short. The merry brown eyes and cupid-bow lips were nearly identical, and again favored their mother's Mediterranean looks.

However, Zak was stockier, more muscular, and carried himself like an athlete. His face was already more rugged than that of his brother, and more olive-colored, like Marlene's. Giancarlo's features were more delicate—not effeminate, just leaning toward classically beautiful rather than ruggedly handsome. Like Michelangelo's *David,* Meyers thought, an impression heightened by his complexion's almost translucent quality.

"Any baseball players between the two of you?" O'Toole asked. "I'm always scouting."

"Me," Zak responded immediately. "Any position, and I can already hit a curveball."

"Impressive," O'Toole commented, then looked at Giancarlo. "And you?"

"He's horrible," Zak answered for his brother. "Can't field, can't hit, throws like a girl. He's afraid he'll hurt his hands."

"At least I have more brains than a golden retriever," said Giancarlo, then acted as if he were throwing a ball. "Here, boy, fetch. Get the ball. That's a good Zak."

With technique born of long practice, Marlene moved between the two potential combatants. "What my little Neanderthal Zak meant to say is that his brother, Gianni, is a gifted musician. He plays several instruments and prefers not to ruin his chances at playing Carnegie Hall."

"Nothing wrong with that," O'Toole responded. "I wish I'd learned to play an instrument."

"Ah, you can always do that when you're old and can't play ball," Zak quipped.

"Out!" Karp commanded before Giancarlo could protest. "You two can continue to impress our visitors with your obnoxious behavior tomorrow. In the meantime, lights out, and I better not hear any squabbling."

Giving each other a dirty look, the twins did an about-face and headed back down the hall to their bedroom. If they engaged in any murder and mayhem after that, at least they did it quietly.

O'Toole gave Karp an amused look. "Quite a handful, those two."

Karp rolled his eyes. "Yeah, any more of a handful and we might all end up in the loony bin. If only they'd put as much effort into their bar mitzvah lessons. They're so far behind, they've had to delay the event until next fall when—if we're lucky—they'll pass into Jewish manhood only a year behind their peers."

It wasn't an entirely fair assessment of his sons' efforts. After all, they'd had to deal with their father getting shot recently, not to mention a half dozen run-ins with terrorists, murderers, and psychopaths over their short lives. Not exactly conducive to studying the Torah, Karp thought, but still they seemed to have plenty of time for their Game Boys and Xboxes.

"They'll be worse tomorrow if they don't get to bed," Marlene said. "Fortunately, it's Saturday so they can sleep in a little."

"Sorry to get here so late," O'Toole apologized. "There weren't a lot of flights from Boise International to New York on short notice. You sure you don't want us to stay in a hotel?"

"Not at all," Marlene replied. "We have plenty of room if you don't mind sleeping on bunk beds surrounded by entirely too much pink, as well as posters of the Backstreet Boys and a hundred or so stuffed animals. It's our daughter Lucy's room. She's currently living in sin in New Mexico with a handsome young cowboy."

"I'm sure it will be just fine," O'Toole responded. "But I got dibs on the bottom bunk. I tend to toss and turn, so the top bunk would pose a hazard."

A few minutes later, the four adults were settled on the couch and chairs of the loft's living room, each nursing a bottle of beer that Marlene had brought from the kitchen. "What's Sawtooth like?" she asked.

"What? You mean you haven't heard of the home of the 'Fighting Nez Perce' at the University of Northwest Idaho?" O'Toole responded. "Well, I guess it's a pretty small town—population maybe forty thousand if you include ten thousand students from the university. The town was originally built in the 1880s to support the timber, mining, and ranching industries of the area. And there's still a lot of that around. But over the past twenty years or so, it's gained a reputation as a fly-fishing and hunting destination. More recently, maybe five years, it's been developing fast as a retreat for city folks trying to get away from it all, mostly from California. The university, of course, plays a big part in the town's makeup and character. So do the Basques."

"Basques?" Karp asked.

"Yeah, there's actually quite a population of them in Idaho," O'Toole replied. "They're from a region between Spain and France, but ethnically, linguistically, and culturally neither Spanish nor French. Apparently, Idaho's mountains are a lot like their homeland. Some of the families arrived more than a hundred years ago, mostly to herd sheep, and many still do. They're good, hardworking people and well thought of in the community, though they tend to stick together and cling to their traditions."

"There's a great Basque cultural center in Boise and a smaller one in Sawtooth," Meyers interjected, "that you should check out if you ever come out our way."

O'Toole shot Meyers a funny look, then continued. "There was a large influx of them after World War Two. Apparently, they deal with a lot of prejudice and animosity, particularly in Spain."

"Speaking of prejudice," Marlene asked, "isn't Idaho one of the states famous, or infamous, for white supremacists?"

O'Toole's eyes grew hard. "I know Idaho gets the rap as the home of the Aryans and neo-Nazis and all that crap," he said. "And for sure, there's some of it. Starting about twenty or so years ago, they began moving to rural areas in Idaho, Washington, and Oregon with the idea that because there weren't many people of color living there, they could create an all-white homeland when the inevitable 'race war' began. In fact, there's a big compound about ten miles from Sawtooth that's home base to the Unified Church of Aryan People. But I've lived in Sawtooth for three years now and the vast majority of people aren't like that."

"So what is the state of race relations between the 'brothers and sisters' and the townspeople?" Karp asked.

"Actually, quite good by and large," O'Toole replied. "To be honest, there aren't a lot of minorities who have been longtime residents of the community, other than a few American Indians. Most blacks and Hispanics are students at the university, and they're there because they play for one of the teams, like mine. But most of the locals are really good to the kids; they follow the teams and are great fans. Like I said, Sawtooth is pretty small, so attending games is a major diversion. The fact is, the average citizen doesn't like these racist assholes—pardon the language—any more than we do, and resent that they moved in from other places and have given Idaho a black eye."

"Sometimes they try to run for office—like mayor or the school board," Meyers added. "But they never get very many votes. A couple of years ago, they held a rally at the city park, and there were maybe ten times more people there telling them to leave town."

Karp glanced at a clock on the wall. Damn, twelve-thirty, better get started or we'll be here all night, he thought. "Tell me about your team."

O'Toole beamed. "They're good kids. Some of them come from pretty rough urban backgrounds, but for the most part have proved that just because you might have an absentee, deadbeat father and live from hand to mouth, it's no excuse to become a criminal or join a gang. Several of them have the talent to play at the Division I level, but didn't have the grades to qualify for a big school. But Division I's loss is my gain. And we've done pretty well, too. Last year, we were a couple of games from going to the College World Series and playing against the big boys. That was our goal for this next spring, but . . . well, unless things change, I won't be there."

O'Toole looked down quickly as he made his comment, but Karp caught the hitch in his voice. "You really love coaching there, don't you?" he said.

O'Toole nodded and took a swig of his beer. "Yeah, I do. When I first got there, I saw it as just a step to something bigger, such as a Division I school that always has a shot at the College World Series. Like my brother, I wanted—still want—to win a national championship. But now I want to do it with the kids from this school. What they may lack in polish, they make up for in heart and desire."

O'Toole gazed at his beer bottle as if hoping to see a vision of a better future in the brown glass. Then he looked up, ready to answer the questions they all knew were coming.

"So how'd you end up in hot water?" Karp asked.

O'Toole took a deep breath, gulped down some beer, and then began. The specifics of the recruiting violations he'd told Karp about were that he'd condoned, even financed with university money, a party at which recruits were plied with alcohol and attended to by girls who'd apparently been paid to have sex with them.

"I'll get to those allegations, which are crap, in a moment," O'Toole said. "But first I need to go back a little ways and put this into context. The main character in this little drama was one of my players, Rufus Porter. He happens to be the prodigal son of one of our wealthiest and most influential citizens, 'Big John' Porter, who owns a couple of local car dealerships and is the real estate mogul of Sawtooth. Big John has his hands in just about every civic organization from the Kiwanis to Friends of the Library, and has dabbled in politics at the state level, though not very successfully because people see through the good ol' boy bullshit."

The event at the heart of the matter had occurred the previous spring during Recruit Week at which a half dozen high school players were brought to the campus to get O'Toole's sales pitch. After the talk and a tour of the facilities, the recruits were sent off to dinner with their potential teammates, who were supposed to return them to the dormitory with lights out at ten o'clock.

"However, two of the recruits were lured out of the dorm by Rufus and taken to this party," O'Toole said. "Sometime during this little gathering, Maly Laska, a female roommate of the hostess who was supposed to be out of town—apparently their rooming together was out of necessity, not friendship—came home unexpectedly. The next day, she reported that she'd been raped by Rufus. I had no idea about the party until it hit the local newspaper the day after the cops arrested Rufus."

"I hate to be the one to say this, but this wasn't a case where the girl gets drunk, has sex and regrets it the next day, and then cries rape?" Marlene asked.

O'Toole shook his head. "No. According to the local district attorney, a good man named Dan Zook, her injuries were consistent with sexual assault and one of the strippers told police that she later saw the girl in her bedroom crying. She told her that she'd been raped by Porter."

"What about the recruits?" Karp asked.

"They both said they saw the girl head back to her room, followed by Rufus a few minutes later. The door was closed and they say they didn't hear or see anything else until Rufus came out and they then left the party. Rufus, of course, claims that the sex was consensual."

"Still, seems like a pretty good case," Marlene ventured.

"It was. Zook charged Porter with sexual assault," Meyers said. "I should point out that doing that was no small act of courage in Big John's town."

"Hell, it took brass balls," O'Toole agreed. "I immediately suspended the jerk from the team. The university was a little slower. The president, E. 'Kip' Huttington III, and university attorney Clyde Barnhill didn't like it—Big John is the number one alumni club booster—but in the end there wasn't much they could do about it either."

"So they put this Rufus away?" Marlene asked.

O'Toole shook his head and took a swig of beer. "Nope. He's free as a bird. The charges were dropped."

"Why?" Karp frowned.

"Well, one thing was that the evidence—the DNA tests and samples—disappeared," O'Toole said.

"What do you mean 'disappeared'?" Karp asked.

"The investigation of the case was originally being handled by the university police," O'Toole said. "Their office is closed at night except for the guys on patrol, and there was a burglary. A number of files and items from the evidence locker were removed. Funny thing, but the burglars didn't touch the pot or cocaine that had been confiscated from college kids and was there for the taking, nor was there any sign of forced entry."

"The prosecutor could have still gone forward on the victim's testimony and that of the stripper and recruits," Marlene pointed out.

"The stripper changed her story after Rufus Porter's lawyer talked to her," Meyers said. "She decided that the victim could have been crying because she'd 'given it up' but then got dumped by Porter. Her new statement indicated that the victim was getting back at Rufus by accusing him of rape."

"And what about the victim?" Marlene asked.

"You'd have to talk to Zook about that, but he's still fuming," O'Toole noted. "She decided not to cooperate at the eleventh hour. Then she just packed her bags and left."

"They got to her," Marlene hissed.

"That's what everybody figures—Rufus runs with some of those Aryans we've talked about, and they play rough," O'Toole replied. "Zook had no choice except to drop the charges. And now he's got to be wondering where his next job will be. Big John doesn't take kindly to anybody being mean to his baby boy."

Karp thought about it for a moment, then shook his head. "Obviously, a gross miscarriage of justice," he said. "But there's nothing we can do about that case. The question for us is how does it tie into your problem?"

"As I said, Rufus was suspended from the team," O'Toole replied. "After the charges were dropped, I got a lot of pressure from the university president, Huttington, and the attorney Barnhill to reinstate him. I still refused."

"On what grounds?" Karp asked.

"On the grounds the asshole raped a girl," Marlene bristled.

"Come on, Marlene," Karp responded, "the complainant took off, the evidence was stolen, the corroborating witness flipped. End of case. We know there was factual guilt, but no legally admissible evidence in the offing. Legally, Zook was left with the presumption of innocence unrebutted."

Marlene growled something inaudible as Karp continued. "I'm asking what grounds you gave to the powers that be to keep the asshole off the team after the criminal charges that got him suspended were dropped. I'm assuming this has to do with why you're in hot water now."

"I understand," O'Toole said, "and you're right. If Huttington and Barnhill had their way, which was to cave in to Big John, Rufus would be back and probably in the starting lineup. However, I was able to keep him off for 'conduct detrimental to the team' because there was plenty of evidence that he set up the party, picked up the booze that was served to guys he knew were underage, and arranged for the strippers. Plus, he knew the recruits were to be in bed in the dormitory by ten."

"Can they make the claim that this refusal to reinstate him was personal?" Karp asked.

"I suppose they can say that," O'Toole agreed. "And I'll admit that I wasn't unhappy to have a reason to remove him from the team. The guy's a racist and a real cancer in the locker room. The only two recruits—and there were six—invited to this party were the two white kids. All the others were black and Hispanic. I think Rufus intended a different kind of recruiting for his friends with the Aryan church down the road."

"A racist, huh?" Marlene said. "I'm sure his attitude didn't go over too well with the brothers on the team."

"No, it didn't, nor with me, or for that matter with the other white players, who get along with all the guys," O'Toole responded. "But Rufus knew better than to say anything out loud; otherwise, he might have had a 'slipped-and-fell' accident in the showers. But his attitude made it obvious. He got the locker as far from the

other players as possible. Came in early to dress. Showered after
they left. Rarely said a word to anybody but me and never attended
team functions. Then he started openly hanging out with the neo-
Nazi/Aryan types."

"Sounds like you have a pretty tight case for 'conduct detrimental to the team' even without the recruiting party," Karp conceded.

"Yeah, I tried to nail him a couple of times even before all of this
went down," O'Toole said. "But Huttington and Barnhill wouldn't
go up against Big John."

"Can he play baseball?" Karp asked.

"What's that got to do with anything?" Marlene said. "The guy's a
Nazi rapist lunatic."

"Because they might try to claim that Rufus was an all-star
player but was being unfairly held to a higher standard than black
players. If the guy can't play ball, all the more reason it's up to a
coach's discretion whether to keep him on the bench, or get rid of
him, especially if he's disruptive."

"Very mediocre—slow, average arm, can't hit a changeup, and
wouldn't have made this team if I'd been coaching when he
started," O'Toole said. "I inherited him from the coach before me,
and I think the old coach pretty much had to take him on because
of Big John."

"Who is this Big John character? He sounds like something out
of a redneck comic book," Marlene said.

O'Toole chuckled. "You're not too far off. As the name implies,
he's a big fella . . . six foot five maybe, maybe three hundred
pounds. Was a Division II all-American right guard for the University of Northwest Idaho, a regular hometown hero. He even got
drafted by the Oakland Raiders but got cut in preseason and never
played another down. He's done all right for himself, though, and
every year he writes a fifty-thousand-dollar check to the university
sports department and that much again to the university's general
kitty."

"What's he like?" Marlene said.

"Sort of what you'd expect," O'Toole said. "Gone to seed a bit.
Hair is thinning. Big paunch and lots of spider veins in his face

from all the drinking. On wife number three. Number one was Rufus's mom, a cheerleader he met during that one season in Oakland. She was dumb as a stick, I hear, but smart enough to abandon them both when Rufus was a couple of years old. Number two just disappeared one night; he claimed she ran off with an old boyfriend, but no one has heard from her since. As for Big John, he wears size sixteen anaconda-skin cowboy boots and a big black Stetson that makes him seem even larger than he already is. Comes off in his car commercials like a loud buffoon. You know the type, 'Come on down to good ol' Big John's car lot and he'll make you a SUPER I'VE GOT TO BE CRAZY deal!' And his face is on most of the real estate signs in the area. He even sold the land that had been in his family for a couple of generations to the Unified Church of Racists and Morons I told you about—claimed he didn't know who the buyer was until it was too late. The place even came with an operating gravel pit that sells sand and gravel to the state highway department, which is apparently how our favorite Nazis make a living."

"I take it he couldn't be overtly racist and stay in business," Marlene said. "What's he say about his son's associations?"

"Not much," O'Toole said. "Calls it 'a stage' his boy is going through . . . sort of like puberty, only nastier. His little Rufus is just reacting, he says, to the perception that I was prejudiced in favor of black players. Rufus is the victim of discrimination, wouldn't you know. He'll tell you he doesn't agree with his son's 'politics,' which is what he calls racism. But by God, he stands by the boy's right to say and do as he pleases . . . as long as he isn't breaking the law."

"So you booted his kid off the team," Karp said, "and Daddy's putting pressure on the administration to get him back on. How does that boil down to you getting suspended by the university and then kicked out of coaching by the American Collegiate Athletic Association?"

"When it became obvious that I wasn't going to let Rufus back on the team, the university attorney, Barnhill, came to talk to me 'as a friend,'" O'Toole replied. "He said that the Porters were going to sue the school and the university. He said that Rufus had also filed a complaint with the university and the ACAA saying that I was the one who encouraged him to take the recruits to the party. I was the one, according to Rufus, who actually sponsored the party, paid for the booze and the strippers. Barnhill said he thought he could make the lawsuit and the complaint go away if I would let Rufus back on the team. 'It's only for his last season,' he said. 'Then he'll be gone.' But I refused. A week later, Barnhill arrived with campus security and told me I had to report to Huttington's office. They escorted me from the floor in front of all of my players, who didn't know what was going on or there would have been a riot. When I got to Huttington's office, it was me, him, and Barnhill, a really slimy character, even for a lawyer . . . just kidding . . ."

Karp smiled and held up a hand. "No offense taken. Sometimes stereotypes are stereotypes for a reason."

"Thanks. Anyway, Barnhill is a golfing buddy and hunting partner with Big John, so I knew that this wasn't going to be pleasant. And it wasn't. They said I was suspended while the ACAA investigated Rufus's allegations and pending any disciplinary action. Barnhill suggested that I find a lawyer. Needless to say, I was struck dumber than a post. They were throwing me under the bus."

As O'Toole spoke, Karp stood up. His wounded leg tended to ache if he sat in one place too long, but he thought best on his feet. "One thing I don't get is, if the object is to placate Big John and get his son on the team, why not just fire you?"

"Well, a year ago, when we almost made the College World Series, and before any of this went down," O'Toole replied, "they gave me a five-year contract extension with fifteen-percent increases every year and a double buyout clause if they wanted to terminate me for anything other than cause. Being suspended by the ACAA qualifies as cause, by the way. The university, meaning Huttington, was also worried about the public fallout of firing me. Most folks were behind me; if they'd just fired me based on a flimsy accusation that I was plying eighteen-year-old recruits with sex and booze, Huttington and Barnhill, and probably even Big John Porter, would have been ridden out of town on a rail. I go to church with these people. They *know* me. But if the ACAA suspended me and I *couldn't* coach, well, the university would be off the hook."

"So, Mikey, tell me about the ACAA hearing and where you're going with this lawsuit," Karp said.

"I better let my buddy Richie fill you in on the legal stuff," O'Toole replied, and looked over at Meyers, who had been silent for the past few minutes with good reason: he was fast asleep with his chin on his chest.

Marlene got up and walked over to the young attorney and removed the empty bottle of beer from his hand. "It's late," she said. "This can wait until tomorrow."

"Marlene's right," Karp said. "It's way past my bedtime, and we'll want clearer heads for this tomorrow."

"What time?" O'Toole asked.

"Well, it's Saturday, and I'm taking the boys to basketball practice in the morning and then to the synagogue in the afternoon," Karp replied. "I teach a bar mitzvah class, plus they're making up for some missed Hebrew lessons. Why don't you and Richie sleep in as long as you like and then do a little sightseeing; we can meet back here, say around six o'clock. Marlene has promised to whip up some of her world-famous sausage and peppers and gnocchi with marinara sauce. Then we can discuss the lawsuit."

"Sounds like a plan, a delicious plan," O'Toole said, then poked his sleeping friend with a finger.

Meyers's eyes flew open and he looked around like a confused owl. "Oh, gee, sorry," he apologized. "Can't believe I did that."

"That's all right," Marlene replied. "Travel can be tiring. Let me show you guys to your room."

Karp watched the two visitors follow Marlene down the hallway. Looking down, he noticed Gilgamesh was looking at him. "What do you say, boy, you smell a rat?" he asked.

"Woof," the dog replied.

"Couldn't have said it better myself," Karp agreed. "But I guess we'll know more about that tomorrow."

9

STANDING OUTSIDE A FORMER TENEMENT BUILDING IN THE East Village, Lucy Karp jumped at the sudden shriek of a passing ambulance's siren. Easy, girl, you'd think you hadn't grown up in the heart of Manhattan, she chided herself. Sirens were your lullabies and yellow cab horns your wake-up calls.

Then again, she had reason to be a little jumpy. Less than twelve hours earlier, in her room at the Sagebrush Inn, Espey Jaxon had given her fifteen minutes to pack a few items and then they headed out the door, which had made Ned a very unhappy, and horny, cowboy. She'd promised to make it up to him, but he'd stomped off.

In a field behind the inn, a black helicopter had been waiting to whisk them to the Taos County airport, where an unmarked black—what else, she thought—jet waited on the tarmac with its engines already turning. They'd arrived at Fort Dix army base in New Jersey in the early morning. Given the hour, Jaxon suggested that they grab some sleep in a small apartment complex on the base.

The sky was just beginning to get less dark in the east when Jaxon knocked on the door of the room she was staying in. When she was dressed, he escorted her to a reception area and asked her to wait while he went off "to make a couple of calls."

Jaxon seemed agitated and distant when he returned. But he quickly buried whatever was bothering him and took her to breakfast in the same apartment complex, where he ate quickly without talking, lost in his own thoughts.

There were only a few other people in the dining room, most of whom sat alone or in small groups, none of them interacting with anybody else outside of their comrades. "What is this place and who are these people?" Lucy asked.

"You don't want to know," Jaxon replied, looking up from his coffee. "It's the sort of place where nobody questions anybody else about who they are or what they're doing. Which is convenient at the moment because I'm officially not here and neither are you."

After breakfast, Jaxon led her to a small office and pointed to the telephone. "It's a safe phone," he said. "Cell phones can be monitored. Is it too early to call your friend now?"

Lucy looked at the clock on the wall: 7:00 a.m. "No time like the present," she said. "He doesn't sleep much." She quickly dialed a number and waited for the answer.

"Hi, Cian, it's Lucy," she said. She listened for a moment, then giggled. "Never say that around my boyfriend, even if it's Irish Gaelic. He has a terrible temper and if he saw me blush, he'd know you were up to no good. Hey, I know it's early, but would you mind if I dropped by? I have something I'd like your help with. What? No, Cian, I do not need any help with that, thank you very much. Good, see you then, and is it okay if I bring a friend? No, *he*, not she, is not an attractive female. Besides, how could you even suggest that you'd have eyes for anyone but me? Uh-huh, okay, I'll accept your apology this time, but don't let it happen again."

Jaxon had followed the conversation with an amused look. Lucy grinned back at him, happy that his scowl was gone. "If you're ready to go, Uncle Espey, I'd like to make this quick. I have a handsome young cowboy to get back to in New Mexico."

An hour later, Lucy calmed herself after the ambulance passed and walked down the worn steps leading to the cellar of the former tenement on East Fourth Street. She arrived at the bottom with Jaxon behind her and pressed the buzzer beneath a small sign that read: Celtic Bookworks, *Go mbeannai Dia duit.*

May God bless you, Lucy translated in her head, and quietly responded, "*Gurab amhlaidh duit.* The same to you."

A shadow appeared behind the peephole. As several bolts clicked and slid open, Lucy was tempted to start humming the *Mission Impossible* theme music. Maybe Tom Cruise will open the door; even if some others think he's gone off the deep end, he's still cute.

Instead, an enormously fat man of about fifty with gray mutton-chop sideburns and wearing a stained wool caftan appeared when the door opened. He squinted at her like an overweight mole from behind thick square-rimmed glasses that rested on top of a small upturned nose. But he was smiling broadly as he fumbled for the key that would open the security gate between him and his visitors.

"My dear Lucy, dear child, do come in," he gushed, unlocking the gate and pushing it open. "How very nice to see you again. You look absolutely wonderful. Apparently your new life in the desert has suited you well. I do believe your breasts are larger."

Lucy stepped forward to give him a hug and a kiss on the cheek that made him smile all the wider, showing tobacco-stained teeth. "*Ciamar a tha thu, Cian?*"

"*Tha mi gu math, tapadh leibh/leat,*" the fat man replied. "*Ciamar a thu sibh/thu fhèin?*"

"*Glè mhath!*"

Lucy turned back to Jaxon, who was standing behind her looking perplexed. "Cian Magee, this is federal agent Espey Jaxon, an old family friend as well as a true *gais cioch,*" she said.

Jaxon reached around and shook Magee's meaty hand. "I have no idea what you two are saying, but pleased to meet you," he said.

"Sorry, it's just the sort of showing off we language geeks do whenever we see each other," Lucy apologized. "I was speaking Scottish Gaelic. Let's see, I started by asking him how he was doing. He replied that he was 'Well, thank you,' and asked how I was. I told him 'Very well.' '*Glè mhath!*' "

"The dirty little minx also tossed a changeup at me," Magee said with a wink. "She switched to Irish Gaelic when she referred to you as a 'true *gais cioch*,' that is, a true warrior. But I didn't fall off the potato truck yesterday, *a ghra mo chroi*."

"So which is it, Cian?" Lucy laughed. "A dirty little minx or 'love of my heart'?"

"I didn't know they were mutually exclusive," Magee said, chuckling. "But come in, come in. Do be careful that my books don't collapse on you or you may not be found until I do my spring cleaning."

"You? Spring cleaning? What year?" Lucy laughed.

"Now, now, I cleaned up the place not more than six or seven months ago," Magee replied. "You'll have to forgive the mess, Agent Jaxon, this hovel serves as both my place of business and my swinging bachelor's pad. But I believe that disorganization is the sign of a fertile mind." He turned and waddled deeper into the passageway of the bookstore-slash-apartment.

Somehow he eased his bulk past precariously perched piles of dusty books—some with bits of papers protruding from their pages, and many of which supported old food wrappers or unwashed plates with a fork or spoon stuck to the surface—and into the main room. It resembled a cave, but made of books and papers. The only natural light came from a small garden-level window to the side of the front door where they'd entered, and another just like it around the corner in the "living room." Otherwise, illumination was provided by an odd assortment of lamps.

In one corner of the room was a large wooden desk upon which the books and papers were only slightly more organized than those in the rest of the room. A smaller table next to it held an ancient manual cash register, the door of which hung open, demonstrating that its contents were sparse. Except for what appeared to be a first-edition La-Z-Boy chair in another corner, not another square inch of open shelf, table space, or chair existed.

Magee stooped, gathered a load of books from the seat of another overstuffed and much-patched chair, and plopped them on top of the larger desk, scattering papers, pens, and food wrappers.

He then picked up a leaning pile of books from a tall stool and, after looking around for a place to deposit them, gave up and dumped them on the floor.

"Sit, please," he said. "I think it's reasonably safe." Clearly exhausted by his efforts, he padded over to the La-Z-Boy and sank into its groaning interior.

Looking around, Jaxon saw that there was another, smaller room, set off from the main area by a gauze curtain, beyond which he could make out a messy bed and a small table on which sat a microwave. Behind the La-Z-Boy he noted a half-open door that he guessed led to the bathroom. The place smelled of old, mildewy books and ancient dust, as well as stale sweat and cooking odors. However, the odor wasn't overpowering, thanks in large part to the sidewalk-level windows that were propped open despite the outside temperatures.

"So Cian's an unusual name," Jaxon noted. "Is it a Gaelic version of Sean?"

"Similar anyway," Lucy answered for her friend. "It means 'ancient, or enduring' in Irish Gaelic. And actually Magee is an Anglicized version of *Mag Aoidh,* which means 'fire.' So we're sitting in the presence of Enduring, or Ancient, Fire."

Magee blushed and mumbled something about names not meaning much. But Jaxon could tell that he was pleased by Lucy's translations.

On the way over, Lucy had filled Jaxon in on the reasons that her friend and fellow "language geek" Cian Magee didn't get out much. "If at all," she'd added. "He suffers from a few phobias, including agoraphobia, the fear of open spaces, which combined with an intense fear of situations from which escape might be difficult—in his case, a fear of crowds—doesn't lend itself to an active lifestyle outside his apartment. Apparently when he was younger, and much before I met him, it wasn't as bad. He tended to go from his parents' home straight to quiet, cocoonlike places, such as the library and small bookstores, especially at odd hours when there wouldn't be many other people around. But at least he got out some. Now, I don't know if he's left the apartment for months. He lives off a partial disability check and what little he brings in at the bookstore, and has everything delivered—food, books, all his necessities. Thank God for the internet, the occasional customer, and a few loyal friends, or he'd have almost no communication with the outside world. However, he is well respected as an expert in Celtic culture and languages, so he is contacted from time to time by other researchers, which gives him something to do."

"What about his parents?" Jaxon asked.

"They died about ten years ago, in an apartment fire over in the Bronx," Lucy said. "It pretty much sealed his fate."

Jaxon glanced at a small portable electric "fireplace" against the wall facing Magee's chair. His host noticed the glance and smiled. "It's my *cois tine*, where, by Irish-Celtic tradition, stories are told and the fate of the world decided. We Irish have always held poets and storytellers in high regard, even as high as our kings. It's part of the reason why we were one of the few literate northern Europeans during the Dark Ages."

He leaned forward as if to cut Lucy out of the conversation. "It's also my poor attempt at ambience for when lovely young ladies stop by to entertain me," he added, wiggling his bushy eyebrows suggestively at Lucy, who giggled.

Suddenly, Magee's face crumbled in despair. "I'd offer you something to eat and drink, beyond the rather foul excuse for water my landlord provides, but the delivery boy hasn't yet come today. I suppose Lucy told you that I'm not exactly a man about town."

"Yes," Jaxon replied. "She did mention that you were something of a homebody. A man after my own heart; I'd much prefer to be home with the wife and kids than disturbing your peace this morning."

"Ah, humph, yes, homebody, that's me," Magee agreed. "Anyway, you're not disturbing me. I do believe that I could probably hunt down a few saltine crackers and perhaps a bit of peanut butter."

"That's okay, Cian, dear. We ate before we came," Lucy said.

"Well, then, I suppose you want to get right to the business at hand," Magee said, slapping his thigh. "I must say, this is all quite an exciting event in my humdrum little life. A visit from a gorgeous sex kitten and a federal agent. I feel like I've fallen into a James Bond movie."

Magee's reaction reminded Lucy that this was not a game. What might be a fun fantasy for readers of spy thrillers or a lonely fat man was a dangerous and all too common thread throughout her life and the lives of her family.

When she heard the recording that Jaxon brought to her in New Mexico, she knew the language was from the Celtic family tree. She was fluent in most of the varieties: Irish and Scottish Gaelic, Welsh, Breton, and Cornish. But with this, she was stumped. However, she'd known who to turn to when it came to the Celts.

Thirty years her senior and obviously no Ned Blanchet, Magee had always been infatuated with her, but not so much out of lust—at least not the standard kind—but more a sort of adoration for a mind that absorbed languages the way sponges absorb water.

Magee was no slouch himself. He spoke all the Celtic languages, plus Old English, which to the modern English speaker might as well have been a foreign language, as well as Nordic languages, including the ancient version used by the Vikings. But like other polyglots, he was fascinated by Lucy's "gift."

Linguists, psychiatrists, and other brain scientists had been studying her since she was a child, trying to ascertain why she, and a very few others like her, picked up languages with such ease. However, they couldn't even agree on how people learned languages, much less what made Lucy such a special case. They all agreed that whatever the means, most people's ability to learn languages deteriorated as they got older, explaining why from puberty on, most people have a difficult time picking up foreign languages, except for words and phrases out of tourist books. But Lucy and other hyper-polyglots, or language savants, not only continued to learn well into adulthood, they became as fluent as native speakers.

Although she'd already informed Jaxon of Magee's credentials, she went over them again for effect. "Cian is the world's foremost authority on Celtic languages, or at the very least, the foremost authority in the United States. He's also someone I would trust with my life."

Magee blushed so hard that for a moment Jaxon thought he might be choking. "The dear girl is exaggerating my bona fides," the fat man said. "However, she's quite right about my willingness to lay down my life for her. She is a true marvel when it comes to languages. I'm a nobody in the linguistics world, but I know many others who consider her the most gifted hyper-polyglot ever."

"Well, her high opinion of you, your abilities, and your character are why I'm here," Jaxon said. "I'd like to ask you to listen to a recording and if you can, translate it for me. But first I have to tell you that this is a very sensitive matter—top secret—so I also have to insist that you keep this confidential. And to that I add my apology for asking you to step into a world that even on the periphery can be very dangerous. I have no right to ask you to do this, and if you want me to leave, I will with no hard feelings and no shame. But I can say that it's possible that this recording will affect the lives of many people."

"Oh my, yes, absolutely secret," Magee replied, nodding emphatically, his tiny eyes bright with excitement. "Not that I really have anyone to confide in, other than a few friends like Lucy. I could use a bit of danger and intrigue in my life. I mean, look at me, a fat, slovenly old man with more phobias than I could shake a stick at, except I'm afraid of sticks, too. No, no, Lucy, I know you're about to protest that, *a ghra mo chroi,* but it's true. We Irish, even Irish-Americans, are great bullshitters, but we know when it's time to tell the truth. I'm okay with it." Then Magee slapped his thigh again and shouted, "Out with it, man! Let's have at this puzzle!"

Jaxon smiled and brought out the MP3 player and disc. Fifteen minutes and a dozen replays later, Cian Magee sat back in his easy chair with a thoughtful look on his face. "First, the language is called Manx, the native tongue of the Isle of Man," he said at last. "However, the men speaking here are not native speakers."

"What do you mean?" Jaxon asked.

"Well, to explain that, I'm going to have to give you a quick history lesson," Magee said. "The Isle of Man sits in the middle of the Irish Sea between Ireland and England. It has been at various times under English, Irish, Scottish, and even Viking rule. Right now it's a British Crown dependency, which means it's a possession of the British Crown but not part of the United Kingdom. It has its own form of government—called Tynwald, which is a holdover from the Viking days. Its inhabitants also have, though only just, their own language called Manx."

"Only just?" Lucy asked.

"Yes, Manx was quite nearly a dead language. It's in the Celtic family and most closely related to Middle Irish, from which it diverged sometime around AD 900. Like with many other peoples whose lands are taken over by invaders, efforts were made to suppress the native culture and language. On the Isle of Man, the English overlords discouraged the use of Manx, and forbade teaching it in schools or using it in public. However, some of the decline can also be laid at the feet of the natives. It's a common theme for the subordinate culture to try to assimilate into the dominant culture in order to prosper; therefore, they look upon those who cling to the native culture—and language—as backward, country bumpkins, uneducated. So it was on Man, where especially by the nineteenth century, speaking and teaching the language took such a sharp decline that by 1974, the last native speaker of Manx was dead."

"But what did you mean that the men on the recording are not native speakers?" Jaxon asked. "If the last died thirty-odd years ago, they couldn't be."

"Well, in some schools of linguistic thought, only small children who have been brought up speaking the language can be considered native speakers," Magee said. "However, that's not what I meant. The Manx being spoken on that recording is a bastardized form of the language. Although the men are fluent, their pronunciations are definitely not the same as what was spoken on Man. Sort of like how the English that an Australian speaks is markedly different from a native of London; they have different words that are

either entirely homegrown—like 'bloke' to mean 'man'—or deriva-
tions of words from a local culture—like billabong, an Aboriginal
word for 'watering hole.'"

"Meaning?" Jaxon asked.

"Meaning that if I had to guess, I'd say that these two people did
not learn their Manx from anyone on the Isle of Man."

"Are there other places where it's spoken?" Lucy asked.

Magee shook his massive head and pushed his glasses back onto
his nose. "Outside of a few scholars, or expatriates, nowhere except
the Isle of Man that I'm aware of."

"I thought you said the last of the native speakers died in 1974,"
Jaxon said. "But some people do speak the language on Man?"

"Oh, yes . . . the history lesson," Magee continued. "Other than a
few recordings, the death of that last native speaker might have
been the end for the language—which is different enough from its
cousins Irish and Scottish that neither can understand it. Making
matters worse, there had never been a written form of Manx. However, about the same time that man died, there was a resurgence of
native pride on the Isle of Man, tied to nationalist goals that some
hoped would lead to complete independence from the British
Crown. With the help of linguists and hundreds of hours of recordings made prior to the 1970s, they began teaching children to
speak Manx in a few schools, though those with any fluency probably still only number in the hundreds."

"So do I need to go to the Isle of Man to translate this?" Jaxon
asked.

"Oh, no, not at all," Magee said. "About twenty-five years ago, I
was approached by the education society from the Isle of Man and
asked to help revive the language. To be honest, it was the best
thing I've ever done." He stopped and shook his head sadly. "I only
wish that I wasn't afraid of flying and of the ocean so that I could
have gone to Man personally. Instead, they brought me the old
recordings, as well as taped interviews with people who remember
bits and pieces from hearing their grandparents."

Jaxon took out a notepad. "Okay, then, I'm ready whenever you
are," he said with a smile.

Magee grinned back. "Okay, I get the hint. Now, there's a couple of words and aspects about the structure that aren't completely clear to me, and perhaps my skills are a bit rusty. It has been years since I heard Manx. However, the two men on your recording seem to be talking in some sort of prose, or a poem."

"A poem?" Lucy asked.

"Well, yes, and given the business of our friend here, I'm wondering if it is some sort of code," Magee replied. "Anyway, in the beginning there's a greeting that doesn't seem to mean much to either of them. But the crux of the message comes from the older man who says: 'A son of Man will march among the sons of Ireland and silence the critic for the good of us all.' "

"It does sound like a code," Lucy said.

"Yes, an instruction of some kind, perhaps," Jaxon agreed. "I wonder if they're talking about patriots from the Isle of Man. You mentioned that there was a nationalist movement on the island. Have you ever heard of any Isle of Man connections to terrorists, say, the Irish Republican Army?"

Magee frowned. "Not that I'm aware of. The nationalist movement was pretty benign when I was involved in the language project. It was more of a cultural pride thing and something that seemed would have a nonviolent political solution. I mean, it's not like the Isle of Man is occupied by British troops or under the thumb of Parliament. Independence would be more symbolic. But who knows? Maybe the nationalists have grown more violent in the years since."

Jaxon bit his lip. "A son of Man . . . so someone from Man will march with the sons of Ireland . . . boy, does that sound like good old-fashioned IRA polemics. Maybe some cross-fertilization? And then silencing the critic. An outspoken politician? Somebody within their own ranks?" He sighed, then added, "I think I better talk to my friends with MI5—the British secret service—and see if they can make heads or tails of it."

Magee shrugged. "Like I said, I'd be surprised if it's nationalists. It's really a sleepy little island—only thirty-three miles long and thirteen wide. It relies on tourism. They are a seafaring people from way back, which reminds me that there is one bit of naughty business associated with the Isle of Man."

Jaxon and Lucy both leaned forward. "Naughty?" they asked.

"Well, for hundreds of years the Manxmen, as they're called, were quite the smugglers," Magee said, happily going back to storyteller mode. "It really picked up in the seventeenth century. Ships from all parts of the world would anchor off the Isle of Man, hidden in any of the hundreds of small bays, and unload their cargoes into the small, fast sloops of the Manxmen. The smugglers would then make the run to remote shores of England or Ireland, where they'd sell their goods for the black market and then slip back out to sea. Of course, the Crown's tax collectors weren't too happy, and the Royal Navy was sent to stop the smuggling. The price of getting caught was pretty steep; some ships were sunk and their crews abandoned in the freezing waters of the Irish Sea, or if caught, they were hanged from the closest yardarm. However, on the Isle of Man, the smugglers enjoyed a sort of Robin Hood reputation. They've a lot of fun stories about the merry chases they would lead the British on."

"Can you tell us one?" Lucy asked.

"Certainly. Let's see, well, many of the stories are attributed to one particularly resourceful scoundrel named Quilliam. I recall one tale of Quilliam, who, when spotted by a British frigate and knowing he couldn't outrun the warship, told his men to go belowdecks. He then grabbed the wheel and ignored orders to stop until the Brits fired a warning shot across his bow. A longboat was lowered from the frigate, commanded by an angry English officer who demanded to know why he'd kept going. Quilliam told the officer that he was dreadfully sorry, but he wasn't feeling well. All the rest of his men, he said, were either dead or dying from what he guessed was cholera. 'You're welcome to come aboard and see for yourself,' he's reported to have said. Hearing about the dreaded disease, the English longboat stayed well away from Quilliam's sloop and skedaddled back to the frigate. Once the British were out of sight, Quilliam ordered his men back to their stations and, after a good laugh, they were on their way again."

"What happened to the smuggling operations on Man?" Jaxon asked.

"Well, the British tried just about everything to put a stop to it," Magee said. "And by 1778 were bound and determined to squash it once and for all. You'll remember they were in a bit of a fight over here in America, and they needed the revenues the smugglers were siphoning off. So they came up with an offer that—as Marlon Brando might've said—they hoped the smugglers couldn't refuse. The British government offered to pardon any smuggler, many of whom had prices on their heads, who volunteered to give up the smuggling life and enter the Crown's service as a sailor or soldier. Legend has it that five hundred turned themselves in and joined up. Those who did not were hunted down on the Isle of Man and sent to prison or hanged. Even at that, it still took another fifty years to stamp out all of the smugglers. It's a well-known fact that many of the wealthiest families living there now owe their fortunes to a smuggler in the family tree."

Lucy looked bemused but then shrugged. "Smugglers from hundreds of years ago seems pretty disconnected to this."

Jaxon nodded. "I agree. But it was an interesting tale."

"Thank you, we aim to please. And well, with your permission, and perhaps Miss Lucy's assistance, I'd like to continue doing a little research," Magee said. "I still have friends on the Isle of Man who I correspond with on occasion. Maybe they could make some sense of the poem. I'll make sure my inquiries seem innocent enough."

Jaxon thought about it as he was standing up. He reached for Magee's hand. "Be careful and don't tell anybody about where you heard the poem. I'll appreciate hearing about anything you come up with."

"It will be my pleasure," Magee said, and turned to Lucy. "You want to give me a call when you're available, my love?"

Lucy also stood and walked over to give Magee a hug. "I will, Cian," she said. "Oh, I almost forgot. What's 'Myr shegin dy ve, bee eh,' mean? It sounded like a sign-off to me."

"What? Oh, yes, you're quite right," Magee replied. " 'Myr she-

gin dy ve, bee eh' means 'What must be, will be.' Sounds pretty dramatic."

"That it does," Jaxon agreed. *"Myr shegin dy ve, bee eh,* then."

"Dia dhuit," Magee replied. "Which is how we Irish say 'God be with you.' "

10

"GOT TO GO, HONEY BUNNY, I'M FREEZING MY SWEET KEISTER off out here, and the cell doesn't work inside the restaurant." Ariadne Stupenagel had stepped into an alley off Brighton Beach Avenue in Brooklyn to escape the bitter wind that was howling in from the Atlantic, but she still shivered in the cold.

"If you come home now, *mon cheri,* I promise to warm it up for you," Murrow said in his best attempt at a sexy French accent, which came off as a fairly accurate rendition of the romantic cartoon skunk Pepé Le Pew.

"You want to warm my cell phone up?" Stupenagel laughed. She adored the man and found him incredibly sexy—but not when he was trying to be sexy and French. Then it was mostly just funny.

"No, your sweet . . . how do you Americans say? . . . derriere," Murrow continued.

"Oooh, Pepe," she squealed, wondering if he would get the joke. "When you talk like so, it makes me purr ze cat."

"Well, my little kitten, sounds like you have need of scratching, *ze l'amour.*"

Stupenagel giggled and sighed. Her boyfriend really did have wonderfully talented fingers and knew just how to use them for *"ze l'amour."* But she had work to do and it was time to focus.

"Sorry, baby," she said. "I need this interview for a story, and this might be the only chance I get. It may take a while, so don't wait up . . . but if you want, I can wake you up, as only I can, when I get back."

"Ah, *oui,* madam, please and most definitely," Murrow mumbled. "Until then . . . *au revoir."*

"Ciao," she replied, and flipped the telephone shut. She allowed herself a smile for a few seconds longer, and then put on her hard-nosed journalist game face. She'd been in the business a long time and knew that her pursuit of the St. Patrick's Cathedral story had her treading in shark-infested waters. She was making someone very nervous and/or very, very angry.

They'd already tried to kill Gilbert, though she knew that she was the real target. However, that hadn't stopped her lover's boss, Butch Karp, from haranguing her over taking chances with "other people's lives."

Stupenagel had told him to mind his own business, though she knew he was just being protective of his aide and friend. Recalling the battle on the rooftop, she did feel a pang of guilt for endangering her lover for the sake of a story. But investigative journalism was more than what she did, it was who she was, and Gilbert had known that going in. And he hadn't tried to blame her for nearly being strangled to death. His only comments had been regarding his concern for *her* safety.

"They tried once, they'll try again," he'd said as they lay in bed that night after the police left.

She'd tried to allay his fears with the old journalism adage that the most dangerous time for a journalist with damning information on a potentially dangerous person or organization, like the mob, was prior to publication. "After it's out, the only thing they'd accomplish by killing me is to bring more of a spotlight on them," she said. "Remember back in 1976 when Don Bolles, a reporter for the *Arizona Republic,* was killed by a bomb planted under his car? He'd been digging into allegations of land fraud concerning the mob and corrupt officials. I was one of thirty reporters from newspapers around the country who went to Phoenix as part of the 'Arizona Project.' We finished the job Bolles had started—a twenty-three-part series on official corruption, organized crime, and land fraud in Arizona. Even the mob now thinks twice before killing a journalist because it focuses too much attention on them."

Murrow was hardly mollified. "I wouldn't care that the job got finished if someone blew you up."

"Ahhh, you're so sweet, Silly Gilly," Stupenagel replied, and then kissed him. His steadfastness in light of his near-death experience touched her. Most of her former lovers would have headed for the hills to protect their hides, much less been more worried about her than themselves. "But you're missing my point. The sooner I can put a wrap on this series, the sooner there's no point in killing me. When I get done with them, the cockroaches will be scurrying for cover, not trying to get to me."

The look on Murrow's face told her that he didn't believe a word of it. He knew that what she'd said was true, but only to a degree. The bad guys were sometimes perfectly willing to kill a journalist out of revenge and to send a warning to other journalists that sometimes the First Amendment was bought with their blood.

The first round had gone to Stupenagel and a wooden baseball bat. The dead man had been identified as Don Porterhouse, a multiple offender with a history of sexual assault, assault, and burglaries. After she read his police jacket, something didn't seem right; Porterhouse didn't strike her as the sort to attack grown men with a garrote, and there was no mention of him being a trained martial artist. But a friend of hers at the Medical Examiner's Office had confirmed that the body he had autopsied had been positively identified as Porterhouse.

The bored NYPD detective who'd been assigned to the case had attached himself to the theory that Porterhouse had intended to burgle and rape Stupenagel and that Murrow had surprised him. "He just grabbed the first weapon he could think of," the detective said of the garrote. When she ventured the possibility that the man had been hired by someone upset with her stories, the cop had politely taken notes, but she could tell that he was doing it to humor her.

The story was the reason she was out on a blustery night to finally meet the man with the Russian accent who had been supplying her with her inside tips regarding Nadya Malovo, the Russian terrorist, and now some character named Jamys Kellagh, who was supposedly in the middle of it all.

She had been trying to meet the Russian source personally ever since the first call, but he'd refused. Then out of the blue, he'd called her that afternoon and suggested that they meet that evening. "I have something to give you in person," he said.

Although she didn't want to look a gift horse in the mouth, Stupenagel was curious about the change of heart. "Why not just mail it to me?" she'd asked.

"Because what I have to give you is one of a kind and cannot be trusted to a third party."

"Can you tell me anything about it? I mean, geez, it's awfully cold outside." There was no way in hell she wouldn't have met the man, but she'd learned from experience to always try to garner as much information while she had someone talking, just in case they didn't show up or disappeared altogether.

"Don't play games," the man warned. There was a pause, and she could hear him talking to someone in the background, although not well enough to understand what was being said. "I will tell you it has to do with Jamys Kellagh."

"You win," Stupenagel surrendered. "Where do you want to meet?"

On the way over to Brooklyn, she'd stopped by the Karp-Ciampi loft, ostensibly to check in on Butch's rehabilitation. But really she wanted to feel him out on the Russian agent, Nadya Malovo. The attack on St. Patrick's had resulted in several murders on his turf, and even if he was cooperating with the feds, she thought, ol' Butchie wouldn't have been too happy to hear that a suspect had been turned over to the Russians and then conveniently disappeared.

However, the district attorney and his wife were getting ready to entertain "a couple of friends from Idaho," and there'd been no time to talk. I didn't know they had any friends in Idaho, she'd thought as she left the loft. Her reporter radar told her to delve a little more into these "friends" when she could get Marlene alone with a bottle of wine.

Stepping back out of the alley and onto the bustling sidewalk, Stupenagel got the impression as she always did in Brooklyn's Brighton Beach that she had awakened in a foreign city. The part of the avenue that she was on ran beneath the elevated subway track, which created a steel cavern that looked straight out of a futuristic movie. But it was hardly the physical setting that was unsettling.

Framed by the community of Coney Island to the west, Manhattan Beach to the east, and the Atlantic Ocean to the south, Brighton Beach was home to one of the largest Russian communities outside of that country, so much so that the inhabitants referred to the enclave as Little Odessa. Hardly anyone on the streets, whether they were store owners, vendors, or passersby, spoke anything but Russian, though the salesmen quickly switched to English when they spotted a visitor with money. The signs above and in the windows of the stores were written in Cyrillic, and even the Dogs Must Be Curbed sign had a Russian translation.

Stupenagel had done plenty of stories on the Russian community of Brighton Beach, and she knew that they were different from the Russian Jews who'd escaped what had been the Soviet Union in the 1980s and 1990s. And she knew that they were different than the wave of Russian Jewish immigrants who had settled in the neighborhood at the beginning of the twentieth century after fleeing the pogroms of tsarist Russia.

While not as openly murderous as the tsarist Cossacks, the socialist regime that the new immigrants had lived under suppressed their culture to such a degree that they conformed to be more like their non-Jewish Russian neighbors than the orthodox Jews of the past. Jew was their ethnicity, but not necessarily their culture and religion. For instance, the fashions they wore—like their non-Jewish counterparts—looked straight out of Boris Pasternak's *Dr.*

Zhivago, at least the winter scenes. Everybody seemed to be wearing expensive fur hats and coats.

Wishing she was as well insulated, Stupenagel pulled her Saks Fifth Avenue wool coat around her shivering body as best she could; she maneuvered down the sidewalk past old crones dressed in black and muttering Russian epithets, and vendors hawking "real Bulova watches" and potato knishes.

Naturally, the area boasted the best Russian restaurants in the five boroughs, and Stupenagel's stomach growled at the thought of tonight's dinner with her "date." The caller had named the restaurant, and she'd immediately known its location, having been there many times in the past.

The Black Sea Café was famous for its mouthwatering dumplings called *vareniki* and *pelmeni. Vareniki* came in a dozen varieties of fillings, from sweet farmer cheese to sour cherries, enclosed in paper-thin dough, topped with sautéed onions, and bathed in drawn butter. When she'd had her fill of them, she would switch to *pelmeni,* which were stuffed with boiled meats and then drenched in a sauce of cheese and eggs and gratinéed.

The plan was to wash it all down with plenty of ice-cold shots of Jewel of Russia vodka. However, the buzz wasn't what she was looking for as much as information. She'd yet to meet the man who could keep up with her drinking ability, though Butch Karp's colleague Ray Guma, a man she'd had a brief and forgettable fling with, was close. She knew that Russians looked at drinking as a sort of competition, and thought she'd have no trouble getting the informant liquored up and talkative.

She knew one other thing about the Black Sea Café. It was owned by a Russian gangster named Vladimir Karchovski and his son, Ivgeny. Brighton Beach was also home to the Russian mob in the United States. It was an interesting aside, and she'd long hoped to interview the Karchovskis, but right now it didn't matter to her who owned the restaurant as long as the dumplings were hot and the vodka cold.

Walking in the door of the restaurant was like being greeted by an old friend with the smell of borscht, the moody dark woods and leathers that made up the interior, and the haunting sounds of the balalaika. Looking around, she noted a group of men who were well into the Russian tradition of extravagant toasts. For a Russian, drinking vodka was a celebration of life in all its joy and grief as only a Russian could express it, full of melancholy and fatalism.

One of the men had just finished a lengthy toast, after which they'd all clinked their glasses and downed the contents before reaching for the *zakuska*—hors d'oeuvres said to bring out the flavor of the vodka. Then they filled their glasses and began another round, or *charka*.

Like any good journalist taking in her surroundings, Stupenagel made mental notes of the other people in the restaurant. Sitting at one table was a fortysomething couple who appeared to be either leaving or returning from a trip. Just one of them, she corrected herself, noting that they sat with a single suitcase between them.

There were also several families in the restaurant. The parents, in the relaxed way of Russians, did little to settle their children, who were running around the restaurant, diving in between the legs of servers and patrons, as if it were a playground. She'd dodged one child when she spotted the man waiting at a corner table beyond where the couple with the suitcase sat. He was looking right at her and inclined his head slightly, indicating the chair across the table from where he sat.

Stupenagel took a deep breath and walked past the table of drinking men. The man giving the latest toast stopped what he was doing and instead raised his glass to her. The other men said something in agreement and also raised their glasses. She smiled and they drank before going back to their business.

Walking up to the table where the single man sat, Stupenagel repeated the phrase she'd been told earlier. "I'm here on a blind date." She wanted to roll her eyes—secret code phrases were too Hollywood for her tastes—but this was his game and she had to follow the rules.

"Then you've come to the right place," the man said, without a trace of a smile that a beautiful woman had the right to expect from such an exchange.

This guy is all business, Stupenagel thought as she took a seat. She took a mental snapshot of his face—the crooked nose and scars around the eyes, as if he'd been a boxer, and the clear, dark eyes that were assessing her just as thoroughly.

The mutual investigation was interrupted when one of the men at the drinkers' table shouted something. He sounded angry.

"What's he saying?" Stupenagel asked.

Her companion listened for a moment and at last cracked a smile. "He said, 'When I was released from prison three weeks ago, not one of you bastards would lend me so much as three rubles. . . . Nobody but Ivan, who is my true friend and not one of you other bastards.'"

"Sounds heavy," Stupenagel said. "But nobody seems to be taking offense."

The man shrugged. "Why should they if it's true? In Russia, we have a saying: 'The first *charka* is for health, the next for joy, the third for quarrel.' We are a moody people who understand that it is better for a man to get such things off his chest than to let it fester inside and someday erupt."

"What if somebody does take offense?"

"They would be in the wrong as long as he does not step over certain lines, or tell an outright lie," the man replied.

Seeing the opportunity for a segue, Stupenagel replied, "Speaking of the truth, thank you for the information you have given me."

The man held up his hand. "I am doing as my employer wishes," he said. "He's asked me to tell you more and to give you something of vital importance. But first, we eat. Are you hungry?"

"Famished." Stupenagel smiled.

"Good," the man said, and clapped his hands sharply, which brought the immediate attentions of a waiter who was obviously nervous. He said something quickly to Stupenagel's companion, who nodded.

Well, whoever this guy is, Stupenagel thought, he's got some pull at the Black Sea, and I'll bet it ain't because he's a big tipper.

"*Vareniki*—all varieties—and *pelmeni*," the man said. "And a bottle of Jewel of Russia."

Stupenagel noted that the man placed the order in English rather than Russian, which everyone else in the restaurant was speaking. It's a message to me, she thought, and acknowledged aloud what it meant. "Well, someone seems to have done his homework."

The man tilted his head to the side and gave her a wry smile. "Yes . . . how do you say in America, 'Knowledge is power.' My employer is aware that you enjoy dumplings and Jewel of Russia vodka. And the waiter told me he remembers you from other visits."

When the bottle arrived, the man filled their glasses and raised his with a short toast. *"Prost.* To health."

Tossing back her drink, Stupenagel savored its warm, smooth course down her throat but noticed that the man wrinkled his nose. "Don't tell me I've met a Russian who doesn't like Jewel of Russia," she said.

"It's *dela vkusa*—a matter of taste," he said, then leaned toward her conspiratorially. "To be honest, I prefer Armadale . . . but it's a Scottish vodka, believe it or not, and they don't serve it here. In fact, if I asked for it, I'd get my ass kicked."

Stupenagel laughed as her companion, who told her his name was Gregory, filled their glasses again. She had the sudden impression that she might have met her match and would not be drinking this man under the table that night. So she resigned herself to whatever happened and was soon happily scarfing dumplings while Gregory kept their glasses filled and regaled her with stories of his time in Afghanistan as a Red Army soldier fighting the mujahideen.

"I hope America kicks the asses of those evil bastards," he said. "These religious zealots will not be happy until every man has been collared and made a dog to their imams and every woman made chattel. I wish we could have killed them all. But we were an army of conscripts, young boys straight off the farms of Ukraine and the streets of Leningrad; we didn't have the heart of men who think they are fighting for Allah."

They polished off dinner with blintzes for dessert and a pot of strong Russian coffee. Through it all, the waiter had been attentive but made no attempt to hand Gregory a bill.

In the meantime, the restaurant emptied. Two families were left, their exhausted children now asleep or fidgeting in their seats. Only two of the men who'd been in the drinking group were left— one staring blankly up at the ceiling with tears streaming down his face, the other snoring with his head on the table. The couple was drinking coffee and waiting on their bill.

Only now did Stupenagel's companion reach inside a leather coat he'd placed on the chair next to him and produce a five-by-seven manila envelope.

"What have you got there?" Stupenagel said, hoping she didn't sound too drunkenly excited. She reached for the envelope.

But Gregory held it just out of her reach. "This is a photograph taken in Aspen, Colorado. The man who took this photograph had been asked to watch for Nadya Malovo. He spotted her and followed her to a meeting in a bar. The others at this meeting were Andrew Kane and Jamys Kellagh."

Stupenagel's sobriety level shot up several notches. She just about jumped across the table for the envelope, but he still kept it out of her reach. "I'm not through," he said with a wolfish grin. "I am told to impress upon you that this is the only known copy—it is not very good quality and our attempts to make other copies have been less than adequate."

"Why not have the photographer make you another?" Stupenagel asked.

Gregory's eyes grew hard, but he waited for the couple to get up and leave before he spat out, "He was murdered. Unfortunately, he was also old-fashioned and used thirty-five-millimeter film instead of digital. He made this and faxed it to my employer. It is not very good quality. He was supposed to send the film, but someone burned his darkroom down with him in it, and the film went with him. So this is all we have, but will be enough, no?"

"Maybe," Stupenagel said. "But now you've got me all excited, and I need to take a whiz before I pee my pants. So just hold that thought, and envelope, for a moment."

Gregory gave her an amused look. "I have nowhere else to go," he said, and smiled.

Stupenagel tottered rapidly to the far back of the restaurant for the bathroom, her mind whirling with the possibilities. First, a Russian spy implicated in the plot to kill the Pope, and now, in a few moments, she would see the face of Jamys Kellagh, the man behind the curtain. Pulitzer, here I come.

Out in the restaurant, Gregory sat back in his chair. As clandestine meetings went, this one had been rather enjoyable. The woman was pleasant to look at, with large breasts and a good sense of humor. Plus, she could drink like a man. Perhaps his boss would find other reasons for him to meet this woman.

Only then did he notice that the couple who'd been sitting near them had left their suitcase behind. He'd been trying to think why the woman had seemed familiar. She'd obviously dyed her blond hair brunette and the glasses seemed phony. Suddenly, though he'd never seen anything but grainy photographs of her, he knew who she was.

"Nadya!" he yelled, and started to rise from his chair just as the suitcase bomb exploded.

It blew the windows out with such force that an old woman standing in front of the restaurant died of a million little cuts that sliced through veins and arteries and bled her dry in seconds. Thousands of ball bearings shredded the two young families and the two friends who'd been drinking together, as well as a reputed Russian gangster named Gregory Karamazov. The simultaneous flash fire from a canister of high-octane jet fuel that took up half the suitcase immediately torched the interior of the café, incinerating anything that would burn, including the envelope and photograph that Karamazov was holding in his hand.

The walls crumbled and then the world was absolutely still for just a split second. The second passed and the vacuum was filled with screams and shouts and the sound of sirens in the distance.

11

ABOUT THE SAME TIME THAT ARIADNE STUPENAGEL WAS downing her first *vareniki* and shot of vodka at the Black Sea Café, Butch Karp opened the door of the loft a second time for Mikey O'Toole and Richie Meyers. "Welcome back," he said to his visitors. "How was your day?"

"Great," O'Toole exclaimed. "We took the boat to see the Statue of Liberty and then over to Ellis Island to check out the immigration museum, which was impressive. We even located the ship's manifest with my great-grandfather's name on it—Seamus O'Toole, steerage class, arrived in 1890 from Liverpool, just eighteen years old and with not much more than the clothes he was wearing. It was really something to stand in the same hall where he waited to hear if he was going to be allowed in or get sent back to Ireland. Must have been nerve-racking. I remember my grandfather talking about Seamus and how there was nothing but poverty, famine, and hopelessness for him back in Ireland. Gives you a real appreciation for the courage it took to leave everything and take a chance on a new beginning."

"I know what you mean," Karp replied. "Marlene's parents were from Sicily and waited in those same pews. So did my grandfather—a Jew from Poland, escaping the tsar's Cossacks. Imagine leaving that for someplace that promised everyone equal protection under the law and opportunity limited only by your willingness to work for it."

"Which I guess is part of why we're here," Meyers pointed out. "So did you have a good day with your boys?"

"It's always a good day if I'm with my boys," Karp said with a smile. "Busy, though."

Actually, it had been busier than he'd expected or hoped. First, there was basketball practice with the twins. As usual, Zak was the star of the team, but Giancarlo was no slouch, with a deft touch for outside shots. It was the only sport where he enjoyed some measure of success when compared to his brother, so at least the good-natured sniping was two-sided.

Then it was on to the bar mitzvah class Karp taught as part of a series presented to the synagogue's youth by Jewish community leaders. Given a free hand by the rabbi, his classes tended to emphasize the impact of events in Jewish history on the American judicial system, or centered on topical moral discussions.

Many of his lessons had raised eyebrows among some of the other parents. And that day's lesson was certain to do it again, as he'd asked the class to consider whether Jews were "culpable in the murder of Jesus of Nazareth."

The question had caused his students to gasp. Then Sarah, who was studying for her bat mitzvah, angrily denounced the allegation. "Christians have used that as an excuse for centuries to murder Jews," she said.

"Exactly why it's important for Jews to examine the allegation and, if warranted, be prepared to debunk its credibility," Karp said.

"But it was the Romans who crucified him," replied Sarah, a plump, precocious teenager whose already well-developed bosoms were the object of great curiosity to her male classmates, much to her disdain.

"But only after Jewish community leaders accused him essentially of sedition against the Roman Empire, of which they were a part," Karp pointed out. "Then when Pontius Pilate said he could not ascertain that a crime had been committed by Rabbi Jesus, those same leaders continued to press for his punishment. And when Pontius Pilate gave them the choice of executing a known murderer—for whom there was factual guilt and legally admissible evidence that led to his conviction—or Jesus, they chose Jesus. So would that make them guilty of conspiracy to commit murder?"

"They were afraid that he might cause trouble for them with Rome," Ben, a thin, bookish scholar noted.

"I thought it was because he was a threat to their leadership in the community," Karp replied. "However, even if we go with your theory, is it okay then to let fear of what might happen dictate how the law is applied? Was that a valid reason, and legally supportable, to conspire with the Romans to murder an innocent man?"

The class had broken down into noisy debate, which Karp was quite sure would be repeated at some of their homes. Especially when their homework assignment was to research the trial and execution of "the Jewish rabbi, Jesus of Nazareth" and then choose whether to prosecute or defend the Jewish leadership for conspiracy to commit murder.

"Why?" Sarah, who came from a very conservative household, demanded to know. "What does this have to do with us becoming adults?"

"Well, I was asked to teach this class as a so-called role model in the Jewish community," Karp answered. "And as you know, my job is to determine whether to prosecute people accused of crimes based on whether they are factually guilty and there is sufficient, legally admissible evidence that is likely to result in a conviction. If it was to happen today, the allegations, trial, and death penalty given to Rabbi Jesus of Nazareth would make an excellent case study with important implications for the American legal system. And as you've pointed out, it has had enormous historical implications for Jews."

"Good one, Dad," Zak said later as they left class. "Hope you're ready for a bunch of angry telephone calls."

Karp shrugged. "Why should the weekends be any different than during the week."

"Well, I think it's an interesting question," Giancarlo said.

"You would," Zak said with an exaggerated rolling of the eyes. "Then again, you think opera is interesting."

The boys were still squabbling when they got back to the loft, where Karp sent them off to their room, hoping to relax for a couple of hours, reading on the couch, before O'Toole and Meyers returned from sightseeing. He'd just settled in with John Keegan's book *Intelligence in War* when the telephone rang.

"Got a minute?" Newbury asked.

"For you, yes," Karp replied.

"I won't keep you long," the head of his white-collar crimes bureau said. "I just need your opinion. It has to do with the 'No Prosecution' files."

Newbury and his gang had been investigating hundreds of "lost" files found in the District Attorney's Office and stamped "No Prosecution." They'd come to light during the initial investigation that brought down Andrew Kane, when he was still just a wealthy attorney, investment banker, and mayoral candidate, and exposed his plans to corrupt and compromise the New York City Police Department, as well as the Catholic Archdiocese, for his own ends.

The files were criminal complaints brought against police officers and members of the clergy. They had been originally sent to Kane's law firm by the city attorney, aka Corporation Counsel, to review and make recommendations on how to make them go away. In most instances, Kane had recommended that the cases be settled (earning large sums of money for Kane). Then, if it suited his purpose, Kane would also recommend against prosecution for the accused. It was something he could use to manipulate the accused as well as the city, the NYPD, and the archdiocese.

Since the "No Prosecution" files had been given to Newbury's Gang, as his cadre of assistant district attorneys and investigators were called, dozens of cases had been reopened and the accused indicted, as should have happened the first time around. Dozens more indictments were expected.

In the course of the investigation, Newbury had learned that Kane had spread the wealth to a few other large law firms. "Whether it was because they were part of what was going on, or he simply couldn't keep up, we don't know yet," Newbury said. However, he'd just learned that his family's firm, run by his uncle, Dean Newbury, had been assigned to a number of cases in which white police officers had been accused of racially motivated crimes in their precincts.

"All the cases were settled and no charges were brought against the accused officers," he said. "However, so far there doesn't seem to have been any irregularities, though some warrant further investigation. Maybe Kane kept the worst offenders for himself—to use as leverage—and shuffled the rest to other firms so as not to raise hackles. Be that as it may, I've assigned one of the other assistant district attorneys, Galen Benson, to handle the investigation of my uncle's involvement. But if you'd like me to step down and move to another bureau, I'll understand."

"Why would I want to do that?" Karp asked, though he knew why Newbury had made the offer.

Vinson Talcott Newbury came from Old New York Money. His family could trace its roots back to the *Mayflower* on his mother's side and the middle 1700s on his father's. (*Though we seem to know little enough about the paternal DNA before that,* he'd once told Karp with a laugh. *I suspect they were black sheep, and it's been kept in the closet.*) Whatever their beginnings, the Newbury side had established themselves as one of the premier white-shoe law firms in Manhattan; their clients included some of the wealthiest, most powerful men and corporations in the country. And V.T. had dutifully followed the predestined course set for him from boarding school to Yale and then Harvard Law. However, he'd then caused something of a minor scandal after law school by going to work for the New York DAO. Years later, they were still looking down their noses because instead of accepting a lucrative position in the family firm, he'd stuck with the blue-collar work of prosecuting Manhattan's criminals.

Extraordinarily handsome with long, blond hair combed back from an increasingly sharp widow's peak, but only about five foot seven, he could also be somewhat sardonic. But Karp knew him as a loyal friend, a man of honor, and one of the best white-collar crimes prosecutors in the country.

Still, heritage meant something and Newbury was the "death before dishonor" type, which is why he'd made the offer to step down as the bureau chief. "Well, there's the potential for the press to see it as a conflict of interest," he replied to Karp's question. "Don't want to start off your new term with a messy scandal, you know."

Karp had brushed it off. "I don't run my office according to what the press may think. I have no doubt that if something comes up with your uncle that you need to bring to my attention, you'll do so," he said. "But to tell you the truth, it is my opinion that you could be trusted to prosecute yourself if you deserved it."

Newbury cleared his throat and seemed to be having trouble speaking, which made Karp smile. He knew that such shows of faith were the sort of thing his friend treasured most. A true throwback to a better time, he thought.

"Thanks, Butch," Newbury said at last. "And I'll keep you apprised. Oh, and by the way, that very same uncle called this morning. He wants me to drop by and meet some of his cronies. I'm sure it's the annual push to get me to join the family practice. Only it's a little more pushy this time since Dad died. I think Uncle Dean is feeling the years and there's no other heir to the family throne. The old man's laying it on thick, all sorts of hogwash about meeting people who could do me 'a lot of good' in the future, whatever that means."

"Take him up on it," Karp chided. "Lot of money in private practice."

Newbury laughed. "No thanks," he said. "I want to be able to sleep at nights after work. I'm not saying he or the firm are scoundrels or crooks. God knows my dad was a good and decent attorney who did plenty of pro bono work. But when your bread is buttered by wealthy, powerful men who think of themselves as being above the law, or at least the IRS, well, the world can be full of compromises. And I'm not the compromising sort."

Karp knew that Newbury wasn't the compromising sort and hadn't wasted any more time worrying about his friend's uncle. His more immediate concern was Lucy's sudden reappearance in New York in the company of S. P. Jaxon. He'd liked and trusted the agent since their rookie years with the DAO. But Jaxon worked in a world filled with terrorists and death, and his daughter had already experienced more of both than any twenty-one-year-old should have had to.

When she arrived at the loft late that afternoon, Lucy had told her parents that she was just in town for a couple of days to help Jaxon with a "translation issue." While she was usually willing to discuss her life in great detail, she'd been taciturn about the exact nature of this problem. However, she had dropped one bomb and that was that Jaxon was no longer working for the FBI. He'd apparently gone over to what the now former agent used to call "the dark side" of private industry.

"Why didn't he tell me?" Karp asked Marlene later as he helped prepare dinner by chopping onions and peppers.

"Maybe because he knew how you'd react," she replied, forming another pillow-shaped gnocchi, a type of pasta made from potato. "You lifer public servants have a way of sneering at those of us former public servants who get tired of bureaucracy and grub for money in the public sector. But I suspect it has more to do with the fact that you're both busy, especially him."

Marlene took a sip of a Piccini Chianti, which she claimed she'd opened early to use as a base for the sausage and peppers, as well as the marinara sauce. "You've been out of the office—or at least you better be or I'll wring your neck and then Murrow's. And Jaxon has apparently been tracking Lucy down in New Mexico and God knows what else. The fact that he's doing something for himself and his family doesn't make him a bad guy."

Karp sighed. Marlene ought to know. She'd been one of the founders of a private security consulting firm for VIPs. It had made her a lot of money, but it had also pulled her into a violent world. All of which got more violent when she turned her day job into volunteer night work, protecting battered women from the men who loved to hit them.

"Still, a call would have been polite," Karp harrumphed. "Especially as he's now flying my daughter about in black jets doing mysterious 'translations' for some private security firm. I don't like this at all."

Lucy had retired to her bedroom, where she was moping about, unable to reach her boyfriend, Ned. When Karp went back to give her a little fatherly advice about dealing with men by "giving them some space," he'd come under attack for allowing strange men to sleep in her room and leave their suitcases "where I'm tripping all over them." She'd then burst into tears.

Retreating in confusion, Karp had asked his wife what was the matter with his daughter. Lucy normally wasn't the sort to cry over some boy.

"You wouldn't understand," Marlene replied, giving him the "men are such morons when it comes to women" look before heading off to console her daughter.

Marlene had returned to the kitchen after placing the suitcases in the twins' bedroom; she announced they would be "camping" on the floor that night. After they arrived and heard about the new arrangement, O'Toole and Meyers had again volunteered to find a hotel, but she insisted that "unless you're allergic to pubescent boys and the smell of dirty socks stuffed under beds," they should spend the night in the boys' room.

"It's only a few days until Thanksgiving," she said. "You'd probably have a hard time finding anything decent, if you can find anything at all, at least without paying next month's salary."

"I don't have a salary next month," O'Toole pointed out.

"All the more reason to stay with us," Marlene replied, pouring two more glasses of Chianti and insisting that the men have a seat while she finished up preparations for dinner.

Two hours later, the adults pushed back from the table with satisfied groans coupled with compliments to the chef and praise for the second bottle of Chianti. The boys and Lucy had been more than happy to eat in their rooms "so that the adults could talk," but the conversation had mostly avoided O'Toole's legal issues until—after helping Marlene with the dishes—the men retired to the living room.

Karp, who'd brought out a legal notepad, quickly got to the point. "So, tell me about the hearing."

As he had the night before, O'Toole deferred to Meyers, who began by shaking his head and saying, "It was a procedural nightmare, a modern-day Star Chamber. Even the room was set up to intimidate anybody with the temerity to challenge the high and mighty American Collegiate Athletic Association: Big, empty white walls with no art, not even a sports poster, and blindingly bright fluorescent lights."

"Bring on the rubber hoses, eh?" Karp said.

"Exactly," Meyers replied. "We were told to sit on one side of a table long enough to seat twenty per side, and even then they kept us waiting fifteen minutes before anyone else appeared."

When they did arrive, the seven members of the hearing panel, their attorney, investigator, and the university's representatives—Huttington and Barnhill—all sat on the opposite side. "I was thinking, 'Now I know how a dying rabbit feels when the vultures start gathering,'" O'Toole said. "I would swear that even their chairs were taller so that they were looking down on me."

The panel was headed by a retired federal judge, George Figa. "He had a reputation in Boise for being strict but fair," Meyers noted. "So I felt pretty good about that, at least until later."

"I recognized one guy, too," O'Toole interjected. "You might remember him, Butch, J. C. Anderson. He was the head football coach at one of the Big Twelve universities for decades . . . retired, I think, in the eighties. He's got to be a hundred years old."

"I do remember Anderson," Karp said. "The man won two national titles, and God knows how many bowl games. But tell you what I remember most was hearing him give a talk once at a camp when I was still a high school basketball player. It was this great, impassioned speech telling us to remember that the real goal of participating in sports wasn't winning, or self-promotion, but the lessons it taught us for later in life about playing fair, following the rules, and sacrificing personal glory for the betterment of what he called 'the team we call our community.' I remember him saying, 'Do that and you're a champion in anybody's book and will go far long after you hang up the cleats.' I never forgot that speech."

"Well, he must have," Meyers said. "Because any hope we had for due process went out the window about as soon as the hearing began."

They'd known the basis of the ACAA case going in because Meyers had been sent the association's investigative file, which contained the complaint, the "evidence, such as it was," and copies of the witness deposition transcripts. "Though as you'll hear in a moment, those were somewhat less than complete," Meyers noted.

The ACAA had been represented by attorney Steve Zusskin. "What's he like?" Karp asked.

"Tall, distinguished-looking," Meyers replied, "wavy, silver hair with deep-set, dark eyes, great voice, almost sounds like he's singing when he talks. Apparently, he used to be a senior partner with a big firm in Boston before deciding to resettle in Idaho. He's about as good as it gets in our neck of the woods. Have to admit, I was a little intimidated."

The hearing began with Zusskin reviewing the accusations brought by Rufus Porter and the contents of the ACAA file by questioning his investigator, James Larkin, a former college football player.

"I nearly lost it and started laughing the first time Larkin started to talk," Meyers said. "The guy's probably six foot four and three hundred pounds, though a lot of it looked like blubber, but he has a voice like a twelve-year-old girl. It was really incongruous to listen to him talk in this high, shrill tone about how under his 'tough' questioning, he got Rufus Porter to 'confess' that he'd taken underage recruits to a party where he knew alcohol would be provided. But, of course, Porter claimed that he only did it at Mikey's suggestion and poor little Rufus felt, and here I'm quoting, 'that his place on the team depended on his doing what the coach asked.' Larkin also said that according to Porter, Mikey even gave him credit for alcohol from the baseball department's petty-cash fund."

The questioning was a real "dog and pony show," according to Meyers, "with Zusskin leading Larkin like a trainer with a St. Bernard at the Westminster Dog Show. For instance, Zusskin asked if women were paid to strip at the party and have sexual relations with the two recruits. Of course, Larkin agreed, and at his master's coaxing added that according to Porter, Mikey paid for it with his university credit card."

"Did they happen to bring up the rape charges brought against Rufus?" Marlene asked.

Meyers rolled his eyes. "Oh yeah. Zusskin made a big show of rustling through his papers and then asked Larkin if during the course of his investigation, he'd turned up allegations of Porter committing sexual assault at the party. Larkin said oh yes, it was that allegation that caused the removal of Porter from the basketball team so he gave it extra special attention. However, as he told the panel, the allegation turned out to be false."

"False!" Marlene sputtered. "The charges were dropped because the evidence in the case mysteriously disappeared and the victim for some reason left town in the middle of the night. I'd hardly call that false even if the charges had to be dropped."

Meyers nodded. "I essentially said the same thing . . . or started to when Judge Figa brought the gavel down and told me I'd get to speak later but I was to refrain from making any more statements while Zusskin and Larkin were trotting around the ring. . . . Well, he didn't put it exactly like that, but you get my drift."

"What did you say to that?" Karp asked.

"Oh, just, 'Fine, your honor, I'll wait for my chance to cross-examine the witness.' "

Karp chuckled. "Bet that went over well."

"Yeah, like a match in a fireworks factory," Meyers said with a grin. "I got an angry glare from the judge, and some nervous glances from the rest of the panel and Huttington. Barnhill was shooting daggers with his eyes, but Zusskin just smiled and went on with the show."

Following Zusskin's lead, Larkin told the panel that he'd interviewed the two recruits in question. "Then he handed out a nine-page transcript."

"Nine pages?" Karp said, furrowing his brow. "Obviously, men of few words. Or are you indicating that this was a somewhat truncated version of a transcript?" The smell of rat from the night before had returned even stronger.

"Yeah," Meyers replied, "for what was supposedly a couple of hours' worth of interviews. But when I complained that the transcript was incomplete, Zusskin said that for the purposes of the hearing, it wasn't necessary to present the entire transcript—only those statements made by the recruits that had bearing on whether Mikey knew about the party and paid for booze and strippers. Oh, and whether he asked the recruits not to cooperate with the ACAA investigation and to lie if questioned. I, of course, asked for the entire transcript and a copy of the tape recording of the interviews. But Figa gaveled me again and told me that the hearing would go forward according to the rules and regulations of the ACAA."

When he finished with the transcript, Zusskin wrapped up his presentation by submitting for the panel's examination his "hard evidence," a telephone record showing that a call had been placed from O'Toole's office to the Pink Pussycat Escort Service on the evening in question and a receipt for five hundred dollars paid to the escort service using O'Toole's university credit card.

"Then the judge asked if there was anything Mikey wanted to say in his defense," Meyers explained.

"Wait until you hear Richie's reply," O'Toole interjected. "He was awesome."

"Not really," Meyers replied. "To be honest, I felt a little overmatched. I'd never dealt with anything like this and had no idea what our rights were."

"Come on, it was a great speech about my right to confront the witnesses against me," O'Toole insisted. "He stood up and said, 'Before this goes any further, I'd like the panel to produce the witnesses so that I can cross-examine them. We'd also like to call our own witnesses and present evidence.' But the judge interrupted and, like he was talking to a naughty schoolkid, said, 'Mr. Meyers, this is a private organization with its own rules for conducting hearings.' Only Richie didn't back down and shot back, 'But how can you reach an honest and independent conclusion if you're the ones who brought the charges?' I don't think the judge was used to being challenged. His face got all red and he told Richie that the ACAA would conduct its hearings according to its rules and that if I wanted to make a statement I should do so before he adjourned so that the panel could deliberate."

"Well, my arguments didn't do you much good," Meyers pointed out, blushing slightly from the praise. "But yeah, Figa as much as said the Constitution be damned. So Mikey got up, told the truth about what happened, and sat down. Anybody with a brain would have seen that he was being honest, but I could tell just looking at the panel that it didn't matter, they'd already made up their minds."

In fact, it had taken the panel all of an hour of closed-door deliberations to return with their verdict. "Figa announced that there was enough evidence to conclude that Coach Mikey O'Toole violated ACAA rules governing recruiting practices and that such violations placed a stain on the integrity of his university and the American Collegiate Athletic Association," Meyers recalled.

"I couldn't believe it," O'Toole said quietly. "It was like my brother's case all over again. They said I was suspended from coaching at the collegiate level for a period of ten years. It pretty much meant the end of my coaching career—at least at the college level; no one will hire me again, even if I could wait ten years."

"We immediately asked Huttington for a public name-clearing hearing at the university," Meyers said. "It was the only chance Mikey had to get his side out to the public. But Huttington put on this long face and said he was sorry, but it wouldn't be in the best interest of the university."

"They fired me the next day," O'Toole said.

"So you filed a lawsuit in federal court?" Karp asked.

Both men nodded. "Yeah, I did some research and thought we

might make a case for a Fourteenth Amendment liberty interest violation," Meyers said.

"Very good," Karp said, genuinely impressed.

"I don't get it," Marlene said, looking puzzled. "I know it's been a while since I've practiced, but how is this a liberty interest case? He wasn't charged with a crime; no one is threatening to deprive him of his liberty."

Recalling his conversation on that very topic a month earlier with the Breakfast Club, Karp looked at Meyers. "Care to explain?"

"Sure, I'll take a crack at it," the young attorney replied. "Marlene, the courts have repeatedly held that the constitutional guarantees first stated in the Declaration of Independence to life, liberty, and the pursuit of happiness include the right of Americans to pursue their chosen profession. Mikey O'Toole's chosen profession is coaching baseball at the collegiate level. Yet, the panel took away that liberty without so much as a nod to the concept of due process. And the public university that fired him denied Mikey a name-clearing hearing, published the false and defamatory charges, and in so doing stigmatized him, which will prevent Mikey from coaching again at the collegiate and probably high school level. How's that, Butch?"

"Well put," Karp replied. "I tried one of these myself during a foray into private practice a few years back on behalf of the city's chief medical examiner. Jury bought into it and it resulted in a hefty check for the CME." He looked from one of the men to the other and smiled. "I have to say that you probably wasted your time and money coming here—not that we haven't enjoyed your company. But I think you're right on track and that, Mikey, you have a fine attorney representing you. I can't think of anything to add, though I'll mull this over, and if anything comes up that might help, I'll call. But the main point is that you don't need me."

O'Toole and Meyers gave each other the same funny look that Karp had noticed the night before. "But that's just it, Mr. Karp," Meyers said, choosing his words carefully. "I think I do need your help. I've never tried a case in federal court, or picked a jury for anything more complex than a burglary trial or a property dispute.

Zusskin has twenty years of trials on me, and he'll have help from whomever the university uses as its attorney, plus the resources of the ACAA and the university."

Meyers stood and faced the picture window, looking out at the lights of Lower Manhattan, and then turned back to Karp. "I'll be honest, my friend's whole future is on the line here, and I'm scared to death that I'll mess this up—not from a lack of effort, but a lack of experience. I'm asking you to please consider being lead counsel; I'd count myself honored to sit second chair."

Karp sat stunned by the emotional appeal. "I'm the one who's honored by the request," he said. "But you'll be fine. You've done the groundwork; keep it up and you'll take it to these guys. I'm the district attorney of New York, and I'm not really free, nor am I sure it's proper for me to take on a civil case in Idaho, no matter how I feel about your client."

"Nonsense, Karp," Marlene said, surprising her husband and the others in the room. "You're on a leave of absence, and I think it would be good for you to get out of Manhattan. Think of it as dabbing your toe back in the water before you jump in feet first."

Karp started to protest but Marlene held up her hand, and this time the look on her face said as much as her words. "And are you really going to let them do to Mikey what they did to Fred?" The comment went right to his heart, as she had known it would. Her smile challenged him to come up with another excuse, but he surrendered.

"I guess not," he said, and turned to his visitors. "Looks like we'll be coming to Idaho. But on one condition, Richie."

"What's that?"

"There's no second seating," Karp said, standing up. "It's an equal partnership, or nothing."

Meyers laughed and stuck out his hand. "Then put it there, pardner."

O'Toole also stood to shake his hand. "Thanks, Butch, my brother was right about you. He always called you his brother."

Karp felt his throat constrict at the word. "He was a good man," he said. "I owe him."

The moment was shattered by the ringing of the telephone. Marlene and Karp both looked at the phone but neither moved to pick it up immediately.

"Late-night calls to the home of the New York district attorney are rarely good news," Marlene said to the confused visitors as she finally moved to look at the caller ID. She picked up the phone and handed it to Karp. "It's Gilbert Murrow."

12

IT TOOK A MOMENT TO GRASP WHAT MURROW WAS SAYING. He was obviously crying and it was all Karp could do to calm him down as he sat on the couch and started scribbling on his notepad.

"There's been a bomb!" Murrow yelled into the telephone. "At your uncle's restaurant in Brighton Beach. The Black Sea Café. And . . . oh my God, what am I going to do . . . everybody's dead . . . I think Ariadne's dead!"

Murrow had broken down again, and there'd been nothing Karp could do except show his notes to Marlene, who was looking over his shoulder. *Bomb at the Black Sea. Ariadne may be hurt.*

"Okay, Gilbert, I know this is tough," Karp said as calmly as he could. "But start at the beginning and tell me what you know is for sure."

His tone seemed to help Murrow pull it together. "Ariadne said she was going to meet someone at the Black Sea Café for an interview. She didn't say who or what it was for but that it had to be tonight. I shouldn't have let her go . . . I should have gone with her . . ."

"Gilbert," Karp said sharply. "I need you to stay with me. I'm sure there's nothing you could have done differently, but that's not what's important now."

Karp heard loud sniffling and throat-clearing before Murrow continued. "Anyway, she had this interview. She called me just before going into the restaurant. She had to have been there for a couple of hours at least. The police have talked to witnesses who saw someone who looks like her having dinner there with another one of the victims—some mob guy. Then the bomb went off."

The phone went quiet and Karp sensed Murrow struggling to remain in control. "I was asleep . . . waiting for her to come home." He choked up. "I . . . I got a phone call—some guy with an accent told me to turn on the news. . . . I think he was trying to help. I turned on the television and this was all over it. As soon as I heard the name of the restaurant, I rushed over here as fast as I could. It's horrible. There's blood and bodies everywhere. . . . Fulton's here, too. I called him on the way down."

"Thanks, Gilbert, let me speak to him for a moment," Karp said.

"Butch?"

"Yeah, Clay. Sounds bad."

"It is. According to witnesses, there was at least one family with kids, maybe two, plus some other folks and the staff. They're still trying to clear the rubble and put out small fires. But they haven't found anybody alive yet."

"Have they identified Ariadne?"

"Nope," Fulton said. "But most of the bodies they have recovered so far are pretty torn up and burned. It may take DNA testing for some of them, according to the crime scene guys. But Gilbert thinks she was here and like he told you, a woman matching her description was seen at one of the tables just before the bomb went off."

"Who do they have for suspects?"

"Not much," Fulton answered. "A couple of NYPD detectives working in organized crime think this was aimed at the Karchovskis. Apparently, some youngbloods from Moscow are trying to establish themselves."

Fulton let the last sentence hang in the air. He was one of the few people in the world who knew that Vladimir Karchovski was the nephew of Karp's paternal grandfather. As a young man, Vladimir had been forced to flee the Soviet Union, leaving his young wife and son, Ivgeny, behind. Ivgeny had overcome his Jewish heritage—definitely not an advantage then in that part of the world, no more than it had been in the past—to become a colonel in the Red Army. But after he'd been wounded in Afghanistan and forced out of the military, he'd immigrated to America to join his father.

There'd never been much contact between Karp's family and the Karchovskis over the years; they had a mutual understanding that their respective careers made it problematic. Karp was the district attorney of New York. The Karchovskis ran a crime syndicate. Granted, it was one of the more benign criminal enterprises—no drugs, no prostitution, just smuggling Russian émigrés and goods like caviar into the United States and exporting U.S. goods into the black market in Moscow. But they'd been known to defend themselves and their turf with swift, ruthless violence.

The Karchovskis had been careful not to let their business affairs cross into Karp's jurisdiction and put him in an awkward position. But over the past year, their paths had suddenly converged. It began when the Karchovskis had come into information that helped Karp nail a gang that had viciously raped and nearly killed a young woman. And, by seeming coincidence, Marlene had proved the innocence of Ivgeny's half brother, a professor of Russian literature, who'd been wrongfully accused of sexually assaulting a student. The cases had brought the families back into each other's orbit and it had grown from there.

Compounding the problem was the fact that Karp actually liked his relatives, not to mention Marlene had been practically adopted by Vladimir as the daughter he'd never had. Thus far, the family connections had been kept a secret from the outside world, but Karp had deemed it necessary to let a few of his closest advisors in on "the family skeleton."

As the keeper of Karp's schedule and office administrator, Murrow had been told of Karp's connection to the Karchovskis, and to

Karp's surprise he had apparently kept the information from his girlfriend; at least it had never appeared in print. V. T. Newbury, Ray Guma, and Harry Kipman, the trio who formed the inner circle of his office confidants, had been told because they were also his best friends and the men he trusted most. Of them, Guma had seemed the least surprised, and Karp surmised that due to Ray's own familial ties to the Italian mob, he might have already known. The other two had taken it in stride. In fact, nothing seemed to surprise anybody when it came to the Karp-Ciampi clan anymore. "The Coincidence Fairy needs to take a Valium when it comes to this family," Butch had told Marlene. "Even fiction doesn't get this weird."

And, of course, Fulton knew about the Karchovskis because he was responsible for Karp's security. His response was typical, a shrug and a comment: *I'm like you. As long as they're not breaking any laws in my neck of the woods, I don't have time to worry about it. Besides, you can't pick your relatives, and you know the rest.*

"Who do you think planted the bomb and why?" Karp now asked Fulton, and could almost hear the big detective again shrug his shoulders.

"This stuff happens in gangland," Fulton said. "There's no saying what Ariadne was up to except that the guy she was with was part of the Karchovski family. She could have been working on a story about the Russian mob. Then again, there are those reports she's been writing about Kane and the hostage situation at St. Patrick's."

Ivgeny Karchovski was convinced that elements of the Russian government were complicit in staging "terrorist" attacks in Chechnya in part through the efforts of Russian agent Nadya Malovo, who'd pulled off Kane's escape. He believed that these elements were using the threat of Islamic terrorism to cast aspersions on the legitimate aims of Chechen nationalists, who happened to be Muslim, in order to control the oil flow through that satellite state.

Karp was about to ask which theory Fulton was leaning toward when he heard a shout in the background. "Hey, Butch! Looks like they found somebody alive," Fulton yelled into the phone. "I'm handing this back to Gilbert."

The next thing Karp heard was the sound of Murrow's breathing as he apparently ran toward where the shouts were coming from. "Gilbert, tell me what's going on," he demanded.

"They've found somebody, Butch," Gilbert replied breathlessly.

Karp detected the hope in his friend's voice and prayed that it wouldn't turn out to be false. This time his prayer was answered.

"It's her, Butch," Murrow shouted. "And she's alive! I think I saw her move her fingers. They're bringing her out on a backboard." There was silence and when Murrow came back, he was more subdued. "She's unconscious and . . . she looks pretty banged up. Sorry, Butch, I gotta go. I want to ride with her to the hospital."

The telephone went dead, but Fulton had called back from his phone a few minutes later. "Hard to tell," he replied when asked about Stupenagel's condition. "Out cold. Unresponsive. They had her strapped to a backboard, but that could have been precautionary. They loaded her up pretty quick into the ambulance."

"Let's get her some protection," Karp said. "I don't want to see what happens when somebody swings a third time."

"Already on it," Fulton said. "A couple of my guys are on their way to the hospital as we speak. Not that any bad guys will get past Murrow. They weren't going to let him on the ambulance, but he climbed in anyway and wouldn't come out. I had to have a word with the driver. I also sent a couple more to watch your place, just in case this is the start of something big."

Karp hung up and told Marlene and their two visitors what he knew. He walked over and looked down at the street from his window just as an unmarked police car pulled up and parked across the street.

"Wow," O'Toole said. "My problems are pretty insignificant compared to something like this. Maybe it's not fair to ask you to help me."

Karp looked at his wife, who was waiting to see how he would answer. "We'll play it by ear," he said. "But for now, I'm still on your team."

❖ ❖ ❖

Two weeks later, Karp and Marlene walked into the room at Beth Israel hospital where they found Murrow sitting next to Stupenagel, reading to her from David McCullough's book *1776.*

"Amazing we ever won the Revolutionary War," Murrow said when he saw them. "I think Americans today could learn a lesson or two from those first guys about courage and faith in the face of adversity." He put the book down and stood to hug them, then excused himself.

It had looked dicey when Stupenagel was brought in. Along with a broken arm, cracked vertebrae in her neck, and burns to her left leg, her skull had been fractured and there'd been significant swelling of her brain that could have proved fatal. But the doctors had induced a coma to allow her brain to heal, and she'd hung in there until gradually awakening on her own.

When she woke, the first person she saw was Gilbert Murrow sleeping in a chair next to the bed. With his round cheeks and pouty lips, his glasses askew on his face, he looked like a little boy, except for several days' growth of beard. He appeared to have been wearing the same clothes for a week.

In that instant, Ariadne's qualms about spending the rest of her life with just one man evaporated. She was content to watch him sleep and get used to the idea that she was completely in love with him. When he finally opened his eyes and saw that she was awake, he smiled and wiped away at a tear that rolled down his cheek, then stood to lean over and kiss her tenderly on her bruised lips.

"I love you, Ariadne," he said quietly. "You are never to go where I can't follow."

"I love you, too, Gilbert," she whispered. "And I would never dream of it."

They had all since learned that it was the call of nature that had saved her. "I was sitting on the damn toilet when the world came apart." She'd been found sandwiched between the steel walls of the toilet stall, which had protected her from most of the flying debris, the flash fire, and the weight of the wall that collapsed on top of her.

"Glad to see you're doing okay," Karp said after his assistant left the room. "But we didn't mean to chase Gilbert off."

"I asked him to give us a few minutes alone when you arrived," Stupenagel explained. "Hearing about all of this upsets him. Anyway, I know you don't have to answer me, Butch, but I need to ask if you've reviewed the evidence from the crime scene?"

Karp nodded. "I'm on the Five Boroughs antiterrorism committee and we got a report. Plus, Fulton and I asked to sit down with the detectives handling the case and review what they'd found to see if we might spot something that would indicate this was something more than gang warfare."

"So you've concluded that this was a terrorist attack, not a mob thing?" Stupenagel asked.

"Do you ever stop being a nosy reporter? Only a few days removed from getting blown up, and you're trying to get a quote out of me," Karp said, shaking his head.

"Nah, I'm not looking for a quote," Stupenagel insisted with a laugh that made her wince in pain. "At least not at the moment, though give me a couple more days and I'll be banging on your door."

"Well—and this is off the record, just in case you 'forget' what you just said—we're not sure yet if this was a turf battle or something else," Karp said. "But we're treating any mass murder, particularly in this fashion, as a terrorist act."

"I think you know better," Stupenagel said. "They were after me and/or the guy I was meeting and what he was about to give me."

"Yeah, and what was that? I heard you haven't been too cooperative about your dinner date," Karp replied.

The forensics guys had told him what they knew. The bomb had been contained in a blue Samsonite Oyster 26" Cartwheel, purchased in 2005 at the company's store in Stratford, Canada. It had contained hundreds of ball bearings packed around a very difficult to obtain, military-grade plastic explosive, and a canister of high-octane fuel. The bomb had been detonated by remote control using a transmitter and receiver from a toy car available at any electronics store—presumably by the couple who had been sitting with the suitcase when Stupenagel entered the restaurant.

Stupenagel's official statement to the police was that she'd gone to the restaurant to interview an unnamed source for a story. "Just a travel piece," she'd said when the detectives asked what the story was about.

Of course, no one believed her. Stupenagel's stories about the St. Patrick's Cathedral hostage crisis and her subsequent investigation into ties to the Russian agent who'd been captured and apparently released had been the talk of the town ever since they first appeared. There were plenty of people in New York City, as well as elsewhere, who believed the conspiracy theory that the U.S. government knew there would be an attack on 9/11 and allowed it to happen as a pretext for the War on Terrorism. Her stories just added to the conspiracy fodder.

"I didn't know who I could trust," Stupenagel now told Karp and Marlene. "No one except Gilbert and my source knew I was going there. So either I was followed, which doesn't make sense because that couple was there before I arrived. Or somebody followed Gregory, but he seemed to be the sort who would have taken precautions against that. Or somebody was listening in on my telephone conversations, and I don't like that one bit."

"So what did Gregory have to say?" Karp asked.

"Nice interview technique, Karp, subtle," Stupenagel scoffed. "What makes you think I trust you either?"

"Then whisper it into Marlene's ear, and I'll get it out of her later," he said.

"Wild horses couldn't drag it out of me, buster," Marlene said with a laugh.

"Yeah, well, I know that Marlene is a Chatty Cathy with a couple of glasses of wine in her, so I'll just tell you what I know and save you the cheap merlot," Stupenagel said. "It's going to be in the newspaper anyway as soon as I can persuade Gilbert to bring me a laptop."

Karp sensed that Stupenagel was avoiding the subject of the people who'd been killed in the attack. Though she was tough and brassy, with the usual journalist's dark sense of humor, he knew that she actually had a big heart and that it had to be tearing at her that others, especially children, had been killed by someone trying to get at her or her source.

"The source, Gregory, was about to give me a photograph that he said showed Kane, Nadya Malovo . . . and Jamys Kellagh meeting in Aspen," she said, watching Karp's face for his reaction. When she saw it, she nodded. "Yeah, I know that would have been big. But that's when I had to take a tinkle, and we all know what happened after that. Which is why I'd like to know if a black-and-white photograph, probably inside a manila envelope, was found in the debris."

"The only photographs I'm aware of that survived were those found inside wallets and purses," Karp said, wondering what part his cousin Ivgeny had played in Gregory's meeting with Stupenagel. "Maybe there's another copy."

Stupenagel shook her head. "I don't think so. He said it was one of a kind and had been faxed to his employer, who I guess are the Karchovskis. Apparently, the photographer has since been murdered and his darkroom burned to the ground."

"Did you see the photograph?"

"Unfortunately, that's when I decided to answer the call," she said. "He said it wasn't very good quality, being a fax and all. But I hoped it would be good enough to smear all over the front page of the newspaper. Maybe we could have smoked that fucking weasel Jamys Kellagh out of whatever hole he crawls into between murders."

"Such language from a lady." Karp smiled. "But I wish your friend had brought that photograph to the authorities so they could arrest that 'fucking weasel' when we had a case to present to the grand jury." Next time I get the chance, he thought, I'm going to have words about this with my cousin.

"Isn't it obvious?" Stupenagel said. "No one is sure who to trust."

"Like me?"

"No, not necessarily. Then again, what takes you off the list of suspects any faster than some other people who have to be on it?"

Karp thought about the columns and names on his legal pad. I don't know who to trust either. Maybe I should put my own name on the lists.

"But it's not a matter of trusting you," Stupenagel went on. "Maybe they don't trust anybody in your office, or maybe they don't trust the people your office has to deal with in other agencies. But I'll tell you what, Butch. This is getting scary. The Karchovskis are nobody to fuck with. Not to mention that whoever did this was perfectly willing to murder a member of the press—tried twice, as a matter of fact—and risk the publicity just to stop me from finishing this story."

"Maybe you ought to cool it for a while," Karp suggested.

"Like hell I will," Stupenagel fumed. "This is going to come down to the last man standing . . . or in this case, the last woman standing."

"That's what I thought," Karp responded, then patted her on the shoulder. "My money's on the woman."

Three days later, it became apparent that Stupenagel had talked her boyfriend into bringing her a laptop. The proof was on the front page:

> One of the victims of the terrorist bombing at the Black Sea Café last week was killed just before identifying the murderous mastermind behind the St. Patrick's Cathedral hostage crisis and other vicious crimes.
>
> Reputed Russian gangster Gregory Karamazov was about to reveal to this reporter a photograph purported to be of a shadowy figure named Jamys Kellagh meeting last summer with Andrew Kane and Russian agent Nadya Malovo in a bar in Aspen, Colorado when the bomb exploded. Eleven people died in the blast, including Karamazov.
>
> A well-placed source told this reporter that the bombing appears to have been a desperate move to hide the identity of Kellagh, and confirmation of Malovo's quiet involvement. According to the source, Malovo was arrested inside St.

Patrick's Cathedral but was handed over to the Russian government.

A spokesman for the Russian embassy in Manhattan denied
that any of its government's agents were involved in the St.
Patrick's debacle. He would not comment on the existence of
Malovo.

"Damn straight, they're worried," the source says. "Imagine
the implications."

Officials with the U.S. government and law enforcement
agencies have also refused to comment. . . .

Karp read the story as he was enjoying peach pancakes at Kitchenette. The Sons of Liberty were carrying on at another table, but
he'd politely declined their offer to join the frivolity so that he
could work.

He looked down at his much-traveled legal pad, which had a
new column headed by thick, dark letters spelling out Black Sea
Café. There were three names beneath it—Stupenagel, Murrow,
Ivgeny Karchovski—the fewest in any of the columns, and he had
to concede that there was a very good chance that whoever knew
Stupenagel was meeting Karamazov at the café wasn't on the list
and might not have been on any of the other lists either.

Someone, or someones, with the resources and know-how to listen in on telephone conversations, and brazen enough—or powerful enough—to feel safe bombing a restaurant owned by a powerful
Russian gangster, he thought. Jamys Kellagh, or whoever he works
for—or she; I don't know for sure if Jamys is male or female.

The conclusions did not sit well with him. Nothing made sense.
It was as if God had taken a giant swizzle stick to the solar system.
The planets were speeding every which way, careening off course,
sometimes on collision paths with other planets, or narrowly missing, but with no discernible pattern to the whole. And every day
seemed to bring new worries.

Karp would have liked to talk to Espey Jaxon about his thoughts.
But the former agent had disappeared after dropping Lucy off at
the loft and didn't answer his telephone messages.

He had recently learned that at least one other person wasn't thrilled about Jaxon's career change. Jon Ellis, the assistant director of special operations for the Department of Homeland Security, wasn't happy about it either.

Ellis had called to apologize for "being an ass" after the St. Patrick's Cathedral hostage crisis by trying to assert federal jurisdiction over the case. Then he asked if Karp could meet him for coffee. Curious as to what he would say, and wanting to get past his aversion to the man that on its face seemed unfair, Karp had agreed.

Five minutes into the conversation, Ellis made his opinion known about Jaxon. "Nice time to quit your country and go for the money," he said, but then he saw the look on Karp's face and quickly backpedaled. "Hey, sorry. Geez, I'm good at sticking my foot in my mouth, or maybe it's my head up my ass. I know he's a longtime friend and that was out of line. God knows he was taking down bad guys when I was still sucking my thumb. And I know the old government pension ain't going to pay for much of a retirement. It's just tough when the good ones leave; we can use all the help we can get. What I get left with are the snot-nosed kids and lazy good-for-nothings who nobody else wants."

Karp told him not to worry about it. He's trying, and I guess they don't teach diplomacy at spook school, he thought. He's not such a bad sort. Just a little overzealous. "I had misgivings about it when I heard, too," he said. "But you're right. I imagine in your business, the burnout rate can get pretty high and frustrating to deal with."

"You got that straight," Ellis said, shaking his head. "Sometimes between the media and Congress, I wonder who's on whose side. Speaking of the media, how's your friend, Miss Stupenagel?"

It was odd to hear Ariadne Stupenagel referred to as his friend. True, they'd known each other for a long time, but most of it had been contentious. He respected her, but he had to think about whether he considered her a friend. I guess I do, he thought.

"Better," he replied to Ellis. "And from what I understand, she's writing again. Sometimes I think she has a death wish."

"Yeah, walking on thin ice with those stories," Ellis agreed. "I'm not a big fan of the media these days, and I worry that she might drive these guys underground. We'd like to get our hands on Jamys Kellagh before that happens."

"You're not the only one," Karp said. "But then you and I might find ourselves in another jurisdictional squabble."

Ellis laughed and held up his hands. "Hey, I learned my lesson. Once you cross the river into Manhattan, one man's word is law. But we will take the leftovers if you don't mind."

Karp had left the meeting with a better opinion of Ellis. He was never going to be a friend, but the guy was trying to do his bit and had his life on the line in dangerous waters. He decided that his original assessment of the assistant director of special operations had been an emotional one. Karp's mentor, Garrahy, had always warned against making decisions based on emotions. *Make up your mind on the facts*, the old man used to preach. *Save the emotional stuff for your friends and family.*

Karp decided to follow that advice with Ellis, which was the reason his name was now crossed off on the legal pad. But it didn't seem to matter; he wasn't getting anywhere with the columns and names. He needed something that tied it all together.

He turned to another blank page and in the center wrote Jamys Kellagh and circled it. He surrounded the circle with a dozen smaller circles, to which he drew lines from the center. Some of the smaller circles he filled with the column headings from the first page. Kane's Escape. Fey's Murder. Aspen. And he added one more: Black Sea Café.

A few of the circles he left blank. Something told him that more of them would be filled in before it was over. However, now that he'd created the new page, he wasn't sure what it meant, except that Jamys Kellagh was at the heart of it all, and he already knew that.

Karp turned the legal pad over and gave the pancakes his attention until Saul Silverstein, the ladies' apparel pioneer, showed up with a copy of the newspaper and began reading Stupenagel's story aloud to the others.

"Now, that is one brave lady," Bill Florence said when Silverstein finished. "I would have been proud to have her on my staff at the *Post*. Met her once, big gal but pretty, nice set of jugs, too. Too bad we're the 'Sons' of Liberty or we could ask her to join us."

"She could be the women's auxiliary, Daughters of Liberty," the artist, Geoffrey Gilbert, quipped.

"To jugs and the First Amendment," defense attorney Murray Epstein shouted, lifting a whiskey and orange juice.

"Jugs and the First Amendment," the others said, joining the toast.

"Hey, are you guys talking about some other bimbo's jugs?" Marjorie the waitress demanded with her hands on her hips.

"Never," the Sons of Liberty shouted. "Show us your jugs!"

Marjorie laughed. "Your pacemakers couldn't handle it. But . . ." she said, leaning toward them seductively.

"Yes?" the old men replied breathlessly.

"I just want you to know that they are *mag-nificent.*"

A table full of old men groaned and poured themselves another round from Florence's silver flask. Karp laughed and began to return to his pancakes when he noticed his friend the priest, Jim Sunderland, and the former judge, Frank Plaut, standing off to the side talking. He couldn't hear their conversation and wouldn't have understood the context anyway unless he'd talked to his daughter first.

"Is it time to send the second package?" Sunderland asked.

"Yes, we seem to have gotten a response for the first," Plaut answered.

"Interesting that Lucy Karp is involved," the priest said, glancing over at the girl's father.

"Yes, but perhaps that could have been anticipated, considering Jaxon's relationship with the family," Plaut pointed out.

"So what's the lucky fellow's name again?"

"Cian," Plaut answered. "Cian Magee."

13

LUCY SAW CIAN MAGEE STANDING AT THE TOP OF HIS STAIR-
well and knew that he had to be excited to have ventured so far
from his burrow. He clutched the iron railing as though afraid that
some ill wind was about to carry his great bulk off into the void.
However, he managed to let go with one hand so that he could
wave when he saw her.

"*Céad míle fáilte romhat*, Lucy," he shouted.

"*Go raibh maith agat*," Lucy thanked him. "A 'hundred thousand welcomes' is certainly a nice Irish greeting. How are you?"

"Very well, indeed, *a ghra mo chroi!*"

"Really, Cian." Lucy laughed as she walked up and gave him a
hug. "You're going to have to stop calling me the love of your life or
I'm going to demand a ring."

"If only that were so, Lucy, I'd have already given you my
mother's ring. In fact, I have it right here in my pocket just in
case." Magee dug into his pants and to her surprise pulled out a
beautiful ring with a large diamond in the center. Awkwardly, he
got down on one knee. "So want to put your money where your
mouth is, *mo chuisle? An bpósfaidh tú mé?*"

"Oh my, so now I'm your 'pulse,' " Lucy said, giggling. She patted him on the cheek. "And no, I can't marry you. I'm already spoken for."

"Ah yes, the cowboy." Magee sighed as he struggled to his feet. "Too bad I'm afraid of leaving this stairwell, and flying in airplanes, and probably deserts, too, or I'd go to New Mexico and challenge him to a duel for your hand. Rapiers . . . except, no, I'm also afraid of sharp objects, too. They can put your eyes out, you know."

"So I'm told," Lucy agreed with a laugh. "Now, what's so exciting that you demanded we come right over?"

Magee looked around as if he were only just realizing where he was and didn't like it. The evening was growing darker and only a few passersby scurried along the sidewalks, trying to get home. He nervously eyed the slow parade of cars that passed, as if he expected one of his phobias to leap out of one.

"Yes, yes, very exciting," he said, and turned to go back down the stairs. "But that's quite enough of the great outdoors. Let's retire to my crib, as the kids like to say. By the way, where's your friend . . . the secret agent man, I thought he was coming."

"He is," Lucy said, following behind. "But Jaxon called to say he was running a few minutes late. He can catch up."

A minute later, Magee was safely ensconced in his easy chair, while Lucy sat on the stool across from him. He was obviously enjoying the moment, and the company, and in no hurry.

Lucy glanced around and noticed the Stouffer's Turkey & Stuffing microwave dinner box in the trash can and felt a pang of guilt. I was home with my family and our friends enjoying the real thing with all the trimmings, and this poor man ate alone out of a box, she thought. It was unbearably sad, but she smiled for her friend's sake and vowed that she'd visit him on Christmas.

"So, Cian. You said you'd received some 'extraordinary' information and that you needed to see us right away."

"So I did," Magee said, picking up an old book with a mustard-yellow cover that may or may not have been the original color. "And here is the reason why."

"A book?" Lucy asked.

"Ah yes, but not just any old book," Magee said. "This, my dear, I believe to be the veritable Rosetta stone to unlock the mystery presented to us by Agent Jaxon."

"You figured out what the poem means?" Lucy asked.

"Well, not yet, but I think this explains a lot about the people involved and may lead us to the answer," he said.

"Where did you get it?"

"Well, I have to admit that it wasn't from any great sleuthing on my part," Magee said. "Two days ago, someone rang my doorbell and when I answered nobody was there. However, they'd left a package, containing this book."

"That's odd," Lucy said. "And kind of creepy."

"Yes, indeed," Magee agreed. "But as it was helpful, not hurtful, I have to think that the messenger was sent for benevolent purposes and perhaps knew of our quest."

Lucy's eyes narrowed. "I still don't like all this clandestine stuff," she said. "I wish Jaxon was here. He might have an idea where it came from."

"Yes, well, perhaps he'll be able to explain it when he arrives," Magee said. "In the meantime, let me give you a taste." He made a great show of blowing dust off the cover and then using a piece of plastic to gently open the book to the title page. "You, of course, are aware that the acids found in the oils on your fingertips can damage old manuscripts. This book isn't particularly ancient—from what I can tell, probably only seventy-some-odd years or so. However, my research on the internet indicates that this may be one of a kind and needs to be treated with TLC."

In spite of her misgivings about the book's delivery, Lucy was intrigued. Magee had inherited the storytelling ability his Irish forebears were known for and was using it to full effect. "So what's it about?"

"What's it about?" he repeated, looking about mysteriously, which made her laugh again. "I'll tell you what it's about, little *deirfiúir.*" He stopped and appeared to be listening to the sounds outside the garden-level window opposite his chair and above Lucy's head. "I believe it's a sort of unauthorized edition exposing an organization so secretive that they make the Freemasons look like publicity seekers."

"I see, turn down your marriage proposal and suddenly I'm no longer *'mo chuisle,'* I'm your little sister," Lucy complained. "Oh well, fickle man, tell me more."

"I have to do something to protect my wounded heart," Magee sniffed. "Thinking of you as my little sister, and therefore unsuitable for carnal pleasures, will help me heal. But before I go further with the book, I think the occasion calls for better ambience." He rose halfway from his chair and turned the switch that started his electric fireplace. The glowing "coals" and "flames" cast an orange pall on the room and strange flickering shadows on the walls. "Ah, that's better," he said.

"Much," Lucy agreed. "Now tell me the name of this book and this mysterious group."

"Such an impatient child," Magee complained. "If you're not careful, you're going to ruin the mood. But as to your question— they are one and the same, the title and the group." He turned the book to where she could see what it said.

"The Sons of Man," Lucy read aloud. "From the poem?"

"Exactly. 'A son of Man will march among the sons of Ireland to silence the critic for the good of us all.' Only I think we should be reading that as 'Son' capitalized."

"So the Sons of Man is the name of the group," Lucy said. "What's the book say about them?"

"It's a history book," Magee said. "Remember what I told you about the Isle of Man and how it was home to inveterate smugglers?"

"Yes, you said that the wealthiest people on the island today owe their fortunes to smuggling."

"And you'll remember how in 1783, the British, who were tired of being made fools of by the smugglers, as well as needing money to carry on war against the Americans, offered amnesty to the smugglers?" Magee continued.

"Yes, and five hundred took them up on the offer," Lucy said.

"And those who didn't and remained on the island were hunted down," Magee added. "Well, it appears that there was a third group of smugglers who refused to join the British armed services, nor were they willing to live as hunted men on their own home island. These people . . . what was that?" Magee stopped his monologue and tilted his head to the window behind Lucy.

Lucy turned in her chair to listen, but hearing nothing, she scolded Magee. "Stop that, Cian," she said. "You're giving me the willies."

"I thought I heard something at the window," Magee protested. "But never mind. It could have been somebody walking by or one of the rats from the alley. I swear they're getting bigger and more aggressive. I had to battle one for my peanut butter and jelly sandwich the other night. Fortunately, rats are not one of my phobias and I was victorious."

Magee reached into a box next to his chair and pulled out a meerschaum pipe and a large plastic bag of tobacco. "Do you mind?" he asked. "I know it's extraordinarily bad taste these days to subject someone to secondhand smoke, but it's my one real vice and it adds to the story, I think."

"Go ahead, Cian, I like pipe smoke," Lucy said.

"Oh, good," he said, lighting the bowl with great dramatic puffing. He sank back in his chair with his eyes closed and a look of satisfaction on his round face. "Anyway, this third group of smugglers, with all their kin—led by twelve heads of families— fled across the Atlantic to America, where the war was winding to a close. Patriots might have been fighting for freedom and ideals, but the smuggler families saw opportunity in the form of miles and miles of open coastline along which to ply their trade. They smuggled goods from Europe and the Caribbean—rum, tea, and even arms for the revolutionaries—not because of any patriotic zeal for their new homeland, but the desire for cold, hard cash."

In the orange glow and swirling smoke, Lucy imagined the seafarers running British blockades as Magee continued his story. After the Americans won their war, the smuggler families continued their business with even greater ease. The fledgling government was having a difficult time collecting taxes from honest men, and had no navy to speak of. "So they grew wealthy."

Smuggling remained the cornerstone of the empire they built, but it wasn't the entire building. "They were no different from other immigrant groups that founded crime syndicates—the Irish mob, the Mafia—in that they saw the wisdom of funneling the ill-gotten gains into legitimate enterprises," Magee said. "They also began to assimilate into society. Perhaps to disguise their roots, they changed their Manx names to English or Scottish, and using their fortune as bargaining chips, they began to marry into the best families. However, they continued their secret ways, organized into a council made up of the leaders of the twelve original families. Places on the council were passed from first sons to first sons. Other family members could be involved in the secret organization, if they were trusted, but only in unusual circumstances could someone who wasn't a firstborn son ascend to a place on the council."

"The Sons of Man," Lucy said.

Magee nodded. "Yes, that's where the name came from. As I said, their historic business was smuggling, and that apparently included a wide variety of commodities over the years, including slaves. But their operations remained diverse—rum from the Caribbean, diamonds from South Africa, whatever they could get past U.S. customs and make a lot of profit from. They also exported products made in the good old USA and smuggled them into other countries, especially weapons that went to foment revolutions and wars. They apparently made quite a killing smuggling liquor into the United States from Canada and Mexico during Prohibition. However, they seemed to be content with just getting their cargoes in or out and let others—like Al Capone—do the distributing, which I suspect avoided unnecessary conflicts with other armed groups."

"Wow," Lucy said. "This is all so out of left field. What else?"

"Well, the history stops just before the Second World War," Magee said. "But if the Sons of Man stayed true to form, I suspect that their ventures evolved to smuggling drugs and God knows what else. However, what I find particularly interesting is that they weren't just content with their smuggling empire. Somewhere along the line—maybe to protect what they had—they began to broaden their reach into politics, the legal system, the military, and financial institutions. First sons, the heirs to their fathers' seats, were expected to pursue careers in these areas—so they became politicians, and lawyers, and judges, and bankers, and captains of industry."

Magee patted the book. "And it's all in here. The original Manx names and the name changes; the history and the general outline of their purpose. Up to the late 1930s anyway. It's rather frightening, really, how a focused organization that is willing to bide its time and wait for the right moment can become a potent political and economic force. Maybe alter the course of history."

Lucy looked skeptical. "You're kidding me. A group no one has ever heard of?"

Magee nodded solemnly. "Yes, a group no one has ever heard of—or few people, because somebody obviously sent me this book, and I assume that was so that I could help you and Agent Jaxon."

"Speaking of whom," Lucy said, looking at her watch, "I wonder where he is. He's going to want to hear all of this."

Magee smiled. "That's quite all right. A good tale only gets better the second time around, and I suspect the two of you will want to borrow my book and delve into this yourselves."

"So who wrote the book?" Lucy asked.

"A good question," Magee said. "There is no credited author. No publisher listed after the title page, and no record of it in the Library of Congress or any public library I could find. I tried to find a record of the Sons of Man on internet search engines and got a few hits. One was an incredibly bad song by a band called Killswitch Engage. I believe the lyrics go something like *You son of man I am here as a witness/You son of man can't you see what burns inside me.* Not exactly Bob Dylan and no apparent help with our poem. But that was about the most interesting of the lot."

"Did you try to find any references from the Isle of Man?" Lucy asked.

"Yes, and nothing there either," Magee replied. "I even wrote an email to their tourism bureau asking if they knew anything about a group called Sons of Man, but that was a dead end, too. Obviously, it was written by someone with insider information—maybe one of the Sons."

"So if Sons of Man is capitalized," Lucy wondered aloud, "I wonder if the poem is also referring to another group that calls itself the Sons of Ireland?"

"I thought of that myself," Magee said. "And I did find a non-profit association called the Sons of Ireland in Monmouth County, New Jersey. But it was founded in 2002 after the World Trade Center attack, as their internet site states, based on 'the principles of brotherhood, charity, and community service.' Their big annual event is the Polar Bear Plunge on New Year's Day, when the brave ones jump in the Atlantic to raise money for charity. In other words, they don't seem to be in league with the nefarious Sons of Man."

"Can I see the book?" Lucy asked.

"Yes, of course," Magee said. "This has certainly added a bit of spice to my mundane little existence, but I'm sure I'm merely the conduit and this should be in your hands."

Lucy got up off the stool to get the book. "If that's the case, why not just send it to me?" she wondered as she sat back down.

"That I can't answer," Magee said. "But I expect it will be revealed in due time."

Lucy looked at the cover. It was embossed with a symbol consisting of three running legs joined at the hip inside a circle, as if forming the spokes of a wheel. "I've seen something like this before, only there was a Medusa's head in the middle," she said. "It's on the flag of Sicily. I think it's called a triskelion."

"Or triskele, from the Greek for 'three-legged.' It's quite an ancient symbol and has been found on pottery dating back thousands of years, including one piece depicting Achilles with the triskele on his shield," Magee said. "It's also on coins found in Sicily that date back to 300 BC. You've already seen the one on the Sicilian flag. But it's also on the flags of Brittany and . . . as you might imagine . . . the Isle of Man. They're each a little different. Besides the Medusa, the legs on the Sicilian version are nude; those on the flag of the Isle of Man are like the one on the front of the book, gold-armored and spurred. Notice that whoever published this book went to the expense and trouble of using real gold leaf on the armor. Isle of Man banknotes also feature the *tre cassyn,* as it's known in Manx, above the Latin phrase *Quocunque jeceris stabit.*"

"Wherever you will throw it, it stands," Lucy translated, and grew quiet. *He bears the mark that stands wherever you throw it. Look for it.* She could hear Andy's voice warning her from her peyote vision.

"Exactly," Magee beamed, then noticed that Lucy had grown pale. "Say, is there anything wrong?"

Lucy pulled herself out of the memory. "No. Just recalled something. Not important."

"Okay, if you're sure," Magee said, then turned back to his story. "The oldest known version of the *tre cassyn* on the Isle of Man is found on the ancient Sword of State that once belonged to Olaf Godredson, a king of the southern Hebrides and the Isle of Man in the 1200s."

Lucy smiled. "You've been doing a lot of research."

Magee blushed. "Oh my, yes, and one discovery seems to lead to another. For instance, there are stylized versions—such as a triskele where the legs are represented by spirals. The earliest of those discovered so far were found on Neolithic carvings in County Heath in Ireland."

"Think that's the tie to the Sons of Ireland?"

"Who knows?" Magee shrugged. "But other than the use of the triskele, I couldn't find any definitive connection between the two. However, the more I looked, the more I was surprised at what a common symbol it is."

Magee explained that the triskele was also the symbol of nationalist movements of indigenous groups of Spain, including the Galizan, Asturian, and Cantabrian. "There's a four-branched version called the *lauburu* that is used by the separatist Basque movement."

It had also been adopted by Wicca and other neo-pagan groups. "It's quite popular with the bondage and sadomasochism crowd, too, especially after it appeared in the movie *The Story of O*. I suppose you and I could rent it and watch it together," Magee said, looking sly. "Just in case there's some hidden message in all that heaving, naked flesh."

Lucy rolled her eyes. "The only hidden message is in your pants, you dirty old man."

"*Maireann croí éadrom i bhfad*, eh?" Magee chortled.

"Yes, Cian, 'a light heart lives longest,' but on with your story," Lucy said.

Magee laughed and swiveled in his chair to the wall of books behind him and removed a small book from the shelf. "*Mein Kampf*," he said. " 'My Struggle,' Hitler's little master-race manifesto. Originally it was published with a photo of that madman on the cover. This is a reprint, but the point is, I want you to look at the symbol on the front."

"A swastika." Lucy nodded. "Four-legged, but yes, I see the similarity."

"Quite unfair really," Magee said. "In many cultures, the swastika is a benign symbol, such as in the Hindu religion. But unfortunately, the triskele was doomed to become a symbol of hate once the Nazis got a hold of it; a trilegged version was also the symbol of the Waffen-SS division in Belgium. More recently, white racist death squads in South Africa have used it as their symbol, as have Aryan and neo-Nazi groups in western Europe and the United States. There is also a cousin of the triskele favored by these racist groups called the Valknut—three interlocking triangles—a terrible fate for something of innocent Norse origins."

"So are the Sons of Man racist?" Lucy asked.

"There's some indication of that in the book," Magee replied. "Part of which seems to have emerged during the slave-smuggling years, when there was little regard for the welfare of their cargo other than keeping them alive for sale. But while there are racial overtones, I think that the philosophy that evolved simply holds that their interests are best protected by a white state, preferably of Celt-Nordic-Germanic origins. I have to say as an Irish-American who is proud of his Celtic roots, I'm ashamed that such a connection exists. They can kiss my ass, *Póg mo thóin!*"

"Every race has its racists," Lucy said with a shrug. "And most every society has had men who seek dominion over other men, or think they know what is best for all—especially if it is best for them. The Sons of Man seem to be just one more, though if they still exist, they might be more dangerous than most. Maybe the recording and the book was sent as a warning, like you said, a Rosetta stone to translate what they're up to. . . . God, I wish Jaxon was here."

Lucy checked her cell phone. It was working, but there was no message. "He's almost an hour late, which is not like him," she said. Then she stood up, walked over to Magee, and kissed him on the cheek. "Especially after you've done so much work."

Magee blushed the color of a ripe tomato and tears jumped into his eyes. "Be still my heart," he said. "Thank you, but I was just doing what I could to help." Embarrassed, he hauled his bulk out of the chair. "Perhaps I best fix us a spot of tea while we wait for Agent Jaxon."

As Magee puttered about near his microwave, Lucy looked at books on the shelves and piled on chairs. When she glanced over at the hallway leading to the front door, she was startled to see someone standing there. Then she saw that the 'person' was actually St. Teresa.

Oh no, Lucy thought. Whether the saint was a figment of her imagination or a genuine apparition, she didn't know. But whichever it was, the saint tended to show up in times of danger, and this was no different. Teresa looked at her and mouthed a single word. *Run.*

At that moment, something crashed through the garden-level window near the door and fell flaming like a meteor in the hallway. The Molotov cocktail then burst and spewed flaming gasoline against a wall of books.

Lucy turned to Magee, who'd come around the corner carrying

two cups of tea. "Run," she screamed to him as he stared in confusion at the quickly spreading conflagration.

"Where?" he cried. "That's the only way out!"

A block away, a man trotted down the alley toward a waiting limousine. He slowed when he approached the car and Jamys Kellagh stepped out. "Is it done?" Kellagh asked.

"Yes," the man said. "I listened for a few minutes. He had the book and had shown it to the girl. They knew far too much."

Kellagh nodded as he thought: That damn book could have ruined us all. Written and self-published by a traitor within the family, only a few copies survived—all in the hands of council members. This one had been, too, until another traitor took it and gave it to the enemy, though he'd since paid the price.

It should have been destroyed a long time ago, Kellagh thought. Folly to have kept it out of some misplaced affection for history. It was only by luck—and technology—that he'd learned that Cian Magee had received the book. His people regularly monitored the major internet search engines, like Google and Yahoo, for a variety of keyword searches that might impact the organization's plans. After the book was stolen, he'd added Sons of Man to the list of keywords to watch out for. There'd been nothing until shortly after Thanksgiving, and then there'd been several hits, all traced to the bookstore.

His first inclination had been to simply visit the shop and, when no one else was around, shoot Magee and take the book back. But the opportunity had not presented itself before Magee called Lucy Karp, a conversation he'd listened in on; then he knew he had to act fast and decisively. He'd decided that a wine bottle full of gasoline and a rag for a wick would accomplish the task of destroying the book and killing the witnesses to its existence.

"Did you wait to make sure no one got out?" Kellagh asked.

"I threw the bottle so it landed right in front of the door," the other man replied. "There are no other doors and it will go up like a torch. You sent me there to buy a book yesterday and even without gasoline that place was just waiting for a match."

"You didn't wait to make sure the job was accomplished?" Kellagh asked calmly but in a tone that made the man tremble with fear.

"Do you want me to go back?"

"No," Kellagh said. "That's what I get for sending an idiot to do a man's job. I'll go have a look. And you better be here when I get back."

Inside the bookstore, Lucy and Magee ran to the other basement-level window. Lucy looked at the narrow opening with dismay. She knew that she might fit through it, but Cian never would.

"You first," he yelled to her. The flames were already spreading into the living room and the smoke was so thick she could only see a couple of feet. "But here, take this, I wanted you to have it anyway. Wear it for me someday, *a ghra mo chroi*, when that cowboy comes to his senses and marries you." He pressed something into her hand that she put in her pocket without thinking.

Magee knitted his fingers together to create a step for Lucy to place her foot. "Up you go," he grunted as he lifted her to the window. Smoke was already billowing from the opening and she coughed and gagged, trying to claw her way out. She felt herself getting weak, but then two hands grabbed her by her forearms and pulled her forward.

Collapsing on the ground outside of the window, she looked up. Jaxon stood there with smoke swirling around him. He looked angry and she shrunk away when he extended his hand to help her up. Instead, she pointed back at the window. "Help, Cian!" she pleaded.

Jaxon turned and rushed back into the smoke. Lucy heard Cian screaming in pain and terror. Retching, she got back on her feet just as Jaxon staggered out. He grabbed her and wouldn't let her get closer to the fire.

"I couldn't get him out," he said. "I'm sorry, Lucy, the window is too small."

As if to confirm that, there was a last wailing cry of a frightened, dying animal. Then there was only the sound of the fire, the shouts of people on the street and people poking their heads out of apartment windows, and the far-off cry of a siren.

Lucy tried again to push past Jaxon, but he held her. "Let me go!" she cried. "I have to help him."

"It's too late, Lucy," he yelled. "Cian's gone. We have to get back, this whole building is going to go."

Jaxon led Lucy across the street, where she sat down on the curb and started to cry. "I killed him," she wailed.

"No, you didn't," Jaxon said. "You didn't start that fire."

"You don't understand," Lucy wailed. "They killed him because of that poem and what he discovered." She looked up, her eyes wild with suspicion. "Where have you been, Espey? You were late."

Jaxon hung his head. "I wasn't responsible for this, Lucy. And I swear to you that I will do everything I can to catch and punish whoever was."

Lucy seemed to weigh what he said. At last she nodded. "For Cian's sake, *nár laga Dia do lámh.*"

Jaxon's brow furrowed. "I'm sorry, I—"

"It's an old Irish blessing," Lucy interjected, "and means 'May God not weaken your hand.'" She reached in her pocket and pulled out the object Cian had given her, knowing that it was his mother's ring. She put it on her finger and started to sob.

14

THE QUIET TAPPING OF THE STENOGRAPHER'S MACHINE stopped as Richie Meyers checked his notes. The others in the room—Marlene Ciampi, Mikey O'Toole, Kip Huttington, and Clyde Barnhill—remained silent, like actors at a rehearsal waiting to deliver their lines. They were an hour into the deposition of Huttington, the first half covering O'Toole's history at the university, including his success and standing in the community, before moving onto the allegations that resulted in the ACAA hearing and suspension. But now Meyers was ready to delve into the heart of the lawsuit.

"Mr. Huttington, were you asked by Coach O'Toole for a public name-clearing hearing at the university following his suspension by the ACAA?" he asked as the court reporter resumed tapping away.

Huttington glanced at his attorney, Barnhill, who nodded.

"Yes, I was," the university president answered.

"And what was your reply?"

"Objection to the form of the question," Barnhill said. "President Huttington is a representative of the university; any reply was officially that of the university."

Meyers gave Barnhill an "are you serious" look. The university attorney had been a pain in the ass throughout the deposition—frequently objecting or touching Huttington on the arm to indicate he wanted to confer before answering the most mundane questions.

"Okay, then," Meyers sighed. "What was the university's official reply through its representative President Huttington when Coach O'Toole asked for a name-clearing hearing at the university?"

Huttington looked at Barnhill, who indicated that they should once again turn away from the others and discuss his answer. When the pair had their backs to him, Meyers rolled his eyes at O'Toole and Marlene. They both smiled and shook their heads; even the court reporter put a hand to her mouth to stifle a giggle.

The deposition was taking place in a meeting room next to Huttington's office at the University of Northwestern Idaho in Sawtooth. Meyers could have demanded that the university representatives come to his office, but given the cramped quarters there, he'd agreed to meet at the university. "Besides," he said, "I think it was enough of a shock when I filed notice that Butch Karp, who just happens to be the district attorney of New York, would be co-counsel. Barnhill even had his secretary call to confirm that I was talking about *the* Butch Karp."

Huttington and Barnhill turned back to the table and faced the court reporter. "The university denied the request," the president replied.

"For what reason?" Meyers shot back.

Apparently, Barnhill had anticipated the question and rehearsed it with Huttington, because he didn't bother to stop him from answering right away. "The university is a member of the American Collegiate Athletic Association and as such is subject to its rules and regulations," Huttington replied. "The ACAA conducted a hearing at which Coach O'Toole was given the opportunity to give his statement; the association then made its decision. The university as an entity was not obligated to provide Coach O'Toole a second forum, and we saw no good purpose—wanting only to get this business behind us for the university's sake, as well as Coach O'Toole's sake."

"You refused to give me a chance to prove that the charges against me were false so that I could clear my name for my sake?" said O'Toole incredulously.

"Sorry, Coach, but we will all have to move on with our lives," Huttington replied. He addressed the rest of what he had to say to the court reporter, as if he needed to explain his reasoning to her and no one else. "Coach O'Toole made a dreadful mistake. But one bad act does not make him a bad man. I wish him the best in his future endeavors."

"Gee, thanks for the vote of confidence," O'Toole said before Meyers could silence him with a look.

"There was no 'good purpose' in allowing him to present his side publicly?" Meyers said to head off any more of his client's remarks.

"Asked and answered," Barnhill replied before Huttington could say anything.

Marlene stifled the impulse to shake her head and say something. She had to remind herself that she'd been introduced as a plaintiff's investigator and was only there to observe.

When Meyers called in early January to tell Butch that he would be deposing Huttington, Marlene had decided to fly out to get acquainted with the players and help with interviews and any loose ends that needed to be tied up.

As much as anything, she just wanted to get out of Manhattan. The murder of Cian Magee had cast a pall over the holiday season. Other than the twins' usual orgy of overdosing on e-presents and other holiday treats, the celebrations had been quiet and contemplative.

Jaxon had taken Lucy to the hospital after the fire, where she was given a mild sedative and treated for burns to her legs. Because of the tears and the drugs, it had been difficult to get the full story from her when Marlene and Butch arrived. Only when she fell asleep was Jaxon able to fill them in on the details such as he knew them. "Which isn't much."

However, it wasn't until Lucy was released and returned to the loft that they heard about the Sons of Man book and its relation to the tape recording Jaxon had asked her to translate. Even then, it all sounded too incredible—a clandestine group of smugglers from a remote island in the Irish Sea who'd immigrated to America and established a crime empire?

"That borders on *The Da Vinci Code* fantastic," Marlene remarked.

Almost as disturbing as the story was Lucy's attitude around Jaxon when he visited the loft to see how she was doing. Marlene noticed Lucy's reticence around him and several times saw her daughter giving him sideways glances, as if weighing something. But Lucy didn't say anything and Marlene chalked it up to shock and grief.

When she got a moment alone with Jaxon, Marlene asked if he'd noticed anything about Lucy's mood since the attack.

"You mean toward me? And yes, I've noticed," Jaxon acknowledged. "I was the one who got her and Cian into this. Then I was late getting to Cian's apartment. I was . . . looking for someone, and it took longer than I thought it would. Lucy hasn't said as much, but I think she blames me. And to be honest, I blame myself, too."

The death of Cian Magee had been front-page news for all of a day. The attack was obviously a homicide and arson, but the police had no suspects or a motive.

Jaxon had "pulled some strings" and kept Lucy's name out of the press, but it hardly mattered. The media could not be bothered with the death of a bookstore owner and the story had died soon after.

Lucy had stayed in New York until Christmas day. After the presents were opened and a quiet Christmas dinner was picked at halfheartedly, she caught a taxi to LaGuardia and left for New Mexico to be with her cowboy.

Now it was January, the twins were back in school, and Butch was preoccupied with the bombing at the Black Sea Café and his obsession with the murder of the schoolchildren during Andrew Kane's escape. Going to Idaho seemed like a great way for Marlene to escape herself.

Marlene had been picked up in an old sedan at Boise Airport by two of O'Toole's players from the baseball team, Clancy Len and Tashaun Willis. The young black athletes had then wasted no time driving her north out of the city on a highway that within a few miles was climbing steadily into the snow-covered mountains.

Initially the land they drove through appeared to be barren—given over to rocks, brush, and stunted juniper trees. But as the road climbed in elevation, the increasingly steep hillsides were covered by a dense forest of pines and firs. "Over on the right is the Payette River," Willis said, indicating the mostly iced-over water in the deep gorge to her right. "It doesn't look like much of a river now, and I know that where you're from, the rivers are big, deep, and muddy, but come spring runoff from the snow and the Payette will be raging."

The higher they climbed, the windier the road became, but it didn't slow Len down much. Marlene, who was no stranger to wild rides, nevertheless clutched the door handle nervously as the old sedan swung around blind corners and skirted sudden precipices. Here and there, patches of snow and ice could be seen on the pavement. To take her mind off thoughts of plunging off the highway and into the river, Marlene asked her escorts their opinion of Coach O'Toole.

"He's the best," Len said. "There wasn't a lot of incentive for me to do well academically in high school. Where I come from on the South Side of Chicago, not a lot of kids go on to college. Those who try hard in school get a bunch of shit from the gangbangers for being 'too good for the hood,' so most just give up. I have to admit, the only reason I wanted to go to college was to play baseball until I could get noticed by a pro scout, only my grades weren't good enough to let me attend a big school. But Coach O'Toole gave me a chance, and when I got here, he found me a tutor so that I could catch up. Now, I'm straight As."

"Still planning on a baseball career?" Marlene asked.

Len took a moment to answer. "Some dreams die hard, and after I graduate, if I don't get drafted, I might try to walk on with some team, just so I can say I gave it my best shot. But I'm not counting on it anymore. Someday, baseball or not, I want to be a teacher . . . just as long as I can make enough money to save my little sister, Tanya, from the South Side."

"What about you, Tashaun?" Marlene asked. "Where are you from?"

"Believe it or not, right here in Idaho," Willis answered. "There ain't many of us brothers around here, but my father was in the air force, based out of Mountain Home Air Force Base down the interstate some from Boise. He was from Mississippi originally, but fell in love with this place and decided to stay."

"He still here?" Marlene asked, hoping she didn't sound nervous as the car swung around a corner just a few yards from the drop-off that plunged down to the river.

"Yep, he and my mom, two brothers, and a sister," Willis replied. "He retired from the air force and teaches computer science at Boise Community College."

"And what about your baseball dreams?" Marlene asked.

Willis laughed. "Hell, I can't hardly get off the pine with the team we got here," he said. "No, I'm a realist. I love the game, but after college, it's going to be softball leagues for me. I want to be a teacher, too, and maybe I can coach a little."

The group rode along in silence for a couple of minutes until Marlene asked, "What about these accusations against Coach O'Toole?"

"They're bullshit," Len exclaimed, " 'scuse my language, ma'am."

"Forget about it," she replied. "I hear worse from my adolescent sons on an hourly basis, though I do appreciate your manners."

"Anyway, it's all a bunch of lies," Len added, "made up by Rufus Porter. He's the one that's stirred this all up because he got kicked off the team. It's a damn shame what they've done to Coach O'Toole; the university and the ACAA ought to be ashamed of themselves. I hope he wins his lawsuit for more money than they got."

Marlene caught the hitch of emotion in Len's voice. O'Toole's players love him. Just like his brother, she thought. I remember from the funeral how devastated his former players were. She was about to comment on that when Len, who was looking in the rearview mirror, spoke.

"Looks like we got some crackers for company."

A few seconds later, a big Ford pickup truck roared up alongside the sedan. Inside were three young men, all as bald as billiard balls. Two sat in the front seat but the third was leaning out of the cab window, pantomiming pumping a shell into the chamber of a shotgun. He aimed the imaginary weapon at Len and pulled the imaginary trigger, laughing as he looked back at his companions.

The two cars went around a blind corner and the faces of the three young men changed from laughter to panic. A semitruck bearing a load of timber was coming head-on from the other direction, and they were seconds from being obliterated. The driver of the pickup gunned the engine and swerved in front of the sedan just in time to avoid being crushed. For a moment, the pickup remained in front, as if the driver was recovering his wits, and then it rocketed off ahead.

"Speak of the devil," Willis said with disgust. "That clown leaning out the window was good ol' Rufus Porter himself, and those were some of his Aryan nation friends. That timber truck almost did the world a favor."

A few miles farther, Len turned off onto another two-lane highway and headed northeast. They'd gone about twenty more miles, much of it paralleling a railroad track, when they passed a gravel road with a gated entrance and guard station. No people were visible, but they could see the Ford truck pulled off the road on the other side of the gate.

"That's the property of the Unified Church of the Aryan People," Len said contemptuously. "As you can see, our friends are the religious types."

Another ten miles brought them to the town of Sawtooth, which, Marlene noted, had managed to retain at least some of its history. The entrance to Main Street was dominated by a tall wood-sided building that proclaimed in big white letters on a red background to be the Sawtooth Mercantile and Livestock Feed Store. Across the street was a saloon called the Cowboy Bar; as if on cue, two young men in ten-gallon hats and cowboy boots sauntered out.

"I love it here," Len added. "I hope to live here someday. The air is clean, the water doesn't smell like the sewer, and for the most part, people treat you the same way you treat them. That's one of the things that Coach O'Toole emphasized to all of us players: Be good members of the community if you want to be considered part of the community."

"Sounds a lot like his brother," Marlene replied. "How much farther to Coach O'Toole's house?"

Willis pointed to a small mountain that rose beyond the town. "About a half hour," he said. "Coach lives up there, past the university campus."

As predicted, a half hour later, the group arrived at the entry of a long driveway that led to a large log home where smoke was curling up from the chimney. A pair of curious horses watched them from a snowy pasture as they rolled up to the house. Tall, red-haired Mikey O'Toole and his attorney, Richie Meyers, were waiting on the wide porch.

"I hope my two young friends here didn't show you too wild a time," O'Toole shouted as he walked down the wide steps to embrace Marlene. "Clancy is a city boy, but he seems to have lost all inhibitions about driving fast on our treacherous mountain roads. He's the Mario Andretti of the University of Northwestern Idaho."

"Please, coach, maybe 'the Wendell Scott,' at least he was a brother," Len said, laughing. "But don't worry, Coach, I took it easy on her. We did have one small run-in with some of our friends from the Unified Church of Racists and Morons, including favorite son Rufus Porter."

O'Toole shook his head and apologized. "Sorry, Marlene, they really are in the minority, but our Aryan neighbors do like to make themselves stick out like sore thumbs."

"Say, Coach, you mind if we go downstairs and watch the TV while you old folks catch up?" Len asked.

"Watch it with the 'old folks' comments, Clancy, unless you want to be running suicide sprint drills every day for a month when I get reinstated," O'Toole said, laughing. "But go ahead, you know you don't have to ask, and you've probably behaved yourselves about as long as you can stand. There's beers in the fridge, but leave your keys with me, you're spending the night. I'm about to throw some steaks on the barbecue. How many cows do you think the two of you can eat?"

"No more than two or three each," Len said, and tossed his keys to O'Toole. "I'm not too hungry. . . . What's for breakfast?"

O'Toole sighed theatrically. "I've gone into massive debt trying to feed these guys," he said. "And there are a couple dozen more just like them on the team. But come on in, I'm forgetting my manners, making you stand out in the cold."

Without being asked, the two baseball players took Marlene's suitcases into the house, followed by the others. Then with a wave to the 'old folks,' they disappeared down a big spiral staircase, and the sound of a game on television soon wafted up.

The next day while sitting in the university meeting room, Marlene smiled at the memory of O'Toole's banter with his players. Not exactly the sort to use sex and booze to recruit youngsters, she thought, and looked over at Huttington and Barnhill. So why were these two so willing to throw him under the truck for some racist jerk just because some fat-cat booster wants his boy on the baseball team?

Two hours after the deposition began, Meyers asked for a quick break so that he could go back over his notes and make sure he didn't miss anything. Back on the record, he asked a few housekeeping questions and then finished with a question that Karp had suggested during their telephone conversation.

"We're about finished here," he said, and looked directly into Huttington's eyes. "Is there anything else you can think of that would be relevant or significant regarding this case? Something I might have missed or was omitted?"

Barnhill scoffed. "What kind of a question is that? President Huttington has been completely forthcoming with both the ACAA investigation and your rather lengthy deposition today."

Up to this point, Meyers's demeanor had been polite and reserved. But now he fixed Barnhill with an angry glare, which made the other attorney laugh nervously and look quickly away. "Mr. Huttington, I asked you a question," Meyers said tightly. "This is a deposition and you must answer my questions, even if your attorney objects. And do remember you're under oath."

Barnhill scowled and began to say something, but Huttington waved him off. "That's okay, Clyde, we have nothing to hide here."

"Yeah, that's right, Kip," Barnhill agreed, though the smile he tried to assume looked almost painful. "Nothing to hide."

Marlene got the distinct impression that a message had just been passed between Huttington and his attorney. Indeed, it made her wonder what they were hiding.

"Your answer?" Meyers demanded.

Huttington blinked at the tone. Nice timing, Marlene thought. Richie's sending his own message.

"Uh, no, I can't think of anything to add that would be relevant or significant," the university president replied.

Meyers smiled like he'd just caught Huttington in a lie. "You're sure?"

Recovering his nerve, Barnhill angrily retorted, "Are you implying that President Huttington is lying?"

"Not at all," Meyers replied, his tone suddenly light again. "People sometimes forget when they're asked something in an uncomfortable circumstance, such as a deposition. So I was just making sure he'd had plenty of opportunity to answer the question completely and honestly."

"Then your question has been answered."

Meyers grinned. "Indeed. Thank you, that's all."

Huttington and Barnhill stood up quickly and left the room without saying anything more. Meyers looked at Marlene. "How'd I do?" he asked.

"Perfect," she replied. "Butch would tell you he couldn't have done it better himself."

"He's a great coach," Meyers replied.

"He had a great coach, too," Marlene noted, looking out the window. Big flakes of snow were floating gently to the ground. She shivered. "Someplace around here where a gal can get a hot cup of coffee?"

"You bet," O'Toole replied. "There's a great little Basque coffee shop around the corner."

They got up from the table and walked out into the hallway just in time to see Huttington and Barnhill confronted by an olive-skinned man wearing a bright red beret and carrying a wooden cane. "Where is my daughter?" the man demanded in heavily accented English.

"I'm sorry, Mr. Santacristina, we've been over this; I have no idea regarding the whereabouts of Maria," Huttington replied. "Now, if you'll excuse me." He started to move toward his office but Santacristina blocked his way.

Barnhill took a step toward the man. "I believe there is a restraining order that prohibits you from coming within one hundred feet of Mr. Huttington. Now, do I need to summon the police?"

"Summon whoever you want, Barnhill," Santacristina shot back angrily. "I'm sure the newspapers and television stations will enjoy the story of the father who was arrested for asking a married university president what happened to the student he was having an affair with."

On cue, a campus police officer appeared from inside the president's office. "Is there a problem here?" he said to the men.

Marlene expected that Huttington would have the angry man thrown off campus or in jail, but instead the university president shook his head. Glancing nervously in the direction of Marlene, O'Toole, and Meyers, he said, "No, it's all right, Officer. Mr. Santacristina's daughter, Maria, was a student intern in my office. She was reported missing by her father last spring, and he now labors under the mistaken impression that I know something about her disappearance."

"She was more than a student intern, wasn't she, Huttington?" Santacristina demanded. He pointed to the university president with his thick wooden stick. "This man used his position and smooth words to lure a young woman into an illicit affair. What would any father think?"

"Thinking might actually be wise before 'any father' goes around making more wild accusations," Barnhill retorted. "Or shows up drunk at a university dinner party thrown in honor of Mr. Huttington and makes a scene in front of all the guests, which is what got him slapped with a restraining order . . . an order, I might add, I am about to invoke if he doesn't get out of our way. Or maybe it's the Immigration and Naturalization Service I should call."

Santacristina glared at the two men. "I will leave," he said. "But I will never stop haunting you until justice is done." He turned to go but hesitated when he saw Marlene looking at him. His eyes narrowed as if sizing her up; then he headed for the exit, with the police officer following to make sure he left. Huttington and Barnhill glanced once more in their direction before walking into the president's office.

"What was that all about?" Marlene asked.

"Well, it was pretty big news here for a little while when Maria Santacristina disappeared late last spring," O'Toole said. "But that's the first I've heard that she was having an affair with Huttington."

"Do you believe it?" Marlene said. "Or is . . . what's his name—Santacristina?—a desperate father grasping at straws?"

O'Toole shrugged. "Believe what? That good ol' Kip was having sex with a student? What's not to believe? She was a lovely girl; he's a good-looking, well-spoken older guy. But I'm sure he wouldn't want that to get out. Sawtooth is a pretty small, conservative town—screwing students, excuse the imagery, would not go over well. Plus, he married into big local money, and knowing his wife, Suzanne, she'd leave him penniless. But the part about Huttington knowing what happened to her? That's not something I've heard about, either."

"Do you know the father?" Marlene asked.

"Not really. His name is Eugenio Santacristina," O'Toole replied. "He's one of our local Basque sheepherders, but well respected in their community from what I gathered from the news reports when Maria disappeared. Otherwise, quiet, keeps to himself like a lot of the other Basques."

Marlene recalled seeing a group of swarthy, mustachioed men

standing outside the Navarre Restaurant in Boise wearing white
leggings beneath red skirts and red berets. Willis had pointed them
out and said they were Basque dancers taking a break from a festival taking place at the Basque Cultural Center on West Grove
Street.

Marlene followed the other two out into the cold and headed
for the Basque coffee shop. Several inches of snow had fallen
since they'd gone into the university building, and Marlene was
shivering by the time she spotted the sign for the restaurant. She
stepped inside, gratefully basking in the warmth and the smell of
fresh roasted coffee. However, as they made their way to the
counter to order drinks, she noticed that the other patrons and
waitresses were nervously eyeing four young men sitting in a corner booth.

What made them stand out was the "uniform" that, as much as
their shaved heads, identified them as either skinheads or neo-
Nazis. They wore baggy jeans held up by red suspenders over
white T-shirts emblazoned with the Iron Cross, and completed the
ensemble with heavy, steel-toed Doc Martens boots. They'd piled
their long wool coats, which looked like German army issue from
the Second World War, on a table next to them.

"If I'm not mistaken," she said, "that's Rufus Porter sitting over
there with several of his friends."

Meyers didn't turn to look. "You're not mistaken, that's him, but
best we ignore him."

However, as if he understood that he was the subject of their
discussion, Porter and his friends got up and walked over to where
they stood. "Well, well, if it isn't my dear old coach, Mikey O'Fool,"
Porter sneered. "I'm looking forward to getting back on the field
this spring, but guess you won't be there."

"Don't count on it, Rufus," O'Toole replied. "The only way you'll
get back on that field is if you get a job mowing the lawn."

Porter's eyes blazed at the insult and then noticed Marlene's
smirk. "What are you smiling at, bitch?" he snarled, and started to
poke at Marlene with a finger.

A moment later, Porter was yelping in pain as she grabbed his index and middle fingers and bent them backward, locking his elbow and forcing him up on his toes. With her attacker off balance and unable to do anything except respond to the pain, she propelled him back into his friends, silently thanking Jojola for the jujitsu training.

Porter's face changed into a mask of rage. He'd been humiliated and now he and his friends intended to settle the score, but their attention was diverted when the front door opened and Eugenio Santacristina walked in.

The Basque's dark eyes immediately took in the situation. He strolled over, placing himself between the skinheads and the others.

"You and your friends are not welcome here," Santacristina said calmly.

"Fuck off, spic," Porter spat.

Santacristina's face grew grim as he gripped his wooden cane around the middle and tapped it lightly into the palm of his free hand. "Say that again," he replied. "And I promise that you will not walk out of here on your own. I will break both of your kneecaps, and those of any of your friends who interfere."

"And I'll be glad to help," O'Toole added.

Santacristina glanced at the coach and smiled before turning his attention back to Porter and his friends. "Now, what is it to be? A future as a cripple, or merely a moron?"

Porter seemed to be weighing his options. His former coach was a big man, and even the small attorney looked pretty tough. The woman knew some sort of trickery, too. But it was the Basque and his stick that worried him the most.

"Let's go, Rufus," one of the other skinheads suggested. "We'll settle this some other day when there's not so many witnesses."

"I will look forward to that," Santacristina said.

Porter did his best to look tough and as though he would have still preferred to battle. But he said, "You're right. Too many witnesses." He stepped back from Santacristina and snapped a Nazi salute with his right hand raised, exposing a tattoo on the inside of his right bicep that appeared to be some Aryan symbol. "Death to niggers, kikes, spics, and race traitors."

"Get out," Santacristina said, infuriated by the salute but still keeping his cool.

"Got to get our coats," Porter said.

"Esteban," Santacristina said to someone behind the skinheads, who turned to see that four other Basque men had emerged from a back room and had positioned themselves behind them. "Bring these dogs their coats."

The youngest of the Basques responded by grabbing the coats, which he held at arm's length as though they smelled, and tossed them to the skinheads. "Now leave," Santacristina ordered, "or I will beat you like the mongrel dogs you are."

The skinheads made their way to the door and left. Porter, who was the last to leave, shouted an epithet but fled as the Basque men moved toward him.

When they were gone, Santacristina introduced himself, extending a hand to Coach O'Toole. "I was sorry to hear what happened to you. I do not believe these things they say."

"Thank you," O'Toole replied. "We're planning to fight back."

"So I have heard," Santacristina said. "I hope you win."

On impulse, Marlene asked, "Would you care to join us?"

Eugenio Santacristina inclined his head slightly and flashed a smile that looked all the brighter for his tan skin and created a whole series of smile lines around his mouth and eyes. "I would be delighted." He turned to the other Basque men, thanked and dismissed them in their language, and they left for the back of the restaurant again.

Some shepherd, Marlene thought. There's a man used to giving commands and being obeyed out of respect. "I noticed that you don't need the cane to walk," she said.

Santacristina held up the four-foot-long piece of gnarled but polished oak. "This? No, this is not a cane," he said. "I am a shepherd. This is a walking stick I use to keep up with my charges on the steep hillsides. However, I admit that at nearly sixty years old, I lean on it more than I used to."

"You're sixty?! I would have guessed much younger," Marlene said.

"Chasing sheep keeps one youthful," he replied with a laugh.

The three men and one woman were soon talking over steaming cups of rich, dark coffee, which Marlene would later swear had the consistency of motor oil but was the richest, smoothest, most flavorful coffee she had ever tasted.

Santacristina signaled to the waitress and ordered something. The language sounded similar to Spanish, or perhaps Portuguese, but with some other intonation—more like what she'd heard once on a visit to Romania.

A few minutes later, the waitress returned with a plate of cheese, bright yellow in color but streaked with blue veins.

When Marlene asked about the cheese, Santacristina replied, "This is Onetik, a traditional type of Basque cheese made from sheep's milk. It is best with a red wine, but seeing as how I am with another man's wife, and tongues may wag, we will stick with coffee." He laughed and said something to the hovering waitress, who laughed, too.

"Are all Basque men so charming?" Marlene asked.

"It is ingrained in us by our mothers from the day we are born," Santacristina said, and smiled.

As Santacristina and the other two men chatted, Marlene used the opportunity to study his facial features, which were strong—a prominent nose between deep-set eyes that flickered with intensity below thick, dark eyebrows. His tan face was framed on the bottom by a five o'clock shadow that she suspected might be permanent. But his most striking physical characteristic was the color of his eyes, almost amber against a darker background. When he turned to meet her gaze, she noticed a jagged white scar that started just below the hairline on the left side of his forehead and disappeared into his full head of jet-black curls.

Marlene hesitated, not wanting to be rude, but then asked, "If I'm not being too nosy . . . we saw your confrontation with Huttington and Barnhill today. What happened to your daughter?"

Santacristina's smile fell from his face, and he hung his head and appeared to be studying the depths of his coffee. "It is not a pleasant story," he replied. "I may not show it always on my face, but my heart is broken. I do not wish to burden you with my tears."

"I'm a good listener," Marlene answered.

Exhaling, Santacristina explained why he'd confronted Huttington. Indeed, why he'd been asking the same question of the man for the better part of a year, ever since his Maria had disappeared without a trace.

"She was a good girl," he said. "An angel given to my dear wife and me. She was attending the university and majoring in early childhood education. All of her life she wanted to be a teacher. But I am a poor man and unable to pay for her education, so she made her own way through work-study programs, including as an administrative assistant for that *sasikumea* Huttington."

Huttington had begun his pursuit by lavishing praise on her for her work and then finding reasons to keep her after hours and reward her with dinners. "I started to notice that she was spending more and more time with him, and then he started taking her on these little trips. She told me they were for 'university business,' but I could see that she had fallen in love, and my heart ached for her. He was a married man and twice her age. But she was as headstrong as her mother—who married me against the wishes of her family—and would not listen to me."

"Where is her mother?" Marlene asked, though she suspected the answer already.

Santacristina shook his head sadly. "She died four years ago, when Maria was seventeen," he said. When he looked back up at Marlene, his eyes were shiny with tears. "It was ovarian cancer. I was, of course, devastated. But it was even harder on Maria. Her mother doted on her, and they could talk about anything. Maybe if Elena had lived, she could have talked sense into our daughter. But I would not have wanted Elena to have the pain that I endure now."

"I'm so sorry," Marlene commiserated. "Was your wife Basque, too?"

"Yes," Santacristina replied. "I met her shortly after I arrived in this country and came to Idaho, which you may have heard has a large Basque community. My Elena was much younger than me and very beautiful." He stopped and pulled out his wallet, from which he produced photographs of two strikingly beautiful women. "This is my Elena and my Maria." He replaced the photographs. "They were my reasons to live. But now they are both gone, and I live only to find my daughter so that I may lay her to rest beside her mother."

"And you think Huttington has something to do with Maria's disappearance?"

Santacristina nodded. "I last saw her two days before she disappeared. I dropped by unexpectedly and it was evident that she had been crying. But she assured me it was nothing, and that soon everything would be all right. The next day, I called to check in on her, but there was no answer. And there was no answer the next day or the next, either. . . . It was not like her. She called me almost every day. She knew how lonely I was without Elena."

He'd driven to his daughter's apartment and talked the landlord into letting him in. "All of her books for school were piled neatly on her desk, ready for class," he said. "Even her clothes were laid out and waiting. Everything you would expect of a young woman going to school. But the most important clue that something was wrong was that her cat was almost crazy for want of food and water. She loved that cat and would have never left it to suffer like that."

"Did you go to the police?"

"Yes," he replied. "They were polite and took my information down. But they seemed to think that she was just a silly college girl who ran away from home."

"Did you tell them your suspicions about Huttington having an affair with your daughter?" Meyers asked.

"No," he said. "I was sure he had made her pregnant. But I did not yet suspect him. I was afraid that he had spurned her and . . . and she had, perhaps, harmed herself. Or maybe let her guard down in her grief and was attacked by a stranger."

"Have the police done anything?" Marlene asked.

Santacristina nodded. "Yes," he said. "As much as they could. When Maria did not return, a young detective was assigned to her case. He filed a report with the FBI and registered her with a national crime computer in case someone saw her, or she tried to leave the country, or . . . or a body was found that matched her identity."

The Basque stopped talking for a moment to compose himself, then smiled at some memory. "Her mother was always afraid of losing her, so she had Maria fingerprinted when she was a young child when the police were promoting such a program. But there was nothing."

Santacristina said he began to wonder more about Huttington. "I called and asked to meet privately with him. I wanted to ask him when he had last seen her and what had happened. But he would not see me without his attorney present, and there is something about that man, Barnhill, that makes my skin crawl. I did not want to discuss my daughter's sexual life in front of him."

Marlene frowned. "But what makes you think Huttington was responsible for her disappearance?"

Santacristina was silent for a long moment. "I believe that she was pregnant," he said. "I found a box for a pregnancy test kit in her bathroom trash can. There was a positive result on the indicator strip. I think that the child was his. But he is a married man, an upstanding—oh, what is the term?—pillar of the community. Getting a young college girl pregnant would have been a great embarrassment, and maybe cost him his job. I think this is why my Maria is . . . she is gone."

He'd crashed a university dinner party and attempted to talk to Huttington, but Barnhill had him thrown out and arrested for trespassing. "The charges were dropped, but I was told to stay away from him or go to jail. This seemed to me to be the acts of guilty men, so I went back to the young detective and told him what I believed."

"Did he look into it?" Meyers asked.

"Yes, or at least that is my understanding," Santacristina said. "He told me he talked to Huttington—though Barnhill had insisted on being present—but the *sasikumea* . . ."

"What is *sasikumea*?" Marlene interrupted.

"Bastard," Santacristina replied. "And he is one and worse. He did not show the slightest concern about Maria's disappearance, not even the sort a university president would for his intern. All he ever said to the press was that he hoped she was all right and had simply 'moved on.' Anyway, Huttington denied having an affair— saying that I had jumped to conclusions—and that he had not seen Maria for more than a week before she disappeared. He said he assumed she had quit."

"Did you ever tell the press about your theory?" Marlene asked.

Santacristina shook his head. "There is no proof," he said. "And if I made it public, Barnhill would go after me, and as you may have guessed from my conversation with them this afternoon, my immigration status is somewhat questionable. I would not care about that if it would help find my daughter, but I fear that if I am deported, there will be no one here who will remember Maria and seek justice for her."

"But what I don't get is why Barnhill hasn't carried out his threat to report you," O'Toole said.

"They are not anxious for the publicity," Santacristina replied. "So far the newspapers and television stations have not caught wind of this, but if I was arrested, they would pay attention to what I said. So we have this stalemate."

Santacristina hung his head and his shoulders shook. When he brought himself back under control, he apologized for crying. "It is a sign of weakness."

"No, it's not. It's a sign of love and heartbreak," Marlene replied. "But we can change the subject if you like."

Santacristina nodded. "Yes, please," he said with a weak smile. "Tell me why you are here with these gentlemen."

Marlene smiled at the gallantry, but let Meyers and O'Toole talk to him about the lawsuit. "So I guess we both have problems with Huttington and Barnhill," O'Toole said when they finished. "But unlike you, I don't know why they turned on me."

Santacristina suddenly furrowed his brow and then looked intensely at Marlene. "Maybe we were intended by God to meet," he said.

"I'm always open to the possibility," she replied. "But why do you say that?"

"Bear with me, as I have not thought this out entirely," Santacristina said. "But Coach O'Toole, you said you were surprised at the lack of support from Huttington, someone you once considered to be on a friendly basis with, no? What might that indicate to you?"

"I see where you're going," O'Toole replied. "That somebody has something on Huttington and is blackmailing him to support Porter and get rid of me."

Santacristina nodded emphatically. "Yes. And what if this blackmail ties Huttington to what happened to my daughter?"

"I guess that's one possible theory," Marlene said slowly, then shook her head. "But on its face, I think most people would say these are two unrelated events, and we'd only be guessing at a connection."

"Perhaps," Santacristina agreed. "Perhaps I am just a father driven mad with grief. But I believe it is true."

"And you know what," Marlene said. "Something in my gut tells me it is, too." She looked at the other two men and thought of Butch. "The question is what can we do about it?"

Two hours later, Clyde Barnhill was about to call it a day when the telephone in his office rang. Sighing, he answered it.

"What in the hell is that Jew bastard doing getting involved in this?" said the voice on the other end.

"Hello, John," Barnhill replied. "I told you before. The 'Jew bastard' knew O'Toole's brother. They were roommates in college."

"Yeah, so the fucking district attorney for New York just happens to take a case in Bumfuck, Idaho," Porter complained. "You don't find that a little coincidental? I don't believe it for a minute. And now his wife is out here—hanging out with that Basque motherfucker."

Barnhill did not like Big John Porter, nor his idiot son. But they served an important purpose for his friends back East, and so he resisted the urge to tell him to stick it up his ass.

"Calm down, John," Barnhill said. "We checked it out with friends in New York. Karp is on a leave of absence. He got shot but the shooter was not accurate enough. O'Toole obviously called him and asked for help. I wouldn't worry about his wife, obviously just some bored housewife who wants to play investigator."

"Yeah, and maybe you don't know, maybe she's working with Santacristina," Porter said. "She and O'Toole and that attorney fella, Meyers, were about to mix it up with my boy and his friends when Santacristina showed up. That a coincidence, too?"

"I've said it before, John," Barnhill replied, letting a little anger seep into his voice. "Your boy needs to lay low and stay away from those 'friends.' It draws attention to him right now and won't look good if it gets into this trial."

"Yeah, yeah, I've told my boy that he has to watch out for what he does in public. But he likes those fellas, and they, at least, treat him with respect," Porter replied. "Tough to keep an eye on him 24/7."

"I understand," Barnhill said. "We just need to be careful around the woman. She's the wife of the district attorney. If something happened to her, there'd be a lot of eyes looking this way."

The phone went so silent that Barnhill thought he could hear the poorly greased wheels in Porter's head grinding slowly. "Yeah, you're right," the big man agreed at last. "But nobody messes with my boy and gets away with it forever."

If your boy was any dumber, Barnhill thought, he'd be a donkey, and not a very smart one. "Well, my advice right now is that we all sit tight. There are more pressing concerns than Marlene Ciampi."

"I ain't so worried about her," Porter replied. "But like you said, she's the wife of the fucking Jew bastard district attorney of New York, and that ought to worry everybody. If you know what I mean."

"I know, John," Barnhill said. "And our friends are monitoring the situation. Now go have yourself a nice Jack Daniel's on ice, and I'm going home to do the same."

"All right, Clyde," Porter said. "And oh, hey, we going to get any huntin' in this winter? We can use the Unified Church property anytime we want and no fucking game wardens to worry about."

"Sounds like a plan, John," Barnhill said. "I wouldn't mind shooting something . . . I wouldn't mind that at all."

15

A STIFF BREEZE SWEPT DOWN THE CONCRETE CANYONS, STIR-
ring up old leaves and litter as the few tourists willing to brave
the elements on a chilly Sunday evening to window-shop along
Fifth Avenue pulled their coats tighter and tugged their hats
down around their ears. Despite the cold, V. T. Newbury hesitated outside of the towering skyscraper as the sun slipped into
the cloud bank somewhere beyond New Jersey. He'd been going
in and out of the skyscraper most of his life, but the only reason
he had was now gone, and he felt as if he no longer belonged
there.

A sudden gust of frigid air slapped him in the face, like someone
trying to get him to come to his senses. He considered turning
around and taking a taxi back to his place in the Village, but taking
a deep breath, he pushed through the revolving doors. Normally,
they would have been locked on a Sunday, but not when Dean
Newbury's nephew was coming to visit.

As V.T. walked up to the security desk, the guard smiled and
hooked a thumb toward the private Newbury, White & Newbury
Only elevators behind him. "Good evening, Mr. Newbury, your
uncle is expecting you," the young man said pleasantly. "And by the

way, I was sorry to hear about your father. A nice man. Always had time to ask how I was doing."

"Thank you, uh"—Newbury glanced down at the man's name tag—"David. Yes, he was a good man. I miss him." Not trusting himself to talk about his father's death without crying, he entered the elevator and pressed the button for the top floor of the seventy-story building.

The family firm occupied the entire floor—and that was just for the senior partners and their secretaries. The entirety of the next two floors below also housed the firm's junior partners, as well as the foot-soldier attorneys, paralegals, investigators, secretaries, researchers, and, occupying a wing of its own, the all-important billing department.

When the doors opened again, V.T. stepped off the elevator and waved to the pretty receptionist at the front desk, who smiled and pointed toward the office of his uncle, Dean Q. Newbury, the impervious, flint-eyed, most senior of senior partners.

"They got you working on a Sunday?" he asked the receptionist as he headed in the indicated direction.

"If your uncle's here, I'm here, Mr. Newbury," she called after him.

V.T. hurried down the hall, but then slowed as he approached the office opposite his uncle's, which had been his father's for nearly fifty years. The door was open and the lights on, so he stepped inside.

It was a magnificent office, as befitted the number two partner of the nearly two-hundred-year-old firm. The entire office was four times the size of his quarters at the District Attorney's Office. The furnishings were much nicer, too—soft couches and chairs done in light tan leather, with accents of wood around the library and the trim.

The main room was dominated by an ancient rosewood desk, said to have once been owned by George Washington when the ragtag Continental army was holed up on "York Island," awaiting the armed might of the British Empire. There was also a full kitchen with oak countertops and a refrigerator on which photographs of V.T. and his mother hung from magnets. The walls were tastefully decorated with art, including a large oil painting of V.T.'s parents and himself as a five-year-old boy, enjoying a picnic on the beach at the family's Cape Cod oceanfront house.

More photographs of the family were propped along the bookshelves, which were full of various texts. They weren't just law books, either, but the sort of books a bright young son might choose to read during a visit to his father's office while the old man worked. Dickens's *Tale of Two Cities.* A first-edition copy of Hemingway's *The Sun Also Rises* with the inscription *"to my fishing buddy, Vincent, Warmest Regards, Ernest."* History books. Poetry books. Copies of the Bible, the Koran, and the Torah, plus treatises on Buddhism and Hinduism.

There was even a much-thumbed copy of Jack Kerouac's *On the Road.* Its hard use indicated that his father would have preferred a transient life spent in smoky coffeehouses, listening to Beat poets, to his penthouse suite and corporate law. But that was simply not an option for Newburys, for whom duty to the family firm was cast in stone—at least not until V.T. and his cousin Quilliam broke the mold.

As always, the most impressive part of the office to V.T. was the view of Central Park. The gray crowds of trees stretched away to the north in the dimming light outside, but within a couple of months would be leafing out, an oasis of green in gray old Gotham. Even in winter, the scenery before him reminded V.T. of how the contrasting views from his father's and his uncle's offices matched their personalities.

His father spent many of his lunch hours walking in the park; he called it "getting in touch with sanity." Winter mornings sledding with his son gave way to summer mornings playing catch or taking a stroll with his wife while their boy wobbled ahead on a new bicycle.

Dean Newbury's office, on the other hand, faced south. Still a fantastic view, but one dominated by edifices of granite, concrete, glass, and steel. Fitting, V.T. thought, for a man with the emotional capacity of a rock.

Then again, he knew that his father also had reaped the benefits of a big-money law firm without complaint. He'd never had to worry about how to pay the mortgage or send his son to the finest boarding schools and Europe for "fine tuning."

His wife's family, who were quick to remind the Newbury side that they could trace their American beginnings back to the Pilgrims, were wealthy New England bluebloods. But the Newbury family was richer still, though considered by their in-laws to be "newcomers," having only reached America sometime around the Revolutionary War.

Neither side was known for its warmth. Public demonstrations of affection were frowned upon. But the New Englanders were puppy dogs compared to the Newbury branch. In fact, V.T.'s paternal grandfather, a one-eyed monster named Haldor, made Uncle Dean Newbury seem warm and cuddly as a koala bear. Not once could V.T. remember having received a pat on the head or a kind word from the time he was born until the old man's death. In fact, his most vivid memory of Grandfather Newbury was how the family patriarch would follow him with that one eye as he walked past, like a vulture sizing up a dying rabbit.

When V.T. asked his father why Grandfather Newbury didn't seem to like him much, his father laughed. *So you noticed that, too, eh?* he'd said. *Don't let it bother you, it's just the way he is; he treated me the same, and I don't think he knows any better.*

The only person who ever really seemed to matter to Grandfather Newbury was Uncle Dean, who, V.T. gathered from his mother, spent much of his time after adolescence in his father's company. *But I daresay there's little affection between them,* she'd added. *It's more like they're in business together. Just remember you have a mother and father who love you very much.*

V.T. had considered himself lucky that he got his pair of parents. While still patrician in many respects, they were odd ducks in their respective families, with all sorts of unsavory habits like laughing out loud and kissing in public. Their child was considered insufferably unruly—likely to speak before spoken to, and loud. But his parents ignored their families' admonishments to take him in hand before it was "too late."

When V.T.'s grandfather passed away there was a large funeral on what was a fittingly gloomy, misty day, attended by a host of severe, important-looking men and their dour, faded wives. But he couldn't remember anybody actually crying except for his dad. The others simply stood or sat beneath umbrellas with their faces unmoving, as if set in stone. And when the brief service was over, they simply turned away, got in their limousines, and returned from wherever they came.

V.T. and his father were the last ones left at the grave site. They'd stood there holding hands and looking at the casket as raindrops struck it and rolled off. The boy had looked up at his father and been surprised to see tears also rolling from his face. *Goodbye, Dad,* he'd said at last. *I wish I could have known you.*

With the passing of the old man, V.T.'s uncle had been next in line for what his dad called *the throne. . . . And he's welcome to it.*

Dean Newbury was a chip off the granite block that was his father. He made it clear at every opportunity that his brother was a disappointment to the family and argued incessantly with him about taking on pro bono cases on behalf of indigent people or causes Vincent supported, such as Greenpeace.

One such argument V.T. overheard when he was twelve or so. It was one of the few times he ever heard his father raising his voice, and the exchange stuck. *Pro bono, Dean, do you know what that means? For the good, Dean, for the good. I'm trying to save the soul of this firm, if there was ever a soul to be saved.*

Dean Newbury shouted back. *This firm doesn't need a soul. What it needs are billable hours, big settlements, and huge fees. And senior partners who remember their responsibility to their family.*

Damn this family's responsibilities, Vincent shouted *A murky tie to the past that for all I know was full of pirates and scoundrels, and now full of secrets that even its members are not privy to know.*

The argument ended when V.T. poked his head in the door. The two men glanced at him, then glared at each other, before dropping the argument. However, V.T. got the clear impression that the battle was not over, merely postponed.

Like Haldor, Dean Newbury spent a lot of time with his son, Quilliam, particularly after the boy became an adolescent. But that, too, seemed to be a relationship that lacked any connection beyond that of proctor and pupil.

After Quilliam went away to college, V.T. only saw him at the obligatory family gatherings at Thanksgiving and Christmas, which were for the most part quiet, joyless occasions more for show than substance. It was easy to see at such times that the relationship between Quilliam and his father was growing increasingly strained, and they could often be seen off by themselves on the grounds, gesturing and arguing.

The final breaking point between father and son occurred when Quilliam refused to go to law school after graduation and instead joined the U.S. Marine Corps. In a private moment before Quilliam shipped off to boot camp, V.T., a freshman at Harvard, asked his cousin why he would join the marines with the unpopular war in Vietnam picking up steam. *This family has always taken from this country and sacrificed nothing,* he'd replied bitterly. *Sooner or later, all bills come due.*

Whatever bill he thought the family owed, Quilliam paid when he was killed by a sniper in Danang shortly after the start of the Tet offensive in January 1968. His body had been shipped home for services complete with a flag-draped coffin and a marines honor guard. At the conclusion, the honor guard folded the flag into a triangular bundle and tried to present it to Dean Newbury with the condolences "of a grateful country." But Dean had turned away and refused to take it, so his brother Vincent accepted it from the confused marine sergeant.

V.T. had at first misinterpreted his uncle's reaction as a political statement regarding the war. But when he saw his uncle's face, the expression wasn't one of sorrow or even bitterness over the loss of a son in an unpopular war. It was anger. Anger directed at the coffin. Anger at his son for disobeying. Later, when their eyes met at the reception hosted by his parents, V.T. got the distinct impression that his uncle was thinking: If someone had to die, it should have been you. The firm could have done without you.

That impression had gone a long way toward V.T.'s choice of law careers after he graduated and passed the bar. Not that corporate law had ever interested him, but he didn't feel that he belonged at a family firm in which billable hours became the litmus test for good lawyering, and whose leader couldn't mourn the death of a son.

There had been plenty of tears at the funeral for V.T.'s father the previous month. But most of those were shed by Vincent's friends and the employees of the firm who'd worked closely with him. Those in attendance from his mother's side at least looked sad, but those who attended from the Newbury side were as emotionless as ever. And when the memorial service was over, they turned away, got in their limousines, and drove back to wherever they came from.

Most did not show up at the wake, which, V.T. thought, was just as well. They would not have understood or appreciated the tearful toasts to "a good man" and the laughter as various people related stories about his father, who, unbeknownst to V.T., had been quite the practical joker in college.

V.T. had spent much of the memorial service and wake in stunned disbelief. His father had complained of chest pain some ten years before, right after V.T.'s mother died. It turned out to be mild arrhythmia. He'd changed his diet and exercised regularly, and took digitalis to deal with any reoccurrences of the arrhythmia. After a recent physical, the longtime Newbury family doctor had pronounced him as fit as any octogenarian had a right to expect. But a month later, Vincent Newbury collapsed and died from a massive heart attack.

It had taken time to get over the shock, but V.T. had come to accept that his father had lived a long life and that old men sometimes died unexpectedly. He was just grateful that their relationship had been such that after the other mourners left the grave that day and he was alone, he hadn't wished he could have known his father better.

More of a surprise when he thought about it was how his uncle had suddenly warmed up to him after his father's funeral. It had started with invitations to lunch, at which Uncle Dean strained to be jovial and warm but, as he'd never had much practice at it, came off as stiff and phony. Yet, when his uncle kept trying, V.T. decided he was being too hard on the old man and decided to give him the benefit of the doubt. He even told his boss and friend, Butch Karp, that he had decided the old man, a widower, was feeling the end of his days and realizing that his nephew was the only real family he had left.

Karp had been sympathetic about his loss. He reminded V.T. that it was their fathers who first gave two young assistant district attorneys of such disparate backgrounds something in common besides the law. One of Karp's favorite stories was how he'd learned to love the law while sitting at his father's knee in the living room of their Brooklyn house in the fifties. Butch's father, Julius, had graduated from law school as one of the best and brightest of his class. But the realities of supporting a wife and family had steered him into the business world, where he'd become moderately successful. However, he'd never lost his passion for the law, and the family living room was the scene of Saturday night gatherings of some of the best legal minds in the five boroughs. Over glasses of whiskey and through a fog of cigar smoke, they'd debated the great cases of the day and argued questions of constitutional law as if they were preparing to go before the U.S. Supreme Court.

One of those who regularly attended the gatherings was Vincent Newbury, at least until his duties with the family firm had put an end to his participation. It had been V.T.'s father who years later pointed out the connection when Karp and Marlene visited the Cape Cod beach home with V.T. *I wish I could have spent more time with those folks, like your dad,* he'd said. *But I was expected to spend my time at the family firm.*

V.T. also suspected that part of his uncle's warming trend was the lack of a Newbury heir to take over the firm. In the past, the annual invitation to join the firm had come from his father, as both a wistful idea to be closer to his boy and a private joke between them, knowing what V.T.'s answer would be: No thanks.

However, the sales pitch he got from his uncle over dinner at Harry Cipriani, one of New York's most expensive and exclusive restaurants, following his father's death had bordered on the pathetic. Dean began by lauding V.T.'s "noble efforts" on behalf of the public. However, he said, no one could hold it against a longtime public servant "who in the twilight of his career opted to ensure his own golden years by taking over the family business." The comment had caught V.T. by surprise, as he didn't really consider himself to be in the "twilight of his career." Nor had he considered that with his father gone and his uncle going, he might be considered to be in line for "the throne."

Sensing V.T.'s uneasiness, his uncle had quickly noted that nothing needed to be decided at that moment and that all he was asking was that his nephew keep an open mind. He'd then requested that V.T. drop by the office so that he could introduce him to "a dozen or so friends and associates . . . important people who could be of considerable help to a bright young man such as yourself." As a show of good faith for the turnaround in their relationship, he'd agreed.

That's why V.T. was now looking at a photograph of himself with his father on a deep-sea fishing adventure off of Nova Scotia some twenty years earlier. A voice behind him interrupted the memory. "This could be your office, you know—or if you wait just a bit longer, you could have mine, if you prefer that view."

V.T. turned and saw his uncle. He felt a little guilty, as if his uncle had read his mind about the contrasting views and personalities. He held out a hand. "Good to see you, Uncle Dean."

The old man's hand was cold as ice but his face was the picture of bonhomie. "Welcome. Welcome," he said, clapping V.T. on the back. "Thanks for coming. I think you'll find this evening's meeting very interesting."

As usual, Dean Newbury was impeccably dressed, in a five-thousand-dollar Armani suit and what V.T. presumed to be hand-made calfskin shoes, which probably added another grand to the ensemble. He looked every bit the elder statesman; his hairline had receded until he was bald on top with a fringe of snow-white hair around the sides, but his Aqua Velva–blue eyes were as sharp and piercing as when V.T. had been a boy.

Dean took him by the elbow and ushered him across the hall into his own office. "I wanted a minute alone with you before we meet the others," he explained.

V.T. looked around with interest. All the years he'd been going to the firm to see his father, he'd only been in his uncle's office once, and all he remembered was the view. The room had none of the warmth of his father's, either. The office had a kitchen, done in black granite and stainless steel, all of which looked like it had never been used.

There were the usual law office diplomas on the wall. A photograph of Dean standing on a podium with then president Richard Nixon—one arm around the president's shoulders and both of them raising the V for victory sign. However, two sets of paintings on the walls seemed incongruous with the sterility of the rest of the decor. One set was a series of portraits in oil that he knew were the senior partners of Newbury, White & Newbury dating back to the early nineteenth century. The second set was three oil paintings of sailing ships that were hung on the wall opposite the portraits, along with what appeared to be a primitive old map depicting Great Britain, Ireland, and Scotland surrounding the Irish Sea.

"I didn't know you were such an avid ocean lover," V.T. said, pointing to the paintings.

Dean glanced at the paintings and grunted. "I'm not," he said. "Matter of fact, anything smaller than a luxury liner like the *QEII*, and I'm seasick as a dog. I inherited those from your grandfather Newbury, who insisted, as had every head of this firm before him, that they hang in the office of the next in line to remind us that our paternal roots were in seafaring folks."

Closing the door, Dean turned to his nephew. "I wanted to again ask you to keep an open mind about joining the firm," he said, moving over toward his desk. "But I do want to warn you, joining the firm is not an automatic ascension to the head of the firm. The men you're going to meet are my most trusted advisors, and I can trust them to be honest when they let me know what they think of you."

"So this is a test?" V.T. said, wondering why that made him feel so irritated when he knew that this was going to be either a sales job or a job interview.

"I suppose, but it's because they're being protective of me and this firm. Many of our families have been close for a very long time, and we look out for one another," Dean replied.

The little speech took V.T. aback a bit. He'd never heard that much emotion for the death of his own son or brother. Then again, maybe he does have it in him and just doesn't know how to show it, he thought. "That's a great sentiment," he said.

"Sentiment?" Dean snorted. "Call it self-interest. Our affairs are closely linked, and they just want to make sure whoever is in this office holds up their end of the bargain. But in the end, I will make my own decision."

Dean turned to gaze out the wall of windows facing south, like an ancient king surveying his kingdom. "I'm an old man, Vinson," he said, using V.T.'s Christian name for perhaps the first time in his life. "And I guess that your father's death has reminded me of my own impending mortality, so I am trying to get my affairs in order. As you know, you are my only heir . . ."

V.T. thought he detected a note of bitterness in the statement but kept his expression unchanged.

". . . and it is my preference—the preference, really, of all the men you see on that wall," he said, pointing to the portraits of his predecessors, "that this firm's leadership be passed on to a New-bury. So I thought that, perhaps, we might spend more time to-gether, get better acquainted. And . . . perhaps . . . you'll come around to understanding that you have a legacy here that a great many people—more than you know—are counting on a Newbury to continue."

V.T. smiled. "Thank you. I'd like the chance to get better acquainted. However, as I always told my father, I enjoy working at the District Attorney's Office. Like I said before, I feel that I make a real difference there."

For a moment, the smile faded from the old man's face and it was a struggle to replace it. "Yes, yes, of course, and you certainly have put in your time with little enough reward, but maybe it's time to hand the baton to the next generation so that they can champion the cause of an ungrateful public."

V.T. started to protest the description but Dean held up a hand. "Please, why argue? Has the public ever thanked you for taking on the dregs of society?" he said. "No, they elect politicians who coddle criminals and pass laws so that after all your hard work their new 'friends' can go right back on the streets murdering, robbing, stealing, raping. That has to be tough on you. Nonetheless, it's your life. I just want to make the point that you can make a difference here, too. The law isn't just about putting criminals in prison. We also protect the rights of all citizens, which I might add— though perhaps it isn't politically correct—includes the rights of people who have worked hard for their success and have the right to enjoy the fruits of their labors and to pass those fruits on to their descendants if they so choose. These people create more than great wealth. They create jobs, pay wages, build an economy and a nation. And in the end, they pay a far greater percentage of their income in taxes than does, if you'll excuse the term, 'the average Joe,' or for that matter, welfare mothers and gangsters who pay no taxes at all, build nothing, are simply anchors on the ship of society."

V.T. understood the argument, at least the rational side of it. He'd actually had it before with his father many years ago when he was a teenager and railing against "the establishment." Expecting his father to take his side and not toe the company line, he'd been surprised and at first upset when his father actually defended the role of white-shoe law firms and their clients. By the time his father finished, V.T. had reluctantly conceded that the firm's clientele had important, legitimate interests that required legal experts to protect. And, his father pointed out, he would have never been able to take on as many pro bono cases as he did if some wealthy real estate developer with a tax problem wasn't footing the bill with his legal fees.

Like his father before him, V.T. had certainly enjoyed the benefits of having the best of anything money could buy. Education. Opportunity. Freedom to choose. He didn't believe that money was the root of all evil, just—as the Bible actually said—the "love of money." He didn't love money as such, but he certainly enjoyed what it could buy—fine wines, frequent travels with first-class accommodations, and a nicer home than he could have afforded as just an assistant district attorney.

Yet, working for the DAO, he was acutely aware that money could buy a more equal protection for some than for others. Money paid for dream-team lawyers and armies of investigators; it greased palms and on occasion had been known to buy a public official, a witness, a juror, or even a judge. It was probably why he'd gravitated toward prosecuting white-collar crimes, to level the playing field.

V.T. didn't like his uncle's social-issues rant. But for the sake of familial cordiality, he just nodded and said, "I understand completely."

Dean smiled broadly, pulled open the center drawer of his desk, and withdrew a small item. He held it out and V.T. saw that it was a ring. "As a token of a new relationship between us, I wanted to give you this," he said. "It belonged to my son. That symbol has been a sort of family coat of arms for centuries."

"A coat of arms? I thought the Newbury coat of arms has ducks and crosses or something on it," V.T. said.

"Well, yes, perhaps coat of arms isn't the right term," Dean said, pressing the ring into V.T.'s hand. "More like a fraternity ring. A very old fraternity, and if you play your cards right, I'll let you in on our deepest secrets someday."

Holding the ring up, V.T. noted the three gold spirals joined at the center against a black background of onyx. "It's beautiful," V.T. said. "And it does look old. Is it Celtic?"

"Indeed. It's called a *tre cassyn*. You'll see that the men you're about to meet also wear these, as do I. The symbol fits our motto: *'Quocunque jeceris stabit.'* "

"Wherever you will throw it, it stands," V.T. interpreted. He saw his uncle's surprised look and added, "One of the requirements in boarding schools when I was a boy was that we study Latin. I have to confess that I was one of those geeks who actually enjoyed the class."

Dean laughed a bit too loud. "Well, good to see someone's education didn't go to waste. Anyway, it would make me proud if you'd accept it . . . if for no other reason than as a reminder of Quilliam."

V.T. thought the comment about wasted educations in the context of giving him Quilliam's ring was a jab at both his son and anyone who wouldn't jump at the chance of ending a legal career on the top floor of a Fifth Avenue skyscraper. But his uncle was already heading for the door. "Now let's go meet the others. They're not the sort who like to be kept waiting."

Dean Newbury then pulled up short. "Oh, we also have another motto you may hear from time to time. It goes back to the first American Newburys. 'What must be, will be.' A bold statement, don't you think?"

16

THE SAME STIFF BREEZE THAT HAD BUFFETED V. T. NEWBURY nearly half the length of Manhattan to the north caught up to Ariadne Stupenagel and Gilbert Murrow when they stepped out of the Whitehall Street subway station at the southern tip of the island where the Hudson and East rivers meet. "Maybe we should go home and call it a night," Murrow suggested hopefully. "The doctors said you're supposed to be taking it easy."

"I can't, sweetie," Stupenagel responded as she pulled the sling supporting her cast around to cover her fingers better. "But really, you go. I don't need an escort from here, and I promise to take a cab home when this is over."

"No way," Murrow replied. "Wherever you go, I go, too. Remember?"

"You're sweet, pookums," Stupenagel replied, and kissed him on the nose. "But haven't you ever heard the saying 'Fools rush in where angels fear to tread'? There's no reason for two fools to be rushing around on a night like this."

"Well, I'm a fool for love, so let's quit gabbing and get this over with," Murrow replied.

The pair made their way across the street to the entrance of the

Staten Island Ferry. They paid the fare and boarded the ferry, which on a Sunday night was nearly deserted. Any other day or time, and there might have been a few hundred commuters with homes on the island or tourists aboard. In the past, the ferries had carried cars, but all that had changed on September 11, 2001. It was too easy to hide a bomb in a car or truck and so it had been closed to all but pedestrian traffic.

Stupenagel and Murrow were neither commuting nor sightseeing. Several hours earlier, while enjoying a quiet late Sunday afternoon snuggling in the Fifty-fifth Street loft, Stupenagel had received a call on her cell phone from a male whose accented voice she recognized as belonging to her Russian source, the employer of the late Gregory Karamazov. He wanted to know if she would meet with him.

How do I know this is legit? Stupenagel had asked. *I'm getting a little sick of people trying to kill me.*

The unexpected reply caused the caller to laugh bitterly. *I don't blame you,* he'd said. *This is a dangerous business. I believe that you told Gregory, who by the way was my dear friend, that you were there on a blind date and he replied that you'd come to the right place. But I wouldn't blame you for having had enough. If you like, I can see if what I have to say would interest one of your competitors.*

Ooooh, that's low, Stupenagel had replied. *Okay, when and where?*

The caller had not invited Murrow, but she'd made the mistake of admitting where she was going. Only afterward had she stopped to ponder if the sudden inability to lie to him—she'd always prided herself on being a fabulous liar when necessary—was yet one more sign of the strength of their relationship. He'd insisted on going and no amount of arguing or promising could change his mind, so she'd given in.

Now, as the ferry pulled away from the pier, she was having second thoughts again. You have no right to put him in danger, she admonished herself. But she had to admit, she was glad he was there, standing with her on the exposed stern of the ferry.

All the other passengers were inside, and Stupenagel was about to suggest that they go there, too—despite instructions to remain outside—and get out of the cold, when a tall, strongly built man suddenly appeared out of the shadows. She did a double take, for standing in front of her was a man who, except for the scars on his face and a patch over one eye, bore a marked resemblance to Butch Karp. She glanced at her boyfriend, but he gave no indication that he saw what she did. She shrugged it off as coincidence.

"It is very cold out here," the tall man said.

Here we go again with the corny codes, Stupenagel thought. It might have been funny in a *Get Smart* television spoof way, except it brought back painful memories of the Black Sea Café and the people who'd died there.

"Not as cold as it gets in Siberia," Stupenagel replied.

On the other side of the ferry, Nadya Malovo had worked her way close enough to hear the exchange and smiled. Nor as cold as the grave, Ivgeny my love, she thought, signaling her men to take up positions.

Her spy inside of the Karchovski crime family had called two hours earlier and told her about this meeting. The man had been trembling with fear when he spoke. He was well aware that the last traitor in the Karchovski family had died at the hands of Marlene Ciampi, during a failed attempt to kill father and son Karchovski. The best this traitor could expect if the Karchovskis got wise was a bullet. Or it might be much worse.

However, there was no telling what even a coward would do for the right enticements of sex and money. She'd had to provide both, even though the former had disgusted her. She much preferred sex with women, but it was a powerful tool to use with men. She'd known that since she was a young KGB agent assigned to a Red Army unit in Afghanistan commanded by then colonel Ivgeny Karchovski. He'd used her to relieve the stress of an unwinnable war as much as she'd used him to try to further her own ambitions. But that was more than twenty years ago, and a lot had changed since.

For one thing, Ivgeny Karchovski, a popular officer and recipient of the Soviet Red Star, the nation's highest military honor for courage, was now a crime boss in Brooklyn. But not just some ordinary gangster. Somehow, in a manner she had yet to discover, there was some connection between the Karchovskis and the New York district attorney Karp, who had proved to be a resilient enemy, as well as the man's wife, Marlene Ciampi.

Meanwhile, Malovo was convinced that it was the Karchovskis who had helped track down Andrew Kane at the hideout in Aspen. If not for an eleventh-hour warning from Jamys Kellagh, the plan to take the Pope hostage and blow up St. Patrick's Cathedral might have ended right then.

Malovo had cursed herself for letting her then lover and accomplice, the Palestinian terrorist Samira Azzam, plan the murder of the Karchovskis. Azzam preferred bombs, which Malovo knew had their place as a weapon of terror due to their psychological impact on civilians. But bombs were too inexact and impersonal for Malovo's tastes. She'd discovered in the KGB torture chambers of Kabul that she enjoyed killing on a one-to-one level. She preferred to look her prey in the eye when she shoved a knife into their heart, or put a bullet in their brain. That was the fate she planned for Ivgeny tonight. After that, it would be easy to kill his father, the old man Vladimir.

The icing on the cake would be the death of the reporter Stupenagel. The plot against the Pope would have been at least a partial public relations success—the object being to place the blame on Muslim Chechen nationalists. However, the reporter's stories had thrown the spotlight back on herself, as well as the "shadowy" Jamys Kellagh, and implied that Malovo worked for certain interests who were using Islamic terrorists as the bogeymen to justify the brutal occupation of oil-rich Muslim states in southwest Russia.

It was all true, of course, even if the reporter didn't know the half of it. The Soviet Union was gone, and Malovo didn't work for the Russian government anymore. At least not the "official" Russian government. However, there were certainly among her current employers highly placed and important men in that government, just as there were highly placed and important men among her employers in the Russian mob, as well as among the military and industry.

Their goal was to return to ruling their part of the world with an iron fist that would have made Joseph Stalin proud. But they entertained none of his ideals of a socialist state; their fist embraced greed and their own power over the state. It was a fist that would encourage terrorist acts to blind the already frightened Western world so that there would be no opposition to Russian occupation of the Muslim states and, when the time was right, the extermination of the "Muslim problem"—like the extermination of cockroaches.

Although not directly allied with them, Malovo's masters had found common ground with those for whom Jamys Kellagh worked. They, in turn, were affiliated with those groups in north and west Europe, as well as white supremacists in South Africa, who saw themselves in direct competition with Islamic theocracy for world domination, and who sought to stem the tide of brown-skinned subhumans who bred like rodents and threatened to over-run the planet.

Malovo agreed in principle with the philosophy; however, she left the intellectual debate to those better suited for it. On the other hand, her counterpart Kellagh was a true believer in the cause of the nameless organization that he dedicated his life to but would never discuss. Yet, he killed just as easily as she did.

Now they had a mutual problem, the reporter Stupenagel. Instead of universal condemnation of the Chechen nationalists for the attack on the Pope inside St. Patrick's Cathedral in Manhattan, she'd exposed the plan as a ruse to use terrorism as a scapegoat for political gain. And it had only gotten worse.

Malovo didn't use that name in her day-to-day business, preferring the Chechen name Ajmaani, so she had been incensed that the reporter had been given her real name and that it had then appeared on the pages of newspapers. But identifying her as a Russian agent had caused shock waves in Moscow, just as publishing Jamys Kellagh's name with the implication that he had ties to U.S. law enforcement had put the heat on him.

Her capture inside of St. Patrick's had angered her employers nearly as much as the ultimate failure of the plot. They had been forced to pull more strings to get her "transferred" to Russian custody, exposing their position. The official story they gave in Moscow was that she'd actually been working undercover to expose the plot against the Pope but had been discovered and held hostage by the terrorists. However, Stupenagel's stories—forwarded to Moscow from the Russian embassy in New York—had put that story in question, and Malovo dared not return home.

It was obvious to Malovo and Kellagh and the people who controlled them that Stupenagel's anonymous federal law enforcement source was feeding her the information. But that was Kellagh's problem.

Her target was the unnamed source with access to high-level intelligence in the Russian government and army, as well as the Russian mob. And that source was Ivgeny Karchovski, which had been confirmed when the spy warned her about the meeting between Gregory Karamazov and Stupenagel. She'd become even more alarmed when she learned that the purpose of the meeting was to hand over a photograph of herself with Kellagh and Kane at the bar in Aspen.

With Kellagh's help in obtaining the plastic explosive, she'd quickly assembled the bomb and then arrived at the café in the company of an accomplice, to complete the picture of a couple having dinner before leaving on a trip. When she was sure that Stupenagel and Karamazov were occupied with their drinking, they left the restaurant. She'd then walked across the street and away from the direct line of flying glass and ball bearings before detonating the bomb.

The bomb was intended to kill everyone in the restaurant, and was to be followed by a fire that would incinerate paper, including photographs. She could hardly believe her eyes several days later when she read the story by Stupenagel, who had somehow survived.

In a rage that had terrified the Muslim terrorists with whom she was staying at a safe house in New Jersey—they believed that she was Chechen—she cursed the phenomenal luck that seemed to surround Karp, his family, and their associates. Even the hardened, cold-blooded killers with whom she worked were speaking in frightened whispers that Allah favored these infidels. They were particularly afraid of David Grale, the madman who was hunting them. He, too, had apparently survived repeated attempts to kill him, and the superstitious idiots were calling him a *shayteen,* a devil, and attributing supernatural powers to him and his subterranean army.

The supernatural crap was all nonsense, of course, Malovo told herself, but there was no denying the luck of her adversaries. And in the case of her former lover, Ivgeny, and the Ciampi woman, she was troubled by the fact that they were not only lucky, they were dangerous.

After getting the call from her spy in the Karchovski organization, she'd met with Kellagh to discuss her options. The spy had told her that Ivgeny would have only one bodyguard with him, and who knew when Ivgeny Karchovski would thus expose himself again? As for the reporter, it would look like she had stuck her nose too far into gang warfare.

Kellagh had called an accomplice working security on the ferries to have a trunk filled with weapons deposited belowdecks on the ferry. But he'd then had to rush off to a meeting with his employers. It seemed he was always running late, including when he was to attend to the death of the bookseller in December, which could have exposed the organization he worked for and their March plans.

Of course, Malovo was not immune to spies and traitors. After Kellagh left to deal with the bookseller, one of her own men had been caught calling the enemy and giving away their position. She'd cut the man's head off with her own knife and left it for her would-be captors to find, laughing as she watched them storm the building from another apartment across the street. She imagined them looking in the grocery bag she'd left in the middle of the floor with its grisly contents.

However, just in case the traitor had passed on more than her location, Malovo had Karchovski and Stupenagel followed. But her spy had been telling the truth—Ivgeny was traveling to meet the reporter with only his driver-slash-bodyguard, and even that would mean a surprise for her former lover. Stupenagel had brought only her boyfriend.

Now Malovo waited in the shadows for her men to get set, smiling as the reporter gave the response: "Not as cold as it gets in Siberia."

Karchovski held out his hand, which Stupenagel shook. "It is time to introduce myself," he said. "My name is Ivgeny. I believe you know who I am." He turned away and leaned over the rail of the ferry, facing the water, forcing Stupenagel and Murrow to do the same. He then spoke very quietly.

"I ask that you keep your voices low so that we can't be overheard," he said. "There are others listening. In fact, you are about to meet the subject of some of your stories, as well as the woman who planted the bomb in my restaurant. Her name is Nadya Malovo."

"You set me up?" Stupenagel hissed.

"Actually, the plan is to set up Malovo," he explained. "But I did need you, and myself, as bait. I will apologize later, but this woman is responsible for the death of many people, and unless she's stopped, the death of many more."

"This was the woman with the suitcase at the Black Sea Café?"

"Yes."

"Good. Put a cap in her for me," Stupenagel said. "What do you want us to do?"

"When the shooting starts, just get on the ground and try to avoid getting killed."

"Great," Murrow groaned. "Doesn't anybody around here want to live to be a hundred?"

Before anyone could answer, a woman spoke behind them. "Put your hands in the air, Ivgeny, and tell your man to obey. The other two as well."

The party did as told and turned slowly to face Malovo. She was accompanied by several men, who spread out around them but remained out of earshot. She smiled and pointed her gun from Ivgeny to Stupenagel to Murrow. "Who should I shoot first?"

"Wait," Karchovski said. "I want to give you a chance to surrender before there is any more bloodshed."

Malovo opened her mouth in surprise and then started to laugh. "Ah, Ivgeny, you haven't changed," she said. "A killer with a sense of humor, and one who actually places a premium on life."

"Unlike you, I take no pleasure in destroying," Karchovski replied. "Do you really think your bosses' use of terrorism will cow the world into giving them a free hand?"

Malovo shrugged. "Why not? Most people are sheep, especially in the West, where they are so fat and happy they think that everything will be okay if you talk nicely to people who believe that God has appointed them to convert infidels or put them to the sword. You refuse to see that by being soft, the current governments of the West and Russia are allowing the lowest common denominator—the illiterate, the filthy, the plague of Africans, Asians, Arabs, and Latins—to inherit a world built by their superiors."

"So you would stoop to killing thousands of innocent people to get the rest to place their lives in your hands instead?" Karchovski asked.

"Yes. Unless they are afraid, they will cling to their 'rights' and hamper the efforts of more intelligent people who are trying to protect them from that plague," Malovo scoffed. "But enough of this. I didn't come here to debate. I came here to kill you and this stupid woman. Now, in memory of our romance in Kabul, I'll let you choose who dies first."

"And I'll give you one last chance to lay down your weapons," Karchovski replied. "You are surrounded."

"What sort of fool do you think I am?" Malovo sneered. "My men are in complete control of this ferry. At this moment, they are holding the captain, the crew, and the other passengers captive. Watch, I will even stop the boat."

Smiling, Malovo waved a hand over her head. She waited for the engines to shut down, but instead the ferry continued to proceed across the water as normal. She scowled and looked up to where her man was supposed to be watching for her signal. He was there, and she angrily signaled again. But instead of the expected response, he plunged forward over the rail and onto the deck of the ferry.

The sentinel was replaced by a tall, thin man who appeared to be wearing a robe. His pale face glowed yellow in the ferry's running lights, which gave him a ghostly appearance that shook the men with Malovo. *"Shayteen,"* one of them mumbled in fear.

Of the people standing on the deck, only Ivgeny was not surprised to see David Grale peering down at them.

After the restaurant bombing, the Karchovskis had quickly dismissed the idea that some other Russian gang was behind the attack. Gangsters were first and foremost businessmen. While friction and territory could lead to killings, even outright warfare, they all knew that it was bad for business. It attracted the police and put a stop to normal transactions. And usually, there was some indication—threats or reports of hostility—that preceded violence.

It led the Karchovskis to conclude that they had another mole within their organization. From there it had been easy to figure out who. In fact, the traitor was the man standing next to him, his bodyguard. How Malovo had turned him, Ivgeny did not care. In fact, in one way, he owed the man his thanks for giving him this opportunity to kill the woman who had tried to murder him and his father. Yet, it had been all he could do not to strangle the traitor with his own hands when he thought about the death of his friend Gregory, with whom he'd served in Afghanistan, and the other innocent people who died in the café.

The traitor had been fed the information about the meeting with Ariadne Stupenagel and then left alone to contact Malovo. Ivgeny had felt a twinge of remorse for exposing the reporter, and unexpectedly her boyfriend, to danger, but he knew that the bait had to be too tempting or the rat might smell the trap.

Even then, there were great risks involved. Malovo might have tried to plant a bomb on the ferry, but he dismissed this, knowing her preferences, and counted on her wanting to kill him herself up close.

He'd also had to leave his other men behind and bring only the traitor. Where there was one rat, there might have been another who might have warned Malovo of a trap. However, he'd arranged for backup by having a go-between contact Grale with his plan.

Grale was something of a business associate. The mad monk's network of street people were spread throughout Manhattan, and to a lesser degree the other boroughs, and provided excellent intelligence. In exchange, Grale sought medical supplies, weapons, and food for his followers. The arrangement worked well, though even his own men, as tough as they were, didn't like dealing with Grale and his so-called Mole People. It was an added bonus that he and Grale had discovered that they had mutual enemies.

The appearance now of Grale at the railing above froze Malovo for an instant. But she was trained to deal with the unexpected and whirled to shoot Karchovski. However, he, too, was a trained fighter and knocked the gun from her hand with a telescoping baton he'd had up his sleeve.

Stupenagel and Murrow dove to the deck just as Malovo's men were suddenly overwhelmed by robed fighters who'd appeared like wraiths out of the shadows. Terrified, the Muslims didn't put up much of a fight, screaming, *"Shayteen! Shayteen!"* before being cut down.

Karchovski moved in to follow up his advantage and narrowly missed being eviscerated by a palm knife that appeared in Malovo's hand. He jumped back in the last instant and flipped open a butterfly knife that he carried.

"Put down the knife, Nadya," Karchovski ordered as they circled each other. "Your men are dead or captured. It's your decision to live or die."

Malovo laughed but the sound was bitter and harsh. "What? And submit to your tender mercies? I don't suppose you would be turning me over to the U.S. or Russian government?"

Karchovski shook his head grimly. "No, that mistake will not happen again. But your death will be as painless as I can make it after I have from you what I want to know."

Suddenly, a speedboat roared out of the dark and pulled alongside the ferry. A spotlight from the boat picked out Karchovski and Malovo, and then someone opened fire.

Ivgeny dove to his right just in time to avoid a bullet that rang off the metal hull. He looked up to see Malovo activate a red light on her shoulder harness and then run for the side of the ferry, diving into the black waters.

Cursing, Karchovski jumped up and ran to the rail. But the speedboat and the red light that bobbed in the wake of the ferry were already far behind. He picked up Malovo's gun and fired until it was empty, then heaved it at the escaping woman in frustration. He pulled his cell phone from his pocket and dialed a number. He spoke rapidly in Russian, then flipped it shut.

With Stupenagel and Murrow trailing him, he ran up to the bridge, where the captain and his crew stood in stunned silence. Two terrorists in black lay dead on the ground, the work of Grale's men.

"I apologize for all of this," Karchovski told the captain. "But I need you to stop the ferry. I have a boat picking me up on your port side in a moment."

The captain looked down at the dead men. "All engines stop," he told his crew, then turned back to Karchovski. "I guess we owe you thanks for saving us from these two. But who are you people?"

"It's not important," Karchovski said. "Please allow me to disembark before you get under way again." With that, he took off running, again with Stupenagel and Murrow on his heels.

They reached the stern on the port side just as a motorboat was pulling alongside. "I'm sorry," Karchovski said to Stupenagel as Grale and a half dozen of his fighters climbed down into the motorboat. "You are welcome to join us in case you don't want to answer questions from the authorities."

"I think that's a good idea," Stupenagel said. "And maybe you have time for a few questions?"

"Some other day, perhaps," Karchovski said. "But we'll drop you back at Battery Park."

"What about me, boss?" asked Karchovski's bodyguard, who'd remained standing on the stern of the ferry with two of Grale's men.

Ivgeny turned to the man, his eyes blazing with anger. "What about you, traitor?"

Before the bodyguard could respond, Grale nodded to his men. One struck the bodyguard on the back of his head with a blackjack, knocking him to the ground.

"Tie his hands and feet," Ivgeny instructed.

They did as told, then hauled the man to his feet. "Please, Mr. Karchovski, why are you doing this?" The man started to cry.

Karchovski, however, was unmoved. "My only regret is that I do not have the time to deal with you properly," he said, and spit in the man's face. "But this is for my friend Gregory, and the others whose blood is on your head."

"No, I did nothing, I swear to you," the bodyguard blubbered as Karchovski grabbed him by the lapels of his coat.

"Tell that to the fish," Karchovski replied, and launched the man over the side of the ferry. Weighed down by his clothes and a bulletproof vest, the man kicked violently in an attempt to keep his mouth above water. He was still kicking, his eyes wide with terror, as he slipped beneath the surface and disappeared into the depths.

The gangster leader turned to Stupenagel and Murrow. "You will forget that you saw that, no?"

"No," Murrow said, and was nudged in the ribs by Stupenagel. "I mean yes. Never saw a thing. Besides, I believe these are New Jersey waters. No jurisdiction."

"Honey bunny," Stupenagel said. "Now would be a good time to be quiet."

"Right."

Ivgeny Karchovski smiled and shook his head. He would never understand these Americans and their sense of humor. "You have nothing to fear from me," he said. "But so you know, he was the man who betrayed you and all the other people at the Black Sea Café."

"Good riddance to bad trash, then," Stupenagel said.

"Ditto," Murrow agreed.

"Then please, climb down," Karchovski said.

A few minutes later, Murrow and Stupenagel were standing on the dock at Battery Park, watching Karchovski's speedboat roar into the darkness. Murrow sighed. "Well, that was exciting," he said. "I guess you'll have another story on the front page."

Ariadne tousled his hair. "You are one cool cookie, Gilbert my love. Let's go home . . . I've a deadline to make."

17

WHILE IVGENY KARCHOVSKI WAS DROWNING A TRAITOR IN New York Harbor, V. T. Newbury's uncle led him down the hall, past the still smiling receptionist and through a pair of frosted glass doors. Now they were standing in a vestibule outside another elevator and a set of stainless steel doors that looked like the entrance to a bank vault.

His uncle noticed him look at the elevator and said, "VIP. Goes straight to a private area in the parking garage. Sometimes our clients are trying to avoid the intrusions by the overzealous press. They like their privacy, even those who otherwise must lead public lives, and we respect that."

Dean Newbury turned to the steel doors and paused. "As a matter of fact, I hope you will honor my request to keep the identities of my associates confidential. You may recognize some of them, but all are important men who have to be careful about how their lives are reported, as well as where they go from a security standpoint."

"You may count on it," V.T. promised. He saw no reason to want to discuss his uncle's cronies, and he had to admit that all the buildup was making him curious.

"Good lad, knew I could count on the old Newbury discretion," Dean said, smiling, and pressed the palm of his right hand against a pad next to the door. There was a slight click and the door slid open, revealing a large meeting room dominated by a round wooden table around which sat eleven men.

Most of the men rose when they entered, except for those who appeared too elderly to rise without assistance. They were all white and ranged in age, he guessed, from forties to nineties.

"Gentlemen, may I introduce you to my nephew, Vinson Talcott Newbury," Dean said. "The son of my late brother and the last male member of this line of Newburys."

Eleven pairs of eyes focused on V.T., who felt like a crown prince being presented at court for a throne he wanted no part of.

Dean walked V.T. around the table to introduce him to each man. As they moved from one to the next, V.T. was increasingly impressed by the credentials of this set of "cronies": a U.S. senator from Tennessee, a congressman from Utah, a general at the Pentagon, the assistant director of an unnamed intelligence agency, a commentator from a television network, two federal judges, two bank presidents, a wealthy entrepreneur, and another prominent attorney, who'd been a recent past president of the American Bar Association—and, of course, his uncle.

V.T. knew several of the men on sight, and a couple more by reputation. But it was safe to assume, as his uncle had pointed out, that this was a council of equals. He thought he recognized several of the older men from his grandfather's and Quilliam's funerals.

And now gathered here to meet little ol' me, V.T. thought. I don't know whether to be flattered or to try to make a run for it. Looking down at the table, he noted the symbol on Quilliam's ring—the *tre cassyn*—was also embossed in gold in the wooden top. He glanced around and noticed that all of the others were, indeed, wearing rings like the one he'd just been given. The thought suddenly made the ring seem very heavy and he longed to take it off, but didn't out of deference to his uncle.

The members took their seats and V.T.'s uncle continued with the introduction. "Gentlemen, I've taken the liberty of explaining that we are members of a sort of ancient fraternity with ties back to Old Europe," he said. "But I was just thinking that a more apt description might be a 'think tank' that meets from time to time to discuss, and perhaps take some action to deal with, issues that confront this country. You will never hear about us in the news, Vinson, but you might be surprised at what we have accomplished behind the scenes for a great many years. But we'll leave the discussion of history for another day. Am I right, gentlemen?"

The gentlemen nodded their assents, and he continued. "As you all know, I'm trying to persuade my nephew to return to the family fold and possibly take up the mantle of his family's law firm. I would like nothing better than knowing that when I pass from this world, the firm of Newbury, White & Newbury will be left in the good hands of someone who understands the great responsibility of this charge."

"Hear, hear," the others replied, though V.T. thought the "vote" was less than fully enthusiastic.

"To that end, I wanted him to meet you, my most trusted associates and advisors, and perhaps in the company of such an august group, he may also come to understand that there is much he could accomplish at the helm of this law firm and as part of this 'fraternity.' "

Another round of "Hear, hear"s ended the introduction, and the rest of the meeting was spent chatting while dinner was served. While this was less formal, with one-on-one and small-group conversations, V.T. got the impression that it was actually the more important phase of the "examination."

Most of the questions seemed aimed at finding out where he stood on the political spectrum. He considered himself somewhat conservative, though with definite liberal tendencies when it came to social issues.

He answered honestly, including what he thought of the Patriot Act, which was that in times of war, a country's government sometimes needed extraordinary powers. "Especially against such a difficult enemy as global terrorism," he said. "However, it's a balancing act between giving government enough tools to protect us from enemies without, and protecting us from the government overstepping its bounds in regard to intrusions into private lives."

After dinner, his uncle escorted him back out of the room and to the elevators that would take him to the lobby. "Well done," Dean said, shaking V.T.'s hand. "I think that went rather well for a start. Please remember what we agreed regarding our little meeting. Mum's the word."

"I promise," V.T. replied. "Not a peep. So the others are staying?"

Dean looked back toward the stainless steel doors. "Yes, we have a number of business items and housekeeping matters to attend to," he said. "A regular Rotary club meeting with minutes and reports. It's boring stuff and, unfortunately, likely to take up the rest of the night. Due to the distances involved, and busy schedules, we don't get the opportunity to meet face-to-face very often and have to seize the opportunity when it presents itself."

Placing a hand on V.T.'s arm, he looked his nephew in the eye. "This is an important trust you've been offered. Our aspirations for you go beyond this law firm, such as eventually a seat on the U.S. Supreme Court. And why not, there are kingmakers in this room who might be able to help."

V.T.'s mouth fell open. "You're telling me that this 'fraternity' or 'think tank' can arrange to have me appointed to the highest court in the country? I thought that was the prerogative of the president and confirmed by Congress?"

Dean Newbury spread his hands as if to say stranger things have happened. "I wouldn't say 'arrange,' or even guarantee that such a thing could be done. Of course, you would have to be qualified, perhaps by starting with an appointment to a federal bench for a bit of seasoning. But we do have a certain amount of influence in the political arena, as well as with the American Bar Association, which as you may know has for the past fifty years issued its evaluations of the credentials of nominees to the federal bench and particularly the Supreme Court."

"Yes, I know the ABA issues a report to Congress on whether they believe a candidate is 'well qualified,' 'qualified,' or 'not qualified.' But they have no official standing in the selection process," V.T. pointed out.

"Perhaps not, but a 'well qualified' usually leads to confirmation," his uncle replied. "Presidents and the Congress can't be expected to know the qualifications of every nominee. As in any other business, they rely on advisors, including the ABA."

V.T.'s mind was reeling. He'd promised his uncle that he would keep an open mind, but that was when he thought the job offer was going to be a senior partnership and eventual control of the family firm. He wasn't naïve enough to think that such things as nominations to the U.S. Supreme Court were free of political maneuvering. Anybody who read a newspaper knew how rancorous and partisan the proceedings could be once the nominee got to the congressional hearings. But something that a few powerful men could arrange?

V.T. thought that the group was a little carried away with its self-importance and influence. Then again, he thought, I'm sure the demagogues of the Christian right sit around convincing themselves that they have more influence than they do. Just like the left-wing appeasers in the Democratic Party think the public will follow them like lemmings just because they rail nonstop against everything the incumbent Republicans try to do, particularly as it relates to counterterrorism. Which is, of course, why they keep getting disappointed in November.

"Well," he said, flustered. He cleared his throat to give himself a little more time to find the right words without insulting his uncle. "This is certainly unexpected, and I don't really even know how to respond without a great deal more thought. But I do appreciate the honor that you consider me worth the thought."

"Well, my boy, I have to admit there's a little ego involved," the old man said. "There's been a Newbury on that council for nearly two hundred years. We don't want to mess up that run now, do we?"

The elevator opened and V.T. stepped in. He turned around

and nodded. "I'd hate to be the one to do that. I'll give it a fair hearing."

When the doors closed, Dean Newbury stood for a moment pondering his next move. He turned and reentered the meeting room and immediately addressed the others. "So, gentlemen, your thoughts?"

"Dangerous, this fire you're playing with," the television commentator said. "His father betrayed you . . . us . . . and your nephew works for the enemy, the Jew Karp."

"Well, I believe the old, overused saw is 'Keep your friends close and your enemies closer.' But I am not sure that my nephew cannot be turned to a friend," Dean Newbury replied. "You better than most of us understand how easily opinions can be swayed with the right choice of words and enticement. And besides, haven't we always held that blood is thicker than water?"

"Blood of firstborn sons," the senator pointed out. "He was not brought up in the brotherhood."

Dean Newbury understood the argument. He'd heard it before. The seats around the table had been passed from firstborn son to firstborn son for more than two hundred years. Ever since their ancestors had first arrived, fleeing the reach of the British Navy. But the line of succession had not always been straight. Some of their predecessors had been childless or had not produced male heirs. Or the firstborn son had died, like Quilliam, and there'd even been several who rejected the cause, like Quilliam, and had to be watched carefully for any sign of disloyalty.

Therefore, sometimes the seats had been filled in other ways. Second sons had been indoctrinated and accepted into the brotherhood to replace their fathers, or, as would be V.T.'s case, a first son of a second son. But they usually started the process of "education" much younger than V.T., when the mind was easier to mold.

However, Dean Newbury had been forced into the present situation by several betrayals. The first was his own body, which had failed to produce any more male heirs, only two daughters, who themselves had only produced daughters. The second had been Quilliam, who'd recoiled from his rightful place and joined the marines.

The third betrayal, or actually a series of betrayals, he laid at the feet of his brother, Vincent. Their father had never trusted Dean's younger brother, who had not been given much more than a basic understanding of the family's history and did not know the true source and extent of their wealth.

It had been a struggle just to get him to go to law school so that he could at least help the firm's pantheon of rich and important clients. Then they'd had to wean him from the radical clique of do-good lawyers who met in Brooklyn at Julius Karp's house and spent their Saturday evenings prattling about a sacrosanct Constitution, when anybody with any intelligence knew that adjustments needed to be made to the document to reflect modern concerns.

However, Vincent had learned more than he should have about the family's business. Never the full story or the details, or the names of the other members of the council, but enough to be dangerous. Then he'd somehow made it past the state-of-the-art security system, gained access to Dean's office, and stole the old mustard-colored book that was kept on a shelf. He'd berated himself for keeping the book, or at least for keeping it where someone might see it. But then he hadn't expected to be betrayed by his own brother.

The reasons for keeping the book were uncharacteristic for Dean Newbury. Most copies of the self-published book had been destroyed before they could get out to the public. It had been written by another traitor in the late 1930s, who had met an untimely end sleeping off a bender inside a warehouse where he kept most copies of the book. The warehouse mysteriously caught fire, killing the author and destroying all other copies of the book and the printing plates that made them. However, several copies had been saved by the arsonist to present to members of the council, including Dean's father.

How long the book was missing before he noticed it was not in its place, Dean didn't know. He wasn't even sure at first who took it because the security camera tapes, which were recycled once a week, had already been wiped clean. It had remained a troubling mystery until a security guard saw his brother on one of the monitors enter the office and remove something from under his desk.

Nothing was found on a subsequent security sweep, but Dean suspected that his brother had removed a listening device. There'd been a moment of panic, when he recalled a recent conversation he'd had with Jamys Kellagh regarding "the project." But he calmed down when he thought about the fact that they'd been speaking in the ancient tongue, which few would know how to translate, and even if someone did, they'd spoken in code.

What had been done after that was necessary in regard to his brother's betrayal. Vincent's chef had been instructed to prepare a stew with a large amount of foxglove stem cut up in the mix. Foxglove was of course a natural source of digitalis—a useful medication for heart disease, but also fatal if taken in too great an amount. A cursory examination, however, would have led to the conclusion that Vincent was the victim of an accidental overdose. But even that wasn't a worry, as the Newbury family doctor had pronounced the death was due to a massive heart attack, and then the family's contact at the Medical Examiner's Office rubber-stamped the death certificate.

However, the book was not found in Vincent's office, his apartment in Soho, nor the beach house in Cape Cod. Dean had spent many sleepless nights and countless hours in the day second-guessing himself for not torturing his brother to find the book before he was killed.

Then luck turned their way. Kellagh traced the book to a store in the East Village. However, he also reported that the owner of the bookstore was a friend of Lucy Karp. Kellagh had then made a unilateral decision to destroy the book and kill the people who knew of its existence, a decision that worried the council, though nothing could be done about it at that point.

The book and Magee had perished in the fire, but the Karp girl survived—yet another example of the infernal luck surrounding that family. Dean considered having Kellagh kill her; he was certainly close enough to do it. But on reflection, he wasn't worried about what she might reveal now that the book was gone. It had been written in the 1930s, the names chosen for disguise were common, and even with the book it would have been difficult to trace them to their current descendants—and, in the case of those members who'd failed to produce male heirs, many of the family names were different. But murdering the daughter of the district attorney would have brought far too much unwanted attention, and his "fraternity" had done everything it could for two hundred years to avoid detection.

As Cian Magee had guessed, the small band of Manxmen smugglers with their families had created an empire more powerful and wealthy than many of the world's governments. They'd learned the art of deception from the past, and had the patience to await the right tides and fortuitous winds that would enable them to slip past British men-of-war.

Avoiding any publicity outside of their legitimate roles as successful businessmen, lawyers, politicians, and military officers, they'd slowly shifted the family business away from purely criminal enterprises to a balance between legal and illegal endeavors. However, they'd never abandoned their smuggling roots—from bootlegging liquor during Prohibition to providing arms to Fidel Castro during the Cuban revolution.

In the early 1960s, they'd recognized the enormous potential of the drug trade and arranged with the organized crime syndicates like the Mafia, and newcomers such as the Crips, to provide the transportation and border-crossing expertise. They'd been smart enough to be satisfied with their piece of the pie and never got into dealing drugs, which might have brought them into violent competition with their clients. But they could also be ruthless if someone tried to cross them or cut them out of the loop.

Drugs had been lucrative and remained so, as well as a way to control the mud people in their ghettos and barrios. But currently the greatest profits were in smuggling the second most traded commodity in the world behind oil. Weapons. Always a good money-maker, going back to the days of supplying American Indians and the

Confederate army. World events in the last half of the twentieth century had made arms dealing more profitable than ever.

In fact, the end of the cold war had been a godsend. The fall of the Soviet Union had freed all those little states to buck Russian rule, and they needed guns for that. Dean Newbury and his associates had found high growth markets in the Balkans and Africa, and then a new surge with the rise of Islamic extremism. At times they'd even cooperated with governments, like the United States when it wanted to supply rebels in Afghanistan with the arms to fight the Soviets. Dean Newbury and his partners could have cared less who got hurt. If Slavs and Arabs and Jews wanted to kill each other, more power to them—as long as they had the money to buy weapons.

The families' worldview had evolved with their fortune and time. Dealing in slaves had taught them that the Negro was an inferior species, hardly human. And Arabs could boast all they wanted about being the originators of algebra or ancient civilizations, but this was a "what have you done lately" world. And the answer was: little more than breed like vermin and remain ignorant slaves to a seventh-century dogma.

The Sons of Man had bigger plans . . . plans Hitler and Stalin had failed to realize, but that were possible and headed in the right direction. The first major step would be the control of the U.S. government and the American public. There had been some among them who prior to World War Two thought that the time was near for taking over in the United States. Hitler had been on the rise in Germany, a man who truly understood that Jews and subhumans would someday overrun the world and drain the resources if there wasn't a "Final Solution." And the council had energetically supported the American Nazi Party and, ironically, the isolationist and peace groups who wanted to keep the United States out of the war in Europe. The hope was that a United States government controlled by the Sons of Man could join hands with Nazi Germany and rule the world. But the dream was ruined when the damned monkey-men in Japan attacked Pearl Harbor and brought the United States into the war on the other side.

The next opportunity had been the rise of Senator Joseph Mc-Carthy, a demagogue whose anticommunist fear mongering had convinced the American public that the communists and lefties were at the door. They'd spent a lot of money wooing the senator and tried to influence him, with some success, but that moment, too, had passed when the senator flamed out.

After President Dwight Eisenhower warned the American public about the growth of the "military-industrial complex," there were those on the council who felt he was hitting too close to home and wanted him assassinated. *We are the fucking military-industrial complex,* one of the older men had snarled. But cooler heads had prevailed by pointing out that there'd be hell to pay for a popular president's murder.

Now there were new opportunities to cement their power. White America was growing paranoid about unchecked illegal immigration and the growing numbers of mud people. And they were frightened of terrorism perpetuated by Islamic extremists. Using the bogeymen of the public's fears, the Sons of Man had seized on the moment to push the populace of the United States into easing the grip on their precious rights in exchange for the safety of an all-powerful, all-knowing government. A government influenced covertly by the council.

The current strategy was to use the terrorists until the Sons of Man could consolidate their power, and then with their friends in Russia, who had similar designs on controlling that part of the world, they'd crush the Muslims along with any other troublesome people in the world. And they'd do it with nuclear bombs and other WMDs if necessary. After all, who could stop them— moral arguments against such necessary slaughter were for the weak.

However, the terrorists weren't always easy to control. The council received the warning that the World Trade Center was about to be attacked with barely enough time to sell off stocks that would be negatively affected and buy into companies whose stock would rise. But those are the breaks when dealing with sand niggers, Dean Newbury reminded himself.

The road to ultimate power was not a smooth one. A case in point was the continued existence, and even interference, from the Jew Karp and his family and friends. Somehow they kept escaping the best attempts to eliminate them, and they'd managed to foil what should have been major steps forward in the plan.

However, the latest failure could be chalked up to one of those firstborn sons who some of his fellow council members were arguing were so important. "Have you forgotten that Andrew Kane was a firstborn son of a firstborn son?" he asked the others.

"An abomination," the general snarled. "The bastard kid of the father fucking his whore daughter. Kane should have never been allowed to inherit his father's seat."

"My point exactly," Newbury said. "A useful tool, and if he'd pulled it off, we might be singing a different tune. But my point is that from time to time we've realized that we should not be iron-bound to the canon of first sons if the candidate is defective or untrustworthy. We seem to be forgetting that until Kane's personality disorders got the best of him, he was our golden boy—the next mayor of New York City, and a strong candidate for a run at the White House."

"Well, at least he was brought up in our ways," one of the bankers said. "Your nephew is fiftysomething and a lifelong 'public servant' known for his fundamentalist views on the Constitution. And then there's his friendship with Karp. I don't see how it can work."

Dean shrugged. "Granted, it may be a difficult sell," he said. "Unless he can be convinced that it's for the good of his country."

"Brainwashing?" the congressman scoffed.

"A version, perhaps," Dean replied. "But gentlemen, I'm not suggesting that he be initiated straight into the council. We can bring him along slowly and see what sort of candidate he makes. Perhaps blood will tell. If not, there is a spot next to his father in the Newbury plot."

"And what will you do for an heir if this experiment fails?" the senator asked.

"The daughter of one of my sisters has a ten-year-old son who seems bright enough. The family might prevail upon his parents to let him live under my wing, where he can be provided with all of life's best advantages." And maybe persuade them to allow me to adopt the boy so that the Newbury name is not lost, he thought.

"A wiser choice, I think," the television commentator said.

"Perhaps if I had the time to raise another boy," Dean replied. "But I want the wheels set in motion for our great triumph before I die."

With that said, Dean moved to put the debate over his heir aside for the time being. They had a more pressing matter to attend to: Senator Tom McCullum. Bad enough that he was questioning the legitimacy of the Patriot Act; the council had supported the act as a small step forward toward a government they'd control. But now he was also calling for a full-out congressional probe into the attack at St. Patrick's Cathedral, the involvement of the Russians, and allegations—all true—that the "act of terrorism" had been arranged to turn world opinion against Chechen nationalists. McCullum had gone so far as to hint that he believed that certain factions in both governments were using Islamic extremists for their own ends. And that was really hitting close to home.

McCullum was one of the most persuasive speakers on the Hill. He had a way of uniting both liberal and conservative factions, especially as a champion of the Constitution. After much debate, and going back and forth—after all, assassinating a U.S. senator was not to be taken lightly—the council had decided that it could not risk the potential that a congressional hearing might lead Senator McCullum to them.

The council's plan had been set in motion by Newbury's conversation in Manx with Jamys Kellagh. The Sons of Man would march with the Sons of Ireland to silence the critic for the good of all.

Kellagh was next on the evening agenda. Dean pressed a button beneath the table and spoke so that the receptionist could hear. "Miss Rauch, would you let Mr. Kellagh know that we are ready to see him."

A minute later, Jamys Kellagh entered the room. It was not his real name, but he had not used that since he was a teenager and it had been determined what career path he would take. He was the son of a male family member but not a first son, and groomed to be a second-level operative like his father.

Kellagh remained standing while the others questioned him about his mission in the East Village that December.

"Do we know for certain that the book perished with the book-keeper?" the old general asked.

"I was there when the girl climbed out of the window," he said. "She did not have the book, and the place was gutted."

"Good," the general said. "But are we confident that what she was told does not compromise the bigger mission?"

Kellagh shook his head. He hated reporting failures to this group, both because he believed in the cause and because it could be dangerous. Too many things had already gone wrong. It started with the mess at St. Patrick's because of Kane. But it continued when the man he'd sent to murder the reporter in her apartment had tumbled off the roof. The man's name wasn't Don Porter-house, a piece-of-shit rapist who'd been killed and his identity switched with Kellagh's man, one of his best assassins and a former colleague at the agency, years earlier. Then the bitch had survived another attempt to kill her at the café in Brooklyn, though that he could blame on Nadya Malovo.

"I don't think there's a problem," he said in answer to the general's question about Lucy Karp. "She heard a story about some odd group from history about which there's never been anything more up to date than the book. They were able to translate a message in the old tongue between Mr. Newbury and myself, but they had no clue what it means. I think we are safe to go forward as planned."

"What about Butch Karp?" a banker asked.

"He's supposed to be taking it easy, doctor's orders, and is occupying himself with a civil case in Idaho of all places," Kellagh replied. "Right now, he's still here in New York, but he doesn't go to the office and about the only other activity he seems to have is breakfast with a bunch of retired old duffers who sit around arguing about the Constitution. To be honest, I wonder if the latest attempt on his life didn't take some of the fire out of him."

"And your counterpart with our Russian friends?" one of the retired judges asked.

"She is taking care of the reporter and the gangster herself," Kellagh said. He looked at his watch. "In fact, I would say they are no longer an issue."

"I wonder if we should concentrate more on removing these impediments, Karp and his associates," the other lawyer said.

Kellagh shook his head. "I wouldn't recommend that," he replied. "For one thing, these missions have put them on a heightened alert, and we cannot account for all of their friends. The Indian and the Vietnamese gangster have disappeared, and of course, tracking David Grale is impossible. My advice is to wait while we concentrate on accomplishing the main mission. We can deal with these issues later."

When Kellagh left the room, the retired general turned to Newbury. "There seem to be a lot of excuses for failure these days from Mr. Kellagh."

"He's your nephew, what would you have us do? Up until now he has performed well."

"Yes, but any more failures and we may have to rethink his position," the general said. "Too much hinges on him and we can't afford weak links that fail us. Keep that in mind with your own nephew, Mr. Newbury."

"I will do that," Newbury agreed icily. "Now, if there's nothing else that anyone needs to discuss, I call an end to this Tynwald. . . . *Myr shegin dy ve, bee eh!*"

"*Myr shegin dy ve, bee eh!*" the others replied.

18

THAT SAME NIGHT, MARLENE AND BUTCH WERE CUDDLING on the couch when she told him about Santacristina and his theory that there might be a connection between his daughter's disappearance and Mikey O'Toole's case. She'd just returned from Idaho following Huttington's deposition and some initial inquiries at the Sawtooth police department regarding Maria's disappearance, and it was weighing on her mind.

Karp was skeptical. "I'm sorry about what he's going through," he said. "It doesn't sound good. But I don't see the connection except that Huttington is involved in both at least at some level. You know as well as I do that parents of missing children will grasp at any possibility. Every time the cops catch some serial killer—no matter what part of the country he may have terrorized or when—these families converge on the off chance that the killer might know what happened to their son or daughter. But thousands of these cases go unsolved, and their bodies are never found, and—while Santacristina might not want to hear this—sometimes people do run away."

"I understand that," Marlene conceded, "however"—she began ticking off her counterpoints on her fingers—"her passport was found in her apartment. No one has used her credit cards or her checking account. She'd laid out her clothes and her books, like any good student getting ready for school the next day. Also, I did some nosing around in the Basque community, which is like one big family, and by everybody's consensus, Maria and her father were as close as we are to our own children. Do you think Lucy or the boys would 'run away' and leave us wondering what happened to them?"

"No, of course not," Butch replied. "If I had to give an opinion, I'd agree Maria's dead. I'm even willing to concede that it's a plausible theory that the reason she is dead is because she was pregnant and Huttington was the father. But it's just one theory and there's another that says she's the victim of a complete stranger who saw a pretty girl and took her into those mountains, killed her, and left her body there. It's a big country. What I'm having a harder time wrapping my arms around is that her disappearance, and probable murder, is somehow connected to Mikey's case."

It was a fair point, and they'd dropped the conversation. Then the telephone rang. It was Murrow calling to alert them to a forthcoming story by Ariadne in the next morning's edition of her newspaper.

"Let me read you a little of it," Murrow said. "It's, uh, written in the first person and starts with Ariadne meeting with an anonymous source on the Staten Island Ferry this evening."

This reporter and her source were ambushed last night on the ferry by terrorists led by alleged Russian agent Nadya Malovo—the same woman captured after the hostage crisis at St. Patrick's Cathedral and turned over to Russian authorities by U.S. law enforcement.

Malovo confirmed to sources that she was responsible for planting the bomb at the Black Sea Café earlier this month. She also boasted that she worked for powerful individuals in Russia who were encouraging acts of terrorism by Islamic extremists. Their aim is to frighten the public in Russia and legitimize their violent suppression of Chechen nationalists to

Western governments by claiming to be fighting the world-wide "War on Terrorism."

"Wow, heck of a story," Karp said.

"Um, yeah, but boss, I feel like I better tell you something . . ."

"Uh-oh, I'm not sure I like the sound of that."

"Yeah, well, it probably won't get out," Murrow replied. "But in case it does, I wanted you to hear it from me first. . . . I, uh, well, I was there when this all happened."

Karp wasn't the only one who swore after the story hit the streets. There was an immediate storm of criticism aimed at Stupenagel from congressmen, federal law enforcement agencies, the State Department, and the Russian embassy. They dismissed her story as "fantasy" and "fabrications." It was pointed out that all the men found dead on the ferry were from Muslim countries and several were on the Homeland Security Department's list of terrorism suspects. A few days later, a spokesman for the department announced that an investigation had determined that the purpose of the terrorists on board the ferry had been to take over the boat and blow it up. "Any reports of a more massive conspiracy have been discounted," he said without referring to Stupenagel's story specifically.

The rest of the media—stung once again by a Stupenagel scoop—was only too happy to run with the "official" version of events and snipe at their competitor. Their stories implied that Stupenagel was embellishing her story to pump up her role in the action. Several papers printed editorials lambasting her for "irresponsible and the 'me-first' journalism . . . that sullies the good name of our profession."

Stupenagel did have one defender. Senator Tom McCullum was quoted as saying that the intensity of the criticism following the publication of Stupenagel's story "probably is a good barometer of the veracity of her reports." He then announced that he wanted to expand his call for a congressional inquiry into the "debacle at St.

Patrick's Cathedral" to include the bombing of the Black Sea Café and the attack on the Staten Island Ferry.

Stupenagel had just laughed off the criticism as "professional jealousy and political butt-covering." Then, in a reversal of their usual roles, she had sworn Marlene and Butch to "off-the-record" secrecy before she would reveal the entire story, including identifying Ivgeny Karchovski and David Grale as the leaders of the so-called antiterrorism squad.

When she was finished, Karp had started in on her but Stupenagel shut him down. "I didn't want him to go, either," she said. "But he insisted out of concern for me. It's his life, Butch, and like it or not—and I'm not entirely sure how it happened—we seem to have found a connection. He didn't do anything illegal, nor was this in the DAO's jurisdiction. We kept his name out of it, and no one else knows he was there. So lay off."

A few days later, Marlene returned to Idaho to continue preparations for the trial. Butch wouldn't be coming for another couple of weeks, but she wasn't alone. Detective Clay Fulton had insisted on accompanying her. She suspected that her husband had asked him to keep an eye on her, but Fulton made it sound like it was his idea and that he needed a vacation away from Manhattan.

When she asked how it was that a New York City detective could justify working on a civil case in Idaho, he explained that like his boss, he was taking a leave of absence. He, too, was still rehabilitating from leg wounds after being shot by Andrew Kane during the sociopath's bloody escape a year earlier. "Besides, Helen's never seen that part of the country," he said of his wife, "and she has a notion to try skiing at Sun Valley when the trial is over."

Ostensibly, Fulton was working on the O'Toole case, but after talking it over with Marlene and Butch, he'd also volunteered to nose around a little regarding the disappearance of Maria Santacristina. "Just in case there's something to this theory that they're connected," he said.

As it turned out, Fulton had once again proved why he was one of New York's finest. In fact, Marlene had driven to Sawtooth from O'Toole's house that night to meet with Eugenio Santacristina because of what Fulton had recently learned.

The fresh layer of snow squeaked beneath Marlene's boots as she walked from the SUV she'd rented to the Basque Cultural Center in Sawtooth. All she'd told Santacristina was that she had some news that might interest him. He'd asked no more questions, but suggested that they meet at the cultural center so that she could see a real Basque festival. "And no one will bother us there."

A few lonely flakes still filtered down, but otherwise it was a clear February night in the mountains, with stars so brilliant that they shimmered like bits of crystal against the ebony backdrop.

Stomping the snow off her feet, she entered the center just as a dance was beginning in the main hall. A wide circle of men and women held hands, twirling, stomping, and laughing as they moved counterclockwise to the music. The women were dressed in loose white blouses with dark vests and long, full red skirts that blossomed like giant roses as they swung their hips and kicked their legs. The men wore red berets, white shirts, and white pants accented by a red sash.

In the center of the circle, young men took turns performing wild, acrobatic leaps and spins to shouts of admiration from those in the circle, as well as from the spectators. The energy and music reminded Marlene of gypsies, or some wild mountain tribe whose customs and origins were lost in the depths of time. She spotted Eugenio Santacristina standing across the hall with a group of similarly dressed men and waved when one of the men touched his shoulder and pointed to her.

Now Santacristina circled the dancers and took both of her hands in his. "It is good to see you," he said, kissing her lightly on both cheeks before turning back to the dancers. "It's called a *romeria*, a traditional Basque dance. The energetic ones in the center are the *dantzaris*. We are a dancing people; my Maria loved to dance, as did her mother. In fact, I fell in love with Elena the first time I saw her dancing."

Marlene looked up at Santacristina as he watched the dancers. His mouth was turned up in a smile, but the amber eyes were sad and lonely. And why not, she thought, he's lost the two people in the world he loved the most, both of them far too young.

When the song ended and the dancers took a break, Santacristina gently touched her arm and led her back to a room off the main hall. On the way, they passed a table around which men were smoking cigars and playing cards. They were tough-looking men, young and old alike, and dipped their heads when they saw Santacristina.

Closing the door of the room, Santacristina turned to her and said, "So, you have some news?"

"I do," she replied. Several days earlier, Fulton had been digging into Huttington's background at her request to "see if there are any reports of domestic violence toward his wife or other troubles at home."

There were no such reports. But while he was at the police department, he'd asked to see the police reports regarding any crimes around the time of Maria's disappearance. What he was looking for were such things as a rash of burglaries, or reports of a serial rapist—something that might indicate that perhaps Maria had surprised a burglar or been targeted by a sex offender. Again, the line of inquiry had come up negative, but he had discovered one unexpected bit of news.

"Two days after Maria disappeared, Huttington called the police to report that his Cadillac had been stolen," Marlene now told Santacristina. "He claimed he'd left the keys in the ignition and the car parked outside of his garage."

When Marlene called and told the same story to her husband, he'd pointed out that a possible scenario was that Maria took the car to embarrass her lover. "She might have thought that he would have had to reveal his affair with her. Then she runs into a bad guy who carjacks the Cadillac and takes her someplace to kill her."

It was a valid point, but Marlene could tell that Butch didn't believe it. He was just being his usual thorough self and trying to keep her mind open to all the possibilities. It was one of his strengths as a prosecutor.

"The majority of stolen cars eventually get found and identified by the vehicle identification number, even if they've been stripped down for parts," Marlene told Santacristina. "However, there's been a national BOLO for the Cadillac since it was reported missing, and there's been nothing. Same thing with the national crime computer concerning Maria; no one has applied for a job using her Social Security number, used her credit cards—or applied for others—no one has been pulled over for a traffic infraction or showed up at a hospital fitting her description or matching her fingerprints. It's the lack of anything at all that indicates to me, and Detective Fulton, that the missing car and your missing daughter are connected."

As she talked, Santacristina had walked over to the window, where snowflakes were fluttering against the pane like moths trying to reach the light inside. "Maria would not take his car, not even to embarrass him," he said. "She did not run away and leave me and her friends, and her cat, to wonder what had happened." He tapped on the window. "She is still out there somewhere, waiting for me to find her and lay her to rest next to her mother."

Even though Santacristina had his back to her, Marlene knew he was crying again. Her eyes were filled with tears also when she walked up and placed a hand on his shoulder. "We'll find her, Eugenio. Somehow, we'll bring her home to you."

Santacristina hung his head and then turned to her. "Marlene, I have to tell you something, something about my past. It is a hard thing, but you need to know before you continue helping me."

"You don't have to tell me anything, Eugenio," Marlene interrupted. "I have far too many skeletons in my closet for me to be passing judgment on anybody else. I think I understand the character of the man you are."

But Santacristina clapped his hands on Marlene's shoulders,

guided her to a chair, and made her sit. "You are a true friend," he said. "But I need to get this off my chest, or I cannot allow you to go any further."

Marlene started to protest but saw the look on his face and closed her mouth. "I'm listening," she said.

"Good. To start, my name is not Eugenio Santacristina," he began. "My name is Jose Luis Arregi Katarain, and I am not who I pretend to be—a simple shepherd with an immigration problem, although that is what Barnhill believes. The real reason why I avoid stirring up too much attention, even with my beloved daughter missing, is that I am wanted by the government of Spain and have been for more than twenty years."

As a young man, he'd joined a Basque separatist organization known as the ETA. "For Euskadi ta Askatasuna, which means 'Basque Fatherland and Liberty.' I don't know how much you know of our history, but culturally and linguistically we are not Spanish, though we have always lived in the mountains between Spain and France."

Basques had dreamed for a long time of an autonomous country of their own and hoped they might get it when they fought on the side of the Spanish Republic during the Spanish Civil War prior to the outbreak of World War Two. The enemy was the fascist forces led by Generalissimo Francisco Franco, and the Basques felt that right was on their side. However, the Basques and the Republic went down in flames when Hitler's Nazi Germany came to the aid of Franco, using his enemies' cities for trial runs of the Nazis' technologically superior weaponry.

After World War Two, Franco, who when he saw the way the tide was turning had declared Spain to be neutral, was kept in power by the governments of the United States and western Europe. They appreciated his strong anticommunist sentiments and were willing to overlook his early alliance with Nazi Germany.

For his part, Franco never forgave the Basques for opposing him and suppressed, often violently, any public expressions of Basque culture or nationalism, including outlawing the display of the Basque flag. "We were forbidden to speak our language in public or teach it to our children in our schools. Our children had to be baptized with Spanish names only. Those who protested were arrested and disappeared into the dungeons of Franco's secret police, and often never seen again."

The ETA had been created in 1959 by young student activists as a discussion group seeking ways to promote Basque traditions despite the oppression. But the discussion groups soon evolved into a Basque nationalist movement; then when Spanish forces reacted violently, it became an armed rebellion.

"My father was a professor at the university in Navarre, a Basque state," Santacristina said. "He was convinced that with a reasoned, pacifist approach, the world would see that the Basques deserved a homeland of their own. He wrote many papers and was featured in prominent magazines. But one night, men wearing masks and uniforms kicked down the door of our house and took my father away."

As he spoke, Santacristina/Katarain had returned to the window, where he now etched a name in the frost on the pane: Luis. "His body was found the next day; he'd been shot in the mouth and left in an olive grove. The Spanish government, of course, denied any involvement. They blamed it on the ETA, saying that his peaceful nationalist views were anathema to more violent revolutionary aspirations, so his own people had killed him. But the men who kicked in our door were speaking Spanish, not Euskara. We knew better."

The year was 1971. "The same year I joined the ETA," he said, "which was portrayed by the government-controlled media as terrorists, responsible for bombings and assassinations."

"Were you?" Marlene asked.

The man she had known as Eugenio Santacristina shrugged. "One man's terrorist is another man's patriot. I will say that unlike the Franco government, which made war on women and children and university professors who dared to write papers, our targets in those days were the army, government officials, and the national

police, which unlike the FBI in this country was a paramilitary organization that carried out attacks on civilians."

Katarain pointed to the scar at his hairline. "I received this because I was clinging to my father's leg, begging them not to take
him. But certainly the violence went both ways. It was an unde-
clared war—the ETA against Spain and its fascist dictator."

The war heated up when a dozen Basque *independentistas* were
executed by a government-sponsored death squad. In retaliation,
the ETA had assassinated Admiral Luis Carrero Blanco, who was
Franco's heir apparent and the man behind the secret war against
the Basques.

"Ironically, when Franco died a short time later, he had no one
to replace him as dictator," Katarain said. "So he handed back the
government to the monarchy, which in turn created a democracy in
Spain. It was so ironic. There we were, trying to win our freedom
from what we considered a foreign power, much as you Americans
did from the British, and we handed freedom to the Spanish people, who despised us."

The advent of democracy did nothing for the Basque cause. By
the 1980s, the war was becoming more vicious, especially with the
creation of Grupos Antiterroristas de Liberacion, or "Antiterrorist
Liberation Groups, also called GAL." The group was sponsored
and protected by the Spanish government as a supposedly coun-
terterrorist organization.

"They were capitalizing on concerns in the United States and
western Europe with the growth of terrorism," Katarain said. "By
lumping us in with Islamic extremists, and even the IRA, they were
actually encouraged to carry out a program of assassinations, kid-
nappings, torture, and murder against suspected ETA members.
Many of their victims did not belong to the organization, but it was
enough just to be suspected."

Katarain sighed and traced a heart on the pane next to Luis. "By
this time, I was in my thirties and tired of all the bloodshed. I
wanted a life and the cause of Basque freedom seemed as remote
as ever. But then the GAL arrested my younger brother and his

pregnant wife, who were betrayed by a coward. He told the death squads that they could be used to get to me."

Bowing his head, Katarain continued. "I was supposed to get the message that if I gave myself to the GAL, they would be freed. I would have done it, but I was hiding in the mountains and did not hear about the offer until it was too late. When we found them in the same field where my father's body had been dumped, they were dead—tortured first and then nearly decapitated with piano wire."

Katarain buried his face in his hands and groaned as if reliving the discovery of the bodies of his brother and sister-in-law. "They called us terrorists," he said, "because we wanted to speak our own language and enjoy our culture and have our own country. Of course, when it is the government committing the crimes, it is not terrorism, it is 'national security.' "

Katarain found the traitor who had betrayed him and strapped him into a vest bomb filled with nails and dynamite. "I sent him to the local police station where the GAL was holding their meeting."

"Why would he agree to go?" Marlene asked.

"Because I had a gun pressed up against the forehead of his five-year-old son," Katarain replied bitterly. "I told him that if he did not go, I would shoot the boy and leave him in the same field where they left my brother and his wife."

"I don't believe it," Marlene said. "You would never harm a child."

"We will never know, Marlene," he replied. "You do not know the anger and the hatred that burned inside of me, but I did not have to find out if I was capable of such a thing. It was enough that the betrayer believed my threat and walked into the police station and detonated the bomb. I returned the boy to his mother and left again for the mountains."

It had not taken long for the Spanish national police to figure out who had put the traitor up to the bombing, and the price was increased for the capture of Jose Luis Arregi Katarain. But friends helped him escape in 1985 to the United States, where he made his way to Idaho to lose himself in the largest Basque community outside of their homeland.

"I became a shepherd, and as I walked through the beautiful mountains that reminded me so much of home, gradually my anger began to subside," Katarain said. "Then came the day when I saw Elena dancing a *romeria* and fell in love. And when Maria was born, I was sure that I was done with all violence. But now . . . now that she's been murdered by a man who used her like a whore and cast her aside, I burn with hatred and anger again. I could easily kill him."

Katarain's shoulders slumped. He reached into his shirt pocket and pulled out a pack of cigarettes. "Do you mind?"

Marlene shook her head. "No, in fact I'll take one myself if you have a spare."

Shaking a cigarette out of the pack for Marlene, he lit it for her, then lit one for himself. "So now you have heard my story and understand why I am reluctant to press the authorities about Huttington and my daughter," he said. "But it's not because I'm a coward. If I thought that it would help find my Maria, I would do it. But all it would accomplish is my extradition to Spain and no justice for my angel."

Katarain stopped talking and inhaled deeply off the cigarette. He looked up at Marlene, ready to accept whatever accusation he thought he would find in her eyes. "I would not blame you if you walk away from this now and turn me in to the authorities. But I ask one thing and that is you wait until I have brought Maria home to her mother."

Marlene looked back at Katarain and thought about his comment regarding how thin the line was between a patriot and a terrorist. He may have killed men who had nothing to do with his father's death or that of his brother and sister-in-law. Perhaps some innocent father had not gone home to his children that evening. But she could not condemn him.

"As I said before, I'm in no position to judge you," she replied at last. "It's not for me to turn you in. In the meantime, we have a child to bring home to her mother and justice for a loving father and, I believe, a good man."

Katarain passed a sleeve across his eyes and held out his hand for her to shake. "When Elena died, I cursed God," he said. "And when Maria was taken from me, I doubted that God existed, unless as an angry deity punishing me for the sins of my past. But now I believe that God led me to you. When I leave here, I will return to church for the first time in a long while. And there I will light a candle and on my knees thank Him for you."

Marlene smiled and was about to hug him when something started to buzz in her coat. "Sorry, forgot to turn off the cell phone," she said.

"Go ahead," he nodded. "I'll finish my cigarette."

Marlene looked at the caller ID on her phone and smiled. "Why, hello, Clay Fulton, how's things?" Listening to his reply, she said, "Have you told Butch? No? Why, I'm flattered. What's that? I shouldn't be . . . it's too late to call New York? Well, he's probably asleep, but I'm sure he'll be delighted to hear from you in the morning. Nice work, Clay, you are the very best detective there ever was."

Flipping the phone closed, Marlene was lost in thought until Katarain spoke.

"Something wrong?" he asked.

Marlene shook her head. "Well, no, actually something's right," she said. "It has to do with Butch's case. That was Detective Fulton, who just met with a couple of very important witnesses." She walked over and, standing on her tiptoes, kissed Katarain on the cheek.

"I have to run," she said. "And I may not be back for a few days. But promise me you won't tell anybody about Huttington's Cadillac and especially that you won't try to go after Huttington. We're going to do this the right way. Agreed?"

Katarain didn't answer. From her own violent past, she knew what emotions were broiling beneath the surface. She grabbed his hand and looked him in the eyes. "Eugenio Jose Luis Arregi

Katarain Santacristina, I am asking you for the sake of our friendship and respect for the trust I've placed in you. You cannot go after Huttington. Butch may need him at the trial, and revenge is not the same as justice."

The Basque bit his lip and looked at her. His amber eyes were hard and angry, but after a moment, they softened, and he squeezed her hand. "I promise to wait. But if there is no justice for Maria in the courtroom, then all bets—as you Americans like to say—are off."

19

THE SUN WAS RISING ABOVE THE COAST RANGE TO THE EAST, casting a golden glow across the Pacific Ocean off the Oregon shore. Marlene fixed the pair of binoculars on the surfers who were sitting on their boards a hundred yards away, waiting for the next set of waves. Two began paddling fast when an eight-foot swell rushed in from the west.

Picking up speed down the face of the wave, the faster of the two popped up into a wide stance while the other gave up. Marlene focused on the rider. Definitely a woman. Although she only caught a glimpse of the surfer's face as she finished her ride and began to paddle back out to the lineup, Marlene was pretty sure that she had found who she was looking for: Maly Laska.

"She'll be the only girl out there," her roommate had said. "The currents are pretty strong right now and the swells are big—you have to be ready to play with the big boys . . . or not give a shit what happens to you if you mess up. She's a little of both."

When Fulton called her at the Basque Cultural Center and told her what he'd learned, Marlene knew that she needed to find Laska, the young woman who claimed Rufus Porter raped her. It had taken a week of digging, but she'd located the girl's parents in

Huntington Beach, south of Los Angeles. They'd only just moved there and had been reluctant to say anything until Marlene convinced them that she worked for the good guys. Even then, all they would admit to was that she had moved away months ago. "She's scared and just wants to forget about the whole thing," her mother said. "I wish you people would leave her alone."

Marlene put herself in the young woman's shoes. You've just been raped, reported it to the police and gone through that humiliation, only for the justice system to fail you miserably. Then something happens—a threat?—so you pack up your bags overnight and hightail it home to Mom and Dad. But you're still afraid enough that you don't stay. Where do you go?

The question bothered Marlene for several days until she woke up next to Butch, who'd flown in to begin preparing in earnest with Meyers, at O'Toole's house in Idaho after a restless night. Come on, Marlene, she was originally from San Diego, so you're a beach-girl surfer type who goes to school in Idaho. You're outdoorsy. You go home to your parents, who live in Huntington Beach, but it's not safe for you or them . . . so . . . ? Sooooo . . . you return to the ocean and find someplace "safe" to surf.

Of course, that only left a couple thousand miles to search—just counting the West Coast—but it gave Marlene someplace to look. She began by doing database searches of library systems in California, Oregon, and Washington. That turned up a few hits for M. Laska, Mollie Laska, and one Maly Laska living in Lincoln City, Oregon. A quick check of the Lincoln City chamber of commerce website indicated that the town was promoting itself as a "little known but definitely on the rise" spot for surfing.

Two hours later, Marlene was on a flight to Portland, Oregon, where she rented a car and drove to Lincoln City. It was night when she arrived, so she'd waited until morning to head out. The library entry had provided a street address, which led to a pretty little cottage on the cliff above the beach just south of Lincoln City.

The roommate had answered the knock on the door. Marlene identified herself as representing Dan Zook, the prosecutor in Sawtooth, which she'd okayed with him before leaving. "I just need to ask her a few questions."

At first the roommate denied knowing any Maly Laska. But Marlene had pointed out that the broken-down VW bus in the driveway was registered to Maly, a fact she'd been able to ascertain by getting Fulton to call the Oregon Department of Motor Vehicles before she approached the house. "So what," the roommate said, and began to close the door.

Placing her hand on the door to keep it open, Marlene said, "Look, I don't want to hurt her or put her through any more than she's already been through. But you know and I know, and Maly knows, that guys like Rufus Porter will just keep doing what he did to her until somebody stands up and puts his ass in prison. I know she's scared. I'm sure she's been threatened. And if she wants me to go away, I will and I'll forget I ever knew where she lives. But I've got other people I'm worried about right now, too—an innocent man who is having his life destroyed by Porter's lies, and a father who's looking for a daughter who disappeared and thinks—however remote the chance is—that somehow this is all connected."

The roommate looked at her and seemed to be debating in her mind before she bowed her head and nodded. "We heard from Maly's folks that you might be up this way," she said. "You might as well come in."

As Marlene entered, she saw the roommate put a handgun back into a drawer of the stand next to the door. The other woman noticed the look and said, "I keep this here, hoping that asshole Porter shows up looking for her someday. I'm going to let him in the door just to make it legal in terms of the 'make my day' law, and then I'm going to shoot him in the balls and watch him die slow."

They'd talked for a few minutes, and then the roommate told her where to look for Maly at the beach several miles north of Lincoln City called Cascade Head. "She usually surfs until about nine. Then she has to come back and get ready for work at a local restaurant."

An hour later, after spotting Maly out on the water, Marlene took off her shoes and went for a walk along the beach. That way she could enjoy the morning and keep an eye on her subject without raising suspicions until Maly stopped surfing.

Marlene picked up a rock and skipped it out toward the breaking waves. It reminded her of days she spent with her father as a young girl, skipping stones into the water at Coney Island. He was at a difficult stage in life now—suffering from dementia and mourning the loss of his wife, Marlene's mother, Concetta. She was still lost in thought, skipping stones an hour later, when she noticed that Laska had caught one last wave in and was paddling to the shore. The young woman reached the beach, picked up her board under one arm, and began crossing the sand on muscular legs to the parking lot. There she rinsed under an outdoor faucet, unzipping her wet suit to reveal a tan, athletic body.

Marlene moved to intercept the girl as she picked up her board again and started to walk toward the highway leading back to Lincoln City. As she approached, the girl gave her a glance and then slowed her pace, as if trying to decide whether to continue on or run back to the water.

"Maly Laska?" Marlene asked as she caught up.

"Don't know her," the young woman replied, and picked up her pace again.

Marlene had to run to keep up. "I'm sorry, I know who you are, but I'm not here to hurt you or give away your hiding place—though to be honest, anyone with a computer could find you if they wanted."

The young woman stopped and studied Marlene with eyes dark green like the ocean she'd just come from. "You with the District Attorney's Office in Sawtooth?" she asked angrily. "I told them I was done with it. I will not press charges and if I'm subpoenaed, I won't show."

"I can appreciate that," Marlene replied. "And no, I'm not with the District Attorney's Office, though he's given me permission to say that I am. I am working with the father of a young woman who disappeared several months before you were raped. He thinks that all of this—her disappearance, the rape, and a case my husband is working on to try to salvage the life of the university baseball coach—is connected through Rufus Porter."

At the mention of the young woman who disappeared, Laska had hung her head. But at the mention of Rufus Porter, she started marching off toward the highway again. "I don't know anything about it," she said. "And if I never hear about Idaho again, it will be too soon. Now, if you don't mind, I need to hitch a ride back to town so I can go to work."

"How about I give you a ride back?" Marlene asked. "Saves you the trouble, I get to ask you a couple of questions; I'll drop you off at your house and then drive off into the sunset, you'll never see me again."

Marlene's rapid-fire speech brought a partial smile to Laska's lips. She looked down the highway. There were no cars in sight. "It can be a pretty tough time of year for hitchhiking," she conceded. "All the tourists are gone. . . . Okay, you get to ask a few questions, I'll decide how to answer them, but then you leave me alone and forget you ever found me. Deal?"

"Deal."

The two women walked to the truck Marlene had rented. Stowing the board in the back, they got in and buckled up, and Marlene asked, "Does the name Maria Santacristina sound familiar?"

Laska looked out the window toward the ocean and didn't look back when she answered. "She was the girl who disappeared. I remember the newspaper stories that she was missing, but there wasn't much else. I didn't know her."

Marlene could almost feel the tension in the girl. "Why are you living here in Lincoln City? I mean, didn't you leave the beach to live in the Rocky Mountains?"

Laska half laughed and half snorted. "I went to Idaho because I knew that if I stayed in SoCal to go to school, or anywhere with an ocean and waves for that matter, I'd never go to class," she said. "So I chose the middle of the country. And I loved it. I was getting into snowboarding and backpacking."

"Then why back to the ocean?"

Laska sighed. "Because after what happened, I felt dirty all the time." The young woman's voice grew strained as she struggled to hold it together. "Only the ocean makes me feel clean. If I could, I'd stay in the water all of the time."

"Does it work?" Marlene asked.

"When I'm surfing, nothing else matters," Laska replied. "It's me, the waves, and my friends. I feel strong and good about myself. But at night, I still have to live with the memory and by morning I just feel dirty again."

"Do you have a boyfriend?"

Laska shook her head. "I was always a little shy around boys. Strange, huh, for a California beach girl. Anyway, I wanted the husband, kids, white picket fence—the whole enchilada. But now I really don't trust men, except my surfing buddies, and I'm just one of the guys to them."

Marlene turned off the highway and down the sandy road leading to Laska's house. It was now or never with the tough questions. "Why did you refuse to go forward with the charges against Porter?"

Laska was growing antsy as the ride drew near its end. "I didn't want to go through with the crap of a trial," she said. "It was all falling apart anyway—the evidence disappearing, people changing their stories, and then . . . well, and then it just wasn't worth it."

"Wasn't worth it? He raped you, didn't he?"

The young woman looked out at the ocean, her hand on the door handle as if she just wanted to get out and into the water. "Yes," she whispered at last. "He raped me."

"And you are going to let him get away with it?"

Angry again, Laska turned to face Marlene. "It's done. I just want to go on with my life and hope that someday I can forget. Going back to Idaho won't make it better."

Marlene ached for the girl, but she pushed on anyway. "What about the next girl he rapes, or maybe worse, if Maria Santacristina is also a victim?"

"And what about the protection I needed and didn't get," Laska shot back. "I'm sorry about whatever happened to Maria, but I have a life, too, and parents who have been threatened. Porter's crowd are not nice people."

"All the more reason to put him away," Marlene said as she pulled into the driveway of Laska's house.

Laska reached for the door handle. "I'm sorry. I'm scared and I want nothing to do with this anymore."

Marlene reached out and put a hand on Laska's arm. "Please, I'm not asking you to come back, but if there's anything you can tell me about Porter or what happened after you reported the rape, maybe it would help. Please, Maly . . . Maria's father sets a place for her at his table every night, and every morning he puts it back away until the next night. He's left her bedroom the way it was when she was a child. He can't move on until he finds her."

Laska pulled her arm away. Tears were streaming down her face as she jumped out of the truck and walked to the back to get her surfboard. She got halfway to the house before she stopped and looked up at the sky. Without turning, she said, "Wait here a minute," then walked swiftly to the house, leaned the surfboard next to the door, and went in.

Five minutes passed and Marlene was beginning to wonder if Laska was going to return when she came out of the cottage carrying an envelope. She walked around to the driver's side of the truck.

"This was sent to me after the evidence 'disappeared' from the police station," Laska said, and handed the envelope to Marlene. "Go ahead, open it."

Inside was a piece of white paper with a single typed line and a photograph. "Leave now or take a last ride," Marlene said, reading the paper. She set it aside carefully in order not to disturb any latent fingerprints and looked at the photograph beneath it. When she looked up again at Laska, her eyes glittered with rage. "Can I make a copy?"

Laska shook her head. "Take it, it's yours," she said. "I hope it helps. But either way, I'm done, okay? If you come back here again, I won't be here. And this time I'm going to be a lot harder to find."

"I understand," Marlene said. "I won't try to find you again." She looked out at the glimmering ocean. "I hope you find peace out there."

Laska nodded and smiled grimly. "Thanks. Me, too, if it's possible."

20

MARLENE GASPED AS SHE STEPPED OUTSIDE THE SLIDING glass doors at Denver International Airport. The pilot had warned his passengers that the temperature on that Sunday in early March was "a balmy ten degrees below zero; button up." But looking at the bright blue skies and sun-drenched peaks beyond the windows had convinced her that the pilot was mistaken.

He wasn't. Pulling the edges of her coat around her cheeks, she was convinced that the exposed parts of her face were already frostbitten when an old Lincoln Continental pulled alongside the curb and honked. The driver's-side door opened and a round-faced man with a full white beard poked his head above the roof.

"Hop in, you must be freezing . . . unusual for the second week of March," he said, running around to the trunk and depositing her suitcase. "Sorry, can only offer you the backseat, my wife Connie's riding shotgun with me today. I wanted you two to meet so that she can see that you're way above my speed and can quit accusing me of having an affair whenever I run off to see you about a case."

Marlene laughed, climbed into the backseat, and introduced herself to the tall, angular woman sitting in the front passenger seat. "He's quite right," Connie Swanburg said. "Now that I see you, I know there's no way in hell you'd have anything to do with him." She leaned closer to Marlene and whispered, "Not that I would ever believe it anyway, but it does his ego good to play like I'm jealous every once in a while."

"What's that, dear?" Jack Swanburg asked as he plopped his round body into the driver's seat.

"Nothing, Jackie, old boy," Connie replied, winking at Marlene. "Just a little girl talk."

Heading west from the airport toward Denver, Jack Swanburg explained that they were meeting in a room at the Douglas County Sheriff's Office with the 221B Baker Street Irregulars. "We've helped with a couple of their cases, so the sheriff allows us to use the room," he explained. "One of your gal pals will be there. Charlotte Gates flew in from Albuquerque, and I hear there may be a couple more surprises."

"That's great," Marlene said admiring the view of the mountains just to the west with the sun glistening off the snow on the peaks. She liked Gates, who was the first of the 221B Baker Street Irregulars she'd met.

The Irregulars were an eclectic mix of scientists and cops, many of them retired, who had formed the group more than ten years earlier for the purpose of combining their skills and specialized knowledge to locate the clandestine graves of murder victims. Since the early days when law enforcement agencies had been leery of these "amateur detectives," they'd gained a reputation by performing as promised until their assistance was sought by agencies all over the world. Their methods ranged from ground-penetrating radar to forensic botany and bloodhounds, plus a healthy dose of deductive reasoning made famous by their hero, the fictional detective Sherlock Holmes, who, according to Sir Arthur Conan Doyle, had lived at 221b Baker Street in London.

Marlene had met Charlotte Gates, a forensic anthropologist from the University of New Mexico and director of the Forensic Human Identification Laboratory in Albuquerque, in New Mexico. John Jojola had asked for the professor's help locating and exhuming the hidden graves of Taos Indian boys murdered by the priest Hans Lichner. That was the same time that Marlene and Lucy had met Jojola, who Marlene had assisted in solving the crimes, and he'd thereafter been swept up in the Karp-Ciampi cyclone, as had the 221B Baker Street Irregulars.

After getting the photograph from Maly Laska, Marlene had immediately called Swanburg, who was the president of the group, and asked for their help in finding Maria Santacristina. He'd asked a few preliminary questions, and then asked how fast she needed the Irregulars to get to work.

"Boy, that's fast," he'd said. "But come to Denver, talk to the gang, and let's see what can be done."

Swanburg reached Interstate 25 and turned south toward Douglas County, a rural but rapidly developing area on the tail end of Denver. As they hit the interstate, they passed a big amusement park that appeared to be closed for the winter. When she saw the bright red Ferris wheel, Marlene thought again about her father, Mario, and in particular about a day trip she'd taken the past fall to Coney Island with him.

In the intensity of the search for Kane and the hostage crisis at St. Patrick's, followed by Rachman shooting Butch, she'd had a tough time getting over to see her dad, who was living alone in Queens. Knowing he'd be even less forgiving on the telephone, she'd just gone over to see him and realized that she'd indeed been gone too long when she saw the state of his yard.

All of the many decades they'd lived there and raised a family, Mario and Concetta Ciampi had always been very conscientious about their yard. They had a system, he said. He took care of the lawn and trees; she was in charge of the flower beds. Now it looked like a house where, as he liked to complain, "nobody cares about nothing."

The yard was covered with unraked leaves from the previous fall, and the flower beds and lawn were overgrown, dried up, and brown, even though the neighbors' neatly kept yards were beginning to show hints of green. The neighborhood was once again becoming popular with young families, who exhibited pride of ownership—like her parents once had—and, she imagined, probably looked at the Ciampi house with disdain.

Inside, the house was in even worse shape, with stacks of unwashed dishes in the sink and lying around the kitchen and living room. It also smelled like he hadn't opened a window all winter or taken out the trash regularly. Even the odor of his pipe, which she'd loved as a child, now clung like a stale gray fungus to the walls, furniture, and drapes.

She found him sitting in his favorite chair in the living room with the curtains drawn, watching a rerun of a college basketball game in a stained bathrobe and his underwear. He had a beer in one hand and a bag of Doritos in the other.

"Geez, Pops, do you think you could clean up every once in a while?" Marlene said. She meant it to come out lighter than it did, but the Catholic guilt trip was washing over her in waves and she was feeling a little stressed out.

"Why? It's not like I have company coming over," he replied sarcastically. "And your mother doesn't mind."

The criticism stung Marlene and the comment worried her. Mario was convinced that her mother's soul was trapped in the house, waiting for him to join her before she "went to heaven."

It was one of the reasons he resisted her suggestion that he move into an assisted-living community. He was showing early signs of senior dementia—not as debilitating as her mother's Alzheimer's had been, but enough that she worried about him hurting himself. But every time she brought up the topic of "the nicest community near the beach on Long Island," he'd reacted angrily, and so far she'd left him where he was.

The dementia, which seemed to come and go like the tide, frightened her. By the end, her mother had not remembered Marlene's name and suspected that the "real Mario" had been replaced with an imposter. It was horrible to watch a woman who had always been so strong—the real rock of the family—leave her mind before she left her body.

The thought made Marlene feel even guiltier because she hoped that she wouldn't have to witness the same progression with her father. It would mean an extra visit to the confession booth and yet another promise to be a better daughter.

Determined to start right then and there, Marlene made him get dressed, which he'd done only with a great deal of grumbling. Prying him out of the house, she'd driven to Coney Island for a hot dog at Nathan's. Munching the dogs—which he'd said "are nothing compared to when we used to come here"—they'd strolled down the boardwalk and stopped in front of the Coney Island amusement park, which was also closed for the season.

The sea air and hot dogs had a marvelous effect on Mario's disposition. He pointed at the Ferris wheel with a big grin. "You remember when you and your mother and I would come here?"

"Yeah, Pops, I remember," she said. "I asked you what would happen if the Ferris wheel came off and started to roll to the ocean, and you said, 'Why, it will keep going all the way to France, where they'll pin it to the side of the Eiffel Tower like a giant pinwheel.'"

Mario laughed. "You believed me and demanded to ride over and over again, hoping it would roll to the sea. Finally, they were closing the park and we had to leave, which was a good thing because your mother and I were sick to our stomachs from so many rides. But you were so mad when I pulled you out of the seat that you kicked me in the shins."

"And Mom said you deserved it for telling me such lies," Marlene said, giggling.

Mario gazed a moment longer at the Ferris wheel, then sighed. "Those were great days, eh, Marlene," he said. "Your mother was so young and beautiful. She stayed so beautiful . . . though not so young, I have to say."

Marlene had nestled up against him as he put one of his thin arms around her shoulders. "I miss her so much," he said. "I am not afraid to die. In fact, I look forward to it so I can see her again."

"I miss her, too, Pops," Marlene replied. She felt for just a moment what it was going to be like when he was gone, too, and vowed again to make the effort to see him more often, and bring her kids.

Fifteen hundred miles away, Swanburg was asking her a question for a second time. "How's Butch?"

"Oh, um, great," she stammered. "He still needs to take it easy, but he's recovering and antsy to get back to the DAO."

Swanburg shook his head. "Man, he was lucky that bullet in his neck stopped short of killing him."

"Nonsense, no luck at all," Connie said. "It was the will of God. Don't you think, Marlene?"

Marlene thought about how to answer. Her relationship with God had been improving of late, but it had taken a long downward turn before that and recovery was a long, slow process. She guessed that her current religiosity encompassed the reassuring rituals of the Catholic Church, but with a strong affinity for the nature-based spirituality of John Jojola. "I think that is as good a reason as any," she replied.

"Balderdash!" Swanburg replied. "As a scientist, it's as simple as somebody messed up—fortunately, I might add—at the bullet plant. It's nothing more than an equation: not enough force to move a certain amount of mass at a sufficient rate of speed to kill the man. Sorry, Marlene, your man was saved by physics, not mythology."

"How do you know that God didn't cause the machine at the plant to malfunction?" Connie countered.

"And that one very special bullet happened to end up in the clip of the assassin's gun in just the right order so that it would be the projectile that struck Butch in the neck, and not the one that passed through his leg?" Swanburg turned so that Marlene could see his face and rolled his eyes.

"God would know, he knows everything, that's what makes Him God instead of you, Jack Swanburg, and don't you dare roll those eyes again or I'll poke 'em out."

"Well, then, why not just stick out a big God finger and slow a sufficiently charged bullet?" Swanburg scoffed. "Why go through all that trouble starting at the plant and then selecting the correct bullet when the gun was being loaded?"

"My point exactly," Connie announced triumphantly. "God

didn't need to cause the machine at the manufacturer to malfunction. Not unless that was part of the plan. But God works in mysterious ways, so who knows?"

"Ay-yai-yai," Swanburg cried out, wiping a plump hand over his hairy face. "See what sort of witchcraft and bah humbug I have to live with, Marlene?"

"For nearly fifty years, you old egghead," Connie retorted. "And I'm still trying to save your soul so that we can spend eternity together. . . . What was that? Are you mumbling something under your breath again, Jack Swanburg?"

"No, my sweet," Jack replied innocently. "If converting to the Roman Catholic Church would assure me a spot next to you for all of time, I would confess my sins and, after I finished sometime in the next month, prostrate myself to the Holy See and become one of the pontiff's pious patrons. However, I am not yet convinced, though you are welcome to keep trying."

"And you better believe I will," Connie replied.

Marlene laughed, and when both Swanburgs turned with question marks on their faces, she explained. "Now I know how Butch and I sound when we're together."

Dropping Connie off at a local shopping mall—"I have no interest in Jack's macabre hobby, however noble it might be"—the other two continued to the Douglas County Sheriff's Office. Pulling into the nearly empty parking lot, Marlene smiled when she saw the truck with the New Mexico license plate.

Lucy and Ned made it, she thought. She hadn't seen her daughter since Christmas. She hoped that she'd be able to convince Lucy to return to Idaho with her so they could spend a little time together. Ned, too, if he wants, she thought. Can't imagine what cowboys do in the winter.

The young couple was waiting for her inside the lobby of the Douglas County Courthouse. Lucy was immediately in her arms for the enthusiastic hug that she'd demanded from her mother when she was a little girl but had seemed to not want anymore—until they'd traveled to New Mexico nearly two years earlier and reestablished their bond. She was hoping for a similar road trip, and if Ned had to get back to the ranch, she was prepared to rent a car and drive to Idaho.

Marlene was pleasantly surprised at how good Lucy looked. When she left New York, her daughter looked like a young woman who'd been crying and not sleeping for two weeks. But leave it to her cowboy and the New Mexican air to revive her spirits and console her. Grateful that he was so dedicated to Lucy, Marlene hugged Ned extra hard, which sent him into his usual shy mode, with red face and hands jammed in his pockets as he rocked back and forth on the heels of his cowboy boots.

When Marlene asked Lucy if she could meet in Denver, the idea had been to spend some time with her and maybe talk her into the road trip. Marlene hadn't encouraged her to come to the meeting with the 221b Baker Street Irregulars. Lucy had experienced enough of the dark side of human nature, she didn't need any more, Marlene thought.

However, ever since Christmas, when Marlene had talked about the man she knew then as Eugenio Santacristina, Lucy had been asking a lot of questions about the case. She seemed particularly interested in the fact that Santacristina was Basque.

When Marlene told her about the photograph handed to her by Maly Laska, Lucy had insisted on attending the meeting. "I don't want to explain it now, Mom, but I need to be there," she said. "I'm *supposed* to be there." And she was going to bring Ned if he could get off work.

There was no use trying to talk her out of it, either. Lucy could be as strong-willed as both of her parents, especially if she was convinced that God was directing her actions. Plus, Marlene didn't feel like getting cussed out in a few dozen different languages.

Marlene handed the envelope with the photograph to Jack Swanburg, who took one look at it and headed down the hall "to make a digital copy so that I can project it on the screen in the meeting room. You go on in and say hi to the folks you know and introduce yourself to those you don't."

The first person Marlene saw when she entered the room was

Charlotte Gates, a petite but athletic-looking woman in her fifties with a face tanned to the color of mahogany by decades spent in the blazing sun of the American Southwest. With her opal eyes sparkling, Gates jumped up from her seat and ran up to Marlene for a Lucy-like hug.

Next in line to greet her was Tom Warren, a bloodhound handler she'd met before. He was a sheriff's deputy by day, whose dogs were renowned for finding human beings living and dead. "Hey, Marlene," he called out from the other side of the room. "The gang says hi—Buck, Little Sam, Annie, Ollie, and Wink."

There were also two new faces. One was Jesse Adare, a boyish-looking crime scene technician with a local police department, but his specialty contribution to the Baker Street Irregulars was as an aerial photography buff. As he explained, he used model airplanes—some with wingspans of eight feet—mounted with cameras, or infrared sensing gear, and even a system that could take what the camera lens saw and in real time create a three-dimensional contour map.

The other new face belonged to geologist James Reedy. With his grizzled salt-and-pepper beard and perpetually sunburned face, he looked more like an old-time prospector than a professor of geology at nearby Colorado School of Mines.

"Look out for that one," Gates said, pointing to Reedy. "He looks harmless enough, at least when he's had a bath after a week or so in the desert looking at rocks. But he's one of the practical jokers of this bunch. Nothing's safe or sacred."

Reedy narrowed his eyes. "I'll get you for that one, Gates," he sneered. "Would you prefer short sheets or a rattlesnake in your sleeping bag?"

"You forget, James," Gates growled back. "I know places where not even this macabre group could ever find you, not that they'd try."

When Swanburg returned to the room, he asked Marlene to stand "and tell us a story." She'd been through the group's briefing procedures before, but it always felt like she was having to recite in front of the nuns again.

Marlene decided to start by talking about how she met Santacristina, or Katarain, rather than just jumping straight into the case. However, she left out the part about him being a fugitive from Spain.

When she was done with that part of her story, she went back and talked about the disappearance of Maria Santacristina. She then proceeded chronologically up to what she and Fulton had discovered so far, such as Huttington reporting his car stolen two days after Maria disappeared. However, she left out the photograph she'd received from Maly Laska to see how they would react to Katarain's theory that his daughter's disappearance was connected to Huttington turning on O'Toole.

"He thinks Huttington is being blackmailed," Marlene told the Irregulars. "The prosecutor—a really sharp guy named Dan Zook—is interested in the case, but doesn't think he can get an indictment without a body."

Up to that point the members of the Baker Street Irregulars had remained silent, just sitting back and listening or scribbling notes on pads of paper. But now they started to pepper her with questions.

"What, other than her father's story, do we have to indicate Maria didn't run away?" Gates asked. "It wouldn't be the first time that a young woman leaves without a trace to escape . . . possibly from sexual abuse by her father."

Marlene knew that the question would come; the Irregulars left no stone unturned in these briefings and that included asking the tough ones. But she hated hearing it.

"I'd like to say that I think I have enough of a sense of her father to know that he had a great relationship with his daughter," she replied. "But I know you guys are scientists and this is about 'just the facts.' So I wanted to give you that background. But now I want to show you a photograph I was given recently by a young woman who had accused Rufus Porter of raping her at the party that lies at the heart of the accusations against Mikey O'Toole. This photograph was sent to her with a message to get out of town or this would happen to her, too."

"You said 'had accused'?" Adare asked.

"She left after getting this photograph and now lives in hiding," Marlene replied, and told the group about what had happened in that case with the evidence and changing stories. "I believe that this photograph is the key to finding Maria and bringing justice to her and her father . . . and maybe Mikey O'Toole."

"Amen," Swanburg said, and winked at Marlene. He pressed a button on a remote control and the lights in the room went out except for the photograph that now appeared on the screen at the front of the room.

Marlene was impressed with the clarity of the digital reproduction, which had been blown up to fill the entire screen. The photograph had been taken from above and perhaps fifty feet from where four individuals, apparently all men but wearing handkerchief masks and hats pulled low over their eyes, were posing in front and somewhat to the side of a large sedan. They were dressed in matching white wifebeater undershirts with baggy jeans held up by suspenders. Three of them had their arms crossed gangster style, but the man on the left had his right arm extended and was holding up a beer as if they were tailgating at a football game.

Because the photograph was taken from some height, the group could see that a pit had been dug in front of the car, apparently by the backhoe that could be seen belching a cloud of black smoke in the background. They could not see beyond the top three feet of the pit, but it appeared to be deep.

"It would have to be deep to cover a car," James Reedy mumbled as though to himself.

"And not just any car—a 2002 or 2003 Cadillac Eldorado, I believe, though tough to be absolutely sure of the year from this angle," Adare said. Someone whistled and he mimed a little bow in his seat. "What can I say. Number two hobby after aerial photography is Caddys. I own three. A cherry 1956 Coupe DeVille. A 1985 Biarritz. And a 2004 Eldorado just about like that one. What year did you say Huttington's car was, Marlene?"

"I didn't, because I don't know," she answered. "But anybody want to place a bet on whether the one in the photograph is a match?"

"Not I," said Gates, who squinted up at the screen. "Say, Jack, can you blow up the driver's-side window area behind these nitwits?"

Swanburg did as asked, focusing on a narrow space between the bodies of two of the men and enlarging the space beyond to bring it into view. Staring out with wide, horrified eyes at the men and women sitting in the room, a young woman sat in the driver's seat, a silent plea on her lips.

"Poor girl," Gates muttered, and bowed her head as if in prayer.

"Maria Santacristina," Marlene said quietly. She had no idea how she was going to summon the emotional capital to tell the girl's father about the method of her execution. It would have been a horrible death.

"Jack, can you back up a bit and go to the right arm of the asshole holding up the bottle," Adare requested. "I think we may have what cops call an identifying mark. I'd like a better view."

Again, Swanburg fiddled with the control and zoomed in on a tattoo on the area inside the man's bicep. It looked like three interlocking triangles.

"Sort of a stylized mountain range," Swanburg ventured.

"It's called a Valknut," Lucy said quietly. "I saw one just a month ago." She explained the triskele and the relation to its distant cousin the Valknut. Then, reluctantly, she revealed her last conversation with Cian Magee and the circumstances of his death.

"Do you think this group the Sons of Man are also involved in the death of Maria Santacristina?" Gates asked incredulously. "What are the odds of that?"

"Statistically improbable," Reedy answered.

Lucy nodded. "I think so, too," she said. "Cian told me that the symbol has been appropriated by neo-Nazi and Aryan groups, and there are certainly plenty of them in Idaho. But I don't see a connection to the Sons of Man."

"Okay, that part's not important," said Swanburg. "For the purpose of this investigation, it doesn't matter who is involved at the moment, what matters to us is finding Maria's body. Otherwise, the tattoo just gives the police something to hang their hat on if we can ever accomplish our mission. So, ladies and gentlemen, any ideas on where this photograph was taken?"

"Well, that's definitely a flood basalt geological formation," Reedy said. "See that thin black layer just under the sediment on top, probably no more than four or five inches thick? That's lava, a classic low-viscosity flow."

"What else?" Swanburg asked.

"Well, I'm not the botanist here, but that appears to be a conifer forest in the distance, so if I had to hazard an educated guess as to location, this is typical of our Pacific Northwest," Reedy replied. "A couple billion years ago, there were a zillion big and little volcanoes all over that part of the continent, pumping out lava that cooled into layers like you see in the photograph. It also breaks down into a really rich soil that will support conifer forests."

"Could this be the area around Sawtooth, Idaho?" Marlene asked.

Reedy nodded. "Very likely. You see it a lot around Coeur d'Alene and this is close. We'll want to get whatever the Idaho government has for state geologic maps. They're color-coded and we'll be able to see where the lava flows were in that area to be sure, but I'd be very surprised if Sawtooth isn't sitting on top of a lava veneer."

"The area around the car looks like it could be a dry riverbed—with all those little hills and gullies and not much vegetation except over on the sides and in the distance," Gates noted.

"You could be right," Reedy acknowledged. "But right now, I'd say we're looking at a gravel pit."

Suddenly the professor jumped up out of his chair and ran up to the screen. He pointed to the far right corner of the photograph.

"Right there, Jack, blow up that corner, please!" he exclaimed. When it was done, he shouted and danced a little jig. "Holy shit!!"

"What?" the others asked in unison. They were all looking at what appeared to be a giant Erector set dinosaur. There was a long, thin neck of steel framework that ended with an enormous jawed head. That apparatus was supported by a large body made of wood and steel and appeared to be about the size of a railroad car; the whole structure was perched on massive bulldozer-like tracks.

"That there, ladies and gentlemen, is a ninety-five-ton Bucyrus steam shovel circa early 1900s," Reedy said reverently. "It took seventy-seven of those monsters and another twenty-five or so Marions to dig the Panama Canal."

"So what?" Tom Warren asked.

"So what? So what, you dog-loving SOB," the geology professor replied in mock anger. "Digging the nearly fifty miles that it took for the Panama Canal was and remains one of the largest and most difficult engineering feats ever. More than twenty-seven thousand workers died, mostly of malaria and landslides. That beautiful piece of machinery you so crudely dismissed as a 'so what' chewed through rock like a rabbit through lettuce; it literally moved mountains. There's even a rather famous photograph of Teddy Roosevelt standing on one in the Canal Zone."

"Geez, do you like anything that actually has a heartbeat?" Warren teased.

"My rock hound," Reedy replied, and winked at Marlene. "Living things are too much trouble, give me minerals, give me rocks. Now, there's stability."

The rest of the group broke into smiles at the banter. The two men were best friends and their debates, usually fueled by beers, and hip-deep fishing in a trout stream, were legendary. "Then let me amend my question to 'So what does that mean to those of us in this room and the actual task we are trying to perform?'" Warren asked.

Reedy thought about the question for a minute before answering. "Bear with my little stream of consciousness here. First, Bucyrus International still exists. They're out of Milwaukee and are, in fact, one of the world's leading manufacturers of surface mining equipment. That dinosaur on the screen was state of the art in its day and for quite some time afterward, but the company has long since moved on. I'll bet not more than a dozen of these haven't been scrapped, and I'd be amazed if half of them can still fire up. I don't know if the one in the photograph is still in operating order, but I'll bet you the folks at Bucyrus have records on where their machines ended up, and might be able to tell us if any are in the Pacific Northwest."

Swanburg beamed. "Good work, James. I assume you'll want to follow this up with Bucyrus to narrow down our search."

"My pleasure," Reedy said. "I can't wait to see that baby up close and personal."

"That's still a lot of ground to cover to look for a buried car," Gates noted. "The landscape can change, and I suspect that's particularly true in a gravel pit. If they moved that machine, it will make it more difficult to pinpoint where to dig."

The group was silent as they looked at the photograph. "You said the gravel pit might be part of a dry riverbed?" Adare asked.

"Yep, the gravel may have been deposited by an ancient river or even pushed there by glaciers," Reedy replied.

"Well, my idea is to use the dogs," Adare said. "Remember how they picked up that child's scent in the groundwater downgrade from the actual grave?"

"We've had some luck that way," Warren agreed. "But it depends what time of year we're going to be searching."

All eyes turned on Marlene. "Well, the O'Toole trial is the end of this month and if finding Maria Santacristina has a bearing on that, I'd like to have the evidence available then," she said.

"Well, that could be tough for the hounds," Warren said. "In March, at that latitude and elevation, there may be quite a bit of snow on the ground, which isn't the big problem, but frozen soil can be. As you all know, cadaver dogs are trained to hit on the scent of chemicals released by the decomposition of human cells. In the case of burials, they catch the scent as it comes up through tiny cracks in the ground. But in winter, the snow falls, then it melts, then it freezes, which makes a barrier between the scent and the dog. They might walk right over a grave and miss it."

Again the group was quiet, thinking, until Reedy spoke. "The ground is only frozen two or three feet down," he said. "Below that, the groundwater is moving downhill just like it would be on the surface. That pit would have to be what, six feet deep at least to cover that car. Which means the groundwater at the bottom and even as high as our victim is still flowing."

It looked like a lightbulb went off above Warren's head. "I see what you're getting at," he said as the smile grew on his face. "You want to try our little theory on the pipes. But we've never had the opportunity to test it and see if it works."

Reedy grinned. "No time like the present." He turned to Marlene. "So do you know of any gravel pits in that neck of the woods? It would probably be near a highway to make it easy to supply road material and sand for snowstorms to the highway department."

Marlene nodded grimly. "Oh yeah, I know where I can find a gravel pit." She turned to Lucy. "It's owned by the Unified Church of the Aryan People, which also has its compound on the premises."

"Hmm," Swanburg mused. "I don't suppose they're likely to open the gates and let us snoop about, eh?"

Marlene shook her head. "Doubt it. I think we're going to need a warrant. Like I said, the local prosecutor will cooperate, but he's going to need everything you guys can give him to go before a judge with."

"We can do that," Swanburg said. "In the meantime, we also need to brainstorm about these 'pipes' the boys are talking about, as well as what else we might need to find and excavate a Cadillac with the ground frozen solid." Noting the concerned look on Marlene's face, he quickly added, "But these are the challenges we live for."

"I have an idea about that, too," Adare said.

"So do I," Reedy chimed in. "Especially if those damn dogs could for once pull their weight in Purina and get us close."

"Watch it, Reedy, or I'll bring my new addition to the team," Warren warned. "A pit bull that will love chewing on that tough old ass of yours."

The room was soon buzzing with excited scientists running theories past one another; then Swanburg brought the side discussions to a halt. "These Unified Church folks," he said, "I take it they might react violently if the law shows up and wants to poke around on their property. I can see another Waco, Texas, or Ruby Ridge. I don't fancy getting shot. So what are we going to have for security?"

Again, Marlene felt everybody's eyes on her. "I think you're right to be concerned," she said. "These types aren't always the brightest bulbs in the lamp. And they can get pretty nasty when the government comes calling. I'm not sure if the local police can be trusted either; we have reason to believe that there may be one or two sympathetic Aryan types on the force who might give a warning. I do have another idea, but I'll need to talk it over with Zook, the prosecutor."

The meeting broke up and the group moved down the highway to a roadside grill for burgers and beer, where they regaled Marlene, Lucy, and Ned with stories of their exploits.

The first to get up to leave was Reedy. "I'll call Bucyrus when I get back from my trip, and we can talk about this other stuff," he announced.

"Where are you going?" Marlene asked.

"Actually, I'm heading to your neck of the woods, at least when you're home. I belong to a group of bagpipers called the Irish Society of County Dunbar, Denver Chapter. We're off to march with the other Sons of Ireland in the St. Patrick's Day Parade in New York."

"What did you just say?" The group turned toward the voice. Lucy was just emerging from the restroom. "I didn't quite hear that," she said.

"I was just telling your mom that I belong to an Irish bagpipers association and . . ."

"No, about the St. Patrick's Day Parade?"

"Oh, just that we're going to march with the other sons of Ireland. It's the largest St. Patrick's Day Parade in the world, you know . . ." He would have said more, but Lucy turned white and pulled her cell phone out of her purse as she left the restaurant with Ned.

"What's with her?" Reedy asked. "Did I cuss or belch without knowing?"

"No, nothing like that," Marlene said as she scrambled to collect her things. "But it looks like we may be heading back to Manhattan sooner than I expected. Thank you so much, everyone. I'll explain later, but we have to run. See you at the parade, James."

"I'll be three sheets to the wind on green beer, so I may not see you first," he shouted as she hurried away. "I'm the second guy in on the right in the second row."

Marlene disappeared out of the restaurant door, which slammed behind her. Reedy looked around at the others and shrugged. "What an odd group of people," he said.

21

IT WAS SO SIMPLE, LUCY THOUGHT AS SHE RAN OUT OF THE restaurant. "A Son of Man will march among the sons of Ireland and silence the critic for the good of us all." Of course, it has to mean the St. Patrick's Day Parade!

The line in the poem was obviously a code to proceed with a plan to march in the parade, probably mixed in with one of the legitimate Irish groups, and then . . . And then what? "Silence the critic for the good of us all"? What in the hell does that mean? They're going to kill somebody who's critical? Of what? And kill who?

Lucy called John Jojola and asked him to get in touch with Tran and meet her in Manhattan as soon as possible. "What about Jaxon?" he asked. "You going to call him or do you want me to?"

"Neither," she said. "Please don't call him, not right now. I want to talk to you about this first, but not on a cell phone; they're too easy to intercept. I read about it in *Scientific American*."

In the days following the murder of Cian Magee, Lucy had gone into a deep depression, deeper than she'd let on to her folks, and wanted to return immediately to New Mexico. She'd only agreed to stay until Christmas in the hopes that being with her family would help.

Racked by guilt, she spent hours trying to find any Cian Magee family members or friends she could for a memorial service. Of the former, there were none. And of the latter, there were three she located from a partly burned address book found in his apartment. Two of them had never met him because he didn't go out and they'd never visited his bookstore. *I only talked to him on email,* one told her. *I'm a shut-in over in Newark, and we both liked to talk about the Celts. He loved that saying by an anonymous Roman philosopher, "Celts are the men that heaven made mad, for their battles are all merry and their songs are all sad."*

I didn't know that, thank you, Lucy had said, and hung up. The depth of Cian's isolation ate at her. I should have been a better friend, she thought.

The memorial service had been a miserable affair: a cold, blustery day beneath gray skies that spit hard bits of snow that stung like sand. The only mourners present were the minister for hire, herself, her mother—who had insisted on paying so that Cian could be buried next to his parents instead of a potter's field—and Ariadne Stupenagel, who'd asked if it was okay to write the obituary.

A few days later, the reporter had followed up with a touching narrative about the life and death of Cian Magee that had woven the life of a lonely man into the question marks surrounding his murder. Stupenagel had pushed hard to get the story about why Lucy was at the Celtic bookstore when it was firebombed. But Lucy and her father had agreed with Jaxon that it was not the time for the reporter to write a story about the Sons of Man.

If they still exist, and if they are behind these events, Jaxon had said, *then we have to find out who they are and what they intend to do. We have to solve the rest of the poem's riddle, and we won't be able to do that if they think we're onto them.*

You'd think that any group that has managed to keep its presence a secret for two hundred years, which I'm having a hard time buying, her father had said, *would surely duck back down the rabbit hole before you could say Alice at the first hint of publicity.*

Right, Jaxon had agreed. *If they do exist, we need them to feel like their secret is still safe. I'm not sure how much I buy into all of this, either, but I go back to the thought I had with Cian and that is the possibility of an Isle of Man nationalist connection to the Irish Republican Army. Are you sure you don't remember the names these families adopted from the book?*

No, Lucy had said, shaking her head. *I didn't get to see that part of the book. Cian mentioned them but he was trying to save some of the story for . . . for you . . . and building the dramatic tension for me like any good Irish storyteller. . . . And then there was no time.*

Lucy had not told Jaxon everything Cian had described in the book. She didn't know why she was reluctant to do so, but she just couldn't get past the fact that he arrived at Cian's apartment only after it was too late to save him.

Back in New Mexico, she'd begun connecting dots like her father, though she wasn't aware of his notepad, and hers kept leading to a conclusion that he still refused to see and that was that Jaxon was a prime suspect. *Why would he be so anxious for me to keep quiet about the Sons of Man?* she thought. Then she'd gone to Colorado to see her mother and had been accidentally handed the answer to the riddle. The St. Patrick's Day Parade, when the Sons of Ireland marched!

Returning to New York, she felt like the coyote in a story Jojola had told her: he kept returning to the trap, knowing it was dangerous, but he just couldn't stay away "until one day, he got too close." It was a parable along the lines of curiosity killing the cat, but Lucy wondered if she or the coyote really had a choice in the matter or if it was their fate.

Two days after her return, Lucy got a call on her cell phone. She looked at the caller ID and didn't bother to answer; she knew there would be no one on the other end if she did. Instead, she waited until 7:00 p.m. and then "went for a walk" with Ned.

Leaving her twin brothers in her parents' loft on Crosby and Grand, they strolled to Canal Street, then headed east into the heart of Chinatown. Pretending to be window-shopping like tourists, they suddenly nipped into Chen's Shanghai Emporium on Baxter and walked quickly to the back of the store. The family who owned and ran the store ignored them, even when they passed the sign that read Employees Only and went into a back storage area.

Maneuvering past boxes of silk gowns and rubber-soled slippers embroidered with dragons and flowers, along with crates of "authentic" Mandarin swords and brass Buddhas, they found themselves face-to-face with an enormous Asian man. He was dressed in a bright yellow and red, flower-printed Aloha shirt and baggy jeans; the outfit didn't match his expression, which was essentially no expression at all and never changed as he opened the door to the office he was guarding and indicated they should go in.

Inside, John Jojola and Tran were playing a game of chess. Jojola had just taken Tran's queen and placed his king in checkmate, which set the volatile Vietnamese gangster into a fit of rage. "You cheat, you American pig," he said, and added a few more slurs in Vietnamese.

"You're the contents of a water buffalo's bladder," Lucy translated.

"I've been called worse," Jojola chuckled, "including by him. Now, pay up, you old scoundrel, before I call immigration and have you thrown out of the country."

Still grumbling and giving Lucy the evil eye, Tran yanked a fat wallet out of his pants pocket, plucked a dollar bill from its interior, and flung it at Jojola. "May your descendants look like apes and marry poorly because of your unnatural greed," he cursed.

Lucy hugged both of the men and nodded toward the door. "Shouldn't that guy be like all dressed in black, with his hair pulled back in a ponytail, and aviator sunglasses?"

"How cliché," Tran scoffed. "Why would I want a bodyguard who looks like a bodyguard? Nobody gives a guy in an Aloha shirt a second thought."

"They do when he's six three and weighs as much as my horse," Ned noted.

With the small talk out of the way, Lucy and Ned sat down and she told them about how she'd jumped to her conclusion about the St. Patrick's Day Parade from Reedy's comment.

"You think they might try to plant a bomb along the parade route?" Jojola asked.

"That's what I worried about first," Lucy answered. "Terrorists do seem to like these big statements these days, with lots of blood and innocent people dying. But I think this is a different sort of terrorism. More subtle. The note says, 'a son of Man will march among the sons of Ireland and silence the critic.' Sounds more like one bad guy assigned to assassinate somebody."

"Who?" Jojola asked.

"I don't know," Lucy said. "Maybe the archbishop when he's blessing the marchers. He's certainly been making statements about the war in Iraq that has some right-wingers less than happy with him."

"Are the Sons of Man right-wingers?" Ned asked.

"I don't know, honey," Lucy answered. "I didn't get to hear everything that's in the book. But if you consider how they were marrying into wealthy families and spreading their tentacles into banking, law, finance, the military . . . and seemed to have a thing for power, then perhaps yes, they are righties. But then again, there are lots of crazy lefties with big bucks who seek change through the barrel of a gun."

"What about the mayor?" Tran said. "He's usually at these things."

"And so is every politician running for office from fifty miles around," Lucy said. "Plus the usual assortment of presidential hopefuls and members of Congress trying to remind the public of what they look like. Pretty good pickings."

"So you want to tell me now why you aren't letting Jaxon in on this?" Jojola asked. "It was his recording, and you might just need a bit more backup than an old but virile Indian, a cowboy, and a decrepit, pajama-wearing Vietcong gangster."

"Hey, watch who you're calling decrepit," Tran growled. "But I, too, am wondering about Jaxon. He's not bad for a fed, though I never thought I'd ever say that about any FBI."

"I know this sounds insane," Lucy replied. "But I don't trust him anymore."

Getting up to pace around the room, she outlined her suspicions surrounding the bombing of the bookstore. "But it goes back further than that, and it's a pretty long list. It was his guy, Grover, who betrayed everybody and helped Kane escape. Jaxon also knew where Archbishop Fey was being kept in the Witness Protection Program. He was there at Aspen. You know, maybe he's that Jamys Kellagh guy who Stupenagel says was in a photograph with Kane, and that's why they blew up the café. And before all of that, wasn't it just so convenient that he shows up in New York to take over the antiterrorist desk in the nick of time to ride to the rescue and help stop the terrorists from blowing up Times Square?"

"That's a bad thing?" Jojola asked.

"No, not on its face. But you and David Grale were onto the plot before my dad arrived with Jaxon and his crew in tow. None of the terrorists, by the way, survived that shootout, just like none survived the fight at St. Patrick's Cathedral or when Kane got cornered at the Columbia University boat dock. Maybe Jaxon makes sure they don't so they can't talk."

"Seems like a stretch," Jojola said.

"And why would he have brought that recording to you for translation?" Tran asked. "If he belonged to this Sons of Man, wouldn't he have already known what was on it?"

"I thought a lot about that, too," Lucy admitted. "Then it came to me. What if I've been thinking about this all backward? What if it was the Sons of Man who intercepted the message from someone they were watching, and wanted to know what it said? If Jaxon worked for them, he'd know that I might be able to translate it without tipping off anybody in the FBI. Then when Cian did tell us what it said, the bad guys realized that we both had now heard the name, Sons of Man, and after Cian got the book, something about their history."

"How would they know Cian had the book?" Jojola asked.

"I called Jaxon and told him that Cian had something important to tell us about the Sons of Man," Lucy replied. "He could have put two and two together. Or he may have listened outside the window—Cian thought he heard someone out there—then made a quick decision to destroy the message and the messengers in the fire."

"I don't mean to scare you, but why haven't they tried to kill you since?" Tran pointed out.

"The book is gone and so is the only person who actually read it," Lucy answered. "I'm just a nutty twenty-one-year-old girl who comes up with this story about a secret society she can't prove exists but has something to do with a coded message in a nearly dead language. I'm sure I'll be taken seriously. And as far as Jaxon knows, I'm in New Mexico, so maybe I don't pose a threat."

Lucy hung her head. "I'm sorry," she said. "It breaks my heart, but I can't afford to trust Espey. I hope I'm wrong about him, but a lot of people have died because someone in a position of trust betrayed them and us. And all the signs point to him. I guess this puts you in a tough spot, but I didn't know where else to turn. If you don't want to get involved without him, I understand, but I have to see this through for Cian."

Ned whistled softly and shook his head. "I just can't believe that Mr. Jaxon is a traitor. Even the thought makes me sick to my stomach."

"Me, too, Ned," Jojola agreed. "And I'm not sure I buy it even now. But I have to admit, Lucy's done a pretty good job of showing that he had the opportunity and the inside knowledge to do these things."

"If it's true, this will kill my dad," Lucy said. "They've known each other since joining the DAO back around the Civil War, I think. Ever since he got back to town, Jaxon has been part of his inner circle of the guys at work. He tells them everything and trusts their opinions more than anyone else's in the world except my mom's."

"Which would put him in the perfect position," Tran said. "I'm sorry to say, but there are many reasons why a man would betray his friends and his country. Sometimes it's money or power, but not always. Sometimes the traitor sees himself as the 'good guy' who has realized that he has been on the wrong side. These are certainly strange times and it is difficult to know who is the enemy and who is the friend. If this is true, perhaps like misguided men before him, Jaxon believes that what he is doing is for the 'greater good,' which is usually a euphemism for betrayal and dictatorship."

"So we approach this problem without Jaxon," Jojola said. "What about that other dude, Jon Ellis, with Homeland Security?"

Lucy thought about it. "I don't know. I don't like him personally. But I guess we have to trust somebody who has the muscle to help."

"And your mother?" Tran asked. "She's pretty handy in a scrape."

Lucy didn't answer right away. Her mother had followed her out of the restaurant, having jumped to the same conclusion about the St. Patrick's Day Parade threat. She wanted to fly back to Manhattan with Lucy and Ned, but her daughter had talked her out of it.

"I'll have plenty of support in New York," she'd lied, knowing Marlene would assume she meant Jaxon. "Dad is going to need you in Idaho, especially if his case has something to do with the disappearance of Maria Santacristina. And you have a lot to do before the Baker Street guys show up."

In actuality, Lucy did not want her mom present because she knew that Marlene wouldn't buy her theory about Jaxon and might insist that he be called. So she was relieved when her mom gave in as long as Lucy promised to let others handle "the rough stuff." Marlene had then made Ned swear "on pain of castration" that he'd make sure Lucy followed through.

Lucy felt guilty about not being totally honest with her mother, but she had agreed to contact Ellis, and if there was any rough stuff, she would be happy to get out of the way.

"Mom's in Idaho with Dad," she replied to Tran. "He needs her help right now with the trial only a couple of weeks away."

After meeting with Jojola and Tran, Lucy looked for the business card Ellis had given to her months ago after debriefing her about having been Kane's hostage when he tried to escape. She found it in the bottom of her purse, where she'd tossed it, and gave him a call. He seemed happy but surprised to hear from her.

"I need to talk to you," she said. "I think someone is planning an assassination during the St. Patrick's Day Parade."

Ellis was silent for a moment, then spoke in a low voice. "Don't say anything more. Can you meet me?"

"Yes. Where?"

"You name it."

"Okay, Grand Central Station under the constellations, nine o'clock tonight," she said.

"Pretty public, but I'll be there," he said.

Lucy had arrived early so she could get a seat on the mezzanine above the main terminal floor and watch for anyone "casing the joint." She laughed at herself for going into spy mode with the silly reference to meeting under the constellations. Anybody with half a brain and who knew Grand Central would immediately recognize it as the ceiling of the dome, where lights had been built in to represent a starry, constellation-filled sky.

She saw Ellis arrive and waited for him to turn in her direction before giving a little wave. He didn't acknowledge the wave, but as he looked around he nonchalantly made his way to her table. She got right to her theory about an assassination occurring during the parade but had decided against telling him how she arrived at her conclusion. She didn't feel like being questioned about the Sons of Man or the book, which would have felt like having to defend Cian.

"That doesn't give me a lot to go on," Ellis said. "But tell you what, there's going to be quite a few dignitaries at this year's parade—sort of a show of support for New York after the fiasco at St. Pat's—and I already have a Homeland Security detail assigned to the viewing platform at Eighty-sixth Street. I'll let them know there's a new potential threat."

"What about the archbishop?" Lucy asked. "The tradition is for the archbishop to bless the marchers from the steps of St. Patrick's."

"Well, this can't go any further," Ellis said. "But because of the grim nature of what occurred at St. Patrick's this past fall, the arch-bishop decided that it was too soon to be celebrating on the grounds. So he's decided to join the others on the viewing plat-form. We'll keep an extra guy on him. In fact, I'll be on the plat-form myself."

Lucy picked up her purse to go, but Ellis stopped her with a hand on her arm. "Can I ask why you didn't pass this information to Jaxon?" His eyes locked onto hers.

"He's no longer with the good guys, is he? I mean, he quit the FBI, so what good is he?" she replied, and left before she started to cry.

The morning of the St. Patrick's Day Parade, Lucy rose at five, leaving Ned asleep in bed. She crept out to the living room, where Gilgamesh lifted his massive head and wagged the stump of his tail. "Ssssshhhh, good doggie," she said as she located the clothes she'd secreted behind the couch. She slipped into a pair of long underwear and then several layers of other clothes. Grab-bing her parka from the coatrack by the front door, she slipped out.

So far so good, she thought as the elevator reached the ground floor and the doors opened.

Jojola and Tran stood there with amused looks on their faces. The Vietnamese gangster looked at his watch. "Goddamn, she's ten minutes late," he complained, and handed another dollar to Jojola.

"Ten minutes too late for you to win the pool, you mean," Jojola said, laughing. Just then the elevator bell chimed. Someone above was requesting the elevator. "But save the dollar for our boy, I think he hit it right on the nail."

"He probably found a way to keep her in bed so that he could win," Tran groused, pulling Lucy out of the elevator so that it could go retrieve the winner of the pool. "I shouldn't have to pay for cheating."

A minute later, the elevator doors opened again and Ned stepped out.

"You slept in your clothes?" she asked.

"Nah, you know better than that," he answered. "But tossed them on pretty quick so I could catch a sneak."

"A sneak?"

"Yeah, a sneak."

"I couldn't sleep and was just going out for a walk."

"A sneak and a lousy liar," Tran added, handing Ned the dollar bill.

The four headed out the door with Lucy still trying to proclaim her innocence. "Ned was pretty damn sure you weren't going to sit at home waiting for the feds to stop the people who killed your friend," Jojola explained.

Lucy put up her hands in surrender. "Okay, you got me," she said. "But I was just going to have a look around and see if I could spot anything before they got to the viewing stand . . . if that's where this is supposed to go down. I appreciate that Ellis at least listened, but I think he only half believed me. And besides, he doesn't know what he's looking for."

"And you do?" Jojola said. "So what's your plan?"

"According to the poem, the bad guys are marchers," she replied. "So that narrows it down some."

"Yeah, to a mere hundred and fifty thousand," Tran replied.

"Yeah, a mere hundred and fifty thousand," Lucy agreed. "But they're cooped up on the side streets in Midtown until they march—that's only about a dozen blocks to check out. If we get going early enough, we can get to them all before they start marching."

"And what exactly are we looking for?" Tran asked. "I doubt they have Sons of Man name tags or T-shirts. And I suspect security will be pretty tight, so that rules out spotting their machine guns."

Lucy turned bright red. "I'm not sure what I'm looking for," she said. "I just feel like I will know it when I see it." She turned to Jojola. "I saw some of this before . . . when we were on the butte. I know it's not much of a plan, but it's what I got and I think I'm supposed to be there."

"I'm willing to do this," Ned said. "But not with you. I promised your mom that I'd keep you out of the rough stuff, if it happens."

"Spoken like a true future son-in-law," Tran cackled, which caused Ned and Lucy to blush.

Lucy squeezed Ned's hand. "Sorry, love, but I have to be there, I'm the only one who knows even kind of what I'm looking for," she said. "In fact, you're the one I can't allow to go. But I promise, first hint of anything rough and I'll duck around the corner."

"What do you mean by that?" Ned replied. "You're for sure not going if I'm not."

"I can't let you," Lucy argued, and explained the vision she'd had in her dream of Ned lying on the ground as a man pointed a rifle at him. She could hardly remember any details about the man, but she could still recall the sight of Ned's face as he looked down the barrel, knowing he was about to die.

"Doesn't mean it's going to come true," Ned countered. "And it doesn't matter. You go, I go, or we both stay here and whatever happens, happens."

The pair was about to argue more, but Jojola stopped them. "Look, I'd just as soon you both stayed, but Lucy is the only one with any inkling of what to look for and Ned isn't going to let her come alone. So let's move on." He turned to Lucy. "That's a lot of ground to cover, so I think you should draw us a picture of what this triskele thing looks like so that Tran and I can cover one side and you and Ned can cover the other."

Everyone had agreed to the plan when Tran asked another question. "What do we do if we find something? We can keep in touch by cell phone, but we won't have any weapons; how do we stop these guys?"

It was Jojola who answered. "Same way I stopped you and your buddies back in 'Nam."

"Oh, you mean not very well." Tran smiled.

"No," Jojola replied with a grin of his own. "I mean, any way I could."

The streets of Manhattan were only marginally warmer for the St. Patrick's Day Parade than the plains of Colorado had been. However, that didn't stop tens of thousands of watchers and participants from congregating on Midtown at dawn, nor the myriad Irish pubs around the Fifth Avenue route from opening their doors early to snag the first of the celebrants.

The first St. Patrick's Day Parade in New York was in 1766 when Irish soldiers in His Majesty's army on the "island of York" held a parade of their own, before heading off to celebrate in a more stereotypical Irish way. Two hundred and forty years later, the St. Patrick's Day Parade in New York was the largest in the world and one of the very few where everyone still walked, no cars or floats allowed.

The two-mile-long parade route began at Forty-second Street in Midtown and proceeded up Fifth Avenue to St. Patrick's Cathedral, between Fiftieth and Fifty-first streets, where traditionally the Archbishop of New York would bless the marchers. They would then continue on to Eighty-sixth Street, skirting the east side of Central Park before hanging a right, moving onto Third Avenue for the last hoorah.

Millions of people would eventually line up to watch the 165th Infantry—formerly the "Fighting Irish" 69th—lead the procession of more than 150,000 kilted bagpipers, drummers, drum majors, high school band members, cheerleaders, dance ensembles, representatives of every branch of the services, and the loyal members of the Irish societies, including the Emerald Societies of the NYPD and NYFD, as well as thousands of real Irish folk who'd flown in from Eire herself.

In the grand tradition of those first soldiers, many of the revelers were already inebriated as Lucy and Ned elbowed their way through, and sometimes over, the weaving masses. They were searching for the needle in the haystack and the green beer-swilling straw kept getting in the way.

Moving with any sustained speed was difficult. The side streets had been closed off for a block on either side of Fifth for the first half dozen blocks or so to provide places for the marchers to assemble, every group assigned to a particular spot on a particular street. And each enclave was a party unto its own, with bleating bagpipes competing against blaring horn sections while drummers tried to keep the beat with both and neither. Meanwhile, military honor guardsmen in dark glasses not necessary in the sunless caverns between the buildings watched the pretty girls who strutted about in uniforms of their own. Banners representing the Ancient Order of Hibernians, the Loyal Sons and Daughters of County Cork, the Friendly Sons of St. Patrick, Clan-na-Gael, and a thousand others waved to and fro along with many thousands more tricolor flags bearing the orange, white, and green of Ireland.

They wandered through the crowded side streets—Tran and Jojola on one side of Fifth Avenue, and Ned and Lucy on the other—and got up to Forty-ninth Street when Lucy found what she was looking for . . . or at least hoped it was what she was looking for when her "totem" showed it to her. She was standing in the middle of the crowd with Ned, stamping her feet and blowing on her fingers to ward off the cold when she looked up and saw the owl glaring down.

Actually, it wasn't a real owl, but a plastic or clay version that building superintendents placed on ledges to keep pigeons away. Lucy followed the faux owl's gaze to the big, brightly colored banner proclaiming that bit of street was occupied by the representatives of the Irish Society of County Heath. Like many of the other Irish society banners, this one depicted a religious theme—St. Patrick walking on a green hill between two large, slightly askew stone monoliths. It was the stones that got Lucy's attention, or actually the symbols embroidered on the stones. As clearly as on the day he'd said it, she heard Cian's voice: *There are stylized versions—such as a triskele where the legs are represented by spirals. The earliest of those discovered so far were found on Neolithic carvings in County Heath in Ireland.*

As far as she knew, there was no connection between the County Heath and the Sons of Man beyond a shared, and common, symbol. But Lucy was absolutely sure that she'd come to the right place and pointed out the banner to Ned. "Maybe they just have a flair for the dramatic," she said.

Lucy called Jojola and Tran, explaining her conclusion. "We're off to mingle," she said. "You guys keep looking in case this is a red herring. Then maybe you can follow along when we move out onto the parade route."

The young couple walked over to join the worthies of County Heath, many of whom had been taking liberal advantage of Tully's Irish Pub in the middle of the block. Speaking in perfect Irish Gaelic, Lucy soon had those nearby convinced that she was from the home county itself, and was welcomed as a long-lost cousin to them all. Lucy introduced her "American boyfriend," whose reception was not quite as enthusiastic given that his last name, Blanchet, sounded suspiciously English.

When the greetings died down and the others went on about their business, Lucy huddled against Ned to stay warm and give herself a chance to look around. But outside of the banner with the triskele, nothing seemed remotely linked to any sinister plot by the Sons of Man. She wondered if she'd jumped to her conclusion too swiftly.

The County Heath was represented by one of the larger cadres of bagpipers and drummers, a good fifty in all, led by a huge, red-haired drum major with a tall bearskin hat. His legs stood out like tree trunks from beneath his plaid kilt and he glowered fabulously for the Japanese tourists with their cameras. The county was also represented by two members of a color guard, one bearing a U.S. flag and the other the flag of Ireland. Off to one side, several members of a precision drill team were practicing, tossing rifles through the air to one another.

Lucy looked at the drill team for a moment before realizing what she was seeing. Then it came to her. "Rifles," she said.

"What?" Ned replied. He started to turn to see what she was talking about.

"No," she warned, "don't look. But there's a drill team behind us with rifles."

"Oh, yeah, well, I've seen the kind of rifles they use at the county fair," he said. "They're fakes and can't shoot."

"Are you absolutely sure about that?"

* * *

Someone was watching the young couple who'd arrived late and now stood huddled in the midst of the County Heath representatives. But the girl appeared to be from Ireland—he'd overheard one of the bagpipers saying that he could even place her accent as coming from a small village "to the west of where my people originated from." The boy didn't look like much, just another skinny kid.

Dismissing them as a threat, his attention was drawn to a pair of cops walking through the crowd. His hair was longer and dyed a different color from when he was on the force, and he was wearing sunglasses and a tam, but he turned quickly away just in case one of them might remember him.

Paul Stewart was proud to be a dedicated assassin for the Sons of Man. He was not a first son of a first son, not even a second. He'd been born to a female distantly related to Andrew Kane and had only advanced to a foot soldier for the cause. But that was okay, he was also a true believer and had signed up for the marines out of high school so that when the time came, he would be a trained warrior as well.

Only problem with the marines was that the corps corrupted itself by allowing niggers, spics, and gooks to join. He hated them all and had been dishonorably discharged after nearly killing a black marine. He'd then returned to New York, where his distant cousin Andrew helped get him a job on the New York City Police Department, in part by magically turning his dishonorable into an honorable discharge. He'd repaid the favor by doing anything his cousin asked him to—whether it was roughing somebody up, delivering messages, or reporting anything interesting on the NYPD grapevine. He'd even disposed of the bodies of a couple of teenaged girls after Kane was finished with them.

Whoo, boy, he used to think, if the public only knew what I know about Cousin Kane, who at that time was only a wealthy lawyer and venture capitalist with aspirations to become the mayor of New York City. But Stewart was a man who knew who buttered his bread and kept his mouth shut.

Cousin Kane had saved him again after he'd played a little too rough with a black crack dealer, who refused to pay Kane a "business tax," and left him in a permanent vegetative state. Kane had seen to it that the dealer's family was paid off and that any potential charges against him had been stuck in a file folder and stamped "No Prosecution." The file had been sent on to the District Attorney's Office, where the deal was it would never again see the light of day. That is until that Jew bastard, Butch Karp, arrested Kane, and his pal, V. T. Newbury, started digging into the files.

Stewart had been fortunate that the statute of limitations on his crime was up and he couldn't be prosecuted. However, Newbury had taken his file and many others in the same situation to the chief of police, Bill Denton. Next thing Stewart knew, he'd been drummed off the force. Left with only a partial pension, he'd started drinking heavier and it wasn't long before his wife left him and took the kids.

Abandoned and feeling sorry for himself, he was contemplating sucking on the end of the barrel of his handgun when he got a call from someone working for Kane, who had recently escaped custody. He was to go to a camp in Idaho where he was introduced to his family's history and happily swore allegiance to the Sons of Man. There he'd been trained for his mission until he thought of himself as a perfect killing machine.

Returning to New York, he'd waited to hear if the mission was a go, afraid that his chance at glory and redemption might get canceled. But then he got the call to meet with Jamys Kellagh and heard the words he had been waiting for: It was time for a Son of Man to march with the sons of Ireland and silence the critic. *Myr shegin dy ve, bee eh!*

It didn't even matter to him that he probably wouldn't survive the mission. He was striking a blow for Aryan America and the only leaders who saw the danger of allowing every subhuman from Africa, Latin America, and Asia to invade the country. And the only leaders who were prepared to do whatever it took to wipe out the sand niggers in the Middle East, including using nuclear weapons. Then they'll see whose oil it is.

He daydreamed that his name would live on forever. Two hundred years hence, when little Aryan American schoolchildren read about great patriots who'd sacrificed their lives, his would be right up there with Nathan Hale and Davy Crockett. They would hear how he saved the country from rampant appeasing left-wingers and the threat of being overrun by mud people. And the Jews, don't forget the fucking Jews, Paulie boy, he reminded himself, so ready to die that he hardly noticed the pain of the Valknut he'd branded into the inside of his bicep the last night in Idaho.

Stewart was getting antsy for martyrdom and tired of reviewing the plan. It was pure genius and made use of a talent he already possessed. In the marines, he'd been assigned to a precision drill team; in fact, it was one of the black members of the team whose head he cracked with the butt of his gun. He claimed it was an accident during close order drills, but it was obvious he'd hated the man and had purposely swung the rifle so that it would connect.

Somehow, the Sons of Man had got him an invitation to join the County Heath drill team. He'd heard a rumor that the society had ties to the Irish Republican Army, but the tough part had been getting him a weapon.

The drill team used old M1 carbines rendered harmless by the removal of the firing pin and a metal wedge in the barrel. Otherwise, the M1 was a fine weapon that had served well in World War Two and the Korean conflict. While it didn't have the firepower or fully automatic feature of its descendant the M16, the M1 was deadly in the right hands.

Before they were allowed to bring their useless rifles into the staging area, Stewart and the rest of the team had been required to hand them over at an NYPD checkpoint for inspection. When the rifles passed, they were handed back with the warning to the team not to let them out of their sight.

Taking his time, Stewart had gradually made his way to Tully's, where he ordered a Guinness. As the bartender poured it, he nodded toward the back and quietly mumbled, "Second door on the right. Lock it when you leave."

Stewart casually got up, wandered to the back with his rifle, opened the indicated door, and slipped into a small storage room.

Behind a filing cabinet, he found a perfect replica of his drill M1—only this one was in working order.

He switched guns, walked back into the bar, where he downed the Guinness in a single drain, and went back outside to await his moment of glory. As he stepped off the curb, a drunk grabbed at his rifle.

"Let me show you how to twirl that thing," the drunk slurred.

"Not today, pal," he snarled, and caught the man in the solar plexus with the butt of the rifle. It happened so fast that most of the other bystanders laughed when they saw the drunk on his hands and knees vomiting from "too much, too soon."

Stewart glanced back at the cute Irish girl to see if she'd noticed his martial skills. But she was on her cell phone. Didn't matter, today she'd see what a real man was made of; then she'd really have something to call home about.

He happily pictured her crying over his dying body when she realized that a great patriot had given his all. But the reverie came to a close when the tail end of the parade passed by Forty-ninth Street and those in the staging area marched out onto Fifth Avenue with a great cacophony of bagpipes, drums, and cheers.

If not for the circumstances, Lucy might have enjoyed the walk. At least it brought them back out into the sun, plus there was something about bagpipes and the rat-a-tat-tat of the snare drums that made it almost impossible to march out of step. She waved to the crowd even as she kept an eye on the drill team marching and performing at the head of the County Heath pipes and drums.

As they passed St. Patrick's Cathedral between Fiftieth and Fifty-first, Lucy saw John Jojola moving parallel along the sidewalk. She caught his eye and pointed to the drill team, but added a shrug just in case Ned was right and the rifles were useless. She saw him signal to someone on the other side of the avenue and a few steps farther along spotted Tran on the stairs of the cathedral. He waved to her and she waved back.

Thirty blocks later, Lucy was tired of the parade and growing nervous as they approached the viewing platform set up where the marchers would turn east on Eighty-sixth and head toward Third Avenue. The procession had become stop-and-go as each group put on their best show for the dignitaries.

At last, they were in sight of the platform. Lucy scanned the dais and spotted Ellis standing to one side of a large, red-haired man in a suit who was seated comfortably, obviously enjoying the spectacle, feet tapping to the whir of the pipes. She nearly stumbled into a bagpiper, however, when further inspection revealed that Jaxon was also on the platform, standing next to the archbishop.

Lucy was about to call Jojola and warn him that she thought the archbishop was the target when she was distracted by the bagpiper she'd almost run over. He nudged the fellow next to him and said, "There, Sean, you see the big fellow with the fiery hair . . . that's the grand marshal, Tom McCullum. He's a U.S. senator, wouldn't you know, and a Mick if you can believe it!"

"Aye, Bryan," Sean replied. "I hear he's a regular firebrand and recently spoke at the annual meeting of the Ancient Order of Hibernians. He's calling for an investigation into that little to-do at the cathedral with the Pope and all. Also, gave a speech to the Hibernians about the Patriot Act—was none too fond of it, I hear, in fact was real critical about invasions of privacy and government spying on citizens."

"Well, I don't know what to think about that," Bryan said. "I don't like government intrusion any better than the next American, but maybe it's for the greater good and the only way to deal with these terrorists. We can always get our rights back when it's safe again."

"You have a point, Bryan," Sean agreed. "But when will it be safe again? I heard that they didn't announce Mr. McCullum was going to be the grand marshal until the last minute because there's been threats. But he's here now and that takes courage. . . . Ach, look lively, lads, we're moving forward again. Time to pucker up and blow."

Lucy was suddenly besieged with voices. *He was real critical*

*about it . . . for the greater good . . . silence the critic . . . there's
been threats.*

She flipped open her cell phone and tried to call Jojola. She
thought the phone was answered but she couldn't hear over the din
of the bagpipes. Standing on her toes, she tried to see over the
crowd, but Jojola and Tran were nowhere in sight.

"I think they're going to try to kill Senator McCullum," she
shouted to Ned.

"What?" Ned shouted back.

"I said," she yelled, "I think they're going to try to kill McCullum!" She pointed at the stage and pantomimed shooting. "There!"

"What?"

Lucy rolled her eyes. "Oh, never mind," she shouted, and
started to move quickly through the lines of bagpipers.

"Hey, lass, wait your turn," one of the pipers called out.

Lucy ignored the shouts and confused or miffed looks and
pushed on until only the drill team and the drum major stood between her and the viewing platform. The six-member team stood
in three pairs, each pair tossing their rifles back and forth in cadence to the drumbeat and on command of the drum major who
faced them.

On command, the pipers and drummers stopped at the same
moment while the drill team caught their rifles and snapped to attention, facing the viewing stand. The dignitaries and the crowd
cheered and whistled as the drum major continued to shout commands followed by the instantaneous movement of the team.

"Shoulder arms!" The team brought the guns to their shoulders.

"Present arms!" The team held their guns forward as the drum
major walked stiff-legged down the line for a cursory inspection. As
he passed, each rifleman twirled his weapon and brought it up to
shoulder arms.

Everyone except the man on the end closest to Lucy and Ned.
She saw him suddenly pull down the bolt of the rifle and then slam
it forward with such intent that she knew what was going to happen. Not knowing what else to do, she ran forward and shouted,
"Myr shegin dy ve, bee eh!"

The assassin stopped and turned to see who'd shouted the motto of the Sons of Man. He only knew a smattering of the old tongue, but this phrase he knew because it had concluded every call from handler Jamys Kellagh. However, this time the words had come from the Irish girl who was rushing toward him with her boyfriend close behind.

"Stop! McCullum is no longer the target," she shouted.

The assassin's eyes narrowed. She didn't use the password to call off the mission. And besides, it would have never come from a woman, not with Jamys Kellagh on the viewing stand.

"Wrong," he said, and swung back toward the dais, raising the butt of the rifle to his shoulder. No one on the stand yet realized that something was wrong. His target remained sitting, an easy shot. He started to squeeze the trigger but an instant too late; someone struck him from behind and threw off his aim. Instead, he was looking down the barrel at the stunned face of the drum major when the gun fired.

Stewart spun away from his attacker, the girl's boyfriend, who swung his fist and landed a glancing blow. He struck back, catching the boy on the jaw with the butt of the rifle, sending him crashing to the ground.

Enraged, he aimed the rifle at the boyfriend and was about to shoot him when someone screamed. He became aware of other screams and shouts and remembered that his mission was to kill the senator, and his window of opportunity was slipping away.

In fact, McCullum was being hustled off the stage by security officers along with the other dignitaries, some of whom had decided it was every man for himself and were scrambling in different directions.

The crowd backed away from Stewart, however, giving a clear field of fire. But then a dark-haired plainclothes officer positioned himself in front of the fleeing dignitaries, trying to get a clear shot at him through the crowd. The assassin readjusted and shot the officer, who went down. He swung the gun back to find his target.

"Hey, piece of shit!" The voice came out of nowhere, as did the flying roundhouse kick that caught him square on the side of the head. Dazed but snarling like a lion separated from its kill, he turned on the small Asian man who'd kicked him but fallen to the ground from the effort.

The assassin pointed the rifle to kill the second attacker. And would have, except he was struck such a blow in the back that it seemed to have momentarily stopped his body from responding like the trained killing machine he'd worked so hard to become. He tried to pull the trigger, but his finger wouldn't respond. Then his arms stopped working altogether and the rifle clattered to the ground. He reached behind and felt for the object that protruded from his back directly over his spine, but he couldn't reach it and collapsed to the ground.

"Goddamn, you slowing down or what!" Tran shouted at Jojola. "He almost shot me!"

"Maybe if you brushed up on your kicks you wouldn't fall down every time," Jojola retorted. "Besides, if I let him shoot you, who would pay for my kid's college education a dollar at a time?"

"BOTH OF YOU GET YOUR HANDS UP IN THE AIR!" a nervous police sergeant shouted. He and a dozen others had their drawn guns pointed at the small Asian man and what appeared to be a long-haired Indian. He looked at the body twitching on the ground, the handle of a big-ass knife sticking out of his back. Another body was lying off to the side—the drum major.

"Oh, bullshit," Tran yelled back at Jojola as he raised his hands. "You try kicking some giant lard-ass as hard as I did and see if you stay on your feet. Besides, I think I pulled something in my groin."

"Getting old," Jojola said, laughing.

Lucy rushed up to the police sergeant, who wasn't quite sure what to do about the debate. "Please put your guns down," she said. "He's a police officer."

"Which one?"

"The one with the long hair. He's the chief of police at the Taos Pueblo in New Mexico."

"And who are you, pray tell?"

"Lucy Karp. I'm Butch Karp's daughter."

"Yeah, and who's the other guy?" the sergeant said, then spoke into the microphone on his shoulder. "Can we get some backup and an ambulance, please? I got a regular carnival going on here."

Lucy realized that Tran, a gangster, might have warrants out for his arrest. "I don't know," she said. "I think he is just a bystander who helped stop that guy."

"That guy" had stopped twitching. The sergeant put his gun down and signaled for the other officers to do the same just as Espey Jaxon ran up, flashed a badge at the cops, and turned to Lucy.

"Are you okay?" he asked. "What in the hell are you doing here?"

"Trying to save Senator McCullum's life," Lucy said without looking him in the eye. "And find out who killed my friend Cian."

Before Jaxon could respond, Jon Ellis ran up. "What are you doing here, Jaxon?"

"My firm was hired to provide security for the archbishop," Jaxon replied. "After the fiasco this fall, the church wasn't taking chances."

"I bet that cost a pretty penny," Ellis said sarcastically. "VIP rent-a-cops don't come cheap."

Lucy watched the emotions play over Jaxon's face. He's angry and hurt, she thought, angry at Ellis and hurt because of me.

The tension was broken by a loud groan and the drum major sat up. He'd fainted the moment he saw the rifle pointed at him, which had saved his life. A police officer picked up his bearskin hat, which had fallen off, and was sticking a finger in a hole made by the bullet. "Three inches farther down and you'd be a dead man," the officer said.

Lucy turned to Jaxon. "Was that Agent Tavizon who got shot?"

"Yes, but the bullet just grazed his temple. Other than being stunned and a little bloody, he's a lucky boy who'll live to fight another day," Jaxon replied. "I thought you were in New Mexico."

"I was," Lucy answered.

Jaxon waited for more of an answer, but when it wasn't forthcoming he added, "You want to tell me what you're doing here and, once again, arriving in the nick of time?"

Lucy remained silent, then Ellis took her by the arm. "I believe that's my line, Jaxon. Thanks, but we'll handle the debriefing on this." His men surrounded Tran and Jojola, and another was helping Ned Blanchet to his feet.

Lucy looked over her shoulder at Jaxon as she was being led away. He was standing over the assassin's body. He glanced up and their eyes met. She couldn't tell what she saw in his expression before he quickly looked down again, but his body seemed to sag from some unseen weight.

22

IT WASN'T UNTIL HOURS AFTER THE SHOOTING THAT KARP heard about the assassination attempt. He, O'Toole, Meyers, and Fulton had been holed up in a room at the Grove Hotel in downtown Boise reviewing the case, going over strategy, and running through O'Toole's testimony and what he could expect on cross-examination.

Meanwhile, Marlene had been coordinating the various needs and requests of the 221B Baker Street Irregulars, who would be arriving in Sawtooth a few days before the trial. "We're having a hard time getting the right equipment to the site. It will be there, but it might not be until the day the trial starts," she'd told Karp that day before they heard the news from back East. "Sorry, but we may be pushing it to help you."

"That's okay," he'd replied. "I hope you find Maria Santacristina, but we're not counting on it. I'm going into this thinking we're going to have to dance with the dates we brought to the ball. But I'll save you a spot on my dance card for the second day if you think you can keep up."

"Oh, I can keep up, buster," Marlene responded. "If I remember correctly, it's Marlene, ten, Butch, zero, for who quit first out of our last ten dances?"

"Who's counting," Karp said, and laughed. "Besides, I wasn't talking about that kind of dancing."

Not until he got back up to his room later and turned on the television did he learn about the St. Patrick's Day Parade events in New York City. Stunned, he'd glanced at the telephone and saw that the message light was blinking, which had turned out to be a call from Lucy—saying she was all right and would be in touch shortly—and another from Marlene, who was in Sawtooth, angrily scolding him for turning off his cell phone and then relaying the news from Manhattan.

They tried to assassinate a U.S. senator! Of all the terrorist acts that had been attempted or accomplished in recent years, this one struck Karp as more a thrust right to the heart of what America stood for than all the bloody massacres. Not worse, nothing was worse than the taking of innocent lives, nothing more reprehensible than murder in the name of God. But those events were easily seen for what they were: evil, senseless—serving only to harden the resolve of the West to stand up to terrorists.

This, however, had been an attempt to shake fundamental American values by trying to silence a voice that was warning the American people not to let fear carve away at their civil liberties. A voice that was demanding the truth regarding what was really behind Kane's escape and the attack at St. Patrick's Cathedral, the bombing of the Black Sea Café, the murder of Cian Magee, and the attempted hijacking of the Staten Island Ferry.

It made him wonder if maybe the conspiracy nuts were in some way right, maybe the enemy within was more dangerous than the enemy without. After all, what did it matter if the terrorists were defeated if there was nothing left worth saving? If the Constitution could be ignored, or shelved for convenience, if a senator could be selected for assassination because he demanded the truth, why was he, Butch Karp, in a federal courtroom in Boise fighting for one man's right to those constitutional protections?

* * *

Officially, the Department of Homeland Security had released a preliminary report stating that Paul Stewart, a disgraced member of the NYPD, had been acting on his own. "It appears that Stewart had not selected any particular person," according to the press release. "But that he intended to shoot 'targets of opportunity' in an attempt to avenge his dismissal from the New York Police Department and gain publicity."

Neighbors of Stewart in the Bronx apartment complex he lived in had been quoted by the media as saying the shooter was an angry man whose wife had left him following his dismissal from the NYPD. The reports noted that Stewart had been kicked off the force after being implicated in the burgeoning "No Prosecution" files investigation by the DAO.

"He told me that he was going to get even with the city," an anonymous man was quoted as saying in the *Times*.

Stewart's past and alleged statements had led to widespread speculation that Stewart's intended targets had been the mayor and the chief of police. "He may have also hoped to shoot District Attorney Butch Karp, who he apparently blamed for his dismissal," the *Times* story reported.

Karp, of course, knew better than the "official version" released by the Homeland Security Department. He'd been told the entire story by Lucy and filled in on other details by Jojola. However, Jon Ellis had requested that no one contradict the department "while we investigate Lucy's information about the Sons of Man and see if we can locate them."

The department press release had also indicated that Stewart's plot had been foiled by "concerned citizens, who acted bravely and swiftly in the face of great danger to themselves." The citizens had not been named "out of regard for their safety, in the unlikely but possible event that Stewart had an accomplice."

Even Stupenagel had not yet picked up on Lucy's involvement. Television clips of the assassination attempt had been played ad nauseam. However, most of the cameras had concentrated on the viewing platform or had swung around wildly in the confused melee and had difficulty picking out the shooter and the "concerned citizens" until it was over. Then the television cameras had focused on shots of Stewart lying on the ground with the hilt of a knife protruding from his back and federal agents escorting several people away from the scene with blankets over their heads to protect their identities.

One week removed from St. Patrick's Day, Karp stood in a federal courtroom in Boise, Idaho, still trying to come to grips with the enormity of the attempt to kill Thomas McCullum. He was a few minutes from the beginning of voir dire, the jury selection process for the O'Toole trial, but his mind was back in Manhattan.

If the assassination attempt and the various other terrorist acts associated with it weren't enough to worry about, Manhattan was still serving up plenty of other "normal" crimes to keep the DAO hopping while he was gone. Two days before the O'Toole trial was to begin, Assistant District Attorney Harry Kipman, who was acting DA while he was on leave, had called to let him know that they had a new high-profile homicide case.

Charlie Campbell, the Manhattan borough president and a candidate for the Eighth Congressional District, had returned home to his Upper West Side brownstone to find that his three young children—one of them an infant—were missing. His wife, Jessica Campbell, who was discovered asleep in the master bedroom, woke and happily announced that she'd saved their children from Satan and that they were in heaven.

They haven't found the bodies, Kipman had said. *And the press is all over this one big-time. They're already running stories that Mrs. Campbell suffered from postpartum depression and had attempted suicide after her second child's birth.*

Where's she now? Karp had asked.

Locked up at Bellevue, Kipman had replied. *She wouldn't say what she did with the kids, except that they're in "a better place." And now her husband has her lawyered up. No murder weapon either. Oh, and here's irony for those of you out in Idaho, the family station wagon is gone, too, presumably on the road to heaven. Not to be too obtuse, but I'm guessing we're looking at an insanity defense.*

"I'd bet on it, Karp had replied. *And it's not going to be pretty if we pursue multiple murder charges against a popular borough president's wife suffering from postpartum depression.*

Karp had told Kipman to handle the case like any other homicide. *And no one's to say anything to the press,* he'd added.

Now he needed to concentrate on helping Meyers and O'Toole. Early that morning, a Wednesday, he rose before the sun was up and went down to the hotel's workout room. He hit the weights hard and then spent thirty minutes on the stationary bike, working up a sweat while he filed away the happenings in Manhattan so that his mind would be clear in court. His wounded leg ached as he showered, ate a room service breakfast, and then walked to the courthouse. But the pain seemed to help him focus on the present so that by the time he reached the courthouse steps and saw O'Toole and Meyers waiting for him, he was ready for battle.

They tried to assassinate a U.S. senator! With an effort, Karp turned his attention to the front of the courtroom, where a moment later federal district court judge Sam Allen entered and immediately asked for the jury pool to be escorted in and seated in the pews.

Tall and rangy, Allen was a native son of Idaho who when not in the black robes of his profession preferred a cowboy hat and boots more fitting for his ranch west of town. He spoke in a slow, measured Western drawl, but Karp had found him to be sharp as a Spanish spur, to stick with the Western imagery.

Allen had the bailiff call out twelve names from the pool. Those called rose and made their way to the jury box, where the judge first questioned them to see if any had sufficient reason to be excused, and then told Karp he could begin his questioning.

Karp introduced himself and "my co-counsel, Richard Meyers, and our client, Coach Mikey O'Toole." He then began to set the stage for what he hoped would be the theme of the trial. But instead of the usual mundane personal opinion questions asked of each juror, he'd addressed the twelve potential jurors who'd been seated with a series of questions. At the same time, he made sure that his voice was loud enough for the rest of the jury pool to hear. "How many of you have ever felt you were falsely accused of something?"

Half of the hands, including those in the pews, went up. "I'm not just talking about being accused of something big, like a crime," he added. "Maybe you were just a child and someone unfairly accused you of taking something. Or you were at work and your boss or a co-worker insinuated that you had done something wrong when you had not."

Nearly all the hands were up. "Now, how many of you felt that you weren't given a chance to prove your innocence?" Most of the hands remained lifted. "I see," Karp said. "And how many of you believe that a person should have the right to defend himself from accusations by calling witnesses and presenting evidence that could exonerate him?"

The hands were all up and in the same moment so was the defendant's attorney. "I object to this style of questioning, Your Honor," said Steve Zusskin, who was representing the ACAA. A young woman named Karen Welt was nominally representing the university, but she remained seated, watching Zusskin. "He's making little speeches to the jury."

"I don't believe that there are any hard and fast rules about how I'm supposed to conduct voir dire," Karp replied.

Allen tilted his head and gave Karp a funny look, but said, "I'll allow it. Just tone down the fife and drums, Mr. Karp."

"Yes, Your Honor," Karp replied, and turned back to the potential jurors. "My next question is: Do you believe a person has the right to cross-examine—we in the legal profession call this confrontation—witnesses who make accusations against them?"

Again the show of hands was nearly a hundred percent. "And what would be your opinion of any agency—whether it's the government or a private entity—that refused to grant these basic rights and then deprived a man of his livelihood and smeared his reputation?"

"Your Honor, another speech, and mischaracterizations," Zusskin complained.

"Mr. Karp, I'll allow this, but it's the last of these mass questions."

"Yes, Your Honor," Karp agreed. He could tell by the way the jurors' eyes narrowed at the thought of being deprived of a right to make a living that he had most of them right where he wanted them. He pointed to a woman in the jury box. "Yes."

The woman turned red but managed to stutter, "Uh, hello, my name is Pam Jensen, and my son, Donald, was expelled from high school because a campus cop saw a hatchet in the back of his car. He wasn't allowed to explain that he'd been on a camping trip that weekend and left all of his gear, including the hatchet, in his car. They just said, 'Rules are rules, no exceptions.' And there's nothing we can do about it, so now he's going to have to make up those classes he missed this summer and won't be able to graduate with his classmates."

"I see," Karp replied. "Anybody else?" A middle-aged man with the look and demeanor of an accountant raised his hand. "Yes, sir," Karp said.

"I'm Morty Feldman," the man said. "We used to belong to the Cherry Hills Country Club until I was kicked out because of anonymous complaints that I wasn't wearing the proper shoes on the golf course. It wasn't true, and even if it was, there are members who've broken the rules far worse than that—but, of course, they're not Jewish. But I wasn't allowed to question my accusers. It was just a letter in the mail saying my membership would not be renewed because of 'rules infractions.' My lawyer tried to file a lawsuit for discrimination, but because there are other Jewish members, the case was dismissed."

Several more potential jurors discussed grievances ranging from being unfairly accused of shoplifting as teenagers "just because I was with some friends who were" to allegations of stealing items from work based on circumstantial evidence and hearsay. By the end of jury selection, Karp had used only a few of his peremptory challenges, including dismissing the president of the Boise Rotary

Club, who said she felt that private entities should be allowed to make decisions based on their own bylaws and regulations not withstanding what she labeled "lofty ideals to the contrary."

Zusskin had used all of his challenges to dismiss those potential jurors—including Jensen and Feldman—who'd seemed most aggrieved when answering Karp's questions. But he'd also seemed confused as to how to counter Karp's strategy, except to ask those in the jury pool if they understood the difference between public and private entities.

When it was over, Karp was pleased with how jury selection had gone, but he knew that this wasn't going to be a slam-dunk case. In a civil case, the burden of proof wasn't as high as in a criminal case where a jury had to be convinced of a defendant's guilt "beyond a reasonable doubt." Here, he and Meyers would only have to show that the "preponderance of evidence," a "more likely than not" standard, indicated that the defendants—the ACAA and the university and its representative, Kip Huttington, acting in concert—had wronged O'Toole.

He and Meyers would have to contend with telephone records indicating that a call had been made from O'Toole's office to the Pink Pussycat Escort Service, which had supplied the strippers, as well as the credit card receipt for five hundred dollars to the service, and another receipt for purchases from Campus Liquors. Both were electronic payments so there were no signatures, but the credit card had been issued to O'Toole and was supposed to have been in his possession. There was a new issue as well, because the party's hostess had "suddenly recalled" having overheard Rufus Porter talking to someone he addressed as "Coach" about "paying for entertainment."

Karp thought he and Meyers would be able to deal with those issues. However, the wild card would be how the jury responded to the testimony of the two recruits at the center of the scandal, Steele Dalton and Michael Mason.

They were the reason that Fulton had called Marlene on the day she'd met with Santacristina/Katarain. The detectives had just finished interviewing the two young men and they'd been "very cooperative." So cooperative, in fact, that after jury selection was over and the jurors were sent home, Karp had made a motion challenging the admissibility of the "abbreviated transcript" of the Dalton and Mason interviews that ACAA investigator James Larkin had used at O'Toole's hearing.

"The two witnesses will testify that the transcript is grossly incomplete," Karp argued. "And we've been informed by the defendant that the tape recording of the interviews is no longer available, nor is a complete copy of the transcript."

Zusskin countered that by the ACAA's rules, Larkin had not been required to keep a copy of the tape and "for the purposes of the hearing, the completeness of the transcript was not relevant."

"Not relevant?" Karp scowled. "I guess due process wasn't relevant either."

"This wasn't a court of law," Zusskin said. "It was a hearing before a private entity, operating as it always has under its rules and regulations. When Coach O'Toole took the job, he signed a contract saying, in part, that he would abide by those rules and regulations, which include abiding by the decisions of a duly appointed ACAA panel. The ACAA is like a private club that has the right to kick out members who break the rules of the club. As long as there are no violations of a federally protected class, such as in age, religion, national origin, or race discrimination, normal due process protections do not apply."

"The ACAA was acting jointly, in concert, with a public entity— the university—and participated in creating and disseminating false and defamatory charges pertaining to Coach O'Toole, which have significantly stigmatized him and will prevent him from obtaining future employment as a college baseball coach," Karp said. "It is plaintiff O'Toole's position that indeed Fourteenth Amendment due process applies, and had the university offered Coach O'Toole his requested name-clearing hearing, he would have demonstrated from the evidence—not hearsay or innuendo or speculation, but from the facts—that the charges are totally false."

Zusskin listened to Karp with his arms folded across his chest and a slight smile on his face. "Judge Allen, Your Honor, this is all very interesting, and I'm sure a jury would be on their feet, applauding Mr. Karp's passionate oratory," he said in reply. "But we are trying to focus on a very narrow issue here—the admissibility of the transcript used at the hearing. We want to present it to the jury, as it was heard by the panel that reached this decision. We physically cannot produce a complete copy as the tape recording is unavailable, not because of some sinister plot, but because the ACAA was not required to keep it."

Karp was about to respond again but Judge Allen interrupted. "That's all right, Mr. Karp, I believe I understand your argument," he said. "However, I'm going to allow the so-called abbreviated transcript into evidence, otherwise the jury won't even know what you're complaining about. You'll get the opportunity to call this investigator, Mr. Larkin, and ask him why it appears in this form, and you'll have the opportunity to call the two witnesses to, I assume, rebut or expand on the transcript. Then it will be up to the jury to decide who is telling the truth."

Karp accepted the judge's ruling and winked when he turned to Meyers and O'Toole. Later, as they left the courtroom, he told them that he had not expected to win the motion, "but sometimes even good judges, like Allen, need to be reminded of what's really at stake."

Walking out of the courthouse, they'd almost run into an elderly man who was standing outside the doors, smoking a pipe. Even forty years after he'd seen him as a high school basketball player, Karp recognized the tough, weathered visage of Coach J. C. Anderson. The old man smiled and raised his pipe. "They wrapped up in there? They wouldn't let me smoke this thing inside."

"Yes, we're through for the day," Meyers said. "Butch, this is—"

"Coach Anderson," Karp finished the sentence. "We met once a long time ago." He intended to walk past the man, but then turned. "When I was a teenager, I heard you talk about the importance of fair play and how it would matter when we became adults. It stuck with me all these years, and I've lived a lot of my life by that. What I don't understand is what happened to you?"

The smile disappeared from Anderson's face and his jaw set

tight. "I don't need you to lecture me on principles, Mr. Karp," he said. "I've been part of this system for nearly sixty years as a player and a coach. It's not perfect but it's what we got."

"If this is the system, Coach Anderson, then the system is broken," Karp replied. "No, I take that back. The system isn't just broken, it's become evil and venal. What sort of fair system would take a man's job and destroy his reputation based on a bunch of hearsay and lies without at least giving him the chance to defend himself? I can't believe that you would be part of that."

The old man continued to glare for a minute and looked like he might hit Karp. But then his expression softened and he ran a liver-spotted hand through his white hair. "I don't know what I'm part of anymore," he said. "It's just not the same world that I grew up in. Payoffs. Betting on games. Kids getting recruited on college campuses with sex and drugs. Everybody cheats and commits crimes with impunity. Does any of it matter?"

"Yes, it matters," Karp replied. "And you could have done the right thing. You could have been a voice for fair play."

The coach looked like he was about to say something, but then turned and walked back inside. Karp stood and watched him go, wondering what had caused him to bait an old man. But it had given him an idea for his opening statement in the morning.

"Want to grab some dinner?" Meyers asked.

"Would love to," Karp replied, "but I think I'm eating in the room tonight. I've got to cram for a test."

O'Toole laughed. "Now you're sounding like one of my players."

Karp smiled. "Or your brother."

23

TWELVE EXPECTANT FACES. TWELVE PAIRS OF EYES. SEVEN men. Five women. All white. And all with their attention riveted on Butch Karp as he stood for a moment at the lectern, going over the conclusion to his opening statement in the O'Toole trial one last time in his mind.

Meyers had asked him to give the opening statement. "I'd prefer the closing arguments," the young lawyer explained. "I think if I have any jitters, they will be at the beginning of the trial, but by the end I'll be in the groove."

After the jury was seated and had been instructed by Judge Allen as to their duties, he turned to Karp. "Your opening statement, Mr. Karp."

Karp rose from his chair.

So Karp had started the morning laying out the basics of the case for the jurors, beginning with a brief history of O'Toole's tenure at the university, his accolades and accomplishments.

"Coach O'Toole loved the university and had decided that even should an offer come from a larger school, the University of Northwest Idaho was where he wanted to be," he said. "However, all of this changed in the spring of last year when a former player on

Coach O'Toole's baseball team—a player who'd been dismissed from the team, and whose father is a major contributor to the university's athletic programs—claimed that O'Toole had asked him to show two recruits 'a good time.' According to this player, Rufus Porter, a good time included taking them to a party where they consumed alcohol and engaged in sexual acts with strippers—all allegedly paid for by Coach O'Toole from a university athletic account."

Karp had to be careful how he worded the reasons behind Rufus Porter's dismissal from the team. At a pretrial hearing, Zusskin had successfully argued that the plaintiff and his attorneys should not be allowed to say that Rufus Porter had been kicked off the team because of the sexual assault charges filed by Maly Laska. "The charges were dropped," the attorney had pointed out. "And even if the case had been adjudicated and Porter found guilty, it would be unfairly prejudicial to the rights of the defendants to a fair trial because they would be seen in the same light as an accused rapist."

The judge agreed and said that the plaintiff and his attorneys would be limited to saying that Porter had been dismissed "for conduct detrimental to the team." And that O'Toole had refused to reinstate him despite pressure from the university.

Karp hoped that the jurors would sense that there was more to the story. But at least they would have some motive for Porter to unjustly accuse the coach. "And," he now told the jurors, "only when Coach O'Toole refused to let Porter back on the team did he make these grossly unfair and untrue accusations."

"However," Karp went on, "although we will prove to you that these allegations were false, they are not what this lawsuit is about." He went on to explain how based on Porter's charges, O'Toole had been brought before an ACAA hearing panel "and without the opportunity to confront his accuser, or present evidence, or call witnesses of his own, Coach Mikey O'Toole was summarily suspended from coaching for a period of ten years."

Karp let the number sink in before continuing. "Ten long years, ladies and gentlemen, a veritable death sentence to his coaching career. But the injustice did not stop there. When Coach O'Toole asked the university through its president, E. 'Kip' Huttington, for the opportunity to clear his name at a public hearing conducted at the university, his request was denied. He was told that it would not be in the best interest of the school and—if you can somehow get your arms around this—that it would not be in his own best interest. He was told to move on with his life . . . to move on with his life having been denied the birthright of every American to face his accusers, defend his innocence against malicious lies, and continue to pursue his chosen profession."

Karp hoped that his "little speeches" from his voir dire questioning of the day before were resonating with the jury. "During the course of this trial, you will hear us discuss something called a liberty interest. Now, most of us think of liberty as 'freedom'—for instance, the freedom, or liberty, to live where we want, or do what we want and say what we want as long as we don't commit a crime or infringe on the liberty of other people. However, our courts have also held that there's another type of liberty, and that's the liberty to seek employment in the career of our choice. And it is that liberty, ladies and gentlemen, that was taken from Coach O'Toole without a fair hearing."

It was at this point that Karp stopped to go over his conclusion, which he'd altered the night before after his confrontation with Coach Anderson. "If I may, I'd like to divert for a moment to tell you a story about one of the members of the ACAA hearing panel that so cavalierly acted to destroy our client's life. That man is sitting in the back of the courtroom right now—the white-haired gentleman in the last row behind the defendant's table."

Everyone in the courtroom turned to look at Coach Anderson, whose eyes narrowed and cheeks blushed but who otherwise made no indication that he had unexpectedly become the focal point of Karp's statement. "His name is J. C. Anderson, who some of you may recognize as one of the most successful college football coaches of his era."

"Objection," Zusskin said, his baritone reverberating off the wooden walls of the courtroom as he stood up from his seat between Welt on one side and Huttington on the other. "Coach Anderson is not a participant in this trial. I see no purpose to this little anecdote."

"Mr. Karp?" Judge Allen said.

"Your Honor, if you'll bear with me for a moment, I think it will become clear how this 'little anecdote' applies to what we are doing here today," Karp said.

Judge Allen's lips twisted as he considered, and then he nodded. "I'll allow it; however, please get to your point quickly."

"Thank you, Your Honor," Karp said. "I will." He then repeated the story of hearing Anderson speak at the basketball camp. "I never forgot what he said about life not being a matter of winning and losing, but about fair play. And in the end, fair play is also what this trial is really all about. It was something that Coach Anderson and the other members of that hearing panel seemed to have forgotten."

Karp studied the twelve faces of the jurors and noted their eyes flitting from him to the coach and back. It was time to deliver his message. "We intend to prove by a preponderance of the evidence that the truth of this case is that the American Collegiate Athletic Association and the University of Northwest Idaho and its president, Huttington, acting in concert, created and disseminated false and defamatory accusations that have so stigmatized Coach O'Toole that even should his suspension be lifted, or if he waits ten long years, it will prevent him from coaching again. How do I know? Well, you will hear from athletic directors of other colleges and universities—men who will acknowledge that even though Coach O'Toole is eminently qualified, they would never be allowed to hire him given the nature of the charges brought against him."

Karp looked into twelve pairs of eyes. "We will learn from the evidence the real truth in this case—that the defendants acted with malice, meaning they knew the charges against Coach O'Toole were false and acted with a reckless disregard for truth." He allowed his voice to rise and grow tight. "That, ladies and gentlemen, is the legal definition of malice. Justice cries out, good conscience demands, and common sense dictates that you will not permit this malice to breathe another moment."

Karp took his seat and calmly watched Zusskin rise from his like some great Shakespearean actor relishing the moment before he delivers his lines. "That was a beautiful speech," the attorney said at last. "The sort of speech we might expect on the Fourth of July—all about American birthrights and the Constitution. I myself might have been moved by those words in some other time and place. But ladies and gentlemen of the jury, in this courtroom today, those words were little more than smoke and mirrors intended to disguise what this trial is really about. Allow me to return for a moment to what we believe are the true facts of this case."

Rufus Porter, he said, had been a dedicated member of the university baseball team who "through no fault of his own . . . and with questionable reasoning saw his minutes on the playing field dwindle. As such, he became desperate to please his coach so that when that coach asked him to do something they both knew was not right, he went ahead and did it anyway. He was the instrument of Mr. O'Toole's bid to lure players who might lead his team to a national championship."

The facts will show, he said, that the recruits in question had been truthful when they said that Mr. O'Toole was aware of the party and had sponsored it. "And they told this to an objective investigator for the ACAA shortly after these allegations came to light, not months later when a New York City police detective hunted them down on behalf of Mr. O'Toole and got a different story. You'll also hear from other corroborating witnesses that calls were placed from Mr. O'Toole's office and that alcohol and the services of strippers were purchased using a credit card entrusted to Mr. O'Toole by the university.

"But I agree with Mr. Karp somewhat. The allegations raised by Rufus Porter against Mr. O'Toole are not really what this trial is about. This trial is about whether the ACAA panel, and the university, was acting in accordance with their rules and regulations when they conducted an investigation, held a hearing, and then suspended Mr. O'Toole for violating those rules and regulations."

Zusskin looked up at the ceiling of the courtroom for a moment and sighed. "A few minutes ago, Mr. Karp eloquently spoke about our rights as Americans. Well, he left out some rights, including the right of private entities and institutions to conduct their affairs without undue interference from the government. Let me give you an example. What should be the role of the courts when a member of a country club is expelled for consistently breaking the rules regarding the wearing of a shirt with a collar? Should our courts be tied up because the rule breaker was not given the opportunity to cross-examine or confront the club's board of directors? Or say an employer terminates the employment of someone who is not performing their job in a satisfactory manner or in accordance with the rules and regulations surrounding that employment. What if it was a doctor or an airline pilot who got caught drinking on the job? Should they be able to sue the hospital or airline because they were not afforded a trial? The government will step in to protect certain classes from discrimination based on race, religion, national origin, gender, or age, but do we want the government telling private entities how to conduct themselves at every little turn?"

Zusskin pointed out that the jurors could expect the plaintiff to attack the transcript of the interviews of the two recruits "because it is not the entire transcript of every little thing that was said. For the purposes of the hearing, the transcript only dealt with the questions and answers relevant to the panel. Did Coach O'Toole know about the party? Did he encourage Rufus Porter to take two recruits out of the dormitory and show them a 'good time'? And did Coach O'Toole facilitate this 'good time' by making arrangements with an escort service and paying for them as well as the alcohol that was consumed by these underage recruits? And, lastly, did he then attempt to interfere with the investigation of these charges?"

Zusskin pointed out that the ACAA investigator, Larkin, was following standard procedure when he transcribed only the statements that were relevant and then reused the tape. "There was nothing malicious, a word Mr. Karp likes to throw around, about Mr. Larkin's actions."

Zusskin walked back to the defense table, where, with his back to the jury, he winked at Karen Welt, who was watching him with adoration. As if suddenly remembering something, he turned back to the jury. "If you please, one last comment regarding Mr. Karp's little story about Coach Anderson. I believe that his point was that fair play is as American as apple pie. But in sports, doesn't fair play mean playing by the rules of the game? We might not like all of those rules—heck, I played safety for my college football team and would have loved to pop those receivers before they caught the ball—but we have to abide by the rules or we are not playing fair. My point is that Mr. O'Toole signed a contract agreeing to abide by the rules, including the use of panels to hear complaints and make rulings. And now he doesn't want to play by those rules. We believe that you should insist that he does. Thank you."

Boy, he's good, Karp thought as Zusskin took his seat and Judge Allen asked them to call their first witness.

"Thank you, Your Honor," Meyers said, rising from his seat. "We call Mikey O'Toole."

O'Toole got up from his seat at the plaintiff's table and climbed into the witness stand, where he was sworn in. He then sat and smiled at the jurors. "Good morning," he said quietly. Most returned the greeting and a few even smiled back.

The first part of O'Toole's testimony repeated Karp's opening regarding who he was, how he came to be a coach at the university, and a brief history of his time there leading up to the recruiting event. They then entered the more delicate area of when and how O'Toole learned of the party that led to the dismissal of Rufus Porter from the team.

Karp and Meyers had decided that the best offense was to go after the ACAA case against O'Toole. They didn't want to rely just on a strategy centered on whether O'Toole had received a fair hearing that protected his rights to due process without showing that the allegations against him were false and that the entire case had been a farce from the beginning.

"At what point did you learn about the party?" Meyers asked.

"After Rufus was . . ." O'Toole had been about to say "arrested" but caught himself just in time. "After Rufus violated team rules and was dismissed for conduct detrimental to the team. It was after that I was told by Clyde Barnhill, the university's attorney, that Porter was accusing me of the allegations."

"Did you at any point encourage Rufus Porter to show these two recruits a 'good time' by taking them to a party where alcohol was served and they would engage in sexual conduct?"

"I did not."

"Did you arrange for strippers from the Pink Pussycat Escort Service or pay for such activities?"

"No."

"Did you pay for alcohol?"

"No."

Meyers asked if it was possible for someone else to have used the telephone in his office and have access to the credit card.

"Yes," O'Toole replied. "I let students, including my players, use the office—sometimes to call home, or as a place to do their homework. Sometimes they just hang out there before or after practice, and I'm not always around. I trust them."

"What were your instructions regarding the recruits on the night in question?"

"They were to attend a team dinner and then be taken back to the dormitory with lights out at ten p.m."

After the review of the history, Meyers moved on to the ACAA hearing, asking O'Toole to recall what he could of how it was conducted and what questions he was asked. "How long did it take the panel to reach a decision to suspend you?"

"About an hour."

"An hour. And can you explain to the jury the effect the ACAA decision to suspend you will have on your career?"

O'Toole tried to clear his throat and when he couldn't, he reached for a glass of water and drank before answering. "It's over," he said simply.

"By that you mean it's over at the University of Northwest Idaho?"

"No," O'Toole said, shaking his head. "It's over at the college level, and probably high school, everywhere."

"How do you know that?"

"I've made some calls regarding open positions at other colleges and universities."

"And what's been the response?"

"In at least three circumstances, the athletic directors have said they would like to hire me, but they can't," O'Toole replied.

"They can't?"

O'Toole shook his head again. "They'd never get it past the administration at their schools. . . . I'm the guy who gave recruits alcohol and paid for strippers and sex. I'm damaged goods. The press would tear them apart."

"Have you explained that you're innocent of the charges?"

"Yes, and I think they believe me," O'Toole replied. "But it doesn't matter. I'm a pariah. The publication of the charges against me contemporaneous with my firing has ended my coaching career."

Meyers had intended to ask a few more questions but could tell that his friend was on the verge of breaking down, so he decided to quit. "Thank you, Coach O'Toole," he said, and turned to Zusskin. "Your witness."

Zusskin began his cross-examination of O'Toole by asking if there was a reason Rufus Porter might have wanted to "do anything to get more playing time."

O'Toole shrugged. "I'm sure all athletes want to impress their coaches."

"Was his playing time diminishing?"

"Yes," O'Toole acknowledged. "There are better players on the team."

A loud snort from the spectator section momentarily stopped the proceedings. All eyes focused on a large man in the second row behind the defense table. But with Judge Allen staring at him, Big John Porter made no other sounds.

Zusskin turned back to O'Toole. "It's my understanding that after a final meeting, you essentially just sort of turned the recruits over to your players and you had no way of knowing what happened after that, am I correct?"

"Well, yes. I trusted my players to follow my rules."

"Which included handing the responsibility of watching out for these teenagers to young men not much older than they were?"

"Yes."

"Mr. O'Toole, we've heard a lot about how easy it is to use your office. Would you say there's a lot of privacy in the office?"

"No, not really," O'Toole replied. "There's often quite a bit of activity."

"So it might be difficult for someone to use your office and privately place a call to an escort service, pay for it with a credit card taken from a drawer in your desk, and then call in an order of booze and also pay for that?"

O'Toole shook his head. "Well, not really. They'd just have to pick a time when no one was around. Like during practice there are usually not many other people there."

"I see," Zusskin replied in a manner meant to imply that he did not see at all and neither should the jury.

Zusskin ended his cross-examination by showing O'Toole the contract he'd signed with the university. "Does this contract state that you agree to abide by the rules, regulations, and decisions of the American Collegiate Athletic Association?"

"Yes."

"And would that include the decision reached by the ACAA hearing panel following its procedures?"

"I guess."

"You guess? Is there another possible answer?"

"No. I meant that I guess that would include the decision reached by the ACAA panel."

"Was this a valid contract when you were asked to appear before the ACAA panel?"

"Yes."

"One last question, Mr. O'Toole. I just want to make sure we're clear about this. You were given the opportunity to make a statement in your defense at the ACAA hearing?"

O'Toole nodded. "Yes, but—"

"I didn't ask for an explanation," Zusskin interrupted. "The universe is full of justifications. Just a simple yes or no."

"Yes."

When Zusskin sat down, Karp and Meyers conferred for a moment before the young attorney rose for redirect.

"Coach O'Toole," Meyers said, emphasizing O'Toole's title, which he'd noticed Zusskin had purposefully avoided, "did you think that signing that contract superseded your constitutional rights as an American citizen?"

"No, I did not," O'Toole replied.

"And I think you were about to add to your answer to Mr. Zusskin's question about whether you were allowed to give a statement to the hearing panel."

"Yes."

"Would you elaborate now, please."

"I was allowed to give a brief statement, essentially denying these accusations. But I wasn't—or you weren't, as my attorney— allowed to cross-examine Rufus Porter, or the ACAA investigator, Jim Larkin, or anyone who spoke against me and we weren't permitted to call any witnesses on my behalf, in my defense."

"One last question. Coach O'Toole, is it accurate to say that you were prepared to abide by the rules, as Mr. Zusskin asked you, as long as they were administered in a fair, impartial, and honest fashion?"

"Yes, that would be accurate."

"Thank you, Coach O'Toole, that's it from me," Meyers said, and looked at Zusskin, who didn't bother to look up from his notes when he replied, "No further questions."

The opening statements and O'Toole's testimony had taken the trial up to the noon hour, when Judge Allen called for a lunch break. When court resumed, Karp called the baseball players Clancy Len and Tashaun Willis as character witnesses, although technically the purpose was to ask them if they had any knowledge of Coach O'Toole sponsoring or paying for parties "at which alcohol is served to underage players and strippers are present."

Both young men had replied in the negative. Even at team parties at the coach's house, players were allowed to drink beer only if they were twenty-one or older "and we have to give him our car keys." Although not said in so many words, the love and the respect both young men had for their coach was unmistakable.

Of more importance, however, Karp thought was the testimony of two athletic directors from other colleges and universities who, as O'Toole had indicated, testified under Meyers's questioning that they would have loved to hire him.

"In fact, we were preparing an offer after baseball season last spring to try to lure Coach O'Toole from the University of North-west Idaho to come coach for us," said David Huff, the athletic director of a Division I university known for its baseball teams. "When all of this came out, I was prepared to go to bat for him with my administration and the Board of Regents. I hoped we might even go to the ACAA and get the suspension lifted, maybe with probation. But the administration felt it would be a public relations disaster, and I wasn't allowed to offer him the job."

"Did you end up hiring another coach for the position?" Karp asked.

"Yes," Huff answered, and then surprised him by turning to O'Toole. "Sorry, Mikey," he added. "You know who my choice would have been."

After the athletic directors, Karp called Steele Dalton to the stand. When the young man was situated, Karp handed him a copy of the partial transcript that had been presented to the ACAA panel. After giving the young man a minute to read the transcript, he asked, "Would you say that is a complete record of your conversation with Mr. Larkin?"

"Hell, no," Dalton answered. "A lot of stuff got left out."

"What do you mean by that?" Karp asked.

"I was pretty nervous when the ACAA investigator guy was asking me the questions," Dalton said. "So I was just sort of going, like, 'uh-huh' because I wasn't sure what he wanted."

"Was there any particular reason you were nervous?" Karp asked as if this were the first he'd heard of the claim.

"Well, yeah," Dalton replied, pointing to where Larkin was examining his fingernails at the defense table. "He's a big guy and the ACAA can mess you up as a player if you get on their bad side.

Even before he turned on the tape recorder, he sort of got in my face and said I'd be in a lot of trouble if I lied to protect Coach O'Toole. He said he knew for sure that Coach O'Toole knew about the party and had paid for it. He also said that the underage drinking and sex stuff might hurt my eligibility if I didn't cooperate with the ACAA."

"And this was not recorded?"

"No, it was not," Dalton replied. "Only after he said all that stuff did he turn on the recorder and that's when I just sort of said whatever would get me out of there. But even then we had to stop and start over when he didn't like the way I said my answers."

"What do you mean by that?"

"Well, for instance, he asked me if Coach O'Toole had approved of the party," Dalton answered. "I told him the truth and that was that. When Rufus showed up at the dormitory, Rufus told me that Coach O'Toole sent him to take me and Mike Mason to a party for 'special' recruits."

"What was Mr. Larkin's reaction?"

"I could tell he didn't like it," Dalton replied. "Then he asked me if I was aware that Coach O'Toole had paid for the alcohol and strippers."

"And what did you reply?"

"Again, I said, 'That's what Rufus told me,' I had no way of knowing that myself," he said. "Coach O'Toole never said any of that to my face."

"What did Coach O'Toole tell you and the other recruits?" Karp asked.

"At the end of the day, he thanked us for coming," Dalton said, "and said he hoped that we'd consider the University of Northwest Idaho. He then sent us to dinner with the team but said we had to be back in the dormitory, lights out, by ten p.m."

"Nothing about a party?"

"Nope. Mike and I only heard about the party when we got back to the dorm. A little after bed check, Rufus came by and told us about the 'special party' because Coach O'Toole wanted to impress us. It sounded like fun so we snuck out."

"And you told all of this to Mr. Larkin?"

"Well, as much as he would let me," Dalton replied. "He turned off the tape recorder and told me that I was lying. He said that if I didn't start telling the truth, he would personally see that I lost my scholarship and he'd make sure the story about the party and the strippers got in my hometown newspaper so that my parents and all my friends would see it . . ."

"Was there something you were ashamed of?"

"Well, Rufus said that Coach O'Toole had paid the strippers to give us oral sex and, well, that's what happened," Dalton replied, turning red and keeping his eyes averted from the jury.

"So did he turn the tape recorder back on after that?" Karp asked.

"Yes," the young man said, and held up the abbreviated transcript. "That's what this is. I was scared and just decided that I would just agree with whatever he asked and get the hell out of there."

"Now, Mr. Dalton, according to the transcript provided to the ACAA panel, you agreed with Mr. Larkin's statements that Coach O'Toole asked you not to cooperate with the ACAA investigation and that if questioned, you were supposed to lie. Is that true?"

"What? That I agreed with Mr. Larkin or that Coach O'Toole asked me not to cooperate and to lie?" Dalton asked.

Karp smiled. "Thank you for pointing out for the jury that after more than a quarter of a century, I still don't know how to separate my questions. I suggest you consider a career in law," he said as a ripple of laughter went around the courtroom. "Let's start with whether you agreed with Mr. Larkin's statements that Coach O'Toole told you not to cooperate and to lie."

"Well, first I told him that it wasn't true," Dalton said. "In fact, I called Coach O'Toole after Mr. Larkin contacted me and said he was flying out to interview me about the party and accusation against the coach."

"And did Coach O'Toole tell you not to cooperate and to lie?"

"No, just the opposite," Dalton said. "He said that he had nothing to hide and that I should answer Mr. Larkin's questions truthfully."

"And you did that?"

"I tried," Dalton said. "But Mr. Larkin kept accusing me of trying to protect Coach O'Toole. He said he was going to send a full report of what occurred at the party to my mom."

"Sounds like a schoolyard bully. Have you since told your parents about what happened?" Karp asked before Zusskin could react to the first statement.

"Yes," Dalton replied.

"And what was their response?"

Dalton took a deep breath and let it out. "They were pretty unhappy. That's not the way I was raised. I guess I was just trying to be a big man on campus."

"Did they blame Coach O'Toole?"

"At first," Dalton said. "They thought that there should have been more supervision. But after they heard the truth, they realized that it wasn't Coach O'Toole's fault. I was a man now, and I had to take responsibility for my actions."

"Were there any parental repercussions?"

Dalton nodded. "Yeah, they took my car away and grounded me for the summer." Again, laughter swirled around the courtroom.

"Your witness," Karp said with a smile, and turned to Zusskin.

The attorney approached the stand holding up the abbreviated transcript like Moses holding up the stone tablets. "Mr. Dalton, did you or did you not give these answers to the questions put to you by Mr. Larkin?"

"I did, but—"

"I'm not asking 'but,'" Zusskin interrupted. "You just got done telling us that you're a man now and had to take responsibility for your actions, which means answering my question yes or no. You have a copy of the transcript. Did you give these answers to Mr. Larkin?"

"Yes, sir."

"All right," Zusskin said. "I believe that the bailiff has already distributed copies of the transcript, so let's all read along, shall we? I direct the panel's eyes to line three of the first page."

"Do you mean line three of the page numbered seven?" Karp asked innocently.

"Yes, Mr. Karp," Zusskin replied. "I'll read the part of Investigator Larkin, who asked, 'Was Coach Mikey O'Toole aware that you were going to a party that other recruits were not invited to?' And your reply was?"

Dalton looked at the transcript and recited his line. "I said, 'Uh-huh.'"

"Good," Zusskin said. "Then Larkin asked, 'Did Coach O'Toole pay for the beer and entertainment, including sex with prostitutes, at this party?' And you answered?"

"'Uh-huh.'"

Zusskin turned to the next page. "This is a bit later in the interview . . ."

"Objection," Karp said. "The middle portion of the interview is not here, so Mr. Zusskin is only reading what he wants and out of context."

Zusskin looked at the judge. "Your Honor, Mr. Karp is aware that this was all discussed at a pretrial hearing and knows full well that you have admitted this transcript—the transcript used by the ACAA hearing panel to render its decision, I might add."

"Overruled," Allen said without further comment.

Zusskin nodded and looked back down at the transcript. "The jury will note the following sequence beginning at line thirteen, where Larkin asked, 'Did Coach O'Toole tell you not to cooperate with this investigation?' Your answer, Mr. Dalton?"

"He said I didn't have to . . ."

"Then Larkin asked, 'Were you, in fact, told to lie if someone asked you questions about this case?' Your reply?"

"'Uh-huh.'"

Zusskin closed the transcript. "Mr. Dalton, you told the jury that Mr. Larkin threatened you and that you gave other answers, but there is no record of that, am I right?"

"Well, he recorded some of it," Dalton replied. "So I don't know what happened to it."

"And we have your word on that?"

"Yes."

"But we also have these affirmative answers to Mr. Larkin's questions?"

"Yes."

"And we also know that you are a young man who by his own admission snuck out of a dormitory, illegally consumed alcohol, and—excuse the expression, ladies and gentlemen of the jury—got a blow job from a hooker?"

Dalton nodded. "Yes, I did all those things," he said.

"So now we're supposed to believe a young man who would do those things?"

"It's the truth."

"Which truth, Mr. Dalton? The real truth or what you made up for Mr. Karp—"

"Objection," Karp said. "Counsel knows better than that."

"Sustained," Allen said. "Mr. Zusskin, please rephrase your question."

"Yes, Your Honor," Zusskin replied. "So which truth are we to believe, Mr. Dalton, what you told plaintiff's investigator a couple of weeks ago, or when you were questioned by Mr. Larkin several months ago?"

"I guess now," Dalton replied.

"You guess?"

"Well, yeah, only the stuff that makes Coach O'Toole look bad is on here," Dalton said, thumbing through the transcript.

Karp then kept the redirect short and sweet. "Mr. Dalton, did Coach O'Toole to your knowledge ever tell you that he was aware of this party, or that he arranged for alcohol or strippers?"

"No."

"Did he ask you to lie or not cooperate with the ACAA investigation?"

"No."

"How would you describe Coach O'Toole?"

Dalton shrugged. "He was great. I mean, he told us that if we joined the team, he expected us to work hard, follow the rules, and get good grades or we wouldn't play. But he also seemed fair and like we'd be judged on our ability and work ethic."

"Why didn't you end up signing at the University of Northwest Idaho?"

"Because of all the stuff that happened after this came out," Dalton said. He carefully picked his next words, as he'd been instructed at a pretrial hearing not to mention the rape charges against Rufus Porter. "It looked like Coach O'Toole wouldn't be there anymore. And to be honest, I thought that Rufus Porter was an ass and I didn't want to be on the same team with a guy like that."

"Why, you little . . ."

Karp and the rest of the courtroom turned to see Big John Porter fuming in his seat. He looked like he was about to say something else, but Clyde Barnhill, who was sitting next to him, put a hand on his shoulder and whispered something. Big John closed his mouth and glared at Dalton.

"Spectators will refrain from making comments, or they will be removed from this courtroom," Allen said. "Am I understood?"

Porter nodded but continued to glare at Dalton. When Dalton was dismissed, Big John began to rise to follow him. However, Fulton saw what was happening and got up to escort the young man. The big detective hesitated at the end of the pew with his eyes on Porter, who swallowed hard and sat down.

"Is there a problem?" Judge Allen asked, looking at the two large men.

Fulton turned to the judge and shook his head. "No, sir. No problem here."

24

"THE DEFENSE CALLS E. KIP HUTTINGTON." ATTORNEY
Karen Welt sounded nervous as she turned to look back at the
table where her client, the university president, conferred with her
co-counsel, Steve Zusskin.

Sitting at the defense table, Karp almost felt sorry for the
young woman, who appeared to be in her early thirties and for
the most part had hardly participated in either the pretrial motions hearing or the trial itself. It was obvious that Zusskin was
directing traffic for the defense, and even now seemed to be in-
structing Huttington.

Swallowing hard and nodding to Zusskin, who kept a hand on his
arm, Huttington finally rose and crossed the floor to the witness
stand to be sworn in.

Karp looked at his watch. Almost one o'clock in the afternoon on
Friday. He'd wrapped up the plaintiff's case by calling the former
recruit, Michael Mason, to the stand for what was nearly a carbon
copy of Dalton's testimony, and then a similar cross-examination by
Zusskin, who'd gone through the same exercise of making Mason
read from the abbreviated transcript.

Returning from the lunch break, Karp and Meyers told O'Toole that they felt they had a slight edge but not a clear-cut victory. A lot would hinge on whether the jury believed Dalton and Mason, the two lawyers agreed.

"Still, compared to what we were up against before Detective Fulton found and talked to Dalton and Mason, and we learned the truth about their interviews with Larkin," Karp said, "I'll take what we got anytime."

As Welt began by having Huttington introduce himself and wade through his version of the history regarding the O'Toole case, Karp looked again at his watch and wondered how his wife and the 221B Baker Street Irregulars were doing up in Sawtooth. If things went according to plan, she'd said she would know whether their mission would pan out by the time court was finished for the day. Until then, he couldn't expect to hear anything, as there was no cell phone reception in that part of Idaho.

There was little new or unexpected to Huttington's testimony. According to the university president, he'd only been following the rules and regulations of the ACAA when he first turned over Rufus Porter's complaint, and then when he declined O'Toole's request for a name-clearing hearing. "On the advice of counsel, we thought that any such hearing might breach our standing with the ACAA as the final arbiter of such matters," he said, and then repeated what he'd told O'Toole. "And we wanted the university—and Coach O'Toole—to move on and get this terrible business behind us."

Meyers's cross-examination of Huttington contained no fire-works either. Indeed, by the time his co-counsel finished, Karp thought the jury would think Huttington was a witness for the plaintiff. Under Meyers's questioning, Huttington's testimony was largely laudatory of Coach O'Toole. No, there'd never been a complaint lodged against the coach. Yes, the coach had one of the highest graduation rates for schools the size of Northwest Idaho, and yes, his squads had for the past two years been all-American academic teams because of their high grade point averages.

"Thank you, Mr. Huttington," Meyers said, and sat down to see if there would be a redirect.

Glancing over at the defense table, Karp noted that Zusskin was once again giving orders, only this time to Welt. She looked almost frightened as she nodded repeatedly and then stood to approach the witness stand.

"Mr. Huttington, do you like Coach O'Toole?" Welt asked.

Huttington looked at O'Toole and his mouth twisted as if he'd bitten into something sour. "I would have to say that prior to all of this that yes, I liked Coach O'Toole," he replied.

"What do you mean 'prior to all of this'; have you changed your mind?"

"Well, actually, I didn't believe he was capable of this sort of . . . 'mistake,' is what he called it," Huttington said. "Not until the day he came to my office and said something that changed my opinion of him, which until that time was very high."

This is rehearsed, Karp thought, and whispered to Meyers, "Something's coming out of left field. I can feel it."

"And would you tell the jury, please, what it was that he said," Welt asked.

"Yes, it was quite sad, really," Huttington said, shaking his head. "It was after the news stories broke about Rufus Porter's accusations against Coach O'Toole. He called and asked if he could come see me 'as a friend.' As I said, I liked him and was anxious to help if I could, so I said sure. He showed up at my office and immediately broke down and started to cry."

Karp glanced at O'Toole, whose face was turning red. The younger man reached for a glass of water but his hands were trembling so hard that when he brought it to his lips the water sloshed out and splashed on the table.

"Steady, Coach," Karp whispered. "You're at bat, and everybody is watching. You have to shut it out, focus on the pitch."

O'Toole acknowledged that he heard by nodding. And Karp noticed that his hand was steadier when he put the glass back down.

"Did he say why he was crying?" Welt asked, and looked at the jury as if this behavior was strange indeed.

"Yes, he said he'd made a mistake," Huttington replied. He glanced at the jury, too, and then at Zusskin, before turning back to Welt. "He said that he was responsible for the party and planned it because he was anxious to get Mason and Dalton to sign. As everybody knows, he wants to get invited to the College World Series and 'needed the horses.' "

"Was there anything else he said, something to indicate that there were deficiencies on his current team?" Welt asked.

"Yes," Huttington answered. He looked at the jurors and apologized. "I'm sorry about the language here, but he said that he needed Dalton and Mason because they were white, smart, and better team players compared to the 'me-first, dumb-ass blacks' on his team."

"Did he use the term blacks?"

"No, and again my sincere apologies if this offends anyone, but the word he used was 'niggers.' "

Everybody in the courtroom seemed to inhale at once. O'Toole covered his mouth while in the back row, Len Clancy shouted, "That's a lie. He never uses that sort of language."

Judge Allen banged his gavel to restore order as Meyers jumped to his feet. "I object to all of this, Your Honor. None of this was in any deposition of Mr. Huttington by either the plaintiff or the defense."

"Is that true, Ms. Welt?" Allen asked.

"It just was brought to our attention last week," the attorney replied. "I believe Mr. Huttington had his reasons to hide the truth."

Allen turned to the witness. "Mr. Huttington, is there a reason you didn't report this before?"

Huttington shifted uncomfortably in his seat. "Yes, Your Honor. As I said, I personally liked Coach O'Toole and didn't believe the accusations against him. Even when he made these admissions, I still saw him as a basically good man who made a mistake and was sincerely apologetic. I am a Christian and believe that when a man asks for forgiveness, it should be given. Also, I felt that he came to me in confidence, as a friend, and that I could not betray that trust."

"And that's why you kept this important information to yourself?" Allen asked with a scowl.

"Well, I should point out this isn't the first mention of this issue," Huttington said. "Myself and Mr. Barnhill met with Coach O'Toole and told him that we thought that the ACAA would be more lenient if he just admitted that he made a mistake. I was referring to his admission when we told him that. We at the university hoped all of this could be resolved so that with a lesson learned we could move on. He chose instead to deny the accusations."

"For the record, Your Honor," Zusskin said, rising from his chair. "We intend to call Mr. Barnhill to the stand and will stipulate that we expect his testimony will confirm what Mr. Huttington just said about the meeting with Mr. O'Toole."

The judge turned to Karp and Meyers. "Gentlemen, your response?"

"Just a moment, Your Honor," Karp said, and began whispering to Meyers, who nodded and smiled grimly. Reaching to the shelf behind him for the three-ring binder containing his deposition of Huttington, Meyers stood up. "May I approach the witness, Your Honor?"

"You may."

Meyers strode across the floor and nearly tossed the binder to Huttington. "Is this a copy of your deposition taken last February?" he asked without regard for formalities or manners.

Huttington made a show of opening the binder and leafing through several of the pages. Finally, he said, "Yes, it appears to be."

"Turn to the second-to-last page," Meyers continued.

Huttington did as told. He looked up and tried to smile at the jury, though to Karp it came off more as a grimace.

"Now look four lines from the top, which begins with me asking you a question," Meyers said. "You there?"

"Yes."

"I asked, 'Is there anything else you can think of that would be relevant or significant regarding this case? Something I might have missed or was omitted?' Is that an accurate reading of what I said?"

"Yes."

"You can skip Mr. Barnhill's response, but I then said, 'Mr. Huttington, I asked you a question. This is a deposition and you must answer my questions, even if your attorney objects. And do remember you're under oath.' Is that correct?"

"Yes."

"And you acknowledge here today, in front of this jury that you were under oath to tell the whole truth, just like you are today," Meyers said, letting his anger show.

"Yes," Huttington replied. "I was . . . I am . . . under oath."

"Yes, please remember that," Meyers said. "Now read the next line, which you addressed to Mr. Barnhill."

"I said, 'That's okay, Clyde, we have nothing to hide here.' "

"Nothing to hide," Meyers repeated. "So skip a couple of lines to your answer to my question, which was, 'Is there anything else you can think of that would be relevant or significant regarding this case? Something I might have missed or was omitted?' "

"I said, 'Uh, no, I can't think of anything to add that would be relevant or significant,' and then you asked if I was sure," the university president replied.

"Thank you for adding that," Meyers replied tightly. "And were you sure?"

Huttington nodded.

"The court reporter couldn't hear that, Mr. Huttington. Were you sure?"

"I said I was but that was because—" Huttington began to say, but was interrupted by Meyers.

"I didn't ask you to explain anything, as Mr. Zusskin likes to inform witnesses," the young attorney spat. "However, my next question to you is . . . wouldn't you think that a conversation with Coach Mikey O'Toole in which he admitted he'd made a mistake and had sponsored this party would be relevant or significant?"

"I suppose, but like I said, I was trying to protect him," Huttington replied.

"You suppose? You suppose it might be relevant or significant?" Meyers said, looking to the jury, some of whom had smiles on their faces as they watched the young attorney light into the witness, who was turning paler by the moment.

"Yes, in hindsight, I should not have tried to protect Coach O'Toole," Huttington replied.

"And maybe you should have answered honestly—since I 'suppose' you understood you were under oath—when asked if you could think of anything else that was relevant or significant," Meyers shot back.

"Objection," Zusskin said, trying to sound as if this was all making a mountain out of a molehill. "Counsel should save it for his closing arguments."

"And maybe counsel should warn his client about perjury," Meyers replied.

Allen rapped his gavel once. "Gentlemen, quit the sniping. The objection is overruled. However, if you have anything else to say, Mr. Meyers, please frame it as a question to the witness."

"Yes, Your Honor," Meyers said, and turned back to the witness stand. "So, Mr. Huttington, I believe a few minutes ago you told the jury that during this alleged meeting between you and Coach O'Toole at which he admitted he'd made a mistake, he also said he did it because he was desperate to sign Mr. Dalton and Mr. Mason because, and I believe I have the quote correct here, they were 'white, smart, and better team players compared to the "me-first, dumb-ass blacks" on his team.' Is that correct?"

"Yes, uh, that's approximately what he said," Huttington replied, looking desperately at Zusskin, who looked back without emotion.

Meyers moved closer to the witness stand but turned to face the jury when he said, "Such a vicious, malicious, terrible thing to say . . . and yet you made no mention of it when I asked you if you had anything relevant or significant to add to your deposition."

Huttington looked at the young attorney in front of him and shook his head, then shrugged. "I guess I wasn't . . . I don't know . . . I guess I wasn't . . . ."

"What, Mr. Huttington, you guess you weren't telling the truth?" Meyers finished for him.

"Objection!" Zusskin thundered. "Counsel just asked and answered his own question!"

"Sustained," Allen replied mildly. "Mr. Meyers, please allow the witness to answer your questions for himself."

"Yes, thank you, Your Honor," Meyers replied. "All right then, Mr. Huttington, did you tell the truth when I asked you if there was anything relevant or significant to add to your deposition?"

"I . . . well, no," Huttington replied weakly.

"So why should the jury believe you're telling the truth now?"

Huttington looked at his lawyers, who were looking down at the defense table. "I don't know," he said.

"Neither do we. No further questions for this witness," Meyers retorted, and walked back to the plaintiff's table, where O'Toole and Karp greeted him with smiles.

After Huttington's testimony, Zusskin had called a representative of the ACAA to explain the rules and procedures governing complaints and hearings. It was largely fodder to take up time until the end of the day so that the defense could use the weekend to recoup and plan their counter on Monday, which would be highlighted with the testimony of investigator Jim Larkin.

As the spectators and the defense counsel filed out of the courtroom, Karp looked back and saw that there was one last spectator still standing in the pews. Coach J. C. Anderson looked at him, then shook his head and left. Same to you, Coach, he thought.

However, it turned out that he was wrong about Anderson. An hour later, as he was awaiting a call from Marlene, there was a knock on the door of his hotel room.

Opening the door, Karp found Anderson standing in the hall. Without saying anything, the old coach handed him a large envelope. Inside had been a tape cassette and a large sheaf of papers.

Karp had looked at the papers, which turned out to be a 135-page transcript of Larkin's interview with Steele Dalton and Michael Mason. "But how? Why?" he asked as he invited Anderson into the room.

"The how is simple," Anderson replied. "Zusskin kept the tape in his desk drawer at ACAA headquarters in Boise. The day after the hearing, I dropped by to ask him a few questions you'd raised about the transcript. He had the tape lying on his desk but stuck it in the drawer when he saw me look at it. He told me it had been taped over, but I figured he was lying or he wouldn't have bothered to hide it. So after your little speech about me the other day, I had a friend, a former secretary of mine who I had a thing with a long time ago, borrow it for me. She also made the transcript."

"And the why?" Karp asked.

Anderson looked at him for a long moment. "The why is a little more complicated."

The old man walked over to Karp's window, which faced north into the mountains. "Beautiful view, no wonder Coach O'Toole likes it here," he said, and took a deep breath.

"I believe in the system, Mr. Karp. For most of my adult life, I've abided by its rules and regulations and believed that it had the best interests of the student-athlete at heart. A lot of good people, who believed the way I did, have worked for that organization. Yes, there have been times when the association has been heavy-handed and arrogant. However, I looked at all the good things the association did and decided the good outweighed the bad."

The coach tapped on the window and turned back to face Karp. "But I've noticed a lot of changes with the association over the past ten, even fifteen years. It used to be about the student-athlete, now it's about the association and those in charge, about the power they wield and are unwilling to give up, even when they're wrong. It's a big corporation now, with overpaid executives telling coaches that they can't give a kid money to get home for Thanksgiving or they could be suspended. . . . And in the end, they're just a bunch of hypocrites who along with the universities rake in hundreds of millions of dollars in television revenues and ticket sales off the backs of college athletes."

"What I don't get," Karp said, "is why they went after Mikey O'Toole so hard on such a flimsy case. Even if any of it was true, and it isn't, they didn't have enough incontrovertible evidence to nail him for a parking ticket."

"That I don't know," Anderson said. "I'm aware there's some animosity there, a holdover from Mikey's brother, or maybe what the kid said at the funeral about his brother being blackballed. They got their noses out of joint on that one. Or maybe they did believe Porter based on bad fruit not falling far from a rotten tree. But a lot of it was also driven by the university—it was clear they wanted him out—and by Zusskin, but you'd have to ask him."

The coach stuck out his hand. "But I mostly brought that to you because of what you said to me about my little talk on fair play when you were a kid. I must have given that speech ten thousand times, and I believe every bit of it. You reminded me of that."

Karp shook the coach's hand. "See you Monday in court?"

"I'd rather not take the stand, if that's what you mean," the coach said. "But if you need me to, I will."

"I'll see what I can do to avoid it."

25

THE TWO GUARDS ON DUTY AT THE UNIFIED CHURCH OF THE Aryan People gatehouse peered through their gun slots into the moonlit forest across the highway, sighting along their AR15 rifles, hoping to get a shot at the intruder. A sudden yipping on the left followed by a howl on the right had them swinging their rifles back and forth like pendulums and spurred another argument.

"It's dogs," Andy Vonderborg stated authoritatively. "Or maybe coyotes. I've heared them before on my daddy's farm in Iowa."

"It was wolves, I tell ya," Ernie Hucker replied. "They're all over this part of Idaho. Rufus told me that, and he should know. Lived here all of his life."

Hucker kept lifting and dropping his goggles over his eyes. "I don't know about you, Andy, but these night-vision goggles give me the creeps the way they turn everything green in the moonlight, especially the snow under the trees." He put them back on, looked back through the sights on his rifle, and made little shooting noises. "Pow. Pow. Boy, I'd like to get me a wolf. I'm tired of shooting at paper targets. Maybe the race war will start soon and I can shoot me some niggers."

There was a howl again off to the left and they both swung their barrels in that direction, trigger fingers itching to snap off a couple of rounds. Then something landed in the gravel to the right of the gatehouse. They looked at the flash grenade just as it went off.

The effect through night-vision goggles was about the same as someone sticking white-hot pokers into their eyes. Howling, they ripped the goggles off.

"Ernie, help me, I can't see," Andy cried.

"I'm blind," Ernie shouted. "I can't help you, I'm blind, I tell ya!"

The young neo-Nazis screamed again, once, when unseen forces clubbed them to the ground and gagged them; and before they could say 'Heil, Hitler,' they had their wrists and ankles bound to-gether with plastic wrist cords.

"Done," Tran whispered triumphantly. "You too slow. It's those big fat Indian hands; the fingers get in each other's way. Now you owe me a dollar."

"Like hell," Jojola whispered back. "You had a head start on me and your guy is skinnier. You have hands like a girl, and why are we whispering; we checked it out, there's no bad guys within a mile of here."

The conversation stopped momentarily when Vonderborg groaned. "That was too easy," Jojola said. "These guys are the mas-ter race?"

"Doesn't exactly leave me trembling in fear," Tran agreed, toeing Hucker to make sure he wasn't dead. The skinny youth whim-pered. "Still want to shoot some niggers, tough guy? Maybe I shoot you." He looked at his companion with a grin. "Just like the old days. Shall I give the signal?"

"Be my guest," Jojola replied. "I'll get the gate."

Stepping back outside the gatehouse, Tran aimed a laser pointer up the road and gave two quick flashes. Immediately engines could be heard starting up and approaching at a rapid clip. Jojola opened the gate just as the dark forms of vehicles traveling without head-lights turned onto the gravel road and came to a stop next to the gatehouse.

Marlene Ciampi stepped out of the lead Hummer along with Sheriff Steve Ireland and a deputy. The next two Hummers carried the eight members of the Payette County Sheriff's Department SWAT team, who deployed as soon as their vehicles slid to a stop off to the side and took off running down the road.

"A little dramatic, aren't they," Ireland said, grinning at Marlene.

"Like their boss," she noted.

"Oh, to be young again."

The next two cars, a regular police cruiser and a pickup truck, were driven by Payette County deputies but otherwise occupied by the 221B Baker Street Irregulars. A third truck, driven by Tom Warren, held the kennels of his bloodhounds, who began to bay until he quickly got out and persuaded them to stop with doggie treats.

The scientists got out of their vehicles and stood gazing around, wide-eyed with excitement. Somebody quietly told a joke, probably Reedy, and the others laughed.

Behind the lead cars were four more vehicles, a large black minivan, and a big six-wheeled truck towing a trailer on which sat what looked like a baby bulldozer. The truck driver and the occupants of the minivan stayed in their vehicles.

That was by agreement with the sheriff, a six-foot-five, 250-pound block of granite with an immense dark mustache, who now walked over to Jojola and Tran and nodded toward the gatehouse. "I take it you two reserve deputies served the warrant," he said.

"We tried, but they resisted, sir, and are currently incapacitated," Jojola replied. "I'm afraid we'll have to serve the warrant farther up the road at the main compound, sir."

"Well, thanks for trying," Ireland growled. "Knock off the sir and let's get moving. We're wasting all of this beautiful dark."

Leaving the deputy to watch over the prisoners and the entrance, the three men walked back to the lead Hummer and got in, with Ireland driving and Marlene in the front passenger seat. He looked over at her. "Any ladies want to get off the train, better do it now."

Marlene gave him a sideways glance and shook her head. "Screw you. Let's go, Caveman."

"Yaba-daba-doo," Ireland replied. Putting the car into Drive, he stepped on the gas.

Yeah, look who's calling who dramatic, she thought with a smile as they tore down the road. The "Caveman" had been brought into the picture shortly after Marlene called Zook from Colorado, explained the Baker Street Irregulars plan, and suggested that they were going to need help with security.

Although there were concerns that the Unified Church had sympathizers in the Sawtooth police department, Zook had vouched for Ireland, the sheriff of Payette County.

"If it was up to him, he would have run the Unified Church off a long time ago," he said. "The guy's ex–Green Beret, served something like three tours in Vietnam. All sorts of medals. I once talked to him about what he thought of these Aryans who had just bought the place. He wasn't too happy about it, said that a lot of the guys he fought beside and bled with were black and Hispanic. He had always been known as a good judge of character. After that, all the rest to him was mere cosmetics."

When Ireland first met with Zook and Marlene, he'd listened to their plan and began to laugh. "So you're suggesting that I deputize an Indian police chief who's a thousand miles out of his jurisdiction and a Vietnamese . . . well, whatever he is that you're not saying, but I take it he isn't your typical Asian gentleman. And that with my little crew, we take on fifty or sixty armed Nazis, so that you and a bunch of ivory-towered theorists can dig up a car and a murder victim . . . maybe."

"That's about it in a nutshell," Marlene agreed.

Ireland looked at Zook, who nodded his head. The sheriff laughed again. "I like it. When do we get started?"

After Lucy, Jojola, Tran, and Ned arrived, they'd all met at O'Toole's house instead of the sheriff's office to avoid raising eyebrows and starting tongues wagging. By consensus, they'd agreed that Ireland would be the tactical commander of the security team.

"Colonel Steve Ireland was a legend in 'Nam, even for some of us who also spent a lot of time out in the bush, hunting guys in pajamas like this old fart," Jojola said, hooking a thumb at Tran.

"I will ignore your insults, as my people were building stone temples and delving into the arts and sciences, when yours were living in mud huts and howling at the moon," Tran said. "However, I concur with my esteemed comrade's assessment: Ireland was feared, a ferocious warrior, who some of my men thought could not be killed."

Ireland had brought with him U.S. Geological Survey topographical maps, which he laid out on the dining room table. Pulling a sausage-sized Mancuso cigar out of a side pocket of his camouflage pants, he bit off the end and was about to light it when he looked at Mikey O'Toole. "Sorry, do you mind?" he asked, holding up the cigar.

"Nah, I imbibe every once in a while myself," O'Toole replied. "I was just saying good-bye. I have to drive to Boise to start preparing for the trial with my lawyers. Good luck."

Ireland was soon puffing away as he leaned over the maps from one end so that the others could see from the other. "First thing, we're not going to beat these guys with overwhelming firepower. We've been keeping tabs on the Unified Church, and I'd estimate there's anywhere from forty to fifty of those idiots running around in there. I'd be willing to bet that ninety percent have never been in a firefight and will head for the hills as soon as things get real. But there may be ex-military, and some of these guys we've run into lately for regular crimes like assault and robbery have obviously had some training and are pretty aggressive. They're pretty well armed, too. The main compound and firing range is back five miles from the highway and we've had a tough time getting anyone inside. But we've listened in a time or two from nearby hills, and they've got automatic weapons and what sounds like fifty-cal machine guns."

Ireland began stabbing spots on the map with a meaty finger. "Gatehouse, two guys, usually the numbskulls who fucked up—nothing like putting your best guys out as your early warning system. Guard tower, right where the main road splits—one goes to the compound, right here, the other to the gravel pit, a couple of clicks down that road."

"You've done your homework," Marlene remarked.

Ireland blew a smoke ring up at the rafters. "I've been figuring since day one that we'd eventually have to take these jokers down," he said. "Of course, I thought I might get a little help from the feds. Anybody want to tell me why we're not calling them in?"

Nobody spoke. The big sheriff snorted smoke out of his nose and nodded. "Okay, I don't like dealing with those guys anyway."

Ireland looked back down at the map and drew a rough circle with a black felt-tip pen. "Main compound. Three barracks. Some office buildings. And the private residence of the Reverend Benjamin "Benji" Hamm, the grand pooh-bah of this particular band of morons. Place is surrounded by a twelve-foot chain-link fence topped by razor wire. Another guard post here . . . and here—unknown how many guys are on duty at night, we'll assume at least two."

Pointing back at the barracks, Ireland said, "The one guy we ever got inside said the barracks were made of reinforced concrete, which will take a pretty direct hit from more than I've even got. But if plan A doesn't work, and we have to go to plan B, our job will be to keep them pinned up inside, not try to take them."

"What's the matter, Caveman, are you a cave chicken?" Marlene joked. She and Ireland had been butting heads since they'd met. He was hopelessly chauvinistic and didn't want her involved in case "things get hairy," until Zook took him aside one day and apparently told him what he knew of some of Marlene's exploits against terrorists. The man had continued giving her a hard time, but it evolved into the sort of guff one soldier gives to another. And she'd given as good as she got.

Gagging on a cloud of blue smoke, Ireland chuckled as he wiped his eyes. "Damn, I got to love your moxie, Marlene. Next thing you know, she'll have us going after Osama himself."

Marlene smiled. "That's not a bad idea. Think you could do it?"

Ireland sucked on the end of the cigar and squinted at her through the cloud. "Maybe, with the right men and a plan," he said. "But I don't need to . . . my boys in Special Forces are hunting that little prick right now. It might be a month, it might be five years, but they're patient . . . they'll run him to the ground until he wakes up in his cave some morning with a knife at his throat."

He poked the map. "For the moment, we got plenty to worry about right here. I've got about a half dozen deputies and a pretty good four-man SWAT team I trained myself. With Jojola and Tran, especially if they can pull off plan A, we might be able to keep most of these guys occupied. But I'm worried about your security at the gravel pit, just in case some of these jokers bust out through our perimeter or you run into a patrol. These guys like to play army and maybe they're smart enough to keep some people out in the field."

"Well, I have an idea about where to find more men," Marlene said. But when she said what she was thinking, Ireland shook his head. "We have enough amateurs to babysit. And anybody that's personally involved is a potentially loose cannon."

Marlene dropped it for the time. But after the strategy meeting broke up and the others were off talking, Marlene and Zook took Ireland aside so that she could make her case again. "I know he's had some military training, and I'm betting a few of the others do, too," she said. "And these guys spend their lives walking around in the mountains and won't be tripping all over themselves."

"What makes you think this guy and his pal have military training?" Ireland said.

Marlene hadn't answered that night. But the next day, she introduced Ireland to Katarain, who'd asked to speak to the sheriff when she called the night before from O'Toole's house. Leaving them now in the office to talk, she'd excused herself.

A half hour later, when Ireland emerged, he'd given her a hard look. "This puts me in a funny position, lady," he said.

"I know," she replied. "But you're a father. Put yourself in his shoes for now."

Ireland looked back into the office. "All right, you're in," he said.

"But under those conditions." With that, the sheriff stomped out of the house.

Katarain emerged from the office and gave Marlene a hug. "Thank you."

"You deserve to be there," she replied. "What are the conditions?"

"The same as I asked of you," he answered. "That I be allowed to bury my daughter with her mother. After that, it doesn't matter."

The next step had been to get a search warrant. Marlene, Ireland, Zook, and Jack Swanburg, who'd flown in with the other members of the Baker Street Irregulars team, had gone to see Judge Linda Lewis.

"She's all right. A full-blood Nez Percé Indian who has no reason to like racists," Zook said. "But she's not going to be a pushover for a warrant. Folks around here, including judges, are pretty protective of their privacy and see transgressions against their neighbors as a threat to themselves, even if they don't particularly like the neighbors. There has to be a pretty good reason."

However, Zook had never seen Swanburg in action. In an empty courtroom, the little round man with the Santa Claus beard pulled out his laptop computer and soon had the judge mesmerized with his PowerPoint presentation.

First up was the photograph of the Cadillac and the pit. He pointed out the thin lava shell and gravel deposit, which combined with the conifer forest in the background "makes this a pretty good bet for northwest Idaho."

Next was the blowup of the Bucyrus steam shovel. "My associate, James Reedy, placed a call to the company," Swanburg said. "Their public relations gal was a big help. She said there's only a half dozen still in existence in the United States, one of them located at what was formerly Payette Sand and Gravel until the land was purchased by the Unified Church of the Aryan People. She doesn't think it's still in operation."

Swanburg switched to the blowup photograph of Maria Santacristina at the wheel of the car, staring out at the people in the courtroom. "I turn the floor over to Mr. Zook, Your Honor," he said quietly, and sat down.

Zook quickly went over the series of events, beginning with the disappearance of Maria Santacristina. "There's been no sign that she's alive," he said. "No calls to friends or family. No use of her credit cards or bank accounts. No one applying for work using her Social Security number. No police stops."

He went on to describe Maria's reputed affair with university president Kip Huttington and the positive pregnancy test strip found by her father, and ended with Huttington's report of his car being stolen.

"The car in the photograph is a 2003 Cadillac Eldorado," Zook said, referring to a report provided by Jesse Adare. "That's the same make, model, and year as the car Huttington says was stolen two days after Maria disappeared."

"All right," Lewis said. "I'm convinced. You get your warrant. But have you thought about how you're going to serve this, Steve? I don't expect they're going to welcome you with open arms, not unless it's firearms."

"We're going to sneak up on them when they're sleeping, Injun-style," Ireland said.

Lewis laughed but then her face got serious. "I don't want this turning into a Branch Davidian thing. That just breeds more nuts like Timothy McVeigh et al."

"I'll do my best, Linda, I mean Your Honor," Ireland corrected himself, and winked.

The judge sighed. "Why do I get the feeling that everything I say that you don't like goes in one of those big cauliflower ears and out the other?"

"Maybe 'cause there's not much in between," Ireland said. "Which reminds me, are you going to the Elks club barbecue next Sunday after church?"

"Wouldn't miss it," Lewis replied. "See you there?"

"Probably," Ireland. "Save me a burger if I'm late."

❊   ❊   ❊

The convoy swept down the road until they reached the first guard tower, where the SWAT team waited. Those going on to the compound got out of their vehicles.

"From here we hoof it. Don't want them to hear us coming," Ireland said to Marlene, who also got out of the Hummer. He turned to one of the SWAT members. "Hey, Ryan, any problem?"

Ryan spit a wad of tobacco on the road. "Hell, no," he complained. "They were asleep. So we tied 'em up nice and tight, and let them go back to nighty-night."

"Good man." Ireland looked at his watch and then at Marlene. "All right. We're right on schedule. We've got to cover three miles before dawn, and then we'll see if plan A works. So wait until it starts to get light before expecting to hear from me. If we have to go to plan B, you get ready to skedaddle in case things go bad. Either way, I'll be talking to you."

Marlene stuck out her hand. "Good luck, Caveman."

"Who needs luck when you got looks," he replied, shaking her hand. "See ya on the flip side, and thanks for inviting me in on your little picnic. I haven't had this much fun in thirty years."

With that, Ireland's team formed up and began running down the road at a fast clip. Marlene looked at her watch and walked back toward the other vehicles.

One hour later, the Reverend Benji Hamm woke from a dream in which he heard hounds baying somewhere in the distance, feeling that something just wasn't quite right. He felt for the warm body of the fifteen-year-old girl sleeping next to him, one of the perks of being the Supreme Leader, whose duty it was to propagate the white race. She mumbled something and turned away.

Hamm sat up in bed and squinted. The gray light of dawn was just beginning to slip in through the window, but it was enough to see that a strange man was sitting in the chair at the foot of his bed.

The man, a goddamn slant-eyed gook, put a finger to his lips in the international sign to remain quiet. Any ideas he had about ignoring the warning evaporated when he felt the muzzle of a gun pressed against his temple and heard the hammer being pulled back.

"Good morning, Benji," Jojola whispered in his ear. "We're Payette County sheriff's deputies and we're here to serve you with this search warrant."

Tran held up the paperwork and placed it on the end of the bed.

"You are also under arrest for covering up a murder, which qualifies you for a felony murder charge," Jojola continued quietly. "And if my guess is correct, the young lady in bed with you is a minor, so you're probably looking at sexual assault charges, too."

"How did you get in here?" demanded Hamm, a pudgy six-footer with weak eyes who'd risen to his position mostly due to his gift for demagogic racist oratory and his absolute obedience to his absent superiors.

"That's not important," Jojola said, brushing off a good forty minutes of crawling through snow and pine needles up to the security fence, cutting a hole, and waiting for Tran to pick the lock after getting the signal from one of the SWAT team members that the security system had been deactivated. "Let's just say that your security wasn't state of the art. But for future reference, just remember that you will never be safe from me or my friend here. He wanted to cut your throat, and then serve you the warrant. But I thought we should serve you the warrant and give you a chance to cooperate first."

"You'll never get out of here," Hamm said, trying to summon his famous command of words but having a difficult time swallowing.

"Then neither will you. What's it going to be?"

Hamm considered his options. "I'll play along for now," he said. "After all, my attorneys will tear you to pieces for this intrusion."

"I've had worse enemies, including the distinguished gentleman at the foot of your bed," Jojola replied as Tran waved.

"What do you want me to do?"

Jojola got up from where he'd been kneeling by the side of the bed. "Nothing much. If my guess is correct, you're all set up from here with a public address system. So I'd like you to call an early morning rollout. Tell them you have an important announcement."

"They won't buy that crap," Hamm said.

"Well, then, I guess my friend is just going to have to persuade you to do your best," Jojola said, and nodded to Tran, who stood and slid a knife from a leg scabbard.

Hamm considered his options. There were nearly four dozen men in the barracks; many of them had been training for months. And there were enough weapons—including handheld rocket launchers and machine guns—to make the event in Waco, Texas, look like a walk in the park. He had wealthy friends in powerful places who made sure the compound had the best weaponry money could buy.

Then again, the Asian looked like he meant business. Better to live to fight another day, he decided.

"All right, all right, I'll try," he said. He rolled out of bed, flipped a couple of switches. "Arise, Aryan people, a new day has dawned. Report to the parade field for an important message from your leader. All warriors of the white race must report."

Hamm looked at his captors. "How was that?"

Jojola shrugged. "We're about to find out. But if something goes wrong, and one of my friends outside gets shot, I won't hesitate to blow what few remaining brains you have all over the grass."

Hamm stood and was allowed to pull on his underwear and T-shirt. "It's cold out there," he complained when they wouldn't let him wear anything else.

"Then you'll want this to go quickly," Tran said as he turned him around and bound his wrists.

Jojola's two-way radio beeped once. "We have the reverend," he answered. "What's it looking like out there? Really? Without a fight?"

Suddenly there was the sound of gunfire outside and the phone went dead. Jojola put his gun against Hamm, who promptly wet his underwear.

"Please, I did what you said," he pleaded. "It must be those Valknut guys. They never listen to me."

The radio beeped again. "What happened?" Jojola asked. He listened to the angry voice on the other end, then flipped the phone shut. "All right, let's move out."

Tran pointed to the girl. "What about her?"

"Guess we better wake her up and bring her along," Jojola said.

A few minutes later, Jojola and Tran emerged from the house with their prisoner, trailed by a yawning teenager who'd been allowed to dress appropriately for the weather.

They were greeted by the strange sight of forty men lying on the ground with their hands tied behind their backs. They'd been made to strip down to their underwear and T-shirts and were already shivering as four members of the SWAT team stood guard.

"Wow, quick work," Jojola said to Ireland, then noticed that the sheriff was bleeding from the side.

Ireland noticed the look and shrugged. "Grazed a rib," he said. "About eight of these guys saw us and took off running for that barracks over there. I was dumb enough to run after them when I was talking to you and one of them turned around and shot me. Now the morons have really pissed me off."

"What are you doing about the guys in the barracks?" Tran asked.

Ireland shrugged. "Nothing. Four of my men have all the exits covered and there's no way out. The clowns are probably hoping for a glorious last stand, but we're not going to give it to them . . . at least not at the moment."

"Should we read them their rights?" the SWAT officer asked.

"Yeah, one at a time," Ireland said. "We're in no rush. Set up a little table in the office and take them in one at a time. Get their names, dates of birth, place of permanent residence. Then read 'em the Miranda warning, and if they want to chat, let 'em chat."

"What should we tell them they're charged with?" the officer asked.

"Rampant stupidity," Ireland responded. "No? Well, how about accessory to murder, resistance to a peace officer performing his duty, i.e., serving a search warrant, and I expect we'll discover a few weapons violations when we go through those barracks. The important thing is to take your time and let those folks over in the gravel pit do their work undisturbed."

"They're complaining about being cold," the SWAT officer said.

"Well, are they now," Ireland said with a look of disgust. "Bunch of weekend warriors. Keep them just as they are. Cold men don't think or act very quickly. Those that are cooperative, let them hang out in one of the barracks—as soon as we've cleared it of weapons. The others can freeze their dicks off for all I care."

"Well, things seem to be under control here," Jojola said, and laughed as he turned to Tran. "I wonder how Marlene and the others are doing."

"Let's go see," Tran replied. "If you think you can still walk that far."

"Yeah, yeah, Ho Chi Old Man," Jojola replied. "And by the way, your coyote-speak still sucks."

"Shows what you know, Pocahontas. That was a wolf."

26

ALTHOUGH SHE'D NEVER PHYSICALLY BEEN TO THE PROP-
erty before, Lucy knew where she was the moment the police
cruiser she was riding in turned off the highway and stopped at the
gatehouse. Two-lane highway . . . but rural Idaho, not New
Mexico . . . onto a gravel road.

Then as she waited with her mother and the others at the guard
tower for a signal from Ireland to proceed to the gravel pit, a train
whistled over in the direction of the highway. A train, just like in
the peyote dream, then one mile to where the road splits off to the
right. And I was thinking in Euskara!

Some people might have called it déjà vu, but Lucy had no
doubt that somehow the spirit of peyote had chosen to guide her
through the final torment of Maria Santacristina. But for what reason, she wondered. John's not here, and I'm not going to tell anybody else about this. They'll think I'm nuts. Still, I am supposed to
be here for a reason.

Lucy glanced down the road toward the gravel pit and shuddered. She looked back to her mother, just as Marlene got off the
radio and gave a thumbs-up. "Okay, everybody," she shouted. "Plan
A worked. Let's go!"

Everybody piled back into the cars and the convoy turned right down the road. After about three-quarters of a mile, they reached the entrance and stopped. The gravel pit was huge—more than a hundred acres according to the maps—and now that they were there, it looked bigger than that. Although the snow had melted from the sunny, southern exposures of the barren landscape, there were still large patches on the north sides of hills and in depressions.

"Which way?" asked Swanburg, who was riding in the first car with Marlene, Lucy, and Ned.

"Straight ahead about a mile," Lucy said.

The others turned to look at her. "Just a hunch," she said, and turned to look out the window.

Swanburg shrugged and looked at the small Global Positioning System display on the laptop computer next to him. "Looks like as good a place as any to set up shop."

A mile farther, the convoy stopped again. The Baker Street Irregulars got out of their respective vehicles and gathered around the pickup truck, where they began unloading their equipment from the back. All except for Warren, who opened the kennels, leashed his three dogs, and took them for a walk.

As they worked, Marlene walked back to the minivan, whose occupants were climbing out and stretching. She spoke to their leader. "Are you okay?"

Jose Katarain, aka Eugenio Santacristina, reached up and held Marlene by her shoulders. "I am the most okay I have been since my daughter disappeared," he said. "Today, we find Maria and take her home to her mother. Thank you, my friend."

"We're not there yet," Marlene cautioned. "This science isn't exact, but I feel in my heart that you're right. So let's get started. You know what you're supposed to do?"

Katarain snapped to attention. "Yes, my captain. We six are to set up and patrol a perimeter within line of sight of your people." He turned to the others near the van and snapped off an order they immediately obeyed. One man climbed back inside the van and began handing out rifles to the others, who expertly checked the weapons out and then slammed home the bullet clips like they'd been doing it all their lives.

Marlene nodded with approval. When she first made the suggestion to use Katarain and any Basque men who may have had some paramilitary training, Ireland balked about using civilians. "They're as likely to hurt themselves as the enemy."

Ireland had agreed after talking to Katarain, but he clearly was uncomfortable. "You were right," he told her later, sarcasm dripping from his tongue. "He's had military experience, and so have a few of his friends. I don't have to tell you what kind of experience, though it may come in handy in an exercise like this. But like I told you, it puts me in an awkward position. I'm sworn to uphold the law in Payette County and that man is a wanted terrorist."

"Relax, he's our terrorist now," Marlene said. "And by today's standards of evildoers, he's an Eagle Scout. Anyway, once we find his daughter, he goes back to being a loyal taxpayer. Then the ball's in your court."

Ireland had given her one of his "Give it a rest" looks, then said, "It's the only reason he's not in the Payette County jail right now."

Katarain divided his men into three two-man teams and sent the first two to patrol areas on the far side of the gravel pit. "Myself and Esteban will patrol down toward the entrance to the gravel pit in case there are patrols or anyone escapes from the compound," he said, pointing to the younger man who'd been in the van handing out the weapons. Then with a wave he set off.

Marlene walked back to the last truck in the line, where a small, dirty man in a battered miner's helmet leaned against the driver's-side door, smoking a cigarette. He looked up sideways when she walked up and grinned, exposing a set of crooked, tobacco-stained teeth.

The man's face and head were so covered with long, wiry pewter-gray hair that all she could see was a small dirty space around his yellow eyes and the tip of a pointy nose. So much gray hair also poked out of every opening in the pink, faded long underwear he wore beneath his overalls that she was sure his entire body was as furry as his head.

"So what's next, missy?" he said with a voice that had definitely been ravaged by too many filterless cigarettes.

Marlene looked back at the Baker Street Irregulars. "We wait for them to work their magic and then we dig," she said, nodding at the trailer. "Tell me about your machine."

During their meeting in Colorado, as James Reedy had pointed out, even in late March the ground would still be frozen in that part of Idaho. "Hard as iron; you could swing a pick all day and not get anywhere," he said. "We're going to need an air track drill and someone who knows how to operate one."

He was confident that both could be found, because there were still active hard-rock mines in the area. "Gold and silver, mostly," he said. "I'll call around and see if I can find a miner with the right machine."

Who he found was R. P. Brown, a five-foot-eight, 140-pound gold miner who boasted about not having had a hot bath since the previous December, when he'd treated himself to one for Christmas.

"The man smokes, cusses, drinks, and fights like a fiend—which is why we're pretty familiar with him at county lockup," Ireland said when asked what he knew about the man. "But I'm told he's also the best hard-rock miner in these parts, and while you wouldn't know it to look at him, some say he's been pretty successful at finding gold in them thar hills."

Brown had turned out to be every bit as disagreeable as promised. In fact, about the only person on the team he seemed to get along with was Jojola. They seemed to have an understanding and had even been seen laughing together over some private joke. When Marlene later asked what was so funny, Jojola waved a hand in the air. "Oh, nothing really, the old codger's just got a lot of the trickster in him. As you know, the coyote is my totem, and I suspect his, too, so we get along fine."

No one else wanted to be around "the old codger," but his mine was only five miles from the Unified Church property and he had an air track drill. Not that it was free, mind you.

Marlene had first met him two days earlier. After listening to her describe the search for Maria Santacristina, he'd agreed to loan the machine and run it "for five hundred dollars, half now, half when I'm done digging. And you pay my gas to get there and my diesel to run the machine. And it's five hundred more if anybody starts shootin' at me."

Now he was looking at Marlene through his glittering yellow eyes as if there was something suspicious about her question regarding how his air track worked. But when he realized that she was just curious, he actually looked pleased that she asked.

"Well, missy, that there bitch is a Gardner Denver Model 3100," he said proudly. "It's really just a big fuckin' hammer on tracks. The business end of that baby is driven by an air compressor and will pulverize its way through the toughest rock, and go through this frozen ground like shit through a goose."

Marlene was trying to figure out how shit went through a goose when Brown decided he'd said enough. "Now, if you'll leave me be, I'll get Sally down from her carriage. The others look like they're getting started."

Brown was right about the others. Marlene arrived back at the truck just in time to watch Jesse Adare start the gas-powered motor of the large model airplane he'd snapped together in a matter of minutes. Sounding like a swarm of angry bees, the plane darted down the road and then lifted into the air.

"Turning on the camera," he called over to Jack Swanburg, who was monitoring the laptop computer he'd set up on a portable table.

"Coming in nice and clear," Swanburg yelled back.

Adare had explained to her earlier that day that he planned to send his aircraft up with a specialized camera that would send its images back to the laptop computer as a three-dimensional contour map. The first step would be to locate the Bucyrus steam shovel, and then, by aligning the image the plane's camera was sending back over the photograph taken of the Cadillac, get an approximate direction the photographer on the ground had been facing.

"Then when we've narrowed the search area, we'll look at the contour map and guesstimate the probable flow pattern of the groundwater through the area," Adare said. "That's where the pipes and dogs will come in."

"Of course, that's assuming the steam shovel is a relic and hasn't moved," Swanburg noted. "If it has, then we'll try something else."

The steam shovel had not moved and a short time later, the team was looking across a stretch of the gravel pit toward the ancient mechanical dinosaur, perhaps a mile away. It was still a lot of ground to cover, and the searchers were well aware that as soon as word about the raid on the Unified Church got out, the group's lawyers were likely to come crawling out from under their rocks, seeking injunctions to stop their work.

"We need to get this done today," Charlotte Gates said.

As Adare had said, now was when the pipes and dogs came in, as well as a lesson in subsurface hydrology. As the team gathered around the truck, Reedy pulled a large six-foot-long canvas duffel bag out and explained that "the easiest way to look at what we're going to do is to imagine that you're standing above an underground river.

"Essentially, water flows underground the same way it does above," he said. "Gravity pulls it downhill, and it follows the path of least resistance, although over time, water is a powerful force for change and will make its own path, as in the Grand Canyon."

Reedy went over the facts. One, the car was buried somewhere between them and the steam shovel. However, the photographer had not been high enough for them to be able to accurately gauge the distance between the car and the shovel. "Unless you have more of a perspective from the air, distances can be deceiving in a photograph. Nor do we know if the photographer used a zoom lens and cut out some of the distance between himself and the car."

Therefore, they were going to have to "feel our way upriver, so to speak, and narrow the search area as much as we can. And that," Reedy said, unzipping the duffel and pulling out long, thin pipes, "is where these babies come in. I had them made special by a tent company—titanium, pointed on the end for penetration, and drilled in several places in that first couple of feet to allow water to seep in."

Warren took up the narrative. "We've noticed in the past with the dogs that they would hit on groundwater that came to the surface hundreds of yards below a grave farther up a hill," he said. "Then we had one case where the dogs kept hitting on the leaves of a bush but weren't interested in the ground around it. We dug up the bush, thinking maybe it had grown up on top of the grave. There wasn't a body, but the dogs were all over the water at the bottom of the hole. It was our botanist who said that kind of bush had very deep roots and suggested that the roots had pulled the scent up into the bush and it was coming out of the leaves. That's when we came up with the idea of using these pipes to tap into the groundwater and letting the dogs sniff the tops to see if they'll hit."

Like tag-team wrestlers, Reedy jumped back in. "The idea is to narrow a search area downstream from a suspected grave by placing the pipe in an arc across the flow of that underground river you're standing on. Then, through a process of elimination, we'll let the dogs follow the scent back upstream."

Taking one last look at the contour map, Reedy and Adare set off with the pipes and began to hammer them into the ground, spacing them about twenty feet apart in an arc. Then they moved another fifty feet "upstream" and hammered in another set of pipes.

As they were working, Jojola and Tran arrived and filled everybody in on the operation over at the Unified Church compound. "Ireland's guys have about eight hard-core types holed up in a barrack, but they're not going anywhere," Jojola said.

"How long before our racist friends start calling their lawyers and word gets out?" Marlene asked.

Tran laughed. "Ireland can move fast when he wants," he said. "But he can also move slow. He's taking his time processing everybody. Then he's going to load them all up on the county jail bus and ship them to the 'pokey,' where he'll process them again."

Two hours later, the group was standing with Warren and his dogs. The hounds had followed the scent up and to the right of the main "stream" until reaching a set of pipes the dogs had no interest in. "I'd say we're now upriver from the grave," the dog handler reported.

Everyone turned and looked at the snow-covered field between themselves and the last set of pipes where the dogs had "hit" on the scent. The area was half the size of a football field. They sighed collectively, thinking about the work still to be done, when a snow-white owl flying low above the ground swooped in and snatched a mouse from a spot near the middle of the field. Lucy looked at Jojola, who nodded, but they said nothing.

The next step fell to Reedy, who went back to the truck and returned with an eight-foot-long pole with what looked like white coffee cans attached to either end. He plugged a cable from the pole into a harness apparatus that he slipped on and then opened the chest pack, which contained a readout screen.

Reedy flipped a few switches and began to walk slowly over a piece of ground, then called out to Swanburg, who with Ned's help had moved his table and computer to the search site. "You getting this, Jack?"

"Clear as a bell," Swanburg shouted.

Marlene, who had walked over to stand behind Swanburg so she could see the computer screen, couldn't tell what she was looking at that was so clear. It looked like a bunch of colorful globs reminiscent of the psychedelic poster she'd hung in her college dorm room.

"That's called a gradiometer," Swanburg said, pointing to where Reedy was making adjustments to the machine on his chest. "I won't go into all the scientific mumbo jumbo. But the short explanation is that the earth is essentially an enormous magnet with magnetic fields running north and south. As we all know, ferrous materials—objects made of iron, including the steel used to build Cadillacs—can become magnetized and will have magnetic fields of their own, also running north and south. These can be differentiated from the earth's fields, as well as any objects around them, with the gradiometer, which essentially gives us this colorful map that indicates the intensity of any particular magnetic field. Right now, it's not picking up much of anything, thus the confused blobs."

"Can that thing be used to find gold?" a rough voice behind Swanburg asked.

R. P. Brown had strolled up behind Swanburg, where he'd been trying to act uninterested while still peeking over the scientist's shoulder with Marlene.

Swanburg chuckled. "Sorry, R.P., no. It's only good for objects with iron content."

"Damn," Brown swore. "Then what the hell good is it."

"Well, it has many uses," Swanburg observed. "Obviously, it's handy for finding buried iron, like ore deposits, or utility pipes, or we've even used it to find buried steel drums, one of which had a body stuffed inside, and other illegally dumped toxic wastes. In this case, we're hoping to find a 2003 Eldorado."

Brown was unimpressed and went grumbling back to his Sally. But Marlene hung around and kept asking questions. "So when Jim walks over the car, one of those blobs will suddenly look like a bird's-eye view of a Cadillac?"

"Well, actually no, the lowest values on the readout will be directly above the car," Swanburg answered. "And none of it will look like a car. Remember when you were a kid and someone, maybe a teacher, put iron filings on a piece of paper and then rubbed a magnet underneath? Do you remember the shape the iron filings created?"

"It looked like a butterfly," Marlene said.

Swanburg beamed. "Exactly. The iron filings lined up in a sort of halo around the negative and positive ends of the magnet—sort of like the outer edges of a butterfly's wings."

"So when we find this butterfly's wings we dig down between them," Marlene said.

"Now you're thinking," Swanburg replied. "At least that's the plan."

"Will we know how deep to dig?"

Swanburg shook his head. "Nope. A gradiometer measures magnetic intensity, not depth."

"Okay, set on this end," Reedy yelled. He looked around and suddenly seemed to realize he was one man with a lot of area to cover, and it was already past noon with the sun high overhead and the snow slushy for walking. "Uh, anybody have an idea on where to start?"

"Where the owl caught the mouse," Lucy called out. The others looked at her. "Humor me," she said, and walked across the field until she found where the tips of the owl's wings had left the slightest imprint on the snow where it seized its prey. "Right here, Jim, try right here."

Reedy glanced at the crowd around Swanburg with an amused look on his face. "Actually, I was kidding," he said to Lucy. "We usually divide up the search area into grids so that I don't miss a section. I start in one corner and work from there."

"That will take a long time," Lucy said. "Please, start here. If it doesn't pan out, then go back to your grids."

Reedy tilted his head, looking at Lucy, then shrugged. "Why the hell not," he said, and walked over to Lucy, who bent down and picked something up off the ground.

It was a white feather. "For good luck," she said.

With a half-smile on his face, Reedy began to walk in the direction of the owl's flight path, which had gone from south to north. The smile disappeared and he shouted, "Are you seeing what I'm seeing, Jack?"

"Sure am! You think you got that thing calibrated right?"

Marlene looked at the computer screen and saw the distinctive shape of a butterfly's wings with dark red around the edges, gradually moving to a cooler blue in the middle of the "body."

Reedy walked some distance away from the area and walked a little more. "I got nothing," he yelled.

"Nothing here," Swanburg agreed.

The geologist then returned to the first site and slowly began to pace back along the owl's path. On either end, he bent down and placed pin flags—stiff wires with small plastic squares on the top—along the edge of the perimeter of the "butterfly's wings."

When he finished, he trudged over to the main group and looked at Swanburg's computer. "I'll be damned," he said. "Judging by the length of the anomaly, I'd be willing to bet we just found a Cadillac."

A cheer went up from the group. But Swanburg cautioned. "It looks good. But let's remember, this is a gravel pit with lots of old machinery that could be lying about and even buried."

"Oh, Jack, you're such a wet blanket," Charlotte Gates teased. "This is as good a place to start as any. Let's get that air track over here and start digging."

As they waited for Brown to drive his clanking machine to the site, Lucy walked down and knelt where she'd found the feather. Reedy turned to Marlene. "So you didn't tell me that your daughter was psychic," he said with a quizzical smile.

Marlene smiled back. She was used to Lucy's insistence that her invisible friend St. Teresa was real, as well as the unsettling effects of her almost supernatural gift for languages and for "knowing things."

"I don't know what it is," she said. "I guess that someday science will have explanations for people who seem hyperintuitive or psychic. Maybe some people just pick up more from the environment—they see, hear, or even feel things differently than 'normal' people because their brains are wired differently. I mean, how do idiot savants instantly, and correctly, guess the number of matches that have fallen to the floor, or play a Mozart concerto after hearing it once, or memorize every number in the telephone book after one time through. Yet they can't function well enough to tie their shoes, and only a couple of centuries ago might have been burned at the stake as witches. All science can do is shrug and say that their brains are wired differently. I'm guessing that if there's anything to psychic abilities, we'll learn that there's a similar explanation. Maybe Lucy felt the electromagnetic field when we walked over the area earlier, just like Tom's bloodhounds catch a scent none of us even notices. And, well, there's always God."

"Hey, nothing wrong with any of those theories, even God," Gates said. "As a scientist, I believe that there is a scientific explanation for every phenomenon. But if the explanation for Lucy is that she's wired differently, who's to say that God wasn't the electrician."

"Amen," said Swanburg as Brown and his machine rattled up to the middle of the space between the pin flags.

Within minutes, the crusty little miner had the air track drill pounding away at the frozen ground. And while it might not have gone quite as smoothly as shit through a goose, the crew was astonished at how quickly it broke up the soil, which he stopped to remove from time to time.

"How will we know when he gets to the car?" Lucy asked after about an hour, when the air track was still hammering away two feet down.

"Oh, we'll know," Reedy said. "He has the drill set for the consistency of the soil. When the drill meets something else, like the metal of the car, the machine will behave differently than it does pounding through rock or frozen soil."

As if to demonstrate what Reedy was talking about, the air track suddenly started to buck like a horse at a rodeo, and a screech of metal striking metal filled the air as Brown rushed to shut down the machine.

"What do you think, R.P.?" Reedy yelled.

Brown peered into the hole, then looked up with a grin. "I think a little touching up around the edges to make your job easier, and I'm finished," he shouted. He looked at Marlene. "Better go get your piggy bank, missy, time to pay up."

A half hour later, the group was peering down at the roof of a big car. The walls of the pit had been cleared back to a foot on either side, which Gates now shored up with plastic planks through which she drove stakes to hold them in place.

Gates hopped out of the hole to let Jesse Adare climb in with what looked like a giant pair of tin snips. "Jaws of life," he said. "Cops use them to cut accident victims out of smashed-up cars. I had a feeling they'd come in handy, so I 'borrowed' them from my employers. Just have to get them back by tomorrow night before anyone notices."

It only took five minutes for Adare to peel back the roof of the car and remove it in pieces. There was a space of several inches below where the sand and gravel had not completely filled in or settled, but below that it was packed solid.

"Okay, my turn again," Gates said, and climbed back in the hole with a trowel and a bucket. Probing and scraping gently, she began to remove the material filling the area directly above the driver's seat.

Inch by meticulous inch she placed the material in the bucket, which from time to time she handed up for the others to pour through a screen, to make sure they didn't miss any evidence that remained in the car. After an hour, Gates stopped digging with the trowel and started to brush away at something with her hand.

Perched on the edge of the pit, Marlene glanced up and saw Katarain was standing on the opposite edge, peering in with tears streaming down his dark, suntanned cheeks. His comrade, Esteban, stood next to him with a consoling hand on his shoulder.

One more brushstroke and Gates exposed a lock of long, dark hair. She paused with her hand on top of the hair. "A moment of silence, please," she said. "I believe we've found Maria Santacristina."

As the others bowed their heads, the girl's father sank to his knees and wept. After a minute, Marlene and Jojola moved to his side and with Esteban, escorted him away from the grave.

"I want your memories of Maria to be those of a living girl," Marlene said, looking in his eyes. "That over there is a body we will treat with respect. But she is no longer there."

Katarain nodded and reached up to touch Marlene's cheek. He then turned to Jojola and shook his hand. "Thank you," he said. "I can never repay you for what you have done. Whatever happens from here on out, I want you to know that I am finally at peace."

Two hours later, the sun was getting low in the west as Gates prepared to climb out of the hole. She'd worked her way down to where the girl's chest and hands were exposed. "But I think we're going to have to call it a day and finish up tomorrow."

Although the clothing had mostly rotted into shreds, the anthropologist was surprised at how well the body was preserved with shriveled flesh still on the bones. "I'm guessing the soil is pretty sterile and that there are natural salts present, which have acted as a preservative," she said.

Lucy was staring down at the girl's hands, which were still tied

together at the wrists and clenched in front of her. She was recalling the peyote dream when a man had leaned across her to start
the car and she'd reached up to strike him and instead pulled
something from his neck.

"Sasikumea!" Lucy shouted. The others looked up, wondering
what she was saying. *"Sasikumea,"* she repeated, and pointed.
"Look in her hand."

Gates turned to Reedy. "Hand me a clean towel, Jim." She then
placed the towel beneath Maria's right hand and with a bamboo
probe, she gently pried open the fingers. Something dark fell out
onto the towel.

"Good call, Lucy," Gates said, climbing out of the hole with the
towel wrapped around the object. "That could have fallen when we
removed the body. Then we might have been able to tie it to the
car, but not necessarily to Maria."

The anthropologist walked over to the screen table, where she
carefully rubbed at the sand and soil around the object. She then
held it up for the others to see. It was a medallion in the shape of
three interlocking triangles.

"A Valknut," Lucy whispered.

Gates turned the medallion over and rubbed at the back.
"There's some initials," she said. "R.P."

As everybody turned toward him, R. P. Brown backed away with
a wild look in his eyes and his fists held in front as if ready to fight.
"It ain't mine!" he shouted.

"Don't worry about it, R.P.," Marlene said. "We know someone
else with those initials. His name is Rufus Porter."

Brown lowered his fists with a look of relief. "Oh, I know that
son of a bitch. He's always over at that Unified Church place. Piece
of shit thinks he's real tough when he's hanging around with those
assholes."

Jojola laughed. "Couldn't have put it better myself, old friend."

Brown grinned. "Thanky kindly."

Lucy walked up to Gates and hugged her. "We . . . she . . . was
pregnant. Please make sure the baby is buried with her mother and
grandmother." She then turned and walked away so that only her

mother, who was closest, heard her say, *"Me aflijo para usted y su niño. . . .* I grieve for you and your child."

"Katarain told me that he found a positive pregnancy indicator strip in Maria's trash," Marlene said to Gates, who nodded and turned back to her task. "By the way, where is Katarain?"

Jojola looked back to the road leading to the compound. He pointed to the figures of Katarain and Esteban, who were joined by the other four Basques, as they continued marching.

"Marlene, I think you better get to your radio and let Ireland know that trouble's on the way," Jojola said. He and Tran then took off for the van, jumped in, and roared off in pursuit of the Basques.

A few minutes later, Sheriff Steve Ireland winced as he looked up at the approaching van. The wound in his side, which was more than just a grazing and, he figured, was going to require a surgeon, was starting to stiffen up. However, they were almost done.

Most of the prisoners had been loaded onto the county jail bus and taken to the lockup. The bus had just returned for the last eight, who were the hardcores who'd holed up in the barracks.

He'd cut their power, which had left them with no communications, as cell phones didn't work on the property. He'd then given them a liberal dose of flash-bang grenades and tear gas, which had set off the barracks' sprinkler system.

Dumb thing to have, he thought as the temperature dropped and the shivering, stunned holdouts gave up and surrendered.

The eight were still shivering as they waited to board the bus when the van slid to a stop and Katarain and the other Basques stepped out with their rifles.

Ireland frowned. "I thought our deal was I wouldn't see you," he said to Katarain.

"Deal's off," Katarain said grimly. "We found my daughter. Now I've come for one of her killers. I think he's here." The Basque turned to the prisoners. "Rufus Porter, step forward and meet your justice in the name of Maria Santacristina."

Back in the line of prisoners, Rufus Porter blanched. Up to this point, he'd been playing the tough guy, threatening Ireland with all sorts of dire consequences "when my dad hears about this."

Ireland had just grinned and replied. "Your daddy's going to have his hands full trying to keep his baby boy from serving time in prison as some big hairy hillbilly's girlfriend."

Porter had scoffed and looked at his fellow prisoners. "We'll see who's bending over and taking it in the ass when this is all over."

Now Porter turned to Ireland with a sneer. "I'm your prisoner," he said. "Tell this spic to get lost."

However, before Ireland could do anything, the Basques suddenly pointed their rifles. "Looks like they got the drop on me and my boys," the sheriff said with his hands in the air.

Katarain spoke to the man behind him. "Esteban, the rope." The younger man stepped forward with a rope on which a hangman's noose had already been fashioned.

Porter blanched and started to tremble. "Sheriff, do something! I don't know what the hell he's talking about."

"Sorry, son," Ireland replied. "But your miserable neck ain't worth the lives of me or my men."

Porter stared bug-eyed at the lynch party. "Okay, okay, I was there. But I was only tagging along. That attorney, Barnhill, he called my dad and said Huttington had a problem he needed taken care of. I just got the boys together. Rick, Skitter, and Jonesy, they're the ones that did it."

Porter pointed to three other men in the group, who scowled and cursed him. "You're a dead man, Porter," Skitter spat.

"We'll hang them next," Katarain said as two of his men pulled Porter from the others and he placed the noose over Porter's head.

Porter was pulled roughly over to a large cottonwood tree where Katarain threw the end of the rope over a low branch and tied it off to the trunk. A pickup truck was brought over. Katarain climbed in and hauled the screaming man into the bed, where he was forced to stand.

"Oh God, Sheriff, don't let 'em lynch me," Porter cried as a dark spot grew in his underwear.

"Sorry, boy, nothin' I can do, and by the way, you pissed on yourself, tough guy," the sheriff said, and turned away.

"You buried her alive, *sasikumea*, you bastard," Katarain snarled into Porter's ear. "Quit trying to blame others, Huttington didn't know what you did to my daughter."

"Yes, he did. Yes, he did," Porter screeched in terror. "We sent him a photograph that Reverend Hamm took. Showed the four of us standing around the car with the girl inside. He's the one that mailed it to that girl I raped to scare her. And there's more . . . Huttington let Hamm and whoever he works for use the university's computers. I can tell you more, please, just don't kill me."

"Too late," Katarain said, and pushed Porter off the back of the truck.

"Nooooo!" Porter screamed, and kept screaming when the knot around the tree gave way and he hit the ground. It took most of a minute for him to realize that he wasn't swinging by the neck and slowly suffocating.

The Basques, the sheriff and his men, and even some of the prisoners were laughing. Esteban hauled Porter to his feet and took the noose off his neck, but then stepped back and wrinkled his nose. "I think he shit his pants."

Porter looked around, wide-eyed. Then yelled at the sheriff, who was wiping tears from his eyes. "You tricked me, you son of a bitch," he said. "Ain't no way what I just said ends up in court."

Ireland shrugged. "Fine by me. I think we got plenty to nail you with anyway, ain't that right, Jojola?"

"Oh yeah," Jojola said as he and Tran got out of the van.

They'd intercepted Katarain halfway back and talked him out of murdering Porter on the spot. "Marlene's gone through a lot to do this the right way," he'd argued, and the Basque had finally relented. Then they'd cooked up the "lynch mob" and radioed ahead to Ireland.

"There's plenty to put this piece of shit away," Tran added.

"Good, then I think you can just rejoin your buddies over there, Rufus," Ireland said, pointing to where the Aryans were glaring at their former comrade. "Explain to them your little tirade. You can all kiss and make up in the pokey."

Porter eyed the other prisoners and swallowed hard. "Hey, guys, you know I was just shining these freaks on. Didn't mean none of it," he said, but received only more glares and curses.

A deputy grabbed him by the arm to lead him to the bus, but Porter pulled his arm away. "Uh, Sheriff, can we talk?" he said.

"Why, sure, Rufus," Ireland said. "You can ride back to Sawtooth with me, and if you'd like to give a statement on the way, I'll see what can be done about getting you your own room in my little hotel with bars."

Porter nodded and was led off toward the sheriff's Hummer as Ireland turned to Katarain, who stood in the midst of his men. He appeared to be saying good-bye to them as he hugged each one.

When he saw the sheriff approach, Katarain handed his rifle to Esteban and stepped forward with his arms outstretched.

"I ain't gonna hug you if that's what you're thinking," Ireland said, pulling out a Mancuso and offering one to Katarain.

"No, I was offering my wrists to be handcuffed," the Basque said.

"What the hell for?"

"Our agreement," Katarain replied, a confused look on his face as he accepted the cigar. "I hope you will allow me to attend the funeral for my daughter before I am extradited. Otherwise, I am your prisoner."

Ireland lit Katarain's cigar and stepped back. "Still have no idea what you're talking about, Santacristina." He looked back at the compound, where the prisoners were being loaded onto the bus. "Not a bad day's work," he said. "Minimal bloodshed, too. In fact, only one casualty. But at least it was one of the bad guys—seems the noted Basque terrorist, Jose Luis Arregi Katarain, resisted arrest and died in a hail of gunfire."

A look of understanding passed over Katarain's face and he smiled, but then shook his head sadly. "No, my friend," he said. "The Spanish authorities would demand some proof, and then you would be in trouble."

"Like hell I would," Ireland replied. "Did everything by the book. Fingerprinted the bastard, sent them off to Interpol, who identified the dead man as a wanted terrorist. Story over, book closed."

"You would do this for me?" Santacristina/Katarain said, choking up.

"Hell no," Ireland replied, and clapped him on the shoulder. "I'm doing it for your little girl."

27

THE PARKING LOT AT THE PAYETTE COUNTY DISTRICT Attorney's Office in Sawtooth was empty except for one other car when Kip Huttington and Clyde Barnhill drove up. "You keep your mouth shut," the attorney said. "And let me do any talking."

As they got out of the car, Dan Zook walked out of the building and held the front door open for them.

"I demand to know what this is all about," Barnhill hissed through clenched teeth when he reached the door.

"Let's talk about this in my office, shall we, gentlemen," Zook replied. "Too many ears about."

Barnhill lifted his head and a slight smile crossed his face. No ears even close. I believe I smell someone trying to sell information, he thought. "Well, it better be good. I got better things to do on a Saturday afternoon," he said, allowing his voice to sound a little more agreeable.

All in all, it had been a good week, Barnhill thought. The way he saw it, the trial had been a toss-up and would have hinged on whether the jury thought Mason and Dalton were lying on the witness stand. Then he'd come up with the brilliant idea of having Huttington drop his bomb about O'Toole confessing.

Sheer genius, he thought, mentally patting himself on the back. It had come to him when he was going back over the events before the trial, looking for any little tidbit that Zusskin, who he didn't entirely trust despite their "agreement," might have missed. That's when he remembered the conversation that he and Huttington had had with O'Toole about his resigning to save himself, and the university, the trouble of going through the hearing.

Even with Meyers making Huttington look like he'd lied, or at least omitted important information, in his deposition, Barnhill would take the stand and essentially back up the university president's version. The plan was to recall O'Toole as a defense witness and get him to admit that he had met with the two of them, and they'd asked him to resign. Barnhill chuckled as he imagined himself on the stand claiming that the request to resign had followed O'Toole's admission of guilt and his "nigger" statement.

Heck, it wouldn't even be the end of the world if the university and the ACAA lost the lawsuit, Barnhill thought as Zook led them to the elevator. The university would blame the ACAA for being overzealous when all he and Huttington had done was bring a complaint before the panel for review.

Then the university and the ACAA would all get slapped with some—probably quite large—award for damages. But except for a reasonable deductible, their insurance companies would pay the bulk. And, of course, they'd have to welcome O'Toole back as the baseball coach.

Surely even Big John Porter would see that they'd done everything they could to get his son back on the team. They'd just blame the Jew bastard, Karp. Maybe then Porter would finish the job started in New York and shoot him dead in the courtroom. Now, that would be a happy ending, he thought. But his bosses would just have to find another Big John to act as a liaison between Barnhill and the Unified Church of the Aryan People.

The Unified Church was essentially Big John's baby. He'd set it up secretly as his headquarters for the day the race war started. He even had a bombproof bunker, just like his idol, Adolph Hitler.

The man was a buffoon, but he was a useful buffoon. Barnhill's employers had needed a secret place to train its operatives, and the Unified Church fit the bill. Those sent to the camp by his employers were largely segregated and didn't mix with the usual collection of inbreds, losers, and troglodytes found in the neo-Nazi and Aryan camps. It would have been like mixing purebred mastiffs with mongrel junkyard dogs. The latter could bite, but the former were bred to kill.

Oh, don't be so hard on the Unified Church morons, Clyde, he thought as they got off the elevator and headed to Zook's office down the hall. Their hearts are in the right place, and even Hitler needed cannon fodder and brownshirts for beating up Jews.

Speaking of Jews, Barnhill thought, smiling as he remembered the panic when Karp first showed up in Sawtooth. Boy, howdy, there had been some intense telephone calls from back East, particularly with Jamys Kellagh. Of course, considering all the trouble his employers had had with Karp and Company, including the recent failure of yet another mission headed by Kellagh, he didn't blame them.

However, all the reports about Karp and O'Toole's brother being roommates had checked out. And, he'd pointed out to Kellagh, the case against O'Toole had been in the works long before Karp entered the picture. "I know it's weird," he said. "But it's purely coincidence, and he's shown no interest in our friends out at the Unified Church."

There was more at stake than just keeping Big John Porter and Little Rufus happy and in line. Barnhill had another mission and that had more to do with his position as the university's attorney. He'd been handed the position at the university and told to find a way to force Huttington into allowing the Unified Church and also his employers to launder large amounts of money through university investment funds. All universities invested in the stock market, bonds, and mutual funds, and nobody ever checked their records, especially at some small university in Podunk, Idaho.

The University of Northwest Idaho had also been selected because of its small but renowned Department of Computer Sciences, which had one of the most powerful mainframe Cray computers in the world. His employers had been quite successful at placing their own people within the department. And while he wasn't privy to what they did there, he'd been told that the computer was a match for anything the U.S. government, or anyone else, had at their disposal.

It had not taken much of an effort to find something to hold over Huttington. The man was a sex addict who had seducing coeds down to an art form. A private investigator had supplied plenty of photographs of the university president and several of his conquests, and Barnhill was about to blackmail him with a threat to go to his wife when Huttington got the little Basque bitch pregnant.

Barnhill had hardly been able to believe his luck when Huttington broke down in his office and started crying that he just had to help him. The girl had threatened to go to the Board of Regents and file a lawsuit. His wife would leave him, and he'd lose his job and never find work at a university or college again.

Oh, boo-hoo-hoo, Barnhill had thought back then as Huttington sniffled and sobbed. The whimpering coward would have kissed his ass if he'd told him to after promising to help. "You do know that this isn't a game," he'd warned Huttington. "The girl is going to have to . . . disappear, or you're always going to have that hanging over your head. Can't afford to have her show up in a couple of years with a child that looks like Kip, now, can we?"

"Anything, anything," Huttington pleaded.

"Good," Barnhill replied. "Now, leave the keys to your car with me. You can take my sedan back home, and we'll get you a new ride tomorrow."

"My car? Why?" Huttington said.

"Do you really want to know the answer to that?" Barnhill replied.

Huttington shook his head and sobbed. "Oh God, I'm so sorry."

"Quit sniveling, Kip, and pull yourself together," Barnhill sneered. "Find a pay phone on the way home and call the girl. Tell her you love her and want to see her early tomorrow morning, six a.m., at the overlook out on Saddle Mountain Road. Don't use your home phone—that can be traced. Understand?"

Huttington nodded and placed his keys on Barnhill's desk. The attorney tossed him his. "Now, remember, pay phone, six a.m., far parking lot, you'll be there waiting for her in your car," he said. "Now go home, get some sleep, and come to work tomorrow as if nothing has happened. Oh, and never, ever say anything about this to anyone."

The next morning, Maria Santacristina had showed up on time, only to be forced into the trunk of the Cadillac and taken for one last ride. A few days later, he'd laid out the bill to Huttington, who'd initially balked until he saw the photograph of the Cadillac emailed to him by the Reverend Hamm.

After that, Huttington had been as compliant as a two-dollar whore. He'd given Barnhill's employers the keys to the car, so to speak. Then when Rufus Porter raped a girl and needed help, Huttington himself had gone to the university police station at night, let himself in with his master key, and absconded with the evidence. And he hadn't protested the plan to get rid of Mikey O'Toole so that Big John's kid could live out his baseball fantasy.

Hamm's photograph had come in handy a second time to chase Maly Laska off. In hindsight, the university president probably should have just shown it to her instead of sending it to her as an email attachment. But even if the girl kept a copy, which was doubtful the way she up and left in the night, no one would be able to trace it back to Huttington or Hamm.

It was the perfect murder and blackmail. Except the girl's father had not let it go and seized on Huttington as the only suspect. Nor had he backed off despite threats. Then Marlene Ciampi and Karp had stepped in and started making life difficult.

Thinking about the photograph as Zook ushered them into his office and shut the door reminded Barnhill that he had not been able to raise anybody at the Unified Church all day. The phones were dead and there was no service for cell phones.

Zook sat down at his desk and indicated they should sit at the two chairs that faced the desk. "So what can I do for you, gentlemen?"

Barnhill's smirk disappeared from his face. "What do you mean?"

"Why are we here?"

"What the fuck, Zook," Barnhill growled. "Kip here got a call this morning from Marlene Ciampi, who told him to meet you here or else. To be honest, I'm thinking about filing a harassment complaint. It's obviously because her husband is losing the lawsuit and she's trying to intimidate Kip somehow, which may also constitute witness tampering."

"Really? And what did she say?" Zook asked innocently, looking at Huttington.

"Her message was very short," Huttington replied. He nervously accepted a glass of water the district attorney poured for him from a pitcher on his desk. "She said, 'We found your car,' and that I better show up at your office or else."

"So you thought that it was important to show up?" Zook inquired.

"Well, to be honest, I found her demeanor to be—"

"Threatening," Barnhill said, finishing the sentence for him. "This woman has a reputation back in New York for violence. Check it out. She gets away with it because her husband is the district attorney. But that's not the point. Are you telling me that you don't know what this is about?"

Zook looked surprised. "Oh no, I know what this is all about. I was just listening."

"So?" Barnhill said, exasperated.

"So what?"

"SO WHAT IN THE HELL IS THIS ALL ABOUT?" Barnhill roared.

"Whoa, Clyde, no need to yell," Zook replied quietly. "What this is about is that I am charging Mr. Huttington with two counts of murder in the first degree, kidnapping, and, just because I can, improper disposal of an automobile. Oh, and I'm charging you with most of those, too."

Huttington staggered to his feet, rushed over to a trash can in the corner of the office, and vomited. Barnhill just sat in his chair, scowling and shouting, "WHAT! WHAT! WHAT!"

"What? You want to know what, you slimeball," Marlene sneered as she walked into the office, followed by two Idaho state troopers. She spotted Huttington and walked up to him, holding up the photograph of Maria's impending murder.

"We found her, 'Kip,' you piece of shit." Marlene practically spat the words in his face as he tried to duck away from her. "Just in case they didn't fill you in on the grisly details, they buried her alive in your car. But we found her. We dug her up along with the Cadillac you reported stolen. Want to know how that's going to play to a jury, Kip? Do you? What's the method of execution in Idaho, Dan?"

"Lethal injection," Zook replied.

"Oooh, good one," Marlene said with a smile as she walked over to toss the photograph on the desk in front of Barnhill, who glanced at it and looked quickly away.

"They strap you to a gurney in a bright white room and tilt you up so that a bunch of people sitting in a dark room that you can't see can watch you die. They'll bear witness for Maria Elena Santacristina Katarain, but who will be there for you, Kip? The wife you betrayed with your little fling and then foray into murder? I don't think so, bub. I think you'll be alone, scared as hell, and about to meet Lucifer himself."

"That photograph doesn't prove Mr. Huttington had anything to do with any murder," Barnhill scoffed as he pulled himself together.

"Shut up," Marlene said, which caused Barnhill's jaw to open, but no sound came out of his mouth. Satisfied, she turned back to Huttington. "No, they'll stick needles in your arms and then load you up with the same chemicals they put dogs down with. Supposed to be painless, but I don't know. There's a couple of cases in front of the U.S. Supreme Court right now claiming that in actuality lethal injection is a very painful way to go, but the condemned man is too doped up to show it. You're just lying there looking like you're going to sleep when in reality, your brain is screaming like a cat on fire. And that's how you go into the next life, Kip, like a cat on fire."

Huttington threw up again. But Barnhill jumped to his feet and addressed Zook. "How do you know that's even Mr. Huttington's car?"

"The vehicle identification number, you idiot," Marlene answered. "Right there on the dashboard."

"Well, then," Barnhill said, trying to sound reasonable. "Obviously, whoever took the car abducted the girl, killed her, and buried the evidence. And they tried to make it look like Kip was responsible."

Marlene shot the lawyer a disgusted look and turned back to Huttington. "I know why you did it, Kip. I mean, we already knew because those pieces of Aryan crap, Benji Hamm and Rufus Porter, are singing like the proverbial canaries. But now we have proof to back it up. Do you know what we found inside of Maria this morning, do you, Kip?"

Every time Marlene said his name, Huttington reacted like he was being struck with a whip. "No, I don't want to know," he pleaded.

"We found a fetus, Kip. A baby. Her baby. Your baby, Kip."

Earlier that morning, they'd all gathered around the hole to watch Charlotte Gates remove the last of the sand and gravel from the corpse. The anthropologist had immediately taken the body to the Sawtooth coroner's office. A couple of hours later, she called Marlene. "We have a positive identification of Maria based on dental records and fingerprints."

"Fingerprints?" Marlene asked. "She was that well preserved?"

"Amazingly, yes. Jack Swanburg was able to rehydrate her hands by soaking them in a saline solution and got several usable comparisons," Gates said. "Her parents took Maria to get fingerprinted at the sheriff's office when she was five. It was part of a program for identifying missing children. And barring any injuries, fingerprints remain the same when you get older, they just get larger. So these will stand up in any court."

"Thanks, Charlotte, you guys did a great job," Marlene said.

"I appreciate that and will pass it on," Gates replied. "But don't you want to hear the clincher? . . . Maria's father, you, and Lucy were all right, Maria was pregnant. We found a well-preserved fetus, about three months into gestation. I'm sending tissue off to the lab for blood work and DNA analysis."

"We'll need a DNA sample from Huttington," Marlene shot back.

"Right on, and then we'll analyze them to see if they match," Gates said. "I'll bet Dan Zook will love the idea of presenting that to a jury."

Zook had indeed. He now picked a paper up from his desk and handed it to one of the state troopers. "This is a warrant from Judge Linda Lewis to obtain hair, skin, and blood samples from Mr. Huttington. When we're finished here, would you be so kind as to arrest and escort him to the hospital, where the medical staff will obtain the samples?"

"My pleasure," said the trooper.

"But it's not really necessary, is it, Kip?" Marlene said, picking up the photograph and holding it up for Huttington again. "You know we gotcha. No need to go through the humiliation of some nurse plucking your pubic hairs for testing."

"I, ah, no . . ." Huttington started to say.

"Shut up, Kip!" Barnhill shouted. "Not another word. This is a bunch of—"

"Kip, you tell him to shut the fuck up unless you're looking forward to that hot shot to hell," Marlene snarled. "And just so you understand the magnitude of what you're facing here, you heard Dan say two counts of murder, right, Kip? One count is for Maria. The other is for the fetus. Dan may not be able to make it stick because the courts do not currently recognize the rights of a fetus. But it's certainly not going to go over well with a jury when it considers the death penalty, and there's plenty of slam-dunk charges to get you strapped to that gurney."

Barnhill started to protest again, but Huttington kicked the trash can hard enough to send it and its contents across the floor, where they landed at the feet of the attorney.

"No more, Clyde, no more. Just sit there," Huttington said, pointing at Barnhill.

Huttington looked at Zook. "I take it I'm not already in jail because you wanted to talk to me," he said.

Zook shrugged his shoulders. "Essentially I'm here in case you want to discuss truthfully answering a few questions, and jumping through some hoops for me at future court dates. It might save you from the death penalty, but no guarantees of course. First, let's do this right. Officer, would you please read this man his Miranda rights."

The trooper pulled a small card from his shirt pocket and began to read from it. "You have the right to remain silent," he began. "Anything you say can be used against you in a court of law. You have the right to an attorney . . ."

"I'm his attorney," Barnhill said.

Zook winced as if he was sorry he had to break the bad news. "I don't think you're going to be in a position to represent anybody, unless it's yourself . . . and you know what they say about people who represent themselves."

The prosecutor looked at the other trooper. "In fact, I think we're at that point where you'll want to escort Mr. Barnhill here into that other office I showed you earlier. Read him his rights, too, and see if he wants to make a statement. Then you are free to take him to the county jail."

Zook looked apologetic again. "I'm afraid it's going to be a little crowded down there and you'll probably be sharing a cell with a number of other guys," he said. "Seems that Sheriff Ireland went to the Unified Church compound yesterday trying to serve a search warrant to look for Mr. Huttington's car. Apparently, not everybody was a good churchgoer and some took exception to him being there, so he locked them all up. It's so crowded over there, I hear, they're probably only just now getting to make that phone call to their lawyers."

"This is an outrage," Barnhill blustered as the second trooper clamped a big hand on his arm and pulled him to his feet.

"Yes, it is," Zook said. "Everything about you and Mr. Huttington is an outrage to anybody with a shred of decency. Now get him the hell out of my sight. I believe Mr. Huttington may want to talk to me in private."

❖ ❖ ❖

Two hours later, Marlene emerged from the District Attorney's Office, looked up at the spectacular Idaho sunset, and yawned. A sedan pulled up in the drive and Fulton got out.

"You okay?" he asked.

"Yeah, Clay, I'm great, just tired," she said. "And it's a long drive to Boise. But take me to Butch, would ya?"

Fulton nodded and opened the passenger door. "Your chariot awaits, Athena."

Marlene laughed. "Hmm? Wasn't she the goddess of justice?"

"She was indeed, Ms. Ciampi, she was indeed."

28

ALL CONVERSATIONS STOPPED WHEN KARP ENTERED THE
courtroom with Mikey O'Toole and Richie Meyers on Monday
morning. He looked over at the gaggle of ACAA reps, including
some members of the panel who had railroaded his client, as well
as Zusskin and Larkin. They were all eyeing him like alley rats
keeping track of the terrier prowling through their hood.

Karp considered whether he should feel sorry for them. But in
less time than it took him to blink his eyes, he'd reached his decision. Hell no, he thought, they made this bed of nails. Lie in it.

The Sunday *Idaho Statesman* had blared the headlines all across
the front page, announcing the raid on the Unified Church in
Payette County that had uncovered the clandestine grave of a murder victim from the University of Northwest Idaho. Of course, the
real news was the subsequent arrests of Kip Huttington, Clyde
Barnhill, Rufus Porter, Benjamin Hamm, and several members of
an Aryan gang in connection with the murder of Maria Santacristina. Police were still searching for John Porter, who they
"wanted to question" in connection with the raid.

Another nearly as breathless sidebar story reported that a
Basque terrorist wanted by Spain for a bombing more than twenty

years earlier had been killed in a shootout with the Payette County SWAT team at the Unified Church compound. Jose Luis Arregi Katarain had been identified by fingerprints sent to Interpol by Sheriff Steve Ireland.

"We believe that he may have been training members of neo-Nazi terrorist organizations," Ireland said at a press conference. "He fought like a man possessed, but my boys got him in the end. Afraid he's pretty shot up. Not a pretty sight."

Later, when he was called by reporters and told that some of the other white supremacists arrested at the compound denied the presence of Katarain, Ireland scoffed. "Well, what the hell do you expect them to say. 'Oh, hello, we've been playing army with Osama Frickin' bin Lay-den'? They may not have even known his real name."

Of course, Karp knew the real story. He'd turned in early Saturday night feeling a little run-down and fighting a splitting headache that radiated from the back of his neck. The pain had finally subsided when he heard the door of his hotel room open and a minute later felt a warm female body slip beneath the covers and snuggle up against him.

"Is that you, Lisa?" he mumbled.

A second later he was begging for mercy as Marlene literally had him by the shorthairs. "Shall I just yank them out?" she hissed.

"No, no," he cried. "I promise, it's over between Lisa and me. Ow! Ow! Okay, uncle. I knew all along you were my lovely wife, Marlene."

"That's better, lover boy," Marlene purred.

"So what brings you to Boise so late, my dear? I was expecting you in the morning."

"Carnal desires," she replied. "And maybe to deliver a little good news for my best boyfriend." He'd already heard the report about finding Maria Santacristina; now she filled him in on that afternoon's confrontation with Huttington and Barnhill. "One of the conditions for not seeking the death penalty is that Huttington answer truthfully at any court case he is required to attend, including yours on Monday morning."

"Oh, most beauteous and intelligent siren, this is wonderful news beyond all hope," Karp waxed.

"Now, that's more like it," Marlene said, giggling and allowing her hands to wander.

"I'll say," he replied.

On Sunday, Karp had interviewed a pale and quivering Kip Huttington, who'd been placed on suicide watch in the Boise city jail. They went over Huttington's testimony, which left him staring blankly at the table in front of him as one tear after another splashed down. Karp did not feel sorry for him one bit, either.

The next stop had been to see Rufus Porter, who started to play tough guy again—saying his dad would get him a lawyer "and get my co-urst confession tossed out"—until Marlene dropped his Valknut medallion on the table. "Recognize this, Rufus?" she asked. "We have plenty of bits and pieces, including that tattoo under your biceps, which comes in loud and clear in the photograph Hamm took. Not to mention the feds want to talk to you about some weapons violations with your fingerprints all over them. Ever hear what fed pens are like? State joints are kindergartens by comparison. Now, do you still want to play games?"

Porter's lip started to tremble, and then he started to blubber. "No, what do you want to know?"

Karp looked around the courtroom and saw Coach J. C. Anderson sitting in back, only this time he was sitting on the plaintiff's side. The coach nodded and he returned the acknowledgment. Marlene was sitting in the front row with Fulton, Lucy, Ned, and a young woman Karp did not recognize as he walked up to say hello.

"Oh, there you are," his wife said, and then touched the young woman lightly on her shoulder. "Butch, I'd like you to meet Maly Laska."

Laska appeared nervous, but her handshake was firm. "Nice to meet you," she said, then looked at Marlene. "Boy, when your wife says she's going to do something, she doesn't hold back, does she?"

Karp smiled, thinking of the many ways that applied to Marlene

Ciampi. "No, she doesn't," he said. "Thanks for coming. . . . And thanks for what you did—that took courage."

Laska blushed and mumbled something about it not being a big deal. Karp excused himself and joined his co-counsel and client at the plaintiff's table, ignoring requests by several members of the press who'd followed him down the aisle.

Unlike during the first days of trial, when it was still just a civil lawsuit by a small university baseball coach for what the press had essentially boiled down to wrongful termination, the courtroom was now packed with reporters. They smelled blood and were schooling in preparation for a feeding frenzy.

Karp rose with everyone else when Judge Sam Allen strode into the courtroom, wondering if this was how the Indian war chief Crazy Horse felt when told about Custer entering the Valley of the Little Big Horn. Bring 'em on.

The massacre commenced when Zusskin called James Larkin to the stand, though like Custer, neither the lawyer nor the investigator seemed to sense the impending disaster. Instead, Zusskin reviewed the abbreviated transcript and then asked Larkin why it was only nine pages long.

"Well, my job was to ask only a few pertinent questions and get the answers," Larkin said. "You have to remember, this wasn't for a court hearing, where it's my understanding that both parties receive all of the information. I sometimes interview hundreds of people, and if I transcribed every four-hour conversation and kept every tape, we'd never get anywhere. Think of it as, I was the person asking the questions for the ACAA panel and then reporting the answers. Nothing more."

"And what were those questions, Mr. Larkin?" Zusskin asked.

Larkin held up his big hands and ticked off the questions one fat finger at a time. "Did Coach O'Toole know about the party? Did he contact the escort service and pay for the . . . um, entertainment? Did he pay for alcohol that he knew would be consumed by the two recruits, who were underage? And did he attempt to interfere with my investigation by telling Mason and Dalton not to cooperate or to lie?"

"And those questions were answered in the nine pages of the transcript you provided, in accordance with the rules and regulations of the ACAA, to the hearing panel?"

"Yes."

"Was there anything else that was substantive or relevant that perhaps you should have included?"

"No, not that I can think of. The interviews weren't all that long because, as I said, I was really only after those specific answers to my specific questions."

"So if Mr. Mason and Mr. Dalton testified in this courtroom that your transcript was missing statements in which they denied that Coach O'Toole did these things, your answer would be?"

"What can I say, they're lying," he answered, looking at the jury.

Zusskin gave a meaningful look to the jury and said, "No more questions. Your witness."

As Karp approached the witness stand Larkin tried to stare him down, but he got such a dose of "the Karp Glare" that he wilted, looked over at the jury, and laughed in his high, squeaky voice.

Karp held up the abbreviated transcript. "This is nine pages long," he said. "Steele Dalton and Michael Mason both testified that most of what they said isn't on here."

Larkin leaned back in the witness chair and looked at his fingernails. "Anything substantive, or relevant, is included in that transcript, all in accordance with ACAA protocol."

"And this is the transcript that the ACAA panel that heard Mikey O'Toole's case used to suspend him?" Karp asked.

"Well, that and some other things," Larkin responded.

"And if I recall your testimony at a pretrial hearing regarding the admissibility of this transcript, the tape recording of these interviews was destroyed?"

"No, actually, what happened is I had my secretary transcribe the recording and then I used the tape again for another interview," Larkin replied. "Now I wish I hadn't."

"I see," Karp said with a slight smile. "Then you will be happy to hear that I have that tape and wouldn't you know, you didn't record over it after all." He reached behind him for the cassette tape on the plaintiff's table and held it up.

"Your Honor, it is the plaintiff's intention to offer into evidence this copy of a tape marked on the outside 'Dalton-Mason' and also a certified transcript from that tape, one hundred and thirty-five pages in all. Your Honor, I am compelled to inform the court that we have good reason to represent to you that the defense has been well aware of this tape and its contents. We, of course, have copies for counsel, which"—he turned to see that Meyers was giving Zusskin a copy—"have just been handed to them."

The judge raised his eyebrows and looked over at Zusskin, who sat in stunned silence. He appeared to be unable to speak, so the young attorney next to him shouted, "Objection!"

"Yes, Miss Welt," Allen said mildly. "What exactly is your objection?"

"I, um, I don't know, but I'm sure we have one," the young woman said, nudging Zusskin.

The poke in the shoulder seemed to bring Zusskin to his senses. "What is this nonsense?" he sputtered, rising shakily to his feet and poking the bigger transcript with his finger. "This is a fake."

Karp enjoyed the moment, then turned to the judge. "Your Honor, if the defense will not stipulate to the admission in evidence of the tape and the corresponding certified transcript, then we'll ask that Mr. Larkin step down temporarily so that we can make an offer of proof by calling Coach J. C. Anderson to the stand to vouch for its authenticity and provenance."

Zusskin and the ACAA reps all swiveled in their seats to look at Coach Anderson, who glared right back. "Your Honor, Coach Anderson, as you know was a member of the ACAA panel that voted to sanction my client. He has since had a change of heart and obtained a copy of the supposedly 'destroyed' tape, which he gave to me. If the defense would prefer, we could just play the tape in its entirety. I'm sure the jury will be able to distinguish the voices of the two young men and Mr. Larkin and will be able to determine if it is all part of the same interview. Then they can make a decision if anything substantive, or relevant, was left out."

"I really must object," Zusskin complained. "This is . . ." He groped for a word.

"Unfair?" Karp said helpfully. "Unfair, as in how you stacked the deck against Mikey O'Toole?"

"Mr. Karp," Judge Allen said dryly. "If you don't mind, can we proceed, please? I believe you asked if the defense would prefer you call Mr. Anderson to the stand, or play the tape, or simply stipulate that they are accepting your exhibits without a fight."

"Pretty much, Your Honor," Karp replied.

Zusskin turned to look at the ACAA reps, the leader of whom made a signal with his hands. The lawyer plopped down in his seat and waved a hand at Karp. "Go ahead. We withdraw our objection."

Nice, Karp thought, they just threw Larkin under the bus.

"Well, then, Mr. Karp, please proceed."

"With the court's permission." Karp handed copies of the transcript to the court clerk. Feeling that he now had everybody's attention, he turned back to the witness, who was looking pale as he leafed through his copy of the new transcript.

"Mr. Larkin, have you had a chance to glance at the papers in your hand?"

Larkin looked up like a condemned man at a firing squad. "Uh, yes."

"Good. Now, can you tell us what is on those pages?"

"It's a transcript," Larkin said weakly. He looked over at the defense table, but Zusskin was now almost prone and watching a pencil he was twirling in his fingers.

"A transcript of what, Mr. Larkin?" Karp said, circling in the water.

"Of my conversation with Steele Dalton and Michael Mason."

"And contains the nine pages of transcript that the jury has already seen. Is that correct?"

"Yes."

"Which means there's about another one hundred and twenty-six pages they haven't seen? Am I right?"

"Yes."

"Very good, Mr. Larkin. Now, I'm going to ask you to read from the transcript, but first I want to make sure I'm recalling correctly. You previously testified that there was nothing else substantive or relevant in the interviews with Mr. Dalton and Mr. Mason, except what was included in the nine pages you provided the ACAA panel, am I correct?"

"Well, I meant that in my opinion . . . uh, I," Larkin stammered.

"I asked you a simple question and that requires a simple answer," Karp said. "Nothing substantive or relevant, that's what you said, right?"

Larkin gave up. "That's right. Yes, it's true."

"Okay, Mr. Larkin, let's read together, like a little play. Only I'll read your parts and you read the rest. Let's start with the interview of Mr. Dalton, on page forty-three. You in the right place?"

"Yes."

"Okay, let's see, you said, 'I'm going to ask you again, was Coach O'Toole aware of the party?' "

" 'Uh-huh.' "

"Go on with that sentence, Mr. Larkin. And please remember that the jurors are reading along with us and will notice any deviation from the truth."

"Um, sure. . . . 'Uh-huh . . . well, at least that's what Rufus Porter told us on the way to the party. We asked if Coach O'Toole knew we were going, and Porter told us that the coach knew all about it.' "

Karp nodded. "Very good, Mr. Larkin. Now, again directly from the transcript, you asked the following question and received the following answer. Question, quote: 'Did Coach O'Toole tell you himself about the party or paying for alcohol or strippers?' And Dalton's answer was?"

"Let's see, uh, he said, 'No. We didn't see Coach O'Toole again after the last meeting. We were in our rooms getting ready for bed when Porter showed up and said we could go to a special party only for certain guys.' "

Like shooting fish in a barrel, Karp thought. "All right, let's skip forward about thirty pages, nothing very substantial in there, I'm sure. Now, page seventy-eight, starting about the fourth line down. You there? Good. Okay, question by you: 'Did Coach O'Toole tell you not to cooperate with this investigation?' And his answer was?"

"His answer was: 'No. He told us to cooperate. He said he wasn't worried because he didn't do anything wrong.' "

Karp glanced back at the plaintiff's table as Larkin read. Mikey O'Toole sat with his head bowed, wiping at his eyes. Karp thought of his friend Fred O'Toole and how he'd died.

Jumping over into the interview with Mason, Karp got Larkin to read through the lines that showed that Mason had confirmed Dalton's story. Porter had showed up after bed check and offered to take them to a party. But other than Porter's word, there was no indication that Coach O'Toole knew what was going on.

"This is on page one hundred and twenty," Karp said. "You asked, 'Did Coach O'Toole tell you to lie to ACAA investigators if they asked you questions about the party?' Now, read the next lines."

" 'That's not what he said,' " Larkin read. " 'He told me to tell the truth. He said there's never such a thing as one lie because one lie creates another lie until nobody knows what the truth is.' "

Karp closed his copy of the transcript. "Until nobody knows what the truth is," he repeated. "Mr. Larkin, after what we just heard, do you still feel that the only substantive, relevant information was on the nine pages of the transcript you created?"

Larkin shrugged. "It was my opinion that the boys were lying to protect the coach."

"Nine pages of truth, to a hundred and twenty-six pages of lies," Karp said. "That's a whole lot of lying, Mr. Larkin. So many lies that nobody knows what the truth is, right, Mr. Larkin?"

"Objection," Zusskin said wearily. "Counsel is making a speech."

Karp looked at Larkin, then Zusskin, then the representatives of the ACAA, and snorted in disgust. "I withdraw the 'speech,' Your Honor. And I'm done with this witness."

Zusskin rose tiredly to his feet for redirect, but he seemed lost as he blinked at Larkin without speaking. One of the ACAA reps reached over the bar and tugged on his coat; the attorney leaned back and listened. When he looked up, it was with relief written all over his face.

"Your Honor, we have no further questions for Mr. Larkin," he said. "But may I approach the bench?"

"Be my guests," the judge said, and nodded to Karp and Meyers to join them.

Zusskin smiled at Karp as he walked up, as if ready to offer the deal of a lifetime. "My clients—the ACAA and the university, which, considering the current circumstances of Mr. Huttington and Mr. Barnhill, is now represented by the Board of Regents—have decided that there is no reason to continue this trial. They are prepared to offer a very generous sum to settle the case, as well as reinstate Coach O'Toole to his former position at the University of Northwest Idaho."

"May I inquire as to the change of heart?" the judge asked.

Zusskin spread his hands, shook his head, and smiled. "Just that the jury might misinterpret some of what has been said here. And we are concerned that the complainant, Rufus Porter, may not have been entirely truthful."

"No, as a matter of fact, everything he said was a lie," Karp remarked. "Your clients are just trying to buy their way out of one huge expensive embarrassment."

"So, Mr. Karp, does that mean you are turning down the offer to negotiate a settlement?" the judge asked with an amused look on his face.

"No, I owe it to my client to present the offer," Karp said. "Give me just a moment."

Every eye in the courtroom followed Karp's mission to the plaintiff's table, where he sat and spoke quietly to O'Toole for perhaps thirty seconds with Meyers listening in. Then Karp stood up and returned to the judge's bench with a big smile on his face, which Zusskin misinterpreted.

"We have a deal?" Zusskin grinned.

"No way." Karp grinned back.

"What?" Zusskin replied, frowning.

"No way, Jose," Karp chuckled. "My client wants complete vindication from this jury and this court."

The judge sat back and said aloud so that everyone in the court-room could hear, "Well, then on that note, Mr. Zusskin, call your next witness, please."

Zusskin put his hands in his pants and rocked back on his heels. "Uh, Your Honor, we had intended to call Clyde Barnhill to the stand, but given the circumstances of which I'm sure you've been made aware, we, uh, won't be doing that."

"So are you resting, Mr. Zusskin?"

Zusskin looked back at the ACAA reps, who nodded as one. "Looks that way, Your Honor," he said, and tried to smile but failed.

Allen straightened up. "Well, then, if there are no further wit-nesses, I guess we can move to closing arguments. Yes, what is it, Mr. Karp?"

"Your Honor, there is one request, we'd like to recall Kip Hut-tington back to the stand."

Zusskin whirled and stalked back up to the judge, where, when Karp and Meyers joined him, he whispered, "He can't do that. Mr. Huttington has already appeared and been dismissed. And in light of what happened over the weekend, I doubt Mr. Huttington's lawyer will let him take the stand unless it is to invoke his Fifth Amendment privileges against self-incrimination."

"Au contraire," Karp whispered back. "Mr. Huttington has waived his Fifth and his right to an attorney. Your Honor, I am re-calling Mr. Huttington to correct the record from his prior testi-mony. He will testify, among other things, that he lied when he said that Coach O'Toole confessed to him."

The judge nodded. "Then by all means, let's get him up here and hear what he has to say."

The spectators in the courtroom gasped as a handcuffed Kip Huttington shuffled into the courtroom wearing a jail jumpsuit. A deputy walked alongside with a hand on his arm, though it looked like it was more to support the quaking man than out of concern he might attempt escape.

Huttington kept his head and eyes down as he climbed into the witness stand. Once seated, the judge reminded him that he could still consider himself under oath.

Karp wasted no time. "Mr. Huttington, on Friday you testified that Coach O'Toole came to your office and confessed that he'd known about this party and paid for the alcohol and strippers. Was that true?"

Huttington shook his head.

"Speak, Mr. Huttington," Karp demanded. "The jury can't hear you rattling your head back and forth, and the court reporter is obliged to accurately record your testimony."

Huttington flinched but spoke into the microphone. "No. Coach O'Toole never said that."

"Why did you testify that he did?"

"My attorney at the time, Clyde Barnhill, told me to."

"Why?"

"We were worried about the case."

"Is there a reason you were so anxious to get rid of Coach O'Toole?"

"He wouldn't let Rufus Porter back on the team."

"Was there anybody demanding that you get rid of Coach O'Toole so that Rufus Porter would be allowed back on the team?"

"His father, John Porter."

"So you lied?"

"Yes."

"Why?"

"I was being blackmailed."

"Blackmailed? Whatever for?" Karp acted as if this were the first he'd heard about the issue.

Huttington's head dropped and he began to cry.

"I asked you a question, Mr. Huttington," Karp said, letting his voice rise.

"I got a girl pregnant. Maria Santacristina. She was going to tell my wife, ruin me. I panicked and asked Mr. Barnhill to help. He called John Porter, who . . . who . . . who made the arrangements."

"Arrangements? What arrangements?"

"To have her killed."

Again, the spectators gasped. A woman juror covered her mouth and gave a small cry.

"Do you know how they murdered Maria Santacristina?"

Huttington nodded but couldn't speak. He just kept sniffling and trying to suppress sobs.

"Come now, Mr. Huttington," Karp said angrily. "The court reporter can't hear you nodding your head, nor can she transcribe your sniffles and moans. Do you know how they murdered Maria Santacristina?"

"YES!" Huttington screamed, looking up, his eyes red from tears and hate. "THEY BURIED HER ALIVE IN MY CAR!"

The woman juror cried out. "Oh my God!" Others in the courtroom echoed the sentiment.

Karp waited for the muttering to subside, and then turned to a new line of assault. "Okay, Mr. Huttington. So you were aware that a young woman, who you'd impregnated, was murdered on your behalf. And then you participated in this farce against my client because the murderers were using it to blackmail you. But do you have any idea why the ACAA would be so anxious to participate in this travesty?"

One of the ACAA reps poked Zusskin in the back. He bounced to his feet as if he'd sat on a tack. "Objection. Your Honor, there's no evidence that my clients, the ACAA, were aware of this heinous act. Mr. Karp is painting with too broad a brush."

Allen, who was resting his head on his hand as he listened to the testimony, glanced at Zusskin. "Overruled. Continue, Mr. Karp."

"Thank you, Your Honor," Karp responded. "I believe the brush will narrow. Please answer my question, Mr. Huttington."

"It was easy to get them to believe the allegations against Coach O'Toole were true," Huttington said. "They were still mad at him for his comments at his brother's funeral."

"You heard their representatives say this?"

"Yes, the judge, Figa, said before the hearing that the ACAA was 'tired of the O'Tooles opening their big mouths.' That's a quote."

"Was there someone else specifically who works for the ACAA who you know wanted to get rid of Coach O'Toole?"

Zusskin jumped to his feet. His face was red and sweating. "Your Honor, this is improper examination. Counsel is haranguing this man into making wild statements. I just cannot—"

Allen didn't even bother to look at the attorney. "Mr. Zusskin, sit down."

Karp nodded at Huttington. "So?"

"Yes," Huttington answered. "Steve Zusskin."

"Any particular reason he wanted to do that?" Karp asked, glancing over at Zusskin, who had buried his face in his hands.

"Yes, we paid him," Huttington replied. "We wired two hundred thousand dollars into his bank account from a university slush fund supplied by John Porter. He was supposed to build a case with our help, and Mr. Larkin's, so that the panel would have something to use against Coach O'Toole."

Karp glanced back at Marlene, who was smiling at him with tears in her eyes. "Mr. Huttington, have you been made any promises by me, or anyone associated with the plaintiff, or the prosecutor in Sawtooth, of leniency for any criminal charges you may be facing in exchange for your truthful testimony here today?"

Huttington shook his head. "I will have to testify, truthfully, now and if called upon at any other trial. The only thing I've been told is that if I do tell the truth, the prosecutor will not recommend the death penalty for the murder of Maria Santacristina."

"Do you know where you'll be going from here?"

"Yes," Huttington said, and began to cry again. "I'm going to hell."

Karp was surprised by the answer but recovered quickly. "Well, yes, I'm sure you will," he replied. "But I meant while you're still among the living?"

Huttington blew his nose into a tissue. "Yes. Some of the people I will be testifying against are considered dangerous. I'm going to be placed in solitary confinement in a federal prison for my safety."

"And do you ever expect to walk out of prison a free man?"

Huttington looked up at the jury. There were no sympathetic faces looking back. He glanced at the spectators; there wasn't a smile or a hint of forgiveness there either. Then he looked at Karp. "No. I will spend the rest of my life in prison."

29

"MR. FULTON JUST CALLED FROM THE LOBBY. HE SAYS THE package arrived and he's on his way up."

"Thank you, Mrs. Milquetost," Karp replied to his receptionist, "show him in when he arrives, please." He then sat back at his desk on the eighth floor of the Criminal Courts Building, looking down at the worn yellow legal pad with all of its arrows and balloons and names. Then he tossed it in the trash can. It had served its purpose, but he wasn't going to need it anymore.

Next, he gathered the photographs of the murdered schoolchildren and placed them in a large manila envelope. "Sleep tight, kids," he said. "Tonight we'll get him."

Karp stood and looked out the window. He loved April in Manhattan. The trees in Foley Square across Centre Street were in full leaf and had yet to fade in summer's heat. The city felt young, renewed, ready to take on the world. He should have been enjoying his latest triumph. But even the end of the O'Toole trial had seemed anticlimactic.

First, a representative for the university's Board of Regents had met with him and O'Toole and gone a long way toward "healing" by apologizing for Huttington and Barnhill and what the coach had endured. The representative made no excuses, except to say that the regents had trusted the university president and attorney. So when their attorney, Karen Welt, then offered a large settlement and a lifetime "should he want it" contract as the baseball coach, O'Toole accepted it. "It's where I want to be," he'd said. "And I think we've all learned a great deal."

The ACAA was another matter. The association had replaced Zusskin, who was under indictment for suborning perjury and for the obstruction of the administration of justice. And the defense had switched to contending that the association had been duped by "the criminal masterminds" Huttington and Barnhill, as well as betrayed by Zusskin and Larkin.

"The panel was merely following the rules as set forth in the American Collegiate Athletic Association bylaws," the attorney, a nervous young man, said in his closing argument.

However, by the time Meyers finished his closing—throwing in the word "malice" at least a dozen times—the jurors looked like they could hardly wait to get to the deliberation room and cut his client a big, fat check. Like the ACAA hearing panel, they took less than an hour to return with a judgment in the plaintiff's favor.

If Mikey O'Toole had wanted, he could have retired a very wealthy man. But coaching was in his blood, he told Karp. "I'd just get bored being retired."

Then it was back to New York for Karp and Marlene, where, with a nod from the doctors and a kiss from his wife, Karp returned to work at the DAO. In the meantime, Zook kept them informed about the progress of the cases against those implicated in the Santacristina murder.

Most of it was going well, except for three disappointing developments. The first was that Barnhill wasn't talking, and according to Huttington, he was the link, along with Big John Porter, to who knew how and why the computer system at the university was being used by an unknown group, or groups, connected to the Unified Church.

The second was that before the police could apprehend Big

John, his pickup truck was discovered upside down in the Payette River. The truck had apparently swerved off the road for some unknown reason and rolled down the embankment. He'd managed to get out of the truck but never made it to shore.

"His body was found about a hundred feet downstream," Zook said. "Funny, but he was only a yard or two from shore when he must have slipped and hit his head on a rock. Actually, he hit his head on a rock over and over, if you get my drift. But other than that, we don't have enough to say it was foul play."

The third development had rendered asking Porter and Barnhill about the computers moot. The FBI had flown in specialists to try to break into encrypted files on the Cray computer. However, their attempts triggered a computer virus that had crashed the system, frying every bit of data in the files.

Karp was wondering what was in those files when Fulton popped his head in the door. "I got that tape you wanted," he said.

"Great. Care to stick around while I look at it?" Karp said. "I could use your eyes."

Two hours later, Mrs. Milquetost buzzed to say that Jon Ellis had arrived for his appointment. Karp and Fulton rose to shake the hand of the assistant director of special operations for Homeland Security.

"Thanks for coming," Karp said. "I know this is all short notice."

"No problem," Ellis replied. "Clay here said you needed to talk and might need my help with something important."

Karp nodded. "I got a call from some guy—sounded Russian— said to meet him tonight in East River Park under the Williamsburg Bridge. He says he has a copy of a photograph purporting to be of Jamys Kellagh meeting with Nadya Malovo and Andrew Kane in Aspen. Says it's a fax and not good quality, but good enough to nail this Kellagh character."

"I thought there was only one copy according to that reporter's story," Ellis said.

Karp shrugged. "So did I, but this guy claims that a copy was made. Now he wants to give it to me. But I have to meet him in person at the park, tonight at midnight."

Ellis looked thoughtful, then nodded. "So what do you need from me?" he asked. "Obviously, we're itching to take Jamys Kellagh down."

Karp grinned. "I thought you might be interested. And to be honest, except for my man Fulton here, I'm not sure who I can trust to provide security."

Ellis grinned back. "Well, if you can't trust Homeland Security, then who can you trust?" His face turned serious. "Forgive me if this is out of line, and I asked your daughter this once before, but what about Jaxon? I know he's out of the agency, but he's a friend and, heck, he probably has more firepower and technology as a private guy than I do with the government."

Karp looked troubled, then sighed. "You're right. I've known him for years and I've always liked him. And I'm not saying he can't be trusted. But considering some of the unanswered questions, I'd like to leave him out of it for now."

"Of course," Ellis said. "I think he's one of the good guys, too, even if he went for the money. And hell, I've been involved in a lot of this, you could just as well put me in the same category."

"I've got to trust somebody," Karp replied. "This photograph could break this wide open. But I can't take a chance that it's a setup."

"Yeah, you've got to trust somebody," Ellis agreed. "It's too bad that in these times, you can never be sure who. It's a dirty business, though, when it makes friends suspicious of their friends."

The men stood to shake hands again, then Ellis left, saying he'd be in touch regarding the security arrangement. "With any luck," he said, "tonight we get our man."

A few minutes before midnight, Karp and Fulton pulled into the parking lot of East River Park near the Williamsburg Bridge.

"You ready?" Karp asked as they began to walk toward the bridge. "You gave him the envelope, right?"

Fulton nodded. "Yeah, but I still don't like this. It's too dangerous."

"So is Jamys Kellagh. We had to lure the tiger out of his cave."

"Yeah, but I don't like using you as the sacrificial goat."

Karp and Fulton walked along the path that followed the river, as had been arranged. Up ahead, they saw a tall figure step into the light beneath a streetlamp.

"Looks like him," Karp said.

"Looks like somebody else we know, too, if you know what I mean."

"Yeah, yeah, except I'm a lot better-looking."

As they approached the tall man, Karp glanced around. With all the bushes and trees, there were a lot of places for assassins to hide. He noticed that two bums—one on a bench and the other against the seawall—were sleeping near where the tall man was standing. Dangerous for them, too, he thought, but there was no time to worry about it now.

"Mr. Karp," the tall man said, stepping forward with his hand extended.

"Mr. Karchovski," Karp replied. "You have something for me?"

"Yes," Ivgeny Karchovski said, handing him a large manila envelope.

"I'll take that," said another voice.

The three men turned to see Jon Ellis stepping out of the shadows with a gun drawn and pointing at them.

Karchovski started to turn as if to run, but put his hands up as other men also stepped out of the shadows with guns. He turned to Karp and snarled, "You betrayed me! I'll get you for this, Karp!"

Karp scowled and turned to Ellis. "I thought you were going to stay back and only show if I gave you the signal."

Ellis laughed. "What, hoot twice like an owl? You really are an idiot, Mr. Karp. But look at it this way, *Myr shegin dy ve, bee eh.* In case that brat daughter of yours, who by the way is simply going to have to disappear one of these days, hasn't told you, that means 'What must be, will be.' And what must be is a finish to your annoying habit of getting in our way."

Karp's jaw dropped. "Jamys Kellagh," he guessed.

Ellis gave a slight bow. "My nom de guerre, or one of them," he said. "But I prefer my anonymity, so if you will hand over the photograph, I'll make sure it never sees the light of day."

He reached for the envelope, but Karp pulled it back. "How do you live with yourself?" he asked.

Ellis was at first surprised and then amused. "I sleep like a baby, Mr. Karp," he replied. "There is a war going on and people die in wars."

"Is that what you call murdering schoolchildren to free a man like Andrew Kane? War?"

Ellis shrugged. "Collateral damage. It happens. Get over it, or you should have if you'd wanted to live. And what does it matter if a half dozen kids die, if it prevents the mud people, like your friend Clay here, and Jews, like yourself, and all those prehistoric Arabs from overrunning Western civilization?"

"But you're working with the terrorists?"

"A temporary measure," Ellis said with a shrug. "We will eventually, as the saying goes, 'bomb them back into the Stone Age.' But until then, we need them as the bogeymen. Every time they blow up something, Western democracy slides a little closer to our side of the political spectrum."

"So you're a fascist creep, too?" Karp chided.

"Now, now, name-calling is not nice." Ellis laughed. "We prefer thinking of ourselves as the true patriots. After all, this country was founded by white men."

"White men who created the Constitution so that all men could be free," Karp replied.

"And many of them had slaves," Ellis pointed out. "But let's not argue history. We believe the means are justified. We will do what's best for the American people . . . white American people. It's people like you who endanger this country, so we'll protect Americans from themselves and you."

Shaking his head, Karp replied, "Jon, you got it all backward. And when chicken-shit traitors like you get it wrong, you really get it wrong. And besides, who's going to protect the country from you?"

Ellis looked amused. "Why, no one, Mr. Karp. There will be no bleeding hearts, or constitutional apologists, to lead us all down the road to ruin." He pointed the gun at Karp's face. "But enough of this; give me the photograph."

"Why?" Karp said, holding the manila envelope over the water. "You have to kill us anyway. Maybe somebody finds this photograph in the river—I sealed it in a plastic bag—and takes it to the police. Why should I make it easy for you?"

"Oh, please, Butch, killing you is going to be very easy any way you look at it," Ellis said with a smile. "For one thing, you're a fucking Jew, and Hitler had the right idea about fucking Jews. And as for your Russian friend, they'll probably give me a medal for killing the gangster who lured you here and shot you in cold blood. I arrived too late to save you, or Clay for that matter, but I got the man who got you. Maybe Marlene will be real grateful. She's still pretty good-looking for her age."

Karp's shoulders sagged as he handed Ellis the envelope. "Check it out," he said.

"Oh, I will," Ellis replied, and glanced inside the envelope. He looked back up with a scowl. "What is this, Karp?" He reached inside the envelope and pulled out the yearbook photographs of six children.

"Those are the kids you had murdered," Karp said. "I wanted to show them to you before Clay placed you under arrest."

Ellis's face transformed instantly into a mask of rage and hate. "Fuck you, Karp," he said, and started to raise his gun, but then began to shake violently as the gun clattered to the sidewalk. He collapsed to the ground, where he twitched and then lay still.

At the same time, the men with Ellis who'd started to rush forward to help him were suddenly surrounded by other men with guns, shouting for them to drop their weapons. Karp turned to the bum behind him, who kept a Taser pointed at Ellis. "Cutting it a little close, weren't you, Espey?" he said.

"You said to wait until he saw the photographs and admitted to the murders," Jaxon said with a smile. "I had him in my sights the whole time."

Karp shook his head. That afternoon, when he met with Jaxon and explained the plan, the agent asked, "Why not me?"

"What do you mean?"

"Why don't you think I'm the traitor, Jamys Kellagh?" Jaxon said. "Lucy does. There are plenty of good reasons to think it could be."

"And don't think I haven't considered them," Karp said with a smirk. "But there are a few better reasons why I know it wasn't you."

"Such as?"

"Well, let's start with Stupenagel's stories," Karp said. "I'll bet you're the anonymous government source who's been leaking her the information."

"Damn straight."

"Uh-huh," Karp said, then laughed. "It's probably something you don't even think about, but you've been saying 'Damn straight' ever since I've known you."

"So?"

"So Stupenagel is pretty good at quoting people verbatim," Karp said. "I noticed in three of her stories that the 'anonymous government source' kept ending his quotes by saying 'Damn straight.' "

"Pretty flimsy," Jaxon pointed out.

"On its own, maybe," Karp acknowledged. "But I also asked Clay to get me the tapes of the attempted assassination of Senator Tom McCullum from Channel Nine. They almost didn't let him have them, kept saying they wouldn't release anything that hadn't been shown on television, and even then only if they got subpoenaed. But Clay placed a call to the traffic division and started to tell them about all the illegally parked cars outside the station, and suddenly he had a tape."

"Again, my question, so what?"

"So Clay and I watched them a couple of dozen times, and we noticed something," Karp said. "When the shooting started, Ellis just stood to the side and watched McCullum, as if he expected him to get shot. But one 'former' FBI agent, named Espey Jaxon, jumped in front of the archbishop—the man he was supposed to protect—and it was one of your men who charged the gunman. Not exactly the behavior of co-conspirators."

"Anything else?"

Karp nodded. "Yeah. I think I'm a pretty good judge of character. I knew that murdering children was not part of who you were. Oh, and by the way, it was Lucy who suggested that we watch the tapes. She's a pretty good judge of character, too."

It took a moment for Jaxon to respond to the last statement. He swallowed hard and said hoarsely, "I think I better call my 'niece' the next time I'm in New Mexico and take her out to lunch."

Karp smiled. "If I'd had any other doubts, you just answered them."

A groan escaped Ellis, who was gradually coming around. Jaxon nodded to his men who had patted the agent down and cuffed him. "Glad we could take this asshole alive. The federal government's going to try to claim jurisdiction, you know."

"Been through that fight once recently," Karp said. "They'll have to wait for justice New York DAO style."

Ellis was brought to his feet, still groggy from the fifty thousand watts of electricity that had coursed through his body from the Taser. He suddenly pitched forward as if stumbling and brought his hands to his mouth.

"Grab him! He just ate something," Jaxon shouted to his men. He jumped behind Ellis and began giving him the Heimlich maneuver to dislodge whatever the man had swallowed. "Get an ambulance! Now!"

"Don't bother," Ellis croaked. "Cyanide salts. I'll be dead before he can dial the number."

Ellis crumpled to the ground, breathing deeply but rapidly. A convulsion shook him, followed by another. "Others will follow me," he whispered, his jaw clenched in pain. "They will not fail. *Myr shegin dy ve, bee eh.*"

Ellis vomited and was racked by more convulsions, then his body stiffened and went limp.

Karp reached down and picked up the envelope with the photographs of the murdered children. Tomorrow, he would place it in the evidence file that would be boxed and sent to storage. But he knew he would never forget their faces.

"I'm tired, Clay," he said as the big detective walked up. "I'm tired of all of this."

Fulton nodded, then patted him on the shoulder. "Me, too, boss," he said. "But tomorrow's another day, and it's time to take you home. Your lady's waiting, and so is mine."

Epilogue

BILL FLORENCE RAISED A GLASS OF ORANGE JUICE AND brandy to those sitting with him around the table outside Kitchenette. "The blood of patriots and tyrants," the old newspaperman toasted.

"To Vince Newbury and Cian Magee," Father Jim Sunderland added. "Let's not forget whose blood was spilled in the cause of liberty."

The artist, Geoff Gilbert, took a drink and sighed. "I miss those days at Julius's house when we were all so young, and Vince was still part of our little fraternity." He turned his face to the morning sun on a beautiful, cloudless day in April.

"We were fortunate that Vince remembered those days, and came to us when he began to suspect the true nature of the skeleton in his family closet," Judge Frank Plaut replied.

"He remembered the old oath we took," said clothier Saul Silverstein. "We believed in what the Founding Fathers worked so hard to create and swore to protect it with our lives, fortunes, and sacred honor."

"We were also young, full of whiskey and fresh out of law school or just going into business like you and Mr. Florence . . . or hanging out with the Beats, like our own Geoffrey Gilbert," Dennis Hall noted. "Hell, I didn't even have a year in yet with the U.S. Attorney General's Office, and I'm sure none of us had any idea that our little fraternal oath would end up getting us mixed up in something as big as this."

"I don't know about that," Murray Epstein, the defense attorney pointed out. "Julius Karp was pretty worried about how the ordinary citizen reacts when demagogues like McCarthy dredge up bogeymen in order to secure more power for themselves and the government. I remember him, a little tipsy on the front porch, quoting from Orwell's book, *1984* . . . the part about how the government, Big Brother, used the lie about a false war being waged to keep people in line and stop them from questioning what the government was doing."

"Yes, I remember," Epstein went on. "He thought Ike was saying much the same thing when he warned about the military-industrial complex, an enemy within that could be more of a threat to the Constitution than the enemy without."

"But Islamic extremism isn't a fictional enemy, nor politically compatible with a Big Brother conspiracy . . . though one has to wonder now that we've learned something of the Sons of Man," Sunderland pointed out.

"Bullshit," Hall scoffed. "Islamic extremism is the much greater danger. It cannot be reasoned with. How do you reason with people who believe that God has told them what to do? In fact, God has given them orders to subjugate the world . . . they *have* to obey or go to hell. There's a war for our lives, not just our way of life, going on, and we have to be careful that we don't hamstring the government so much because we're inflexibile—which the Constitution was never meant to be—that we lose both our lives and way of life. We need to keep an eye on government—and beware of those who think like the Sons of Man—but not a foot. There are other books that were as foreboding as *1984* . . . one of them was *Mein Kampf*. The current appeasers on the left, and the

United Nations, could well place us in a position occupied by Neville Chamberlain just prior to World War Two. Now, there's the greater immediate danger."

"Spoken like a true Fox Network propagandist," the defense attorney Epstein scoffed at his friend the prosecutor.

"Oh, a fine thing to say for a CNN lackey," Hall shot back.

"Would you two quit fighting for a moment and tell me why," said Gilbert, "if we know that Dean Newbury is part of this 'evil empire,' we don't tell the FBI or somebody like that?"

"And what would we tell them? That the head of one of the most prestigious law firms in the country—a law firm representing a lot of powerful people and that contributes huge amounts to political action committees and politicians—is really part of a criminal cartel that dreams of taking over the country?" Plaut asked. "We don't even know who else is involved; Vince was never able to get that information for us before they killed him. And the book is gone. I guess it's hindsight and we can blame it on senility and lack of experience at the spy game, but we should have made copies. Now we'll have to try to find another, though we'll have to be careful; they may be on the lookout for anyone asking for it after Cian Magee."

Silverstein shrugged. "We wanted to get it into the right hands, but we didn't know who to turn to. Jon Ellis turned out to be Jamys Kellagh, at least according to our sources, but it could have just as easily been Jaxon. These Sons of Man—sons of bitches, I say—had, or maybe still have, the resources of the government at their disposal and are perfectly willing to kill. We're just a bunch of old farts who stumbled into something much bigger than we anticipated fifty years ago when we were all young idealists. We thought we'd write a few policy papers, protest unjust wars or support just ones, teach law at Columbia like our friend Judge Plaut, support those people and causes, whichever political party they belonged to, that supported the Constitution. Keep an eye out for guys like McCarthy. This group, the Sons of Man, could easily crush us if they knew who Vince gave the tape and book to and that we're onto them. We settled this question a long time ago, after Kennedy. Our role is to watch and work behind the scenes, helping guys like Jaxon do their jobs, while slowly growing a network of others like us."

"Just as long as these others understand what it cost Vince Newbury and Cian Magee," Sunderland said.

"Blood of patriots isn't just a slogan, Jim," Florence said. "But I agree with Dennis that we don't have enough to go to anybody yet. And who would we trust? The FBI? How about V. T. Newbury, the nephew of one of the leaders of this group and an assistant district attorney for New York? We hear he's getting closer to his uncle, especially after this latest bit of news."

"I'd trust this guy," Sunderland said, nodding to the tall man who was approaching the café from the north. "Careful what you say . . . here comes Julius's boy."

Smiles replaced the looks of concern as the Sons of Liberty Breakfast Club turned to greet Butch Karp. "Ah, our good DA has deigned to join us this morning," Florence said. "We understand that congratulations are in order. If Ms. Stupenagel's story about the goings-on in Idaho was accurate, it would appear that once again you've wielded the sword of justice very well indeed."

Karp smiled at the poetic turn but held up a hand. "Other people had a lot more to do with it than I did," he said. "But Ms. Stupenagel's account was reasonably accurate, except where she made more of my role than it really was."

"Such humility," Gilbert said. "But do tell us all about the notorious Basque terrorist who was killed."

Karp wondered if it was his imagination or if the old men did lean a little closer to hear his answer. "I had even less to do with that," he replied. "You probably know more than I do from reading the newspapers." Or maybe not, he thought.

"Phooey," the artist pouted. "I was hoping for something gloriously bloody. . . . So maybe you could tell us instead about the death of that agent, what's-his-name, Jon Ellis?"

Karp smiled and shook his head. "Still very hush-hush," he said, to Gilbert's visible disappointment.

Officially, Jon Ellis had died in the line of duty. It was Jaxon who'd asked that the true story be kept under wraps for the time being. "If anybody asks," he'd said to Karp, "he was working with you and trying to meet up with a source tying the bombing of the Black Sea Café to the Russian mob. You arrived late, and he and his men had already been ambushed."

"What about the men who were captured?" Karp asked.

"They're going to be isolated and detained for aiding terrorism under the Patriot Act," Jaxon had said. "Seems sort of ironic. They wanted to make sure McCullum, or somebody like him, didn't water down the Patriot Act, and now they'll be held incommunicado because of it."

At Kitchenette, Epstein changed the subject from Ellis. "So, Butch, we haven't seen you here much of late. Have we bored you already?"

"Quite the contrary," Karp replied. "I miss the pancakes and the company, but it's back to the grindstone. Got the doctor's permission to return to the office, and I'm still catching up."

"We saw in the paper that you're personally taking on the Campbell case?" Hall asked. "That's going to be a tough one. There's bound to be all sorts of wailing and gnashing of teeth over this 'postpartum blues' defense."

"A terrible thing," Epstein said. "I have to admit that I have problems with prosecuting a woman who was obviously not in her right mind."

"Of course you would," Hall responded. "But the legal threshold for being in her 'right mind' is whether she knew the difference between right and wrong when she murdered her children."

"First, you'll have to prove that she murdered the children," Sunderland noted. "The cops still haven't found the bodies of those poor kids."

"Any comment, Mr. District Attorney?" Plaut asked with a slight smile.

"I'm afraid not," Karp replied. "I'll save my comments for the courtroom."

"So do you have time for peach pancakes this morning?" Sunderland asked, pulling out the seat next to him for a place to sit.

Karp glanced at his watch and shook his head. "I'm sorry," he said. "I wanted to drop by to get a midmorning walk in—the leg's better but still has a ways to go—and because I told Jim I would. But I'm sure you've heard the news about what happened to my associate V. T. Newbury two nights ago."

"Yes, another terrible crime," Silverstein remarked. "Poor man, nearly beat to death by robbers from what I gather. How's he doing?"

"Well, to be honest, beat to death is somewhat of an exaggeration. As he says, 'It looks worse than it is,' though it was bad enough," Karp replied. "He has a broken nose and a fractured cheekbone, plus a couple of broken ribs and a concussion. He'll be in the hospital for a few more days, but looks like he'll recover just fine."

"Still, doesn't sound pleasant, but good to know he'll be okay," Sunderland said. "Give him our best wishes. I don't suppose he's Catholic and in need of a priest? I've discovered that I rather enjoy talking to attorneys with the DAO while they rehabilitate from their wounds."

Karp laughed. "Not a Catholic. I think he's Protestant and not terribly religious at that. But I'll let him know you're available as an enjoyable companion. . . . Anyway, I'll be on my way, but I hope we can catch up soon." Walking over to the curb, Karp lifted his hand to hail a cab to take him to Beth Israel hospital.

"Oh, Mr. Karp," Judge Plaut shouted. "Did I ever tell you that we actually met a long time ago, when you were just a boy?"

Surprised, Karp turned back. "I didn't know that, though I'll say that I've always thought you looked familiar."

"Yes," the judge replied as a cab pulled to the curb. "It was at your parents' house. Some of us used to come over on Saturday nights to talk. You were the mouse listening next to your father's chair."

A memory, distant and fond, came to Karp, who smiled and nodded as he got in the cab and rolled down the window. "I remember," he shouted as the cab pulled away.

Karp smiled all the way to the hospital. Meanwhile, back on

West Broadway, a group of old men sunned themselves, whistled at the pretty girls waltzing past on the sidewalk, and discussed the district attorney of New York City.

About the same time that Karp was walking into the hospital lobby, Dean Newbury was attending to his nephew, who lay in the hospital bed looking somewhat like a beaten raccoon, with two black eyes, a splint on his nose, and a bandage around his head.

"I can't believe those—excuse the expression and you know I don't usually use such vulgar language—niggers did this to you," Dean Newbury seethed. "If I wasn't so angry, I'd find great irony in the fact that a man who has devoted his entire life to putting this sort of trash behind bars to protect the rest of us was so cruelly manhandled by inferiors who probably have a fifth-grade education and three or four children by as many mothers."

V. T. Newbury reached out and grabbed his uncle's hand. "It's okay. I have to admit that I've been rethinking some of my beliefs since this happened. I was scared to death that they were going to kill me, and I hated them for it. I blamed it on their race, and hated them for that, too."

Dean Newbury nodded grimly. "What's the saying? A Democrat is really just a Republican who hasn't been mugged yet." He laughed but saw the look on his nephew's face and quickly added, "Sorry, I didn't mean to make fun of what happened to you, my boy. I'm sure it was terribly frightening, and your reactions are most understandable."

"Don't worry about it, Uncle Dean. I'd have laughed with you at that old saw, except it would hurt too much."

Dean gave his nephew's hand a squeeze and dropped it. "So, perhaps this could be taken as a sign that you might be considering my offer to join the firm? I know it would have thrilled your father."

At the mention of his dad, V.T. fingered the ring on his hand, looking down at the triskele. A few days before he was beaten, Lucy Karp had noticed the ring during a visit to the Karp family loft. "Where'd you get that?" she'd asked. She was smiling but there was something odd about her face, as if she was trying to control her mouth.

"This?" V.T. replied. "It was my cousin's. He died in Vietnam. My uncle, his father, gave it to me recently. The emblem is sort of like a family coat of arms. Why?"

Lucy shrugged and mumbled, "Nothing. Just, uh . . . just wondering." But he'd caught the look she shot her mother, who'd quickly changed the subject.

A few days later, he'd gone to a park in Morningside Heights on the northwest end of Manhattan to meet with a source regarding one of the "No Prosecution" cases. But he'd been attacked in the park by two black men, who'd beaten him unconscious and taken his wallet and watch, but not the ring.

He woke up in the hospital, and to his surprise, it was his uncle who was standing next to his bed. And afterward, the old man had insisted on calling in the best specialists—plastic surgeons for his nose and cheek fracture, and brain specialists with their expensive tests to make sure that the concussion had left him with no permanent damage.

When V.T. tried to thank him, his uncle had waved it off. "We're family, and family take care of each other," he said a little gruffly, but he was making an effort. The old man had hesitated and V.T. even thought he caught the glint of a tear in his eyes when he said, "I know I'm not the warmest person on earth. In fact, you might even think of me as cold and hard-hearted for the way I reacted publicly to the death of my son . . . of my son, Quilliam . . . and again at the death of your father, my little brother. It's just that I handle grief privately; it may not be the best way, but it's what works for me. However, I can assure you that I grieved, and still do."

"I understand," V.T. replied. "Everybody deals in their own way. I do appreciate you saying that, though; I know it wasn't easy." He was quiet for a moment; then, choosing his words carefully, he added, "You know, even before you brought it up, I'd been thinking that maybe it was time I gave the family firm a shot. My father accomplished a lot there. And Butch doesn't need me. He has some great young assistant district attorneys down at the DAO, and my assistant chief is more than capable of filling my shoes."

"Of course he is." Dean Newbury beamed. "Time to let fresh blood have at, eh? And for you to enjoy the fruits of so much experience in the courtroom. You'll make a fine partner and, if things work out well, a great judge who can have a lot of influence on our society, especially if we can get you all the way to the Supreme Court. Of course, you might also consider finding some proper young woman and settling down, even having a son to carry on the Newbury name. It's not too late, you know. You've given it a great run, but you can't be a carefree bachelor all of your life." He chuckled.

"Who can't be a carefree bachelor?" asked the voice at the door, which turned out to belong to Butch Karp, who stiffened when he entered and saw V.T.'s uncle. "Mr. Newbury," he said, and nodded.

"Karp," Dean Newbury replied.

Ignoring the slight, Karp turned to his friend. "So what's this? You thinking about leaving me?" he asked with a smile, but his eyes were concerned.

"As a matter of fact, my nephew is seriously considering joining his family's firm," his uncle interjected before V.T. could answer. "He's put in more than enough time as a 'public servant.' " The old man said the last two words as if cursing.

Karp looked at V.T. Now the concern was all over Karp's face. "So you're thinking it's time to go over to the dark side." He tried to laugh at the old joke, but it came out strained.

V.T.'s reply was unexpected. "What makes it the 'dark side'? Our judicial system isn't just about prosecutors; there's another side for a reason. And my dad accomplished a lot for all sorts of people working at the firm. Meanwhile, what does it matter if I put a few lowlifes in prison; they're out before I can store their files. If I decide I've had enough, then I think I've done enough to deserve it without any smart-assed comments from you."

"Hey, V.T., I didn't mean . . ." Karp tried to apologize.

"That's right," Dean Newbury said before Karp could finish his thought. "Why wallow in the pits with the swine, and for nothing, when he could help mold decisions that could affect thousands, hundreds of thousands, millions of peoples' lives."

"By protecting oil interests and unscrupulous CEOs who loot employees' retirement accounts before jumping ship with a golden parachute?" Karp responded.

"I thought you were the one who said I should consider going with the money," V.T. retorted.

"I was kidding," Karp replied.

"Well, I'm not," V.T. shot back.

The silence that followed was uncomfortable. Karp couldn't remember ever reaching such a point in a conversation—even during heated debate over courtroom strategy or topics of the day—with the normally unflappable V. T. Newbury. "I understand you're under stress," he said, trying to defuse the situation. "Who could blame you? Just remember that if you need someone to talk to, I'm always there for you."

"I think we can do better than that," Dean Newbury said.

Karp ignored the uncle and patted his friend on the shoulder. "Just take it easy," he said. "Give it some thought, and we'll talk about it when you get back to the office." He looked at Dean Newbury, whose eyes were boring into him.

V.T. didn't say anything, but his body language spoke volumes when he rolled away from Karp on the hospital bed. "I'm tired," he said. "I think I'll go to sleep now."

Karp stopped himself from saying anything more. Now, obviously, wasn't the right time. He looked at his watch again. "That's okay," he said. "I was just stopping by to say hello. I'm on my way to a memorial service for Lucy's friend Cian Magee."

"Fellow who burned in that arson, right?" Dean Newbury said. "Too bad. They ever figure it out?"

Karp didn't want to reply. He found the old man loathsome, but for the sake of his friend he shook his head. "No," he said. "It's still a mystery."

"Probably gangs or some neighborhood spat," Dean Newbury said, scowling. "Or the slumlord was looking for an insurance payment. I thought they already buried the victim."

"This is a memorial service," Karp said. "There weren't many people at his funeral."

"And there will be now?" Dean Newbury asked.

"I think so," Karp replied. "Now, if you'll excuse me, V.T., you take care, and we'll talk soon."

"Yeah," V.T. replied without turning back to look at Karp. "See you around."

Karp took a cab to the Irish cemetery in Yonkers and walked as briskly as his leg would allow up a grassy hill to where a crowd had gathered at the gravesides of Cian Magee and his parents. As he approached, the pipes and drums of the Irish Society of County Heath struck up and began playing "Amazing Grace."

Making his way to where Marlene was standing with the guest of honor, Karp noted the great variety of mourners. A "real" memorial service had been, of course, Lucy's idea. "He deserved better than what he got after all it meant," she'd argued, and set to work.

Among the attendees were Espey Jaxon and several of his agents, as well as Tran, accompanied by a dozen shade-wearing Vietnamese gangsters who were giving Ivgeny Karchovski and a half dozen Russian mobsters respectful nods, which were returned. John Jojola and Ned were standing next to Lucy, who'd dressed in black like a widow and was crying softly near the small brass shamrock memorial she'd paid to have placed on Magee's grave. Surprised, Karp also spotted Edward Treacher and two more of the street people who hung regularly around the Criminal Courts Building, the Walking Booger and Dirty Warren, the newspaper stand owner with Tourette's syndrome. Beyond them, standing on a hill in the distance, he noted a tall, thin figure in a dark robe. Unfinished business, he thought as he turned and smiled at Murrow and Stupenagel, who'd been told she could come only if she didn't write a story until Lucy told her it was okay.

There were a dozen or more other faces he thought he recognized as some of Lucy's old friends, plus the twins, Zak and Giancarlo, who looked handsome but uncomfortable in their suits and ties. "Quite the turnout," he said as he walked up next to Marlene.

"Yes, nice, isn't it," Marlene replied, finding his hand with her own. "Butch, have you ever met Senator McCullum?" She turned to the tall red-haired man next to her. "Senator, my husband, Butch Karp."

"Never had the pleasure, though I enjoyed hearing you speak on one occasion," Karp said, reaching across Marlene to shake the senator's hand.

"The pleasure's mine," McCullum said. "I'm an admirer."

"In Montana?" Karp asked.

The senator laughed. "Actually, I hear the Karp name bandied about more in Washington and, of course, when I'm here in New York," he said. "But you can be sure that the news out of Idaho was reported in Montana as well." The music stopped and the senator whispered, "I think that's my cue."

Karp shook his head as McCullum walked over to where Lucy stood and hugged her. Although much of the case was still classified, and would remain that way until Jaxon found and destroyed the Sons of Man, Karp's daughter had asked the agent if he would tell the senator about the man who had uncovered the plot to assassinate him and died for it. When the senator heard about the memorial service, he'd insisted that he attend. His participation had been kept a secret, and quite a few eyes grew wider—especially Stupenagel's—when he stepped away from Lucy to speak to the crowd.

"We've gathered today to honor an American patriot," McCullum began. "And a man who took great pride in his Irish roots, as do I. We should all be proud of where we came from, because it's what made this country great. It's what creates patriots. A land of diversity and a land in which words and ideas are more powerful than bullets or bombs. I'm told that Cian Magee was a man who appreciated words, so I'd like to read you something my grandmother used to say to me whenever I left the house." He pulled a small piece of paper from his breast pocket. "It's an old Irish poem, and I'm going to try this in the mother tongue in honor of Cian. Those of you who speak Irish Gaelic better than I, forgive my mistakes; I've asked Lucy to translate when I'm finished for the rest of you. This is called, *'Go n'eirí an bóthar leat.'* "

"Go n'eirí an bóthar leat," the senator repeated, his voice carrying over the green grass and beneath the oak, sycamore, and walnut trees that lined the roads of the cemetery.

GO RAIBH AN GHAOTH GO BRÁCH AG DO CHÚL
GO LONRAÍ AN GHRIAN GO TE AR D'AGHAIDH
GO DTITE AN BHÁISTEACH GO MÍN AR DO PHÁIRCEANNA
AGUS GO MBUAILIMID LE CHÉILE ARÍS,
GO GCOINNÍ DIA I MBOS A LÁIMHE THÚ.

When he finished, the senator turned to Lucy, who lifted the black veil from her face and said, "May the road rise to meet you."

MAY THE ROAD RISE TO MEET YOU
MAY THE WIND BE ALWAYS AT YOUR BACK
MAY THE SUN SHINE WARM UPON YOUR FACE,
THE RAINS FALL SOFT UPON YOUR FIELDS
AND UNTIL WE MEET AGAIN
MAY GOD HOLD YOU IN THE HOLLOW OF HIS HAND.

Lucy had begun her translation softly, with her eyes on Magee's grave. But as she spoke her voice grew in strength, and she lifted her eyes to the crowd and then to the heavens. She finished and began to cry as the bagpipes wailed.